continued . . .

The Shepherd Kings

"Never one to gracefully deposit the reader at the beginning of a new story, [Judith Tarr] starts this one with a bang. Tarr has once again created a powerful female character ... with the brains to match her beauty. [She] brings all her research skills to the fore as she dramatically describes the final battle. ... *The Shepherd Kings* has more excitement, color, and spectacle, undiluted sex, intrigue, and adventure than one ordinarily finds in several novels by less talented storytellers."　　　　　*—The Washington Post*

Throne of Isis

"In this carefully researched, well-crafted novel about Antony and Cleopatra, Tarr weaves ... a marvelously entertaining tapestry."　　　　　*—Booklist*

"Tarr's historical outline is unexceptionable, her wealth of cultural detail impeccable."　　　　　*—Kirkus Reviews*

Pillar of Fire

"A book that can be savored and enjoyed on many levels—perfect for beach reading, what with its lively portrait of enduring love between two who can never publicly acknowledge their commitment, and for such higher pleasures as those afforded by finely wrought characterizations and insights into the minds and hearts of the mighty."
　　　　　—Booklist

"With her usual skill, Tarr combines fact and fiction to create yet another remarkably solid historical novel. This is a highly entertaining blend of romance, drama, and historical detail."　　　　　*—Publishers Weekly*

King and Goddess

"Pleasingly written ... provides fascinating insights into Egyptian history and daily life. Readers lured by history in general and Egypt in particular will enjoy it."
　　　　　—The Washington Post

"This historic fiction brings the turbulent era alive."
　　　　　—St. Louis Post-Dispatch

KINGDOM
of the
GRAIL

✠ ✠ ✠

JUDITH TARR

A ROC BOOK

ROC
Published by New American Library, a division of
Penguin Group (USA) Inc., 375 Hudson Street,
New York, New York 10014, USA
Penguin Group (Canada), 10 Alcorn Avenue, Toronto,
Ontario M4V 3B2, Canada (a division of Pearson Penguin Canada Inc.)
Penguin Books Ltd., 80 Strand, London WC2R 0RL, England
Penguin Ireland, 25 St. Stephen's Green, Dublin 2,
Ireland (a division of Penguin Books Ltd.)
Penguin Group (Australia), 250 Camberwell Road, Camberwell,
Victoria 3124, Australia (a division of Pearson Australia Group Pty. Ltd.)
Penguin Books India Pvt. Ltd., 11 Community Centre, Panchsheel Park,
New Delhi - 110 017, India
Penguin Group (NZ), Cnr Airborne and Rosedale Roads, Albany,
Auckland 1310, New Zealand (a division of Pearson New Zealand Ltd.)
Penguin Books (South Africa) (Pty.) Ltd., 24 Sturdee Avenue,
Rosebank, Johannesburg 2196, South Africa

Penguin Books Ltd., Registered Offices:
80 Strand, London WC2R 0RL, England

Published by Roc, an imprint of New American Library, a division of
Penguin Group (USA) Inc. Previously published in a Roc trade paperback
edition.

First Roc Mass Market Printing, October 2004
10 9 8 7 6 5 4 3 2 1

Copyright © Judith Tarr, 2004
Excerpt from *Rite of Conquest* copyright © Judith Tarr, 2004
All rights reserved

ROC REGISTERED TRADEMARK—MARCA REGISTRADA

Printed in the United States of America

*For Jennifer Roberson
in honor of guilty pleasures*

*With special thanks to Catja Pafort
for matters geographical*

Well has Merlin spoken the last spell,
worked the last image, gone to his own:
the moon waxes and wanes in the perilous chair,
where time's foster-child sits, Lancelot's son.

—CHARLES WILLIAMS, *Taliessin Through Logres*

PRELUDE

✠ ✠ ✠

BROCELIANDE

Merlin the Enchanter sat alone in the wood. Trees walled his world. They had been young once, slender and small. Now they were old, massive and gnarled, and their branches wove intricate patterns of sunlight and moonlight, stars and clouds and sky.

The patterns of leaf and sky repeated themselves in a shimmer of bright water. The pool was small, hardly larger than a basin, shaped from a bowl of moss-green stone and filled by a spring that bubbled from the roots of the oldest tree, the father tree, that towered above the rest. They were beeches, but the father tree was an oak, more ancient by far than they. Merlin sat in the shade of it, hunched and utterly still.

But his eyes were alive. They were strange eyes, clear gold, set in a face as keen and fierce and inhuman as a falcon's. He was not mad, not at all, but neither was he sane. He never had been. He was too full of magic, too sore beset with visions.

All his world was this circle of trees, this bit of sky, this pool of bright water. Images danced in the water—a whole universe of visions, past and present and to come. They blurred and shifted and changed. They tumbled over one another like silver fish.

He seldom troubled to make sense of them. They were all the same to him in this prison, this cage of wood and water, earth and air. Only the turning of the seasons touched on him, and those but lightly. He did not count them. For if he set number to them, he knew the length of his sentence—and that was far beyond the reckoning of mortal years.

The boy came in spring. The leaves were just unfurling on the beeches. The oak still clung to the last of its sere brown leaves, but even it was yielding reluctantly to the new year. There had been snow not long ago, but it was gone even from sheltered hollows.

Living creatures seldom entered Merlin's prison. Birds flew over it but were not moved to pause. Deer, boar, smaller creatures of the wood, veered away from its woven walls of wood and magic.

And yet on this morning of spring in a year beyond his counting, there in front of him stood a human child. It was naked and brown and as wild as a young stag, and its eyes . . . its eyes were as yellow as a hawk's, and as keen, and as blindly fierce.

Merlin's eyes blinked, gold meeting gold. The child blinked in return. His black brows knit. He tossed his head. For an instant, too quick almost to see, a new-fledged hawk crouched in his place, with wide hot-gold eyes and ruffled feathers; then he was a naked man-child again, scowling at the man beneath the oak.

"And you," said Merlin out of a conversation many years old, or many years yet to be, "look at least as odd as I do. Would your mother's name be Nimue?"

"My mother is dead," the boy said. "My father is a count. He's always away at court. What are you?"

"I am half a devil," Merlin said.

"You look it," said the boy.

"And so do you," said Merlin.

"I look like my mother," the boy said. "I never knew her. Did you?"

"Yes," said Merlin, "and no. She never came to visit me. No doubt she was afraid of me. They mostly have been, one way and another."

"Because you look so odd?"

"Because she had too much magic—and too little. She could never set me free."

"Are you trapped?" the boy asked. "Shall I fetch the woodsman? He can cut you out."

"No mortal man can free me from this place," Merlin said. He said it without sadness, or anger, either. All that was long worn away.

This child of Nimue regarded him with clear golden eyes and said in his clear young voice, "Ah. You are *that* one. I saw you in a dream. I'm supposed to protect you. And feel guilty about you. Because my grandmother's grandmother did something she should never have done, and she could never undo it."

"You dreamed it?" Merlin asked.

The boy scowled. "You don't believe me, either. Nobody does. They all say I'm mad, or touched. Or the Devil's get."

"You are," said Merlin. "But I believe you. I'm the Devil's get myself, after all."

"I probably shouldn't talk to you, then," said the boy. "Father Bran whips me when I talk of things I see. He's beating the Devil out of me, he says. But if God is truth, then how can the truth belong to the Devil?"

"Truth can be hard to stomach," Merlin said, "and the Church only wants to hear its own side of things. The Church wants the world to be simple."

"I go to church when I must," the boy said. "When they can catch me."

"And do you fly up shrieking in the middle of the Mass?"

The boy blinked. He looked more than ever like a falcon. The air blurred about him, but he shook himself and was solid again. "I try not to," he said. "Even when Father Bran drones on and on. And on."

Merlin's face felt strange. It was some little time before he understood. He was smiling. He had not smiled since Nimue trapped him in this wood, built the walls of magic high and made them strong with his own stolen strength. Nimue's daughter—Merlin's daughter, blood of his blood—had never loved him, though she guarded him dutifully. Her daughter and granddaughter had been afraid of him, or had resented him.

There was no fear in this child, and no resentment, though perhaps he was too young for that. He crouched beside Merlin and peered into the pool.

He was the first living thing that had touched the enchanter since he was bound in this place. He leaned across
Merlin's knee, a warm light weight, comfortable as a pup in
a litter. "There are people in the water," he said.

"Visions," said Merlin.

"Visions are the Devil's work, too, Father Bran says,"
said the boy. But he did not recoil from the pool.

Merlin watched him rather than the water. The boy did
not seem to notice, or if he did, to mind. He lived as perfectly in his skin as an animal did, as pure of heart and as
unselfconscious.

Merlin leaned with him over the pool. For a moment it
left off its blur of visions and became only water, reflecting
sky. Sky, and their faces: old and young, grey-bearded and
smooth-cheeked. It was the same face. The same eyes.

Then there was only the one, the man old beyond years.
A falcon soared up on swift wings, leaping toward heaven.

The boy's name was Roland. Having come once, he
came again and again, sometimes in human guise, sometimes on wings. At first he came simply to sit by the pool as
Merlin sat, and to engross himself in its visions. But as the
seasons changed, he wanted to know what it was that he
saw, and why. Then Merlin taught this child as once, long
ago, he had taught Nimue; and before that, a boy named
Arthur, who was born to be a king. It was the same teaching he had had himself, far away in Britain, from old mas-
ters and forgotten Druids, and spirits of wood and water,
earth and air.

Just such spirits came to them at Merlin's calling, and
later at Roland's, to teach him their secrets. Roland drank
knowledge like wine. His mind was as quick as fire. And
everything, to him, was joy.

Merlin began to count the days again, and reckon the
seasons. Days when Roland was not there were as tedious
as the whole of his centuries' imprisonment. Days in
Roland's presence flew as swift as thought. Merlin was
alive again, though still a prisoner.

"I will free you," Roland said. "Teach me. Train me.
Make me strong. Hone my magic till I can break down
these walls."

He said it more than once, so that in Merlin's memory of

that conversation, his selves blurred together: small naked child, long-legged boy, gangling youth. The words were always the same, and the expression, fierce with conviction. And every time he said it, his magic was stronger; but never strong enough.

When Roland was grown out of childhood but not quite a man, he asked the question that Merlin had been waiting for him to ask. He knew the story as people told it: how Merlin the Enchanter had been seduced and made a fool of by the sorceress Nimue, and how she had lured him away into Broceliande and snared him in nets of magic. He knew too from dreams and visions that Nimue had lived to repent her betrayal.

"But why?" he asked in a dreaming noon, halfway between spring and summer. He wore clothes now, because his guardians in the world had impressed upon him, somewhat, that he was a person of consequence, son and heir to the Count of the Breton Marches. He still could not be prevailed upon to keep all of them on, not when the sun was high and the air was warm and the grass was soft for lying on. Somewhere in the wood beyond Merlin's prison lay a heap of lordly garments. Here, he wore a pair of leather breeches, very well worn, and a knife with a silver hilt, plain but fine, and a silver fillet binding his thick black hair.

Merlin, watching him as he lay with his arm over his eyes, reflected in some surprise that the boy was beautiful. Merlin had not been that, that he remembered; wild, yes, and striking in his strangeness, so that some had thought him ugly, but others had found him pleasing. But no one would ever call this boy ugly. His limbs were too long for him now, and tended to tangle; his hair was very much the same; and his nose, as Merlin had observed only the other day, belonged on a notably larger face. And yet he was rather more than mortal fair. The old people of the hills had looked so, before they shut themselves away from human eyes. It was not a human beauty. It had too many edges. His skin was too white, his eyes too strange. But it was beauty to stop the heart.

Roland was oblivious to it. He lowered his arm and sat up with swift grace. His yellow eyes were bright, almost angry. His black brows were knit above them. "Tell me why," he said. "Why did she do it? What drove her to it?"

"Some say," said Merlin, "that she was in league with the king's son, the traitor Medraut; and some, that she simply wanted my power. Others consider that I, after all, am half a devil, and that half of me is never to be trusted. Those say that the quest of the Grail was conceived to destroy the fellowship of Arthur's warband, to break it and scatter it, so that Arthur would be destroyed and his kingdom broken. And Nimue, who was loyal to the king, saw what I was doing, and so lured and trapped me, to save the kingdom; but of course she failed."

Roland shook his head sharply. "That's folly. Devil or no, you devoted your life to Arthur and his kingship. You would never have broken it."

"If Arthur had gone over to the dark," Merlin mused, "I would have."

"But he never did."

"No," Merlin said. He sighed. The boy was leaping with impatience. He was fierce as the young are, without age to dull their edges.

And after all, thought Merlin, it was time. Roland had asked. Merlin would answer.

"Listen," he said. "I have a story."

Roland knew what that meant. He looked as if he might protest, but clearly thought better of it. He drew up his knees and clasped them, and settled as he had so often before, to hear his teacher tell a tale.

"Long, long ago," said Merlin, "in the dawn of the world, when Egypt was young, when Ur of the Chaldees was a raw new city and Babylon but a cluster of huts beside a muddy river, there was a sorcerer, a great master of magic. At first he was a master of the light, but as he grew older and more aware of his own mortality, he turned little by little toward the dark. Then at last, in terror of death, he turned his back altogether on the light, and made a great pact with the Prince of Darkness—no less than that one who is called the Son of the Morning."

"Sathanas," Roland breathed. "The Great Evil."

Merlin nodded. "Yes. That one himself. The sorcerer gave his soul in return for his body's life. He gained much else, too: beauty, wealth, power. Oh, he was beautiful, like a dark angel, and men fell on their faces before him.

"But evil is never content. It was a condition of his pact that he be no king himself, but rule through the power of a king. And so he did, from generation to generation. But men's lives are short and their memories treacherous. For each king who died, he must find another, corrupt him, raise him up, rule through him, watch him grow old, then have it all to do again.

"He grew greatly weary of this endless round. For a long while he withdrew from the world, built himself a fortress with strong spells, and set himself to master all magic that there was in the world. Yet he found he could not do that, for the magic of the light was now closed to him. And that, in its time, drove him nigh mad.

"Then in his stronghold, amid his armies of demons and spirits of the dark, he heard a rumor, a whisper, a tale brought in scattered fragments from the world's heart. The Messiah had come to Jerusalem, or so it was said. He had come, and lived as the most mortal of men, and died as a criminal, hung on a cross.

"And that, said the messengers who brought this word to the world's end, was preposterous; and yet it seemed to be true. For the light is incalculable, and its ways are not mortal ways, and it does as it pleases to do, beyond reason or sense or logic.

"The sorcerer would have regarded this as a curiosity, a fine tale for a long night, except for the rumor that came with it. It was even more fragmentary than the word of the Messiah—who after all was but the incarnation of a minor deity in a very small province of the Roman Empire. And Rome, as every seer knew, was about to destroy that province utterly, and scatter its people to the winds of the world.

"Still, the rumor was this: that before the god's son died, he had celebrated a feast of sacrifice. He had offered up a cup of his own blood, blood of a god, in token of the life that would be given thereafter. And that, as any mage knew, was the greatest of sacrifices, the divine sacrifice, that could redeem or destroy the world.

"Others before him had done this. Osiris, Tammuz, the Green King—their blood bound the chains of earth and

heaven, and strengthened the light in its long battle against
the dark. But none of them had left behind a relic, a remembrance, a vessel that had held his blood. That vessel
was in the hands of a man of Jerusalem, or so it was said; it
was kept hidden, perhaps in ignorance of its power.

"For power it had, beyond any instrument of magic that
had been in this world. It belonged to the light, but it was
not necessarily of the light. In the hands of a master of the
dark, it would be a great weapon, and a mighty force for
destruction.

"The sorcerer wanted it. He wanted it as he had wanted
nothing in all the long ages of his life—even more strongly
than he had wanted to live forever. He wanted this thing,
the cup of a god's blood. He wanted it, and he set out to
take it.

"And he could not win it. It was taken out of Jerusalem
in its fall, when the Temple burned and Roman armies
trampled the holy places. It was spirited away, hidden from
him, taken to the far edge of the world, even to the isle of
Britain. And there he found it, but he could not win it. It
was too well protected.

"He wielded every sleight and wile and power at his disposal. He put on the semblance of mortal man: first a priest
of the Romans, then a Druid of the Britons. But this cup,
this Grail as it was called in Britain, was kept from him,
and hidden away where he could not find it.

"Then at last he conceived a plan. He found a woman, a
meek vessel as he thought her. He summoned a demon, a
prince of his master's court, to lie with her and get a child
on her. For he could not do this himself, much as he might
wish to: that was another price of his deathlessness, to for-
sake all pleasure of woman's body, and all hope of getting
children. But the demon whom he summoned put on his
face, his semblance of supernal beauty, and so seduced the
woman.

"In the passing of time she bore a son, a child without a
father, a strange inhuman creature whose every breath was
magic."

"You," said Roland. "That was you."

"Yes," said Merlin. "I was that child, wrought by a sorcerer to seize the Grail. But he had underestimated my
mother. She was a princess of Gwynedd, a redoubtable

woman even in her youth, and she was a Druid and the daughter of Druids. She raised me as she saw fit, and that was in the light; and when my creator came to claim me, I was already corrupted. My mother had warned me what to expect, and advised me to betray as little of myself as possible. Therefore I seemed a biddable young thing, and dull, so that the sorcerer decided in the end to leave me where I was—but aware of his presence, and ready to do as he bade me, whenever he should have need of me.

"Which in time he did. He used me to make a king as he had done so often before: to raise up Uther as king over Britain, and to seduce him with the lady of Cornwall, and thus to beget Arthur. Arthur was to be his puppet, his kingly servant.

"But I was my mother's son, and from the very beginning I was Arthur's man. I loved him, both the child he was and the king I foresaw. I swore a great oath before the gods, that I would keep him in the light, and never surrender him to the darkness.

"So did I betray my maker twice over. I was not the meek slave he had wrought me to be, nor was my Arthur the puppet king that he was to have been. We had defied him, and worse, succeeded—and made him our bitter enemy.

"It was he who sent the vision of the Grail into Arthur's warband, and so broke the fellowship in its obsession with the quest. And it was he who seduced Nimue and set her to betray me; but she woke to the truth too late, and knew what she had done. She could not free me, but she could protect Arthur, and did, as much as she might. His kingdom fell, but his soul was saved; and his son, who was to have been the sorcerer's puppet, was slain by Arthur's own hand.

"As for the Grail, which was the cause of it all, it was indeed almost betrayed into the sorcerer's hands. He found it in its hiding place in the kingdom of Montsalvat, in a fortress called Carbonek, protected by nine enchantresses and by a brotherhood of holy warriors ruled by a Druid king. The sorcerer corrupted the king's son, maimed and nigh destroyed him. But when the Grail was all but in his grasp, one of Arthur's own warband came bearing the power of the light, and so saved the prince and the fortress and the Grail. The sorcerer was cast down by the might of the Grail. His beauty was rent from him, and much of his strength. The Grail was saved. The light had conquered.

"But it was too late for me," Merlin said, "or for Nimue, whom I still loved. Poor child, she was racked with guilt. She swore to guard me, and bound our daughter to it, too. I would not have permitted that, but she was careful to do it where I could not prevent her.

"For she was convinced that as greatly diminished as our old enemy was, he was not dead; and he would look for me, to destroy me if he could, for I had betrayed him in everything that I did. I had raised Arthur in the light, I had won over Nimue—and yes, I had taught that young warrior, too, the one called Parsifal, so that he came to Montsalvat and redeemed its prince, and saved the Grail. He had a fair store of magic, did Parsifal. His forefathers had brought the Grail out of Jerusalem before its fall; and Nimue was his mother's child, his own sister."

"You taught him deliberately, then," said Roland. "You knew what he would be."

"Ah," said Merlin, lifting his shoulder in a shrug. "I take no credit for that. The gods—or God, if you will— had rather more to do with it than I did. But he was a good pupil. Not as good as his sister, or for that matter as you are, but good enough in the end. He nearly failed, you know. When he came to Montsalvat, his foresight abandoned him. He was silent when he should have spoken, and shrank back when he should have been bold. But for that, the sorcerer would never have found the Grail's hiding place at all."

"But because he did," Roland said, "he was destroyed. Wasn't it a good thing, then, that Parsifal did seem to fail?"

"Some would call it blind luck," Merlin said. "I call it the gods' hand—and their humor, too, maybe."

"You are not a Christian," Roland said, as if he had not realized it long before.

Merlin laughed—and that was something, too, that he had not done in long ages before this child came to disturb his peace. "I am half a devil, boy. Do you think the Church would have me?"

Roland's eyes narrowed. His head tilted. He was not

laughing, but his eyes were glinting. "I think," he said after a while, "that it would try to exorcise you."

"It would indeed," Merlin said.

"And yet you believe in the Grail."

"I believe that it held the blood of a god. The Messiah, if you will. So yes, I believe that your Christ is the son of your God. And he is a face of the light, which I do my best to serve, though I am half a child of the dark."

"That's how she bound you," Roland said. "That's how she did it. She laid the binding on the dark half of you. But she couldn't destroy you—which is what he wanted, isn't it? He wanted you dead and worse than dead. She loved you; and you are half of the light. That half saved your life."

"Such a life," said Merlin.

"You'd rather be dead and in hell?"

"Not likely," Merlin said.

"I will free you," Roland said. "However long it takes me, whatever it costs me. I will set you free."

"You need not bind yourself to that," said Merlin. "I earned this captivity; I had sins enough, when all was told."

Roland tossed his head in refusal. "You did not! I will break the spell. That I swear to you. And if I fail, may the earth gape and swallow me, may the sky fall and crush me, may the sea rise up and devour my bones."

Merlin flung up a hand. But it was too late—as it had been for Nimue. The great oath rolled out of that slender body, made all the more mighty by the strength of the boy's magic. Magic that he had inherited in full measure from Merlin, and from Nimue, who was of the blood of the Grail: light and darkness melded in him, so strong and so fierce and so headlong that even Merlin could not stop or slow him.

Roland had bound himself in ways that he could not begin to understand. Not only to Merlin, but to all that Merlin had done, both good and ill. And—

"Child," Merlin said in the vast silence after the oath, "be wary. Oh, be wary! The sorcerer who made me, who through your foremother bound me, is still alive. He is still powerful, though never what he was before Parsifal cast him down. That is why I was guarded—as the Grail was, to protect me from him. That is why Nimue and our daughter and our granddaughter stayed hidden here. We are all safe in this place, as the Grail is safe in its stronghold. But if we are betrayed—if the sorcerer finds us—"

"Let him find us," said Roland in the arrogance of his youth. "He's grown weak. We're strong. And maybe, if he's destroyed forever, all magics that he made will be destroyed, too. And that will free you from your prison."

"Child," Merlin began, but he could not go on. He should have known. He should have waited till the boy was older to tell him this of all stories—till the boy was a man, and preferably a man of ample years. Youth knew no restraint, and despised prudence.

But it was done, and could not be undone. Nor was Roland strong enough yet to break the spell. Maybe he would never be—and maybe the enemy would never find him. Even when, as he must, he went out into the world; when he took up the lordship that was his by right, and stood up before his peers and his king, and made himself known to them by name and face.

Merlin caught himself praying for that, to a god for whom he had had little use before: the boy's own God, the God of the Christians, who ruled now in this part of the world. Merlin doubted that one of all stiff-necked and narrow-minded divinities would listen to the son of a devil, but he prayed nonetheless, for the boy's sake—this boy whom, day by day and year by year, he had come to love. That he would be safe. That the enemy would not find him. And that his oath not rise up to destroy him, that oath he had sworn in the fullness of his heart, and so bound himself beyond any unbinding.

Unless his God could set him free. *Keep me bound if you must,* Merlin prayed, *but let him be free. God of the Israelites, Lord of the Grail—let him be free.*

PART ONE

※ ※ ※

DURANDAL

CHAPTER 1

✠ ✠ ✠

Olivier had won the toss for the girl. Turpin, who never played, and Roland, who often won, lingered for a while outside the tent. The rest of the king's Companions had wandered off in search of other amusement—and another woman, too, if that was to be had.

It was still broad daylight, though the shadows were lengthening. The warmth of early spring was giving way to a creeping chill. Turpin shivered. Roland tossed a new log on the fire, feeding it till it swelled to a respectable blaze. He stayed there on one knee while the sounds from the tent swelled to a crescendo. The girl, a strapping Saxon, was loudly enthusiastic.

Turpin opened his mouth to remark on it, but shut it again after a moment. Roland seemed lost in a dream, or in contemplation of something very far away from this royal assembly of the Franks. The fire cast ruddy light on his face and lost itself in his eyes. Such odd eyes, yellow as a hawk's. Sometimes he did not look human at all.

He raised a hand idly, slipping it in among the flames. They licked his fingers. He stroked them as a woman pets her cat. They purred as a cat purrs, leaping, curling about his hand, arching under his palm.

Turpin set his lips together carefully. Equally carefully, and with an effort, he turned his eyes away. Roland was not as other men were. All the Companions knew it; and none

of them said a word. Roland was their brother, their com-
rade in arms. They would not betray him.

Roland came to himself all at once, and rose so quickly
that Turpin started. Roland was still oblivious to the man
beside him, or seemed to be, until he said, "Something's
coming."

Turpin frowned. There were always people coming and
going where the king was—and here, at Paderborn, in the
forests of newly conquered Saxony, the whole might of the
kingdom had gathered. People came from all over the world
to speak with or present petitions or offer tribute or threaten
war with the King of the Franks.

But Roland meant something else—something alarming, from the look of him. He was striding away already,
aiming toward the middle of what was now little more than
a camp; but in time it would be a fortress, a strong holding
amid the Saxon forests.

The shape of the citadel was cleared, the line of its walls
marked out. Most of the camp spread outside of it, but the
king's tent stood in its center, and he sat in front of it, holding audience and judging disputes. Roland was well on his
way there before Turpin mustered wits to follow.

Turpin's longer legs brought him level soon enough.
Roland glanced at him and let slip the flicker of a smile.
Turpin suppressed a sigh. People who said the Count of the
Breton Marches was a witch did not know the half of it.

Jehan Turpin, Archbishop of Rheims, Companion and
battle-brother of the King of the Franks, preferred not to
ponder too many complexities when it came to his friends.
If that made him a bad priest, then so be it. God would
judge; and, Turpin hoped, be merciful.

He followed Roland in among the crowd that was always present where the king was. Roland was not a small
man, but he was lighter built than Franks tended to be. He
could slip through gaps too narrow for a man of Turpin's
bulk, and make his way all but unnoticed to a place almost
within reach of the king. Turpin had to push and thrust and
trample toes to do the same.

Rank had its privileges—and episcopal garb cut short
many a curse. Turpin smiled sweetly at the most irate, and
stared down one idiot who would have drawn blade—here,
in front of the king, where he could have his throat slit for

thinking of it—and settled in some contentment just in back of Roland.

Charles the king sat in a chair that he had brought up last year from Rome: a very old chair, a curule chair, such as consuls had sat in when the Empire was alive. It was a chair with broad aspirations, which was fortunate, for Charles was a large man. A giant, the Romans had thought him, as tall as he was, and as broad, and as manifestly strong. Those shoulders could heft a whole ox, and those arms wield a great sword for half the day.

The late sun glimmered on his hair. Bright gold when he was a boy, it was early going silver. What gold was left in it matched the metal of his crown. He sat with chin on fist, frowning at the intricacies of a contention between a pair of freemen.

On another day Turpin might have listened, for he found the law fascinating, and the king's grasp of it was remarkable. But Roland was not watching the king or the petitioners. His eyes were on those who waited their turn, still a sizable company though it was nearing sunset. Most were Franks, and a small number of those were noblemen. A pair of king's envoys stood off to the side, with a small retinue at their backs.

Roland had come to court a hand of years ago, somewhat after Turpin had last seen these two of the king's messengers. They had been away whenever the Companions were in attendance, running the king's errands through the south and west of Francia. It was unusual to see them here in the far reaches of the realm; they must bring news that could not wait for the king to make his way into their own country.

Roland was watching them with peculiar, almost alarming fixity. He looked like a hawk hunting its prey.

The freemen ended their wrangling at last. Charles pondered briefly, nodded, said to one of them, "You take the cow. He takes the calf. And have a care! If you try to take the calf back, I will know of it, and demand an accounting."

Then they were dismissed, and his envoys from Aquitania had come forward, bowing low. Charles rose from his chair to greet them, pulling them erect, laughing and embracing them both. "Riquier! Father Ganelon! Well met, well met indeed! It's not bad news, I hope?"

"Not bad, sire," said Riquier, "so much as interesting."

"So?" said Charles. He laid an arm about the shoulders of each. "Here, let me finish here, then we'll eat. Then you can tell me everything."

Riquier grinned. He was a big florid man, very fond of his wine and his meat—and of a willing woman, too, by all accounts. Ganelon the priest beside him seemed a grey shadow: small, thin, frail, with pallid hair thinning round the tonsure. Only his eyes had any color or substance to them. They were long and dark, hooded under heavy lids. He leaned on the arm of a man whom Turpin recalled as a kinsman of his—brother or nephew—and rested within the protection of two more like the first. They were as gaunt as he, robed as monks, and their faces were empty of expression. As far as Turpin knew, none of the three had ever spoken a word.

Roland gripped Turpin's arm so tightly that Turpin's breath caught with the pain. "That one," he said, low and harsh. "What is he?"

"That's Father Ganelon," Turpin said, "the king's counselor. He comes from somewhere in Italy, he and his kinsmen. He's not much to look at, but he's skilled in keeping the king's peace. The king trusts him."

"Italy? He comes from Italy?"

"Somewhere in—Apulia? Cumae?"

Roland laughed, sharp and short. "Oh, yes. I would believe that he comes from the gates of hell."

"Come now," Turpin said. "Pretty he is not. But he can hardly be a devil."

"The Devil may quote Scripture," Roland said. He slipped under Turpin's arm and was gone, vanished in the crowd of Franks.

"And aren't you a fine one to speak of devils," Turpin muttered to the place where his friend had been.

Roland heard that. His ears were keen—too keen for comfort, sometimes. But he heard no anger in the archbishop's voice. Turpin was remarkably supple of mind for a priest. Whatever he guessed, whatever he knew, he kept to himself.

Roland's flight took him almost out of the tent-city, down the little river that flowed from myriad springs, to the edge of the horselines. The pack animals grazed in a herd, but the warhorses, the big fierce stallions, were tethered one by one near the water's edge. They called to Roland as he came, cries of recognition, welcome, the occasional challenge. He grinned at that, in spite of his heart's trouble.

His own stallion grazed midway down the line, between Olivier's massive bay and Turpin's fine red chestnut. Veillantif was his name. He was not as tall as some, but neither was Roland; and he was a grey, dappled like the moon. His sire had been one of the king's own stallions. His dam had come from Spain, where the horses were the most beautiful in the world. He had his sire's strength and his dam's beauty, and a swift intelligence that delighted Roland beyond measure.

He greeted Roland with a flutter of the nostrils and a toss of the head, pawing imperiously for the bit of sweet cake that he knew Roland would have for him. Roland leaned against the high arched neck and for a little while simply breathed. The temptation to put off his human semblance was so strong that he almost could not bear it. He felt the shifting within, the blurring of his edges. It was all too easy in this place of living waters, in the embrace of the ancient wood.

With an effort of will he stopped it. Now of all times he must not yield to temptation. He must be master of his magic, and of his heart, too.

"He has come," he said to Veillantif in the old tongue of the Bretons. "The old one, the evil one—he is here. He is *here*."

Veillantif snorted and nosed at Roland's tunic, searching for another bit of cake. Ancient evil meant little to him. Sweet cake was here, and it was now, and he wanted it.

Roland sighed. If he had wanted to wallow in terror, he would not have come to this place. He smoothed a tangle in the stallion's long pale mane. He had to think, and think quickly. But first he had to know where to begin.

The guards were talking, out past the line of stallions. Two of the four rode the edges as they should, but the others idled for a while in the shade of a young oak. Roland's ears caught a name, as if the thought had conjured it: "Ganelon? Yes, he's here, and Riquier, too. They're running just ahead of their news. Spain has sent an embassy."

"What, the infidels?" drawled his brother. If Roland had not known better, he would have thought the man had drunk too deep of Saxon ale, but few in the king's army were fool enough to do that while on watch. Charles was merciless toward drunkards.

This one was lazy by nature, that was all, and disinclined to exert himself for anything so trivial as an embassy from heathen Spain.

"The infidels," the elder brother agreed. "It seems they need our king to settle a dispute."

"Everyone wants our king to do that," said the younger. "Now tell me something that matters. Tell me there will be a woman in our bed tonight."

"Not much chance of that," the elder sighed. "The lords have taken what few there are. Me, I'd give gold if I had any, to get me a fine wanton Saxon with long yellow braids."

They yearned together, at length and in tedious detail. Roland pondered what they had said. Spain? A quarrel among infidels? Surely that was not enough to have brought two royal envoys so far out of their accustomed round. There must be more. Something had brought the enemy here. Merlin's enemy, the enemy of the Grail.

Roland shuddered, clinging to the warm solidity of Veillantif's neck. He tried to laugh at himself. He was a lord, a prince, a warrior of renown; and he was an enchanter, if a very young and foolish one. And when at last he set eyes on the one against whom he had sworn the mightiest of oaths, he had run in sheer mindless terror.

He could tell himself that it was more surprise than fear; more astonishment than cowardice. He had not looked to find the enemy here. There were kings enough in the world, and princes, too. The Lombards, the Saxons, the Gascons, the Basques, the infidels in Spain—any or all of them could have fallen under the enemy's spell. But not Charles. Not Roland's bright strong king.

Part of him cried out to rise up, raise all his magics, destroy the sorcerer. But he was not a child any longer. He was a man, and a man knew his limits. He was not strong enough. And if he flung himself into the battle regardless, if he lost his life and his soul in challenging an enemy who, even vastly weakened, was still far stronger than he, then everything was lost, given up to the enemy. Merlin in his prison in Broceliande. Charles the king on his throne. All the bright realm of Francia, and all the realms that Charles might come to rule.

Wisdom was a bitter thing. His heart called it cowardice. He thrust it down and set his foot on it. He would fulfill his oath. But not now.

There could not be a battle. Not yet. But neither could Roland run away and hide. He had to protect the king. Charles trusted Ganelon, Turpin had said. So had other, far older kings done, and been seduced, until they had no will but Ganelon's.

None of them had had Roland to defend them.

And how he was to do that, with the face he had, that was the image of Merlin's in its youth . . .

He could pray. And hide in plain sight. And be very, very careful not to betray the power that was in him. Even if he should be recognized as one of Merlin's children, he could seem both ignorant and harmless, a far distant, feeble off-shoot of that long-fallen tree.

It was a poor hope to hang a king's soul on. But it was the best he had. He would cling to it as he could, and trust that it would be enough.

CHAPTER 2

❖ ❖ ❖

Roland set himself to be the king's most loyal guardian hound. He doubled the guard—staring down any who questioned it—and stood watch himself in the nights. In the days he did his duties as he was bidden, and those, too, often, were to ride out and away from the king.

He wondered if that was Ganelon's doing. But the old serpent seemed content to efface himself among his fellow priests and royal counselors. He had, it seemed, a fair talent for the matters of chancery, and a clerk's love of ink and parchment. Roland never saw or heard him in colloquy with the king, nor was anyone else aware of it.

The day after Ganelon arrived, Roland passed him near the king's tent, going toward the clerks' quarter. Roland was in armor, and armed, ready to ride out hunting bandits. He had his sword and his spear and his great ivory horn, and was, if he reflected on it, rather noticeable.

Ganelon did not look up or acknowledge his presence. He shivered when the king's counselor had passed. Perhaps it was only his own foolishness, but the air felt odd near Ganelon, as if the light had gone all grey, and the warmth been leached from the sun. Then Ganelon was past, and Roland was striding on his way. It was true, then, as he had hoped. Ganelon did not take note of him, or know what he was.

*   *   *

The embassy from Spain rode into Paderborn on a day that shimmered with mist and the soft kiss of rain. They were as exotic as bright birds in that grey light, with their silken banners and their strange marching-music, their beards and their turbans and their dark hawk-faces. They brought falcons in vivid jesses, and hounds of a sort that had never run in this country; and they rode on little light horses out of the east, or on the ram-nosed chargers of Spain.

Roland had been out hunting bandits for the past handful of days, with the king under guard behind him, and Turpin in charge of that guard. When he came back with the bandit king's head on his spear, word was running through that city of tents and half-sketched walls: the infidels were coming.

Roland saw his men settled, the horses taken care of. The grisly object on its spear, he let Ogier keep. Ogier was a Dane, and somewhat bloody-minded. Roland never asked what he did with the trophies he took. It was enough that no one saw them afterward.

People were running now through the streets and alleys of the camp. Roland let himself be caught up in them, plucked away from Olivier and the others, and carried off to the place where the city gates would be.

The king was waiting in the cleared space with its boundaries of builders' twine, dressed in a tunic of crimson silk and wearing the iron crown that he had won from the Lombards. Roland saw Turpin near him, and the complement of guards as Roland had ordered. Ganelon was nowhere in sight.

Two or three people nearby were muttering among themselves, and none too quietly, either. "This is a Christian army. What are we doing bowing and scraping to a pack of infidels?"

"I suppose," someone else said, "we could do as we did with the Saxons. Offer them a choice: the baptismal font or the headsman's axe."

"Douse them in river-water," said a third with a bark of laughter, "and settle it for once and all."

Roland sighed for his father's people, that they should be so narrow-minded. And what would they think if they knew the truth of what he was? These servants of Allah were safely and simply human. His teacher and much-loved forebear was half a devil.

He closed ears and mind to his countrymen's foolish-ness, and turned the whole of his attention to the embassy. He had seen Saracens before in his handful of years with the king, but never so large or so rich a company.

Nearly all of them were men. The few women rode in curtained wagons. Near the end of the line, a little apart but seemingly content in it, a figure rode on a white horse. The rider was dressed like any other man in that company, in silken trousers and embroidered coat, but the face was beardless and the hair covered by a cap rather than a tur-ban. A boy? A eunuch slave, perhaps?

Surely no slave would be mounted on such a horse as this one. It was a stallion of the Spanish breed, white as moon on snow, with flowing mane and a tail that brushed the ground. It did not walk or trot as another horse might. It danced, light as air; yet it was a solid creature, deep of chest, broad of rump, with a strong arched neck. Even Veil-lantif was not so fine as this.

All too slowly it dawned on Roland that the rider was neither boy nor eunuch—that the shape in the bright silks was anything but male. It sat light and easy on the broad white back, as one sits who has ridden since childhood. The slender hand was light on the rein, the fair face fixed straight ahead, taking no notice of the Franks who crowded on either side.

She was as beautiful as the horse she rode, and strikingly foreign. She was no black Moor, but neither was she a fair-skinned Frank. She was a brown woman; warm cream-brown skin, curling brown-gold hair, long gold-brown eyes set slightly aslant in her high-cheeked face. It was a beauty Roland had not seen before. It caught him and held him rapt. Once he had become aware of it, he could not turn away. He wanted to—he would have given much to—

He brought himself sternly to order. This was an infidel, a Saracen. Very likely she belonged to a man who would take great exception to any Frank's interest in his woman. Though what he was doing letting her ride unveiled among unbelievers, Roland could not easily imagine.

Maybe then she did not belong to anyone. Maybe—

He was babbling in his head, captivated by that blessed

glory of a face. And he a man grown, lord and warrior, chosen companion of the king. He had more wits than that, and more sense, too. Was not Merlin his teacher? Had not Merlin taught him to beware the enticements of a woman?

While Roland was so signally distracted, the embassy met and greeted the king and were welcomed into his city. The speeches were not too long, all things considered, or too crashingly dull. When those were over, they all rode together, king and Saracens, inward from the gate to the heart of the camp.

The crowd followed, leaving the gate-space behind. Roland stood his ground. When the last of them had passed, he was standing on the trampled earth, alone but for a bit of wind and a sparkle in the bruised grass not far from his foot.

He bent to take up that sparkle in the grass. It was a silver token on a chain, smooth and round and singing softly in his hand. The singing should have disconcerted him, and yet as he held the token, it seemed the most natural thing in the world. It was a song like water on stone, like wind in leaves, like stars in distant heaven; but like a mother singing to her child, too, and lovers murmuring to one another, soft and inexpressibly tender.

He turned the token in his hand. It was a coin, pierced for a chain, and very old, worn almost smooth. One side portrayed a human shape, a man perhaps, with a spear in his hand. The other was a cup or bowl, a simple curve of silver, unadorned.

"Roland!"

He turned quickly. Before he stopped to think, the token had vanished, hidden away in his tunic. He would find its owner later, he promised himself. Surely one of the Saracens had dropped it. It did not have the feel of a Frankish thing. It felt strange, as if it came from another world than this.

He had no time to ponder it further, not then. Olivier had found him. Olivier his friend, his battle-brother, laid a massive arm about his shoulders, grinned at him with an expression of purest idiot sweetness, and said, "Tell me now and get it over. Who is she?"

Roland flushed. He had not been thinking of the Saracen woman at all, but under Olivier's deceptively witless blue stare, he felt as if her portrait were painted on his forehead.

"I don't even know her name," he said—like a fool, or a man too startled to think.

"That should matter?" Olivier pulled him back toward the tent-city. "Who is she? Is she a Saxon? A royal maid? A—" His eyes sharpened. "A Saracen? You spied one of *those*?"

Roland was not about to tell Olivier that the woman had been riding in plain sight, not if Olivier's eagle eye had failed to find her. He shrugged. "It was just a glimpse."

"So tell me! How beautiful was she? Was she dark, like olives? Or was she fair? They have fair women, it's said—slaves stolen from us."

Roland shrugged again, which he knew would madden Olivier, but he was in a strange and reckless mood. This was not a woman to bandy about among guardsmen.

Olivier astonished him: he shrugged himself, and said, "Very well, keep a secret. I'll find it out soon enough."

"Maybe there is no secret," said Roland.

Olivier laughed. "Yes, and it was nothing at all that made you blush like a girl. She must be quite remarkable."

"And quite, quite thoroughly owned by a bloodthirsty Saracen," said Roland.

"That should stop us?"

"*You* will do nothing," Roland said, "except continue to cut a swath through the women of Saxony. This one is not for us, brother. That, I know in my bones."

"Your bones are old before their time," Olivier muttered.

Roland jabbed him shrewdly in the ribs, which flattened him; but he came up fighting. They roared and tumbled to a very satisfactory conclusion, up again and arm in arm and hunting down a cook who could be wheedled into feeding them at this odd hour.

Once the ceremony of welcome was over, Christians and infidels withdrew to their separate encampments. The infidels had been given a corner of the as yet unbuilt walls, a green meadow by the river with ample grass for the horses. They professed themselves delighted with it, though it was full of buzzing insects. In a little while their bright tents were up, fitted with gauzy draperies that did rather well to keep out the stinging hordes.

Charles the king made his way there without fanfare, not long after the sun had set. He took Roland with him for escort.

They walked together in silence, a tall lord and his smaller, slighter retainer. The night was bright enough for Roland's eyes, but to most men it was black dark, starless and damp still with rain. Charles to passersby would be hardly more than a shape looming in the mist, a big broad-shouldered man among hundreds of his like.

Roland was comfortable in the king's shadow. It was not the first time Charles had trusted him so. Sometimes the king wanted a quieter meeting than royal custom allowed, and for that he needed a man who knew the uses of silence. Roland had learned all of those from his childhood, cherished them and cultivated them.

He had been rather startled nonetheless to be sent for at sunset, when he had thought himself forgotten in the excitement of the infidels' coming. Charles was waiting alone a little distance from the lights and evening clamor of his tent. He smiled when Roland came stepping softly in the gloom, tilted his head in greeting, and walked away without a word.

They passed a pair of Saracen guards, soft-footed silent men with eyes that glittered in a distant flicker of firelight. The guards knew the king. They bowed in their graceful alien way, and with gestures that made Roland think of a dance, guided them through the circles of tents.

The tallest and broadest and brightest housed the leader of the embassy. He was stretched at his ease within, in a glow of lamps and a waft of spices. He rose with a cat's grace and bowed low before the King of the Franks. The others with him, jeweled lords and quiet servants, followed their master's example. They were like a field of grain stroked by the wind.

Suleiman ibn Yaqzan ibn Al-Arabi, governor of Barcelona and Gerona, lord and emir of the Caliph in Baghdad, spoke a quite reasonable Latin. "Welcome," he said in that tongue, "my lord of Francia. Will you sit? Rest? Take a cup of sherbet?"

Charles accepted a cup—to refuse it would have been an

insult. He sipped from it, too, and seemed suitably appreciative, though Roland had not known him to be fond of fruit or sweetness. Wine he enjoyed in moderation, but even that little was forbidden to a Muslim.

Roland effaced himself as was fitting, withdrew to a patch of shadow and stood still. The king would not say what he had come to say, not for a while. There were compliments to exchange, trivialities to consider at considerable length. The exigencies of the journey, the dampness of the weather, the pleasant situation of this new royal city, came under minute scrutiny.

At last and roundabout, they came to it. Charles left off pretending to sip at his third cup of sherbet. Al-Arabi nibbled a bit of confection, set down the rest. Charles said, "Tell me what brings a Muslim of such eminence to the court of the infidel."

Al-Arabi answered with brevity startling in a man whose public phrases tended to be both lengthy and convoluted. "Rebellion. Insurrection."

"The upstart Caliph in Cordoba?"

Al-Arabi inclined his head. "Indeed. Just so."

"And you want my help."

"Baghdad is far away," said Al-Arabi. "The Caliph, may Allah bless his name, has wars nearer home, and a great realm that needs ruling. Francia is strong and its armies are numerous. And its king, as the Protector of the Faithful has taken care to remind me, has been for some time a friend and royal brother to my lord in Baghdad."

"We do find one another congenial," Charles said, "though there are some among my people who would object to that."

Al-Arabi flicked his hand, dismissing the thought. "Certainly they may protest, but the decision is yours to make. Are you not the king?"

"King of the Franks," Charles said a little too gently. "I rule by the will of the people. If they forbid this thing, I can't legally do it."

"Will they forbid it," asked Al-Arabi, "if you offer them the opportunity to advance on our lands as our armies once did on yours?"

Charles' brows rose.

"Not," said Al-Arabi, "that we will ever permit you to

conquer us, but your aid of our Caliph against the rebel could be seen as a blow for Christianity against the infidel."

"That is subtle," Charles said, "but dangerous. For you if we succeed too well. For me if my people discover the lie."

"What lie is there? A Christian king marches into a Muslim country to put down an insurrection. The Caliph's loyal servants invite him; he comes on a mission sanctioned by both his God and Allah. If your more simple people need to be told only of God's will, not of Allah's—is there harm in that?"

"Some would call that devil's logic," Charles said, but lightly. He tugged at his fair mustaches, frowning as he pondered. After a while he said, "Tell me what I have to gain from this, aside from my brother the Caliph's thanks."

"Barcelona," Al-Arabi answered, "and Gerona, and Saragossa, and all their peoples and territories, to hold under Frankish authority. A jewel in the crown of Spain, while my Caliph holds the rest."

"You would bow to me as your king?" Charles asked him.

He looked Charles in the face—striking in a man of so gracefully indirect a people—and said clearly, "Yes. I would. But always in the understanding that I remain a follower of the Prophet, and of his heir the Caliph. You would rule me in the body, but in spirit I remain a Muslim."

"And if I demanded that you convert?"

The dark eyes glittered. "As you converted the Saxons, my lord king? Well then, I would choose to lose my head. But you would lose Spain."

Charles laughed. His voice was light for a man so large, but his laughter was rich and full. Al-Arabi waited courteously for him to finish, and to explain. Which he duly did, through gusts of lingering mirth. "My lord emir, the Saxons were a pack of howling savages who worshipped trees and stones. You people of the Book, who know our Lord Christ and reckon him a prophet, may be somewhat confused as to doctrine, but you'll never be converted by a headsman's axe. You, we'll teach by example, once we share a kingdom."

"Or we might teach you, and you'll profess the Faith."

Charles' grin was wide, mirthful, and he seemed completely certain that such a thing would never happen.

They settled on it then, there between the two of them, though on the morrow there would be a council in which it would all ostensibly be decided. Charles would muster an army and come to the aid of the Caliph. The Caliph in return would make him lord and emir over selected cities of Spain. That would be made palatable to Charles' good Christian people, though he would not lie to them—in that he was adamant. He might shade the truth. He would not twist it altogether.

It was late when Charles left the emir's tent. While he lingered there, the rain had blown away. The stars were out. The moon rode high. To Roland it seemed as bright as daylight.

Most of the tent-city slept. There were still a few people about, seeking the privies or huddled about a campfire. None took much notice of the king.

Roland was calm but alert, as a guard should be. If he used other senses than a man of more mortal heritage might, then all the better for the king's protection.

The corner of his eye caught a flicker in shadow. It was quick, light, supple. Its eyes gleamed on him, fixed for a moment, held with a sharp and piercing intelligence. Then it was gone, hunting some lurker in the night.

Roland remembered to breathe again. It was only a cat, he told himself. It was not friendly, but neither was it hostile. It was as cats were: absorbed within itself.

And yet he could not help but remember those eyes, how clear they had been in the dark, seeing through him as if he had been made of water. One creature in this place knew him for what he was—knew the whole of him, and not only the part that he allowed human eyes to see.

CHAPTER 3

▦ ▦ ▦

Sarissa left her tent in the early morning, just as the first grey light touched the reeds along the river's edge. This country was so rich, so wet—water welling out of the ground and flowing in great slow rivers, pooling in lakes or sinking into marshes. Here where the Frankish king was building his city—did he know what power was in this place? Tenscore springs bubbled from the mountain's foot, feeding a river that fed a greater river.

Water in its softness could wear away stone. Water was great magic. Evil could not cross it. Dark things were washed clean in it.

Sarissa went down to the lesser river, walking barefoot in the grass. It was delicious, wonderful, to do such a thing outside of a garden, on the edge of a wild wood.

Tarik appeared out of the soft and misty air and wove about her ankles, mewing like the cat he seemed. He had a satisfied expression. The hunting had been good, it said.

"Mice?" she asked him.

He hissed. *Snakes,* he said. He licked his lips with a pink tongue, and yawned vastly, so that she might see the full armament of his teeth.

"Snakes? Here?"

He shrugged a cat-shrug, an insouciant flip of the tail. She walked slowly just behind him, her bright mood gone dark.

The strength of wood and water restored her with startling swiftness. Even the oldest of old serpents could not thrive here, though he might slither and slink and do his best to corrupt the weak of spirit.

The sky paled to silver and rose as she came down to the river. She bent to lave her face, to drink of the cold clean water. When she had had her fill, she knelt there for a while, breathing damp cool air, watching the sun spread light across the horizon.

The river caught the flame of it. She trailed her fingers in water as bright as fire. It was clear here, and filling with light. Fishes darted; weeds swayed in the current. Farther out, where the river was deeper, the water darkened to black beneath the sun's brilliance.

Sarissa pulled off her boots and waded out into the icy river. The shock of the cold made her gasp, but she steeled herself to bear it. The current tugged at her. She rooted herself in the earth. The water flowed over her but could not move her. When it lapped her chin, she filled her lungs with every scrap of air that they could hold, and slipped into a strange dark-bright world.

She swam as a fish swims, supple and swift, down and down into that realm of dim green shapes and rippling weeds, lit with sudden flashes of light: sun rising, fish leaping. She passed out of the sun's light, but there was light below her, a gleam in the river's darkness.

Just as she knew that her breath must fail her, her outstretched hand touched the thing that lay on the river's bottom. It was hard, colder than the water, and caught fast in a tangle of weeds and clay. She grasped the end of it and thrust against the current. Her lungs had begun to burn. But she would not let go.

The earth fought for the victory, but the water in its current caught Sarissa and swirled her suddenly upward. Blind, half-unconscious, lungs afire, she burst into the light.

She fell on the green bank with her prize caught beneath her. Out of the water it was a massive, icy-cold thing, but its heart was fire.

She lifted herself to her knees. A sword lay in the grass. It gleamed as if it had come new from the forge, grey rippled steel like the water that had begotten it. Its hilt was plain silver without adornment, but for a white stone set in the pommel.

As she knelt in front of it, Tarik flowed out of the river, licking cat-whiskers, flicking a fish's tail that flowed and stretched and transmuted into a cat's. He inspected the sword with approval. The water had done well, his glance said, and the sun's fire, forging a blade for a champion's hand. If indeed there was a champion in the world, and if, once chosen, he would do what he had been sought out to do.

Tarik, when he was a cat, had a cat's irony. But it was a fine sword, as solid as earth, and as palpably real. Sarissa trusted that the same would be true of the man for whom it had been wrought.

The young Franks were riding in a field beyond the river, a whole whooping pack of them, waging a mock war. Sarissa paused to watch. She let it seem that she was a youth of the Saracens, which won her stares but did not distract people as greatly as if they had known she was a woman. Those whose spears bore red pennons, she managed to discover, were the king's Companions, and the rest, decked in blue, belonged to a great lord of the Franks.

"If you're one for a wager," said the big fair man beside her, "lay your stakes on the Companions. They've Roland and Olivier with them today, and Turpin, too. Those three could conquer Spain by themselves if they had a mind."

"Truly?" Sarissa asked in wide-eyed innocence. "And which are they?"

The Frank pointed them out with a sweep of the hand. They fought in front, all three abreast, in their bright mail and their well-worn helmets. Two were as broad and massive as the Frank who had told her their names. The third, who rode between the others, was not so tall, not so broad, but his spear thrust and swung foremost, and nearly always found a mark.

They rode hard, and they laughed as they rode, sweeping down on their feigned enemies, swirling about them, casting them into disarray. But when the blue pennons were all fallen, the conquerors leaped from their horses and went laughing to the aid of men whom, just moments before, they had attacked with such vigor.

Then at last they had faces, as helmets came off, tucked under arms or hung at saddlebow. Turpin and Olivier were Franks without a doubt, one brown, one golden-fair, but Roland came of a different blood. She had but a glimpse of him amid the crowd of his people, a swift impression of black hair, white skin, strong arch of nose. Then he was hidden behind Olivier's broad back.

Sarissa might have followed, intrigued by what little she had seen, but the king came then, the great lord of the Franks with his hair even fairer than Olivier's, and his incongruously light voice. He was a fine figure of a man, was Charles, Frank of the Franks, a presence as bright and strong as any she had seen. If she had not known already that here was a king, now she would have been sure of it. He ruled in his court and before embassies. But in the gathering of his men he was most truly king.

They did not crowd about him; they had no need to do that. He passed among them, slapping a shoulder here, clasping a hand there. Where a man was wounded, he stopped to see that all was well, and to give comfort if there was need.

A king could heal by the power of his presence. Sarissa watched in a kind of pain. The sight of him brought memories, sorrows, regrets . . .

She shut them away. She turned a little blindly, slipped through the edges of the throng, and left the men to their gathering. They had been a distraction, a diversion from her path. Now she returned to it as she should have done from the first.

There were women in this city of tents and promises. Some were camp-followers, but many were women of respectable family, lords' wives and sisters and daughters, and the queen and her women and—Sarissa had heard—a mistress or two of the king. The queen mother was there, too, Bertha who was said to be the elder image of her son, a woman as tall and broad as a man, with a man's forcefulness, and no little share of arrogance.

Among the women's tents, Sarissa was careful to be a woman, walking as one, carrying herself as one. That was less difficult than it might have been in Spain: women here walked as boldly as men. Maybe they veiled themselves against the sun, but they did not do it to be modest.

Sarissa's foreign clothes and unfamiliar face attracted glances, but she sensed no hostility. Some of those she passed even smiled, and many stared in open fascination. Franks had no guile, people said in Spain. They were like children, honest to a fault.

Children could be cruel, too, and treacherous. And they waged wars as terrible as anything among their elders.

Not until Sarissa had almost come to the queen's tent, set in the middle and raised higher than the others, did someone stop her. A woman stood in her way, tall and robust, with braids the color of wheat, and wide blue eyes. Her face was too blunt for beauty, snub-nosed and wide-mouthed, but Sarissa doubted that the men cared: her breasts were full and her hips broad, and she carried herself like a woman who well knows her own attractions.

Sarissa had not felt dwarfed by the men of the Franks, though they towered over her. Yet in front of this woman she felt unwontedly small and slight. She straightened her shoulders and lifted her chin.

"Are you the physician from Spain?" the woman asked. "Have you come to attend the queen?"

Sarissa's brows rose. "You were not expecting a man?"

"We were expecting someone older," the woman said in the blunt way of the Franks, "but if you have any arts, we would welcome them."

There was indeed a man of respectable years among the emir's people, a physician from Saragossa, but the messenger who had come earlier in the day had not been led to him. Sarissa inclined her head to the Frankish woman. "Take me to her majesty," she said.

The queen was a young woman, strikingly so. She must have been hardly more than a child when she came to the king's bed, for she had children of a good age, and another swelling her belly. This one wore at her, sapping her strength, so that she sat listless in her tent, shut away in the gloom and the flicker of the lamps.

Sarissa took it in with a glance: the dark and musty space, the crowd of ladies and servants, the priest reading in a drone of Latin. There was so little air in that place, it

was a wonder any of them could breathe. She swept the
young queen into the sunlight, brought her blinking and
stumbling to a place arranged as Sarissa ordered it: a chair
covered with soft cloths and banked with cushions, set
under the spreading branches of a tree. It was cool there,
the air clean and sweet, and flowers scattered in the grass.

Queen Hildegarde sank heavily into the chair, though
she was barely swollen yet with the child. Her face was
pale, her fair hair lank. She would be lovely when she was
well, Sarissa thought, but she was wan and lackluster now.

And yet she tried to smile, to speak strongly. "You're
very kind, lady," she said, "but I hardly need—"

A physician might interrupt a queen. Sarissa turned to
the woman who had met her first, and said, "Fetch strong
wine, the best that can be had, and bread to sop in it, and
water heated to boiling. If you please."

The lady's eyes flickered at that belated courtesy, but she
did not refuse to obey. While she was gone, Sarissa saw to
the queen's comfort. The queen's women and her priests
stood back and stared. Not all of them were glad to see a
foreigner—an infidel, as they thought—laying hands on
their royal lady. But she submitted with a sweetness of
spirit that must serve her well in contending with her
strong-willed king.

When the queen was settled as comfortably as she could
be, with even a little color returning to her cheeks from the
light and clean air, Sarissa knelt beside her and laid hands
on the swell of her belly. One or two of the attendants
started forward with a hiss of outrage. The queen's word
stopped them. "This is what she came to do. Will you stop
her before she begins?"

"She is presumptuous!" declared a plump fair child with
a markedly righteous expression.

"She is here at my summoning," said a high imperious
voice. The attendants blanched. The queen mother strode
into the flock of them, scattering the slow or the unguarded, and stood over Sarissa and the queen.

Queen Hildegarde smiled at her, tired but fearless.
Queen Bertha swept a frown round the circle of attendants, till it came to rest on Sarissa. "So. It's true. The famous healer of the Saracens is a child. How much
knowledge can you carry in that head, girl?"

"Enough," Sarissa said. She still had her hands on the slight swell of the queen's middle, sensing clearly the life within. It was strong, as it should be; whatever weakness beset its mother, the child knew nothing of it.

She said so to the queen. She was not surprised to be answered by the queen mother. "Of course the baby is strong. It's my son's. Now tell us why the queen is weak."

That was not so simple. The wine and bread came, and the water. Sarissa sopped wine in bread and bade the queen eat them, which she did slowly, without appetite, but obediently enough. Sarissa poured the water into a cup that she carried at her belt, in which she had crushed herbs from her box of medicaments. Their scent was somewhat sweet, somewhat pungent, and rather more pleasant than not. This she bade the queen drink.

Color rose almost at once to the pale cheeks. Queen Hildegarde sat straighter. She drew a breath; she let it go. She stretched and smiled. "I feel . . ." she said. "I feel whole."

Her women stirred and murmured. Queen Bertha caught Sarissa's eye. That single glance caused the ladies to withdraw to a polite distance, and brought Sarissa in close. "Tell me," the queen mother said. "What ails her?"

"Nothing of the body, majesty," Sarissa said. "The child is well."

"And its mother?"

"Guard her. Pray if you will."

"She is in danger?"

Sarissa frowned. "Perhaps not. But there is something here that saps her spirit. It's recent, no? She was well before?"

"It began soon after we came here," said the queen mother. "Is it this place?"

"No," said Sarissa. "Oh, no. There is great healing among these waters. It would be worse for her if she were not here."

"Then what—"

"I think," Sarissa said slowly, "that you would do well to keep her under guard. Choose guards whom you can trust."

"Someone is ill-wishing her?"

"Something touches on her spirit. Something dark; old

and cold. It may not know or care what it does to her. It will take the child if it can, because that is its nature. She will prevent it if she can, because that is a mother's nature."

"That is hardly work for a company of soldiers," the queen mother said. "A company of holy women, perhaps. Or priests."

"Women," said Sarissa. "Yes. Let them raise a wall of prayer about her, and sing psalms of joy and ease. See that she has sunlight and clean starlight, rest and peace, and no fear."

"And the thing that threatens her?"

"I will find it," Sarissa said.

"Let me see to that," said the queen mother.

"Have you arts and powers, then?" Sarissa asked her.

The queen mother lifted her chin slightly. She looked remarkably like her son the king. "Find it," she said, "but when you do, you will speak with me before you act upon it."

"And if I do not?"

"Would you dare?"

"I will do whatever I judge best," Sarissa said, "majesty."

They met eye to eye like a crossing of swords. Queen Bertha was a woman of great strength of will. But Sarissa had withstood greater powers than this.

King Charles' mother saw it. She would not bow, that was not in her, but she could permit herself to accept the inevitable. To salve her pride, she said, "You will stay here and attend the queen."

Sarissa had intended to do exactly that. But she said, "My tent, my belongings—"

"Our people will fetch them," said the queen mother. "You will live in the queen's tent. Your own can be—"

"No," said Sarissa.

The queen mother's brows rose. That word, her expression said, was not often spoken in her presence.

Sarissa smiled sweetly and said, "I will attend her majesty gladly, and see to her protection. But I will have my own tent, and my own things in it. My art," she said through the uprising of the queen mother's objection, "requires it."

"Please," Queen Hildegarde said. Her voice was soft but clear, and for all its lack of force, it brought the queen mother about. "Please, Mother. Let her be."

"Well," said the queen mother, a sharp eruption of breath. "Well! Have it as you will, then. If only you get better, and she sees to it."

"I will," said Hildegarde. "She will. Is she not a famous healer in Spain, where the physicians are the best in the world?"

In this part of the world, Sarissa thought, but she held her tongue.

"And," said Hildegarde, still with that sweet semblance of innocence, "you did summon her, Mother, out of fear for me. If we are to trust her, we must trust her in everything."

"We will trust her," the queen mother said, as if her word made it law.

CHAPTER 4

✠ ✠ ✠

"Teach me magic."

The king's counselor looked up from the heaps of parchment over which he had been laboring like a common clerk. His face wore no expression at all, until he recognized the king's son. Then it took on one that Pepin could not read.

Pepin's hands were clammy. He wiped them surreptitiously on his tunic, and stood as straight as he could. The hump that deformed his back was aching again, stabbing outrage at being forced to let him stand almost tall. He ignored it. What he wanted, he wanted with all his heart.

Father Ganelon regarded him with a cold dark eye. "And why do you think," he asked, "that a man of the Church would so far transgress as to teach you magic?"

"They—they say," said Pepin, stammering and hating himself for it, "that no one knows it better than you."

"*They* say? And who are they?"

"People round about," said Pepin.

That was not exactly a lie. People did talk of anything and everything. They might talk of magic and of learned priests and of royal counselors, perhaps even in the same breath.

Pepin was not going to tell the exact truth. That he had been walking past this tent in the evening, trying to go quietly as a hunter does, or a shadow. He should have been attending his father the king, but he had escaped—and something, some flicker of movement or glint of light, had made him pause. It was accident, maybe: a gust of wind lifting a tentflap, causing a lamp within to flare.

Inside was a vision of wonder and delight, a golden paradise: a garden of flowers that transmuted into a flock of beautiful women—women in sheerest gauzy drifts of draperies, through which their bodies shone with a wondrous and tender light. Soft white breasts, sweet curve of hip, the exquisite turn of an ankle . . .

Ganelon stood in the midst of them, attended by three tall and motionless figures in antique armor. The nondescript priest of no particular age was dressed in a robe of light. It illumined his face, transformed it as the blossoms had been transformed into women. He had beauty here, and power. He was a creature of gleaming splendor.

Pepin had gone away dazzled, but his mind had recorded every tiniest detail of that vision. It had stayed with him, obsessed him, until he gathered all his courage to approach the king's counselor.

He had never wanted anything as much as this. Not even to be king—though that too he wanted, to the heart of him. If this could bring that about . . .

He was going to be refused. He could see it in Ganelon's eyes. Ganelon was a priest, after all. Priests were forbidden the dark arts.

"I know," Pepin said in a rush, "what you can do. I know what you have done. If the bishops knew, or the lord Pope—he spoke to me, did you know? He was kind to me when we were in Italy. He said that maybe the Lord would make my back straight, if I prayed."

"Ah," said Ganelon, and in that brief sound was a world of understanding. It shattered Pepin's pretensions. It came near to breaking his courage.

"So," said Ganelon in the silence. "You threaten me, as a prince may do. Were your prayers not answered? Perhaps you were simply not patient enough."

Pepin held his temper in check, though it threatened to burst free. He was a prince. He was his father's son. He could master himself, even in this twisted body that God had seen fit to give him.

Ganelon nodded as if Pepin had spoken aloud. "You

have pride enough. But have you discipline? Can you submit to another's will—submit utterly, as if to the will of God?"

"That is blasphemy," Pepin said.

The dark eyes flashed on him and struck him mute. "If you would master the powers of the elements, of earth and heaven and the realms below, you must learn to submit with all your being. Can you do that, prince of the Franks? Can you even begin to try?"

"Can you?"

Ganelon did not strike him down. He was rather surprised, and a little disappointed. He had hoped to see sorcery, a bolt of wrath or at the very least a crackle of lightning. "Pride is the destroyer," Ganelon said coolly, calmly. "Remember that."

"I would rather remember words of magic."

"That is magic," said Ganelon: "potent and ancient."

Pepin did not remember being sent away. He was in the tent with Ganelon and the heaps of parchment. Then he was not. Was that magic? He thought it might have been; but he had no memory of it.

The next day his father sent for him. That was not uncommon. Charles liked to know where all his children were, always. But so soon after Pepin had approached Ganelon, it seemed ominous that the king commanded his eldest son to attend him.

It did not begin badly. Charles was swimming in the river as he always did in the morning, his white body flashing through the dark water. There was the usual flock of hangers-on, gabbling like geese as they loitered on the bank or, if they were very bold or very foolish, swam in the river with the king.

At Pepin's coming, Charles called a greeting with every appearance of gladness, and surged up out of the water. Pepin could never look at him without a stab of— something. Jealousy? Admiration? Both? Charles was tall, straight, magnificent. He was everything that Pepin longed to be.

Pepin's mother said that he was handsome, but a mother would. His face was like his father's, he knew that. His legs were long and strong, and his arms and hands. But his back was a poor crooked thing, twisting him altogether out of true.

Charles never shrank from it. That much Pepin granted him. He laid an arm about it now, freely, and half led, half pushed Pepin to the little pavilion that stood near the river. In it was his bodyservant with cloths to dry him and sweet oil to rub on his skin and fresh garments to clothe him—for Charles never wore the same tunic after a bath as before. Charles was strange that way; obsessive. A little mad, maybe, but one did not say such things of the king.

There was someone else there, too, sitting in a corner, silent, dressed in black. Those cold eyes were unmistakable.

"Father Ganelon!" Charles cried as the servant began to dress him. "Come here, meet my son. Pepin, you know the good Father, yes? He's been one of my wandering ministers for a long while, but now he's back to serve in the court. I've asked him, as a favor to me, to teach you such things as a prince should know."

Pepin lowered his eyes before the light in them betrayed him. Here was his answer after all. Here was his heart's desire.

To his father he said in a low calm voice, "I thank you, Father."

"What, no dancing in delight?" But Charles was laughing. "Come, boy, you've run half-wild since old Albrecht died. Now you'll be a scholar again. You'll learn your Latin and your Greek; and write a fair hand; and you'll learn statecraft, too, and the arts of princes."

"Not the arts of kings?" Pepin heard himself say, just above a whisper.

Charles' ears were keen. "A king is a prince writ large," he said. "Study well, and listen to my counselor. There's much that he can teach."

Indeed, thought Pepin, still with his eyes lowered, pretending to be the sullen prince robbed of his freedom. But his heart was singing. Magic—he would have magic. He would learn more from Ganelon than his father would ever have conceived of.

"I should have trusted you," Pepin said to Ganelon. "I should have—"

"Borel," said Ganelon as if Pepin had not spoken. "Show my lord prince how I prefer my parchment to be scraped. And see that he grinds the ink suitably fine."

Borel was one of Ganelon's kinsmen, people said, tall and silent as they all were, with a long pale face like Ganelon's, and a fringe of colorless hair round a close-shaved tonsure. He did not meet Pepin's glare as he began to show the prince what Pepin had learned from his first tutor when he was a child; and that was a fair number of years ago.

It was a test, Pepin thought. Surely he was not expected to perform duties given an infant who had never set pen to parchment. Pepin could write. He could read. He was no great scholar but he was well enough taught. He knew how to scrape a finely tanned hide to write on, and how to make the ink, too, and sharpen the quill, and write the letters one by one in a fair round hand.

They were very ordinary letters, too: the king's correspondence, no more and no less. Pepin, it was all too clear, was not to be entrusted with secrets.

Not yet.

He endured it with gritted teeth. There was no magic in evidence here. Yet this was the same tent in which he had seen that vision of a garden. There was nothing inside but what one might expect to find in a priest's dwelling: a narrow and ascetic cot, a small chest for belongings, a table and a lamp and a box of inks and pens, and two heaps of parchment, one rough and one scraped clean.

No magical apparatus. Nothing at all that could be taken for such. There was not even a cross, as one might expect of a priest.

Pepin had to trust. He had to cling to memory, and to knowledge that set in his bones. There was magic here, in this man. He knew it. He would find it, learn it. He had promised himself. He had sworn an oath in his heart.

"Wanting is not enough," said Ganelon.

Pepin looked up in startlement. It was only the second day. He had expected it to be much longer before he was spoken to again. He had been scraping parchment and mixing ink, until he was given a new task: to copy a letter of rather stupefying banality, addressed to the priest of a village that Pepin had never heard of.

Ganelon's voice startled him out of it. He had been thinking of nothing, just then, but the shape of the letters, writing each one fair, and none wrong or out of place.

"You must do more than want," said Ganelon as if from the midst of a conversation. "You must will it with your whole heart."

"And how many eons will that take?" Pepin asked him.

"You have an insolent tongue," said Ganelon, but calmly.

"I am a king's son," Pepin said.

"You must forget that," said Ganelon. "You must forget everything but desire. And when all is desire, forget that also, and become pure will."

"No spells? No incantations?"

"Those come after," said Ganelon.

"But—"

"That is the secret," Ganelon said. "That is the truth."

"And you tell it to me now?"

"I tell you that you may begin to know."

"Then you will teach me."

"I have been teaching you," said Ganelon.

Pepin's heart swelled. "Then I will have it. I will have it all."

"If you are strong enough."

"I will be."

"Maybe," said Ganelon.

Pepin did not let himself grow angry or fall into doubt. He was sure. The magic was there for him to take. He would take it. And then . . .

"First you must know how to begin," Ganelon said. "Here, on the page. Ink on parchment. Letters. Words that signify nothing and everything. When you know what the words mean, then you have begun."

"Spells?"

"Chains that bind the world. In the beginning," said Ganelon, "was the word. That is truth."

Pepin shivered. This was nothing holy, his bones knew it, though the words came from Scripture. It was all the more alluring for that. "And can you unbind the world?" he asked.

"That is what we do," said Ganelon, "we who make magic."

"But are there not two sorts of magic? The dark and the light?"

"They are all one," Ganelon said.

"But—"

"No more questions," said Ganelon. "Listen, and learn."

Pepin listened. He was not always certain what he learned, but that was the way of this art. For every man it was different. For every spirit, it showed a new face.

Pepin was not content. It was not his nature. But happy—he was that. Yes, he was happy.

CHAPTER 5

⊞ ⊞ ⊞

A handful of days after the Saracens came to Paderborn, the king called all the lords and commons of the Franks to the great assembly. There in the field under the mountain's knees, by the ever-running river, the gathered prelates of the Franks sang the high Mass, a great rite of invocation and adoration.

When the chanting was still fading away, the plumes of incense scattering in a light wind, Charles told his people what message the embassy had brought. "Spain," he said, "begs us come to its aid. Rebels have taken Cordoba. If we destroy that rebellion, great lands will be ours, and cities, fortresses, treasure . . ."

He had them in his hand. Roland, standing behind him with the rest of the Companions, felt the force of the people's faith in their king. They heard what they chose to hear. Spain—conquest—wealth. And for those who cared for such things, which was a great number, there was another thought, another desire: to restore an infidel country to the light of the Lord Christ.

Those voices rose louder and ever louder. "In God's name! God wills it!"

Charles let them rouse themselves to a fever-pitch. If there were objections, questions, voices of reason, they were all drowned out in that tumult. And that, thought Roland, was exactly as Charles wished it. Charles

wanted Spain—wanted empire. If he won it so, then he
was content.

The emir Al-Arabi did not seem unduly dismayed. Nor
would he be, since he himself had foretold that this would
happen. Al-Arabi, like Charles, wanted what he wanted;
nor did he care precisely how he got it.

When at long last there was something like silence,
Charles' voice rose over it, clear and pitched to carry. "My
heart is glad that you approve this, my people. We will bring
the true Faith into Spain. We will ride in war over the mountains, and conquer a new land for the Lord."

This roar was nigh as long as the first. It ended in a slow
sigh like a surge of the sea. As it faded at last, the emir
spoke. His Latin was purer than many a priest's, and there
were priests to render it in the dialects of the Franks.
Roland heard the overlapping of voices, Al-Arabi's words
rendered in a dozen ways, but all with much the same
meaning.

"In joy," he said, "and in gratitude for the aid that you
offer, I bid you all attend a feast. But first, if you will, in
token of friendship, I offer a contest. Let your best warriors
vie for the prizes: gold and jewels and the wealth of my
people. And for the strongest, for him who conquers all,
there is this."

He beckoned. A turbaned servant stepped forward. In
his hands was a long narrow bundle wrapped in crimson
silk. He shook loose the wrapping with a flourish, and laid
bare a sword.

It was a wondrous thing. Its hilt was plain silver, the
pommel set with a white stone like the moon. Its blade rippled like water.

The servant lifted it, holding it as a priest might hold a
cross. The sun caught it and it flamed with white fire.

Every man in that army loosed a long sigh of pure desire. None of them, not one, was proof against the light of
that sword. It was beauty bare, perfect and deadly. It made
Roland think of ice under the moon, and water in starlight.
It was as pure and strong and dangerous as the highest of
high magic.

A shiver ran down his spine. A sword was a thing of
power, and a truly fine one would carry strong spells and
secrets of the maker's art. But this was more.

His glance caught Charles, standing as still as they all stood, transfixed by that wondrous thing. Not even a king could resist the lure of it.

Not even a king, not even this king, would keep Roland from vying for the sword. Nor was he alone in that desire. All the Companions, the lords and fighting men, knew that same surety.

A stab of alarm brought him up short. Was this a plot against them all? Was it meant to divide them, to set man against man and man against king, and so leave them ripe for treachery?

The sword's gleam offered no answer. Roland's eyes, questing among the gathered faces, searched that of the emir. There was guile there in plenty, but of betrayal he saw nothing. He looked past that lean dark face, scanning the faces of the emir's retinue. Nothing.

Ganelon, he thought. As if the thought had conjured him, he was there among the flock of priests, with his dour monks at his back, and close by him—disturbingly so—the king's eldest son, the hunchback. They were all watching the sword, but not as if they had anything to do with it. Pepin was rapt. His face, so like his father's atop the twisted body, was as full of naked yearning as any other.

This was not Ganelon's doing. Roland did not know if he was glad. Nor, he admitted, did he know that the sword was an ill thing. It did not feel so. It felt clean and rather cold, not a thing of heaven maybe, but not of hell, either. It was made of the elements of the middle realm, of earth and water, air and fire.

Roland would have to stop soon and consider what it meant that Pepin stood so close to the old enemy. Roland had been so preoccupied with guarding the king that he had not been paying proper attention to the king's children. Pepin was not the heir: his mother had not married the king in the eyes of the Church. But he was the king's eldest son. If Ganelon had got at him rather than at the stronger, wiser, far less vulnerable and far more strictly guarded Charles—

Later he would ponder the uses of diversion and distraction. For this moment, all that mattered was the sword.

The assembly hardly waited to be dismissed. They did not, just then, care exactly what they had decided to do about the war. They were all in a fever to prepare for the contest, which would begin after the sun passed noon; then when that was done, the emir would summon them to his feast.

The Companions prepared together as they would for battle, gathered in the tent Roland shared with Olivier, which was the largest. Their servants ran back and forth, fetching clothing, weapons, armor. Only the twins Gerin and Gerer were not there: they stood guard over the king.

"He'll fight for it, too," said Olivier as his servant shaved him—putting that poor man in great danger of cutting his master's throat, but he was used to it. Olivier was seldom silent even when he slept.

"So do we let him win it?" Milun was the youngest of the Companions, younger than Roland, and inclined to fret over matters of precedence. It was his mother's fault, his cousin Thibaut was wont to say. That lady had made a high art of fretting, and she had taught it to her son.

But Milun was a good fighting man and fair teller of tales by the fire of an evening. The rest of them forbore to knock him down and teach him sense. Turpin said, kindly enough, "Of course we don't let him win it. He'd have our necks if we tried. This will be a fair fight. If the king wins, he'll win by his strong right arm, and nothing else."

"But he's the king," said Milun.

Thibaut cuffed him not quite hard enough to fell him. "Stop it, puppy. You'll fight as we'll all fight, for the honor of your name. Maybe you'll win. Stranger things have happened in this world."

Milun growled but subsided. In any case he would not have been able to say much more: two of the servants had brought him his mail-coat. They climbed up on stools on either side of him and hefted the heavy thing above his head. He lifted his arms. They lowered the mail-coat, grunting a little with the weight, working his arms into it and settling it on his shoulders.

Roland, whose own coat was already on, set about helping Olivier with his. Olivier's fair cheeks were scarlet with the razor's burn and the fever of excitement. "Did you see that sword?" he kept asking. "Did you see it? Where do you think it came from? Spain? Araby? India?"

"Fire and water," Roland said without thinking.

No one took much notice. Roland was always saying things that no one else could make sense of; sometimes, as now, not even himself.

"It is a marvel of a blade," Turpin said. "I wonder what its name is."

"Do Saracens name their swords?" Olivier asked.

That stopped them all. After a moment Ascelin said, "No. No, I don't think they do."

Ascelin was a Gascon. They were not always friends to the Franks, and as often as not they were allies of the Saracens. When it came to infidels, Ascelin knew more than most.

"Well," Olivier said, "then how do they acknowledge the power that's in a blade?"

Thibaut snorted. "That should matter? They can fight. The rest is ceremony."

"They'd fight better if they knew who their weapons were," said Olivier.

"Then it's well for us they don't," Turpin said. "Here, are we ready? Shall we go?"

Everyone was ready, even Milun, whose servant handed him his helmet.

"Let us go, then," said Turpin, "and may God bless us all. And if He doesn't choose to grant that I should win the sword—then may it go to another of us."

"Or the king," Milun said, "in the Lord Jesus' name."

They crossed themselves and bowed their heads. Turpin blessed them all, marking a cross on each forehead and sealing it with a kiss.

Roland was last, as it happened. Turpin held him for a moment, smiling a remarkably sweet smile. Roland returned it. His heart was suddenly as light as air.

"Fight well, brother falcon," his friend said.

"And you, brother bear," said Roland.

They laughed and embraced, and followed the others into the bright daylight.

While the Franks prepared, the emir's men together with a great company of the king's servants had readied the field of the assembly for a trial by combat. Its boundaries were marked, and places set for those who would watch. There was a canopy for the queens and their ladies, and another for the Saracens of rank and their attendants.

They would all fight as they were accustomed to do, in mock battle, ranked as they would be in war: lord by lord and company by company. The Companions took places at the king's back.

The emir Al-Arabi rode down the lines on his fiery little mare, with a following of men in Saracen armor. He bowed as he passed the king, and there paused. "My lords," he said, "and men of the Franks, here is the challenge I set you: to draw lots, and so divide, left hand and right. One side, my lord king, of your grace you will command. For the other, let one be chosen who is a strong commander in battle. He who drives his opponent's forces back, even to the border of the field, shall be counted victor."

"And win the sword?" Charles asked.

"Why, no, my lord," said Al-Arabi. "For the victors we have prizes of gold and fine jewels, silks and treasures of my people—and the right to contest for sword when the melee is done, in single combat, man against man."

Charles laughed and applauded. "That is grand sport!" he declared. "Shall we begin?"

Battle was battle, whether mock battle against friends and brothers, or battle to the death against the enemies of the Franks. First the waiting as the captains settled sides and drew lots for command against the king; then further waiting as they took ranks on either side of the broad windswept field. The sun was direct overhead. The sky was clear blue. The wind caught the pennons: gold for the king, green for the other, with Anselm, Count of the king's palace, as lord and commander.

Roland sat on grey Veillantif at the king's right hand, breathing deep to steady himself. The world was preternaturally clear, as it always was before a battle. But his skin quivered and rippled, itching to shift, to sprout wings and fly—and that had not been common before Ganelon came to the king's camp. With an effort he held it in check. His skin quivered one last time, as if in protest, then stilled. His senses sharpened to falcon-keenness.

The horn rang the signal. Roland's lance lowered. On either side of him, lances came down in unison. With a roar of delight, they leaped to the charge.

He set his eyes on a green pennon and a faceless helmet behind it. It did not matter who it was, or what he might be when he was not the enemy in battle. Roland had all the leisure in the world to straighten his lance, to aim at the broad mailed breast, to thrust its blunted end home. The man fell.

There was another behind him, and another. Lances thrust. Swords flashed—not blunted, those, and as deadly as they ever were. There were axes, and here and there a club, whirling about a helmeted head and falling with crushing force.

Roland's lance broke on a shield. He swept out his sword, the familiar blade that had been his father's. It was never as fine as the one that they all fought for, but it was a sturdy thing, and well fitted to his hand. He had grown to manhood with it, and won many a battle, real as well as feigned.

It was like a part of him, a long and deadly arm, smiting men who rose up before him, beating aside lances and swords. People were shouting—screaming. Someone was down; he glimpsed the bright scarlet of blood.

They were falling back—the line was bending, weakening, breaking. Roland glanced aside. Charles' blue glare met his. They needed no word to be in perfect agreement.

Charles on his left hand, Olivier on his right, Turpin beyond the king, gathered and poised and drove in a bright wedge through the massed enemy. They caught him by surprise: off balance, shaped to drive forward, not to fall back. They thrust the ranks back and back, battering them with lance and sword. *"Montjoie!"* they cried together, the king's war-cry. *"Montjoie!"*

The retreat halted. It had found the strength to fight back. Roland mustered himself for yet another onslaught.

There was no need. The green pennants had reached the field's edge. Charles' side had driven them back as far as they could go. The horns rang, halting them, proclaiming the king's victory.

There were gaps in the ranks, men down, stunned or bleeding. But they were laughing, those who were not groaning in pain. It had been a splendid fight, and bravely fought.

In winning it, the king's side had won the right to contest for the sword. Comrades in arms eyed one another warily now, each seeing his companion as his rival for the prize.

"Don't hate me," Olivier said to Roland, "if I knock you about a bit. That sword . . . oh, saints, I want it."

"It's mine," said Thibaut. "Be wise, yield now. Spare yourself a broken head."

"I'll break yours first," said Olivier sweetly.

As the last of the wounded hobbled or were carried from the field, the emir Al-Arabi rode among them again. This time he carried the sword crosswise in his arms, brilliant in its silken wrappings. "You will fight," he said, "man to man. Two by two. As your opponent falls, you will turn and engage the man on your right hand. He who is still standing engages again. And thus until only one man stands. To that man, I give this blade."

They all sighed as they had when they first saw the sword, as no few of them did at the thought of a willing woman.

"Oh, I'll love her," someone murmured indeed, not far from Roland—and maybe it was Olivier's voice, and maybe it was not. "I'll cherish the very heart of her."

Roland had not had a woman in—how long? Not since before Olivier won the toss, the day Ganelon came to Paderborn. Like a fool, his body remembered that now, with urgency that made him catch his breath.

Not now, he told it. *Not till this is over.*

His body was not minded to listen, but he was master of it still. The lines were drawing up, dismounting, horses being led away. Man faced man along the breadth of the field. Those who had lost the melee crowded beyond. They took it in good heart, as far as he could see.

Roland braced his feet on the earth. It was trampled, treacherous. He was a little tired from the melee, but never enough to slow him. This was battle as he had been born and bred to fight it. Single combat, best and most deadly of all.

In the shifting of sides, he found himself face-to-face with a man he knew slightly, a minor lord from the south of Francia. They were a fair match for size and weight, but Roland's eye was quicker and his arm stronger. The man fell in a few swift strokes. And there was one waiting, and one after him, in a blur of clashing steel.

Roland had danced wardances like this, from opponent to opponent to opponent. Sometimes there was a lull: a man down—sometimes laughing, sometimes snarling, occasionally unconscious—but the two on his right fought on. Then he would lean on his sword, or even sit on the ground, and simply breathe.

He did not like to pause too long. If he did, he would become aware of the aches of bruises and the stabbing of wounds, small but sharp.

The Companions were holding their own. So too the king; he did not tire as quickly as other men, and he had a remarkable store of patience. He could husband his strength while others squandered theirs, and be fresh to fight long after they were exhausted.

Roland had learned that lesson from Merlin, but Charles had taught him to master it.

It was no great surprise, then, that as the sun sank, casting long shadows across the field, two pairs remained to fight on it: Olivier and Turpin, and Charles turning from fallen Thibaut to face Roland. Roland smiled at the king. Charles' eyes glinted.

They raised blades in salute. Charles inclined his head. Roland bowed as lord to king. They sprang together, as fierce as if they had been bitter enemies.

Charles was taller, stronger, heavier. His reach was longer. And he was very, very cunning.

But Roland was faster, and he had learned cunning from a devil's son. As wise as Charles was, he still wanted to end this as quickly as he might, with but two opponents left between himself and the sword. Roland could not overwhelm him with the power of his arms, but he could outwait even that king of foxes. He fought only as hard as he must to defend himself, and to keep that heavy blade from beating him down.

Charles tried to draw Roland out, to force him to fight more strongly: hammering and hammering. But Roland was air and water, slipping away from the blows, letting them fall harmless or catch the edge of his blade and dissipate without weakening him overmuch.

Roland waited and watched, and eluded blows that

came faster and faster. Everywhere about him was the blur
of steel. It closed in ever tighter. It drove him back and
back, till like the enemy in the melee, he had nowhere else
to go.

But there was no stricture here, and no requirement but
that one of them fall. He ducked beneath a blow that was
meant to finish him. It brushed him and rocked him, but he
did not topple. Charles half-spun with the force of it.
Roland saw his face clearly as he realized what he had
done to himself: anger, frustration, rueful acceptance. The
flat of Roland's blade caught him neatly beneath the ear
and sent him crashing down.

There was no time for Roland to assure himself that he
had done no lasting harm. Even as he bent to help the king
to his feet, a strong grip on his shoulder spun him about.

Olivier grinned at him. "Brother! I'm winning the
sword."

Roland bared his teeth in reply. "Brother," he said,
"stand aside for me."

"Over my unconscious body," said Olivier.

"Gladly," Roland said.

They were both bloody, bruised, running with sweat,
staggering, but giddy with the delight of the battle. To be
fighting as brother to brother—it was lovely, inevitable.
Roland still had his helmet, by a miracle. Olivier had lost
his. His hair hung lank over his forehead. A great bruise
split his cheekbone.

Roland did not suppose he was any more lovely. Nor did
he care. He firmed his grip on his sword, gathered himself,
swept it up.

Olivier's met it with force that staggered them both.
Olivier grunted. Roland had bitten his tongue: his mouth
tasted of blood.

They knew each other too well. Each knew what his battle-
brother would do next, each move as familiar as the steps
of a dance. For every thrust a parry, for each step forward
a step back.

It could last past the sunset, which was not so far away
now, and all night long, for the matter of that. But they
were both well worn with a long day's fighting, and they
were hardly minded to let it go on as long as that.

Roland could not wait Olivier out. Olivier was wise to it.

Nor could he overwhelm Olivier with his strength: Olivier was his superior in that. He had only his determination, and something that he had not even known was a gift until he became a man and a warrior. In the strongest heat of battle, the world slowed. Each move, each breath, was a matter of great deliberation. Men drifted like fishes beneath the sea. When a sword lifted, there was all the time in the world to meet it and turn it aside. Blows endured for long ages. He could slip beneath them, elude them, return them before anyone had seen him move.

It was not magic. It was something that a man could do, any man, if he was born to it. Olivier had it. He would not have been a great fighter without it. But Roland was quicker than he was.

Even at that, Roland was hard pressed. Olivier fought with all the skill that was in him, till his very soul was battle. Leap, thrust, leap away; spin, whirl, strike. Stamp, shout, stab and stab again, then come round in a great sweeping blow that nigh split Roland in two. Roland barely escaped, twisting, staggering, half-falling. Olivier's foot caught him in the side. Something cracked.

He felt no pain. In this world undersea, adrift in light, he felt nothing at all. He feigned to double up, to crumple. Olivier drew back the merest fraction. For the glimmer of an instant he was unguarded.

Roland darted into the opening, empty-handed, his sword lost, he did not remember where. Olivier was bending to finish Roland, who was no longer where Olivier had looked to find him. Roland's knotted hands smote him at the base of the neck.

Olivier went down like a felled ox. The earth shook as he struck it. Roland staggered but somehow, by God's grace, kept his feet.

The sky was spinning. There was a roaring in his ears: men's voices, shouts, cries, wild cheering.

There was no one else on the field. Everyone was gone, every man, except Olivier. Olivier lay like the dead.

Roland's heart stopped. Then the broad breast heaved. Olivier gasped, coughed, rolled onto his back. He was alive. White-faced, gagging, but alive.

Figures moved, drifting toward Roland. He was still in that time outside of time. He could not seem to come out of it. The people who came seemed to swim as if through deep water. He recognized most of them. The king. The emir Al-Arabi. Turpin and the rest of the Companions. But before them all trod one whose name he had never heard, but whose face he knew as he knew his own: a woman in white silk girdled with silver, with a drift of silver veil over her hair, and in her hands the sword.

After all he had done to win it, he hardly saw it. Her eyes filled the world that was left to him, between the darkness and the narrowing span of light. Beautiful eyes, long, gold-brown, set slightly atilt in a narrow oval face. They were not smiling. They were—angry? Startled? Horrified?

The light was almost gone. He saw his hands reach up to take the sword, for if he did not, it would fall ignominiously between them. He felt it, cold and hard and somehow clean, as if it had been forged of water and not of steel. He could no longer see it. Only her eyes. Her eyes . . . her face . . .

Even in the fall of darkness, she was with him. She stood beside him. She guarded him against the night. She and the sword, the wonderful sword, whose name—yes. He heard it on the edge of hearing.

Durandal. Its name is Durandal.

And then was night, and rest, and such peace as he was ever given.

CHAPTER 6

※ ※ ※

The Frank dropped like a stone at Sarissa's feet. She could make no move to catch him. It was the warrior archbishop who did it, the one called Turpin, whom she had seen fighting beside this man, this Roland, in the melee and after. He was wounded, but not badly, and Roland was a lightweight for his strength; Turpin lifted the limp body, sword and armor and all, with no appearance of effort.

People were murmuring. The shouting and cheering had died. "Is he dead?" someone asked. The word spread. *Dead—dead—dead.*

"He's not dead!" cried Charles the king. "He's alive. Make room now. Make room. Let him breathe!"

People pressed back, falling over one another. Turpin carried Roland through them. The king followed, and the Companions after, and the emir, and all the rest of them in a long murmuring train.

Sarissa was caught among them, borne along with them. There was no thought in her. It was all struck out of her in the moment when she came forward with the sword in her hands, and stood in front of the man who had won it, and he lifted his eyes to hers.

Such eyes. Such a face. Such . . .

No one had warned her. She did not know if she was angry. Perhaps she was. Someone should have spoken. She should have known. All her visions, her forebodings, her powers and her magics, and she had not foreseen this.

That was no human man. Oh, he had mortal blood, no doubt of it, but something altogether different had begotten that face, so white, so keenly carved, and those eyes, so like a hawk's and so little like a man's. And in those eyes lay more power, more sheer raw magic, than she had ever looked to see in a man of this blunt and forthright nation.

Did he know? He must. He had the look of a man who was well aware of what he was. And yet the Franks seemed not to see, or to understand. To them he was only Roland, the Count of the Marches of Brittany, the king's Companion.

Roland the Breton, who had won the sword.

They carried him to the king's own tent, and there laid him down. Servants freed him of his armor. There was blood, though not, she thought, to excess. Red blood, human enough to look at. He was not invulnerable, that one, or perhaps he did not wish to be.

He had a fine young body. Sarissa knelt beside it. Some of them objected, but the king spoke, stilling them. "This is a healer. She healed the queen; she has great skill. Let her be."

Sarissa ran hands over that body, not touching it. Pain was like heat against her palms: bruises, cuts, the stabbing of cracked ribs. Exhaustion was worse, and loss of blood from so many small wounds. And shock—the power of the sword coming upon him when he was so weak, he who of all men must be most open to it.

"Is he well? Will he live?"

Sarissa looked up into a face rather more bruised and battered than Roland's. The man who had contested with him for the sword, the Companion Olivier, was bending over her, swaying with the effort, but grimly determined. "Tell me! Will he die?"

"Not at all," Sarissa said. "He only needs rest and tending."

Olivier loosed a great sigh of relief, so great that he nearly toppled. "Look to him!" Sarissa said sharply.

People obeyed. They carried Olivier off, protesting volubly but too weak to resist.

Most of the others left with him, which was well. She sent for water, cloths, her box of medicaments: and there they all were, waiting, by the king's forethought. She bowed low to him before she went to work.

Charles lingered for a while, but duties called him, and the feast at which Roland should have held the place of honor. But Roland was going nowhere this night, nor was Sarissa.

Even the servants left. But the archbishop, who had sent them away, stayed beside Roland. "When you finish," he said, "lady, you may go. I have some arts myself; I can watch over him."

"I will stay," Sarissa said.

"You need not," said Turpin.

He was strangely insistent. She raised her brows. "I think it best that I stay with him," she said. "He will be well, but he was taken rather strongly. He may need more tending than I've yet given him."

"I can summon you if there's need," Turpin said.

"I will stay," she said.

He looked ready to oust her by force; but she caught his eyes and held them until they looked away.

They settled for the long watches of the night. It was dim and close in this small space, curtained off from the rest of the king's tent. Sarissa could have borne it more easily if she had been raised a Saracen indeed, and lived as their women did, confined forever within veils. But she would endure.

The sword lay at Roland's side. When the servants had tried to move it, his hand had proved to be locked about the hilt. His fingers had relaxed since, but she did not try to take it away from him. It was singing softly, oh so softly, as a mother croons to her sleeping child.

There was another song with it, one that she knew well. Her nape prickled. She traced the song to its source, the heap of clothing and armor that had been taken from Roland. Wrapped in the tunic, tucked deep inside it, she found what she had not even known she had lost.

Her fingers twitched toward the silver coin on its chain. But she hesitated. It had slipped away from her—when? When she had come to this camp?

These tokens went where they would. It had come to this man, as the sword had; as if she needed any clearer proof that he was what she sought.

A champion. A great lord and warrior to fight a war that the world knew nothing of.

And yet, what else he was . . .

She knelt beside him, sitting on her heels, and contemplated his face. Yes, there was other blood than human there; old blood, wild blood, and little of the light in it, either. Even with the wild golden eyes closed, it was not truly a human face.

She reached without thought, to brush a stray lock of black hair from his forehead. He was cool to the touch, no sign of fever. His skin was smooth. Her palm fitted itself to the scant curve of his cheek.

She drew back her hand with a distinct effort of will. "No fever," she said to the archbishop, as if she could excuse herself so easily. Turpin nodded. If he saw through her, he did not show it.

The sword sang. Its song lulled her into a doze.

She roused abruptly. Nothing had changed. Turpin sat motionless but open-eyed. The lamp flickered. Roland slept.

He stirred, murmured. Sarissa's eyes sharpened.

He was shimmering like the light of noon in the hills of al-Andalus. His face shifted: fierce curve of falcon's beak, wolf's muzzle, stag's horn-crowned head.

Turpin set himself between Sarissa and the—man?—in the bed. She met the archbishop's eyes. "If you breathe even a word of this," he said, low and fierce, "I'll wring your neck."

She regarded him with an utter lack of apprehension, which took him visibly aback. "Do you all conspire to protect him?" she asked.

He opened his mouth, shut it again.

"Tell me what he is," she said.

"Why? So that you can destroy him?"

"Don't be a fool," she said, as brisk as if he had been one of her own; and that too caught him off guard. Franks, she thought, had not met the likes of her before—even as strong-minded as their women were.

"Tell me," she said.

"The Count of the Breton Marches. The king's paladin."

"Surely," she said, "and what was he when he was in Brittany?"

"A child," said Turpin. "A count's son."

"And an enchanter?"

Turpin's lips set. He was not going to trust her, his face said.

She almost smiled. Calmly she drew light from the air, shaped it into a globe, and balanced it in the palm of her hand. "Now tell me the truth," she said.

Turpin was not nearly as convinced by the light as she had hoped. "What if you mean him ill? What if you came to break him? That sword of yours—it ensorceled us all. It struck him down when he touched it."

"It was meant for a champion," she said.

"He is!"

"And more," said Sarissa, rocked somewhat by the force of his insistence. "Tell me now. I have to know."

"Why?"

"To heal him," she said.

Turpin was not going to answer. He was a stubborn man, and fierce in his friend's defense.

Before Sarissa could speak again, another voice brought them both about. It was faint, but clear enough. "First tell me who you are."

Roland was sitting up, paler even than his wont, and his eyes less like a human man's than ever.

Sarissa's wits had scattered to the winds. She scrambled them back together. "My name is Sarissa," she said. "I come from Spain."

"My name is Roland," he said, a mocking echo. "I come from Brittany. I won your sword. It is yours, isn't it? Not the emir's. Why? What is it for?"

"For a champion," she answered.

"Yours?"

"Not . . . exactly mine," she said.

His finger ran down the blade, slowly, a gesture so simple and yet so oddly potent that she stood transfixed. "You didn't expect me," he said. "What did you expect?"

"Your king," she said. "He was supposed to—"

"Then you should have simply given it to him. It would have been a splendid gift."

She shook her head. "It couldn't be given. Not from hand to hand. It had to be won."

The black brows went up. "Truly? And you thought we'd let him win."

"That is usually the case, with kings."

"Not here."

"That," she said, "I've come to understand."

"You need a champion for Spain," he said. "My king will do that, with or without a sword. Unless you ask me to—"

"The sword has chosen," Sarissa said. "It chose you. I have to trust its wisdom."

She must have sounded doubtful. His mouth quirked. "You didn't expect a Breton witch. Are you horrified?"

"Startled," she said. "All the foreseeings, the fore-tellings—we saw your king. We never saw you. Except . . ." Her voice trailed off. "Always he had a falcon by him. A golden falcon. Sometimes it perched on his fist. More often it crouched behind him, wings mantling, curved about his head and shoulders—protecting him. Guarding him. That was you, it must have been. But we never—"

"He calls me his defender," Roland said, "and his champion. In battle, you see, we fight side by side. And I am very fast. Blows don't strike him. Arrows don't fall."

"Because you stop them." She nodded. "Yes. Yes, I understand. But we need a king."

"You have a king. You also have the king's champion." He smiled. Dear God in heaven, such a smile. "A yellow-eyed witch from Brittany. I promise I'll devour no children, nor sup on virgins' blood. Plain bread and bad wine will do for me, as for any soldier."

"Are you a Christian?"

The question was so abrupt and her voice so harsh that those golden eyes went wide. And yet he laughed, as if at a grand jest. "Why, lady! I am even baptized—and I didn't fly shrieking at the water's touch."

"No," she murmured. "No, you would not." She shook herself. She turned to Turpin and said, "Now he will be well. Stay with him if you will; see that he sleeps. He'll not need me again before morning."

She was gone before either of them could speak—trying not to run, but succeeding poorly. Her tent was a refuge, as small as it was, and dark, and wrapped in the familiar scents of herbs and spices, sweet grass and smoke and a faint undertone of cat.

Tarik was there, curled in cat-form atop her coverlet. He

opened a lambent green eye at her coming, and uttered a sound halfway between a growl and a purr.

"You knew," she accused him.

His tail flicked slightly: a shrug. He was not accountable for human follies, that shrug said. If Adam's children saw plainly what was to come, and insisted on interpreting it all awry, then that was their misfortune.

"We should have seen that one," she said. "We should have known."

Maybe that one was warded, Tarik observed, sitting up, yawning, licking a soft grey paw. Maybe he was protected, so that even strong magic—especially strong magic—could not touch him.

"Maybe he is a demon's child," she said sharply.

Tarik, who was a minor demon himself, saw nothing objectionable in that. He hissed at her, showed her a splendid armament of claws, and stalked off into the night.

She sank down shivering, wrapping her arms about herself. Very carefully, very clearly, though she was all alone, she said, "The sword shaped itself of water and earth, air and fire, at my will and the will of my people who sent me, to choose and consecrate a champion. All foreseeings, all foretellings, led us to believe that that champion was Charles of the Franks. And if it is not, if it is this one who is not truly a man, how can we trust him? How can we know that he will do what is required of him? What if he turns against us? What if—what if he betrays us?"

The night returned no answer. Her heart was running wild in spite of her, remembering a fine young body and a fine white smile. All the worse for sense or sanity that he should be beautiful. Charles was pleasing to look at, imposing and kingly, but he did not turn her knees to water, or bring her close to forgetting all wisdom or caution.

And for that she almost hated this champion whom the sword had chosen, this Roland from Brittany. She could almost, even, hate the sword; and that was patently absurd. The sword was the greatest hope her people had—the sword, and the one whom it chose to wield it.

CHAPTER 7

❈ ❈ ❈

Roland dreamed, there in the night, lying in the king's tent. He was a boy again, barely a man, just come from Brittany to the king's court. He knew, or so he thought, as much as a young lord needed to know. Above all he knew that if he was to be safe among the common run of humankind, he must conceal his magic. But no one had told him that he would be lonely—he who had been alone and happy all his life—or that he would be so desperately homesick for Merlin's prison in Broceliande.

In his dream Merlin came to him, walking free in the world, and said, "Sword and spear, cup and coin. Remember."

Roland tried to ask him what he meant, but Merlin was sinking away beneath deep water. Roland drifted inexorably toward a glare of light that, when he came to it, proved to be the flicker of a lamp.

She was there, bending over him: the lady of the white stallion, the lady of the sword. She was even more beautiful than he remembered. He was dizzy with her beauty, giddy as if with wine. It made him say things that in his right mind he never would have said. And then he mocked her. He laughed, and she left him, as well she might. He must have given mortal offense.

He tried to follow, but Turpin barred his way. "Not tonight," he said in his deep growl of a voice. "Tonight you sleep."

"I've slept enough," Roland said.

"You'll sleep more," said Turpin, tipping him neatly and all too easily into the bed he had just now abandoned. He snarled, he fought, but Turpin was too strong for him. He had no choice but to yield.

He did sleep. He dreamed again, too, dim confused dreams that he remembered in snatches. Merlin in his wood, Charles on his throne. Jagged mountains towering against a bitter-blue sky. A fortress on a crag; a king dying in a bare stone chamber. Sword and spear, coin and cup—cup full of blood that overflowed and lapped the edges of the world. A shadow rose above it, darkness visible, stretching wings as wide as the sky.

She stood beneath that vast and starless blackness, a slender figure faintly limned in light. The sword lay at her feet. The spear, thrust in earth, burned like a flame in the dark. The coin hung on a chain about her neck, a wheel of silver fire. And in her hands she lifted the cup, the cup of bright blood.

Sarissa. He woke with her name on his lips, sweet as honey, rich as blood. She was gone still. Turpin slept upright in a chair, snoring to wake the dead.

He shook himself free of the rags of the dream, and rose softly lest he wake his friend. He was naked, wobble-legged, but apart from the pain in his ribs, he was as well as ever. His knees steadied soon enough. He found his own clothes, clean and only a little damp, folded at the bed's foot. The silver token was tucked inside the tunic. It sang faintly as it lay in his palm. *Coin,* he thought, *and cup. Yes—and spear.* They meant—something. And there was the sword where it had lain beside him nightlong.

He slipped the silver chain about his neck. The coin settled on his breast, warm and oddly heavy. Its weight comforted him. Guarded him—protected him. It was an amulet, he thought. A defense against harm.

The sword was a defense of another sort, and a great one, too. He wrapped it in the coverlet and carried it in his arms.

It was still somewhat short of sunrise. Olivier was not in the tent they shared. He had found a woman, no doubt, and well for him. Roland would have welcomed a warm and odorous and thoroughly human embrace himself, just then, but there was no one to give it. The tent was empty even of servants. He slipped his father's sword from its sheath and laid it gently on his bed. It was only steel; it had no song for him. Still he felt the pull of parting, as if in laying it aside he had made a choice. Had chosen—what?

He did not know yet. It could be something terrible, something even that would bring about his death. And yet he could not turn away from it. What he had won, he would keep.

His father's worn old scabbard did not fit Durandal too badly. It would do until he could have a better one made. He settled the baldric across his breast—allowing himself to wince, here where he was alone, at the tug on his poor abused ribs—and stepped out again into the morning.

It was an ordeal, that morning, as it always was after a battle. Roland did not set out to be hero or champion. He could not help himself. He endured the flood of adulation with as much grace as he could, drew the sword a thousand times, declined a match or ten against a blade that, its owner swore, was at least as wondrous.

He had duties, but when he went to perform them, the king's messenger met him near the royal tent. "Not today," he said. "The king says rest; heal. Do as you please. Tomorrow is soon enough to be his servant again."

Roland was not surprised; he knew Charles too well. But the messenger made him widen his eyes. The king's eldest son was of age and rank to send servants of his own, not to play the servant before a mere Marcher Count.

Pepin looked nervous. He was not the calmest of men; he had his father's perpetual restlessness without, some murmured, the keen wits that gave it direction. It was difficult to remember that Pepin had been born in the same year as Roland. He seemed much younger, a raw boy, awkward and uncertain.

"Would you like to see the sword?" Roland asked him.

Pepin nodded jerkily. Roland drew it as he had so often already. The sun caught the blade, dazzling him. Pepin threw up his hand against the flame of it, and shrank back with a half-choked cry.

Roland sheathed it quickly. "Ah! I'm sorry for that. I didn't expect—"

"Didn't you?" The question was so bitter, the eyes, blinking still and running with tears of pain, so sharp with resentment that Roland stood astonished. Then Pepin shook himself and laughed, a little painfully, and said lightly enough, "Such a weapon! You don't even need the edge—you can kill with the light glancing off the blade."

Maybe Roland had imagined the resentment—no, more than that: hatred. Maybe it had been meant for the sword, and not for himself. He chose to take it so, for comfort's sake. "I saw you fighting in the melee," he said. "You fought well."

"Our side lost," said Pepin, but he seemed little enough moved by it. He shrugged. "Ah well. Everyone knows how great a warrior you are. My father most of all. I don't think anybody was surprised that you won the sword."

"I was lucky," Roland said.

"God willed it," said Pepin. "We could all see that. My father, too. He's not angry at all, that you defeated him."

"The king is a magnanimous man," Roland said.

"So should we all be," said Pepin. "Go and rest, my lord. You've well earned it."

Roland was hardly minded to disobey, or to resent the dismissal, either. In truth he was a little relieved. He had never been able to like Pepin.

Rather too late, he remembered a thing that had been niggling at him. Pepin in the crowd before the melee, standing close by Ganelon. Standing with the old serpent as . . . pupil to master?

Oh, no. Surely Charles would not have allowed that.

And why not? Charles could not know what Ganelon was. No one did. They all thought him a cold man and odd, but a good priest, learned and wise. Why should he not be chosen to teach the king's son?

It was too late to catch Pepin, to ask him if it was true—if he was Ganelon's pupil. The prince was gone.

Roland could not go to Charles now. He had nothing, no proof, only the certainty in the bones of his magic, from the moment he looked on that pale wise face, that this seeming priest was the ancient sorcerer, the enemy of the Grail.

Tonight he would do what he could. Today, by the king's command, was his own. There were already people coming toward him, smiling, calling to him, besetting him with their mingling of envy and admiration. He turned aside from the path he had been taking toward the king's tent, slipped down a line of tents and dived into the arm of the wood that touched on the end of it.

He had not done such a thing in—years? Indeed. Since the first year he was in the king's court, when for loneliness and sheer homesickness he had run away more than once. Then Olivier befriended him, pressing at him until he was friend and brother in spite of himself, and Turpin made three of them, and between those two he found himself among the king's Companions. Then there was no running away. He was one of them, brother among brothers, and that other part of him was put aside.

She had brought it back—Sarissa, with her wonder of a sword. The sword rested like a familiar hand across his back. The amulet lay warm and strangely heavy on his breast. It was hers, he knew as enchanters know. It had come from her. Its warmth was the warmth of her presence.

He ran light as a young wolf through the thicket of trees. Somewhat within, out of sight of the tent-city, one of the myriad springs bubbled from a rock and ran down in a bright rill. The magic of wood and water danced in his blood.

He left his garments by the rill, hidden under a stone, and the sword buried beneath them. Even as his being shifted and changed, became air and winged swiftness, he remembered the amulet. It swung against his breast, brushing the soft hawk's feathers. He made a sound in his throat, a hawk-sound, that might almost have been laughter. He leaped into the blue heaven.

Freedom was beautiful, glorious. But the man's spirit ruled the hawk's. It brought him back well before the sun set. He was replete with the succulent flesh of a rabbit, and weary, but pleasurably so, with flying high and far. The return to human shape was a bit more of a shock than it usually was: bruises, cuts, cracked ribs, all reminded him forcibly of the battle he had won.

He dressed with care, moving stiffly, but never regretting his long hours' flight. His head was clear, his heart light. He knew what he would do. He would speak to Charles of Ganelon, and tell him the truth; all of it, however difficult, however dangerous. He would trust the king, whom after all he had sworn to serve.

As he laced up his tunic, a flicker of movement caught his eye. He paused. The wood was still. His ears sharpened. Was there a faint, the very faintest hint of indrawn breath?

He moved again with careful casualness, to finish dressing, to sling the sword on its baldric. Someone was watching. Had that person seen him—had he, or she, seen the change?

He bent to dip a handful of cold springwater. The watcher moved—toward him, not away. He gathered himself. Very carefully his hand crept toward the knife at his belt.

Leaves rustled. A supple body slipped between a pair of tree-boles.

He gaped like a fool. For an instant he thought it was she; Sarissa. But this was a taller, slighter shape, and darker, more evidently Saracen. She carried a jar, as if she had come to fetch water; but this spring was a long way from the Saracens' camp.

She smiled at him, long lids lowered over great dark eyes, dark lashes brushing the cream-smooth cheeks. Oh, she was beautiful, this infidel woman, lissome and light, swaying like a young tree in the wind. There was gold on her brows and her fingers, and clashing rings of it on her slender wrists and her delicate ankles.

This one must be a Saracen's prized possession—perhaps the emir's himself. Every fear Roland had had when he first saw Sarissa, he well should have now. Yet they were alone, and she had all too clearly come seeking diversion. And he had not lain with a woman in longer than he liked to remember.

The hawk's mind was still foremost, the man's not yet returned to full strength. A hawk took what he pleased, when it pleased him. When the falcon came into her season, he was ready; he mated.

This woman wanted him. Her smile was full of desire. She ran the tip of her tongue over her red lips and swayed toward him. She let slip the mantle that covered her.

She was naked beneath it, her skin white and rich as cream. Even as slender as she was, her breasts were round and full. Her belly was a sweet curve. Her sex was plucked smooth—so that was true, that traveler's tale. It was white and round, the nether lips just visible, as red as her mouth.

She danced for him, serpent-supple, gliding over the forest mould. Long rays of sun illumined her, casting bars of light and shadow across that face and that wonder of a body.

His own body was burning, his manly parts in outright pain. There was no thought in his head but to take what she so freely, so irresistibly offered. A very distant flicker of sanity cried to him to run, but even as he thought of it, she had him in her arms. She smelled of spices, and of something darker, closer to earth. Her lips fastened on his. Her body wound itself about him.

On his breast over his heart, warmth mounted to heat, and heat to the agony of fire. He reached to tear at the amulet, to cast it away, but his hands were caught, trapped in hers. He could not breathe: she had kissed the breath from him. He was drowning. He was—

Somehow, impossibly, he found strength to thrust her away. But she only wound the tighter, the harder he fought. She did not laugh as a woman might when she had a man in her clutches. The only sound she made was a hiss.

His sight was going dark. He was dying. He was calm, unafraid. She was killing him, crushing the breath from him, sapping his warmth, draining the life from his body. She did it deliberately, coldly, as a snake will take its prey.

No.

It was not even a word. It was pure will. Her arms held him fast, her legs wound about him, her body pinning him to earth.

But she could not hold a falcon. He was too small, too swift. The falcon saw no woman at all but a snake, a supple black-and-silver thing coiled tight round empty space. He soared up and up amid the branches of the trees. The sky was free above him.

He turned his back on it. He clapped wings to sides and plummeted, beak and talons wide. The full weight and force of him caught the serpent where it lay, just behind the flat wicked head.

It thrashed in agony, battering tree-boles, spraying water from the stream. He clung for his life, gnawing, clawing,

grinding down through scales and hide to the supple join-
ings of the spine. To rend, to tear, to break—to kill.

The serpent's throes flung him bruisingly against the
ground. He beat with wings, struggling to catch air, to rise
before the creature crushed him. It was heavy, so heavy, far
too heavy to be an earthly serpent. The weight in it was
magic: old and cold, black and deep.

He was light and fire. He was Merlin's child, the master's
pupil. He was the champion of the sword. He rose up with
all his strength, lifting the serpent with him, high and high.
When he had reached the summit of heaven, he cast his
burden down. He flung it headlong, crashing through
branches, striking the earth with crushing force; he flung
himself after it, dropping like a stone. He cared not at all if
his own body was broken. Only that the enemy was destroyed.

It lay unmoving on the tumbled ground. Black blood
seeped out of it. Its back was broken. Its eyes were flat,
empty of life.

He tore at it with his sharp hooked beak. Its blood tasted
of grave-spices and of old tombs. He gagged on it in revulsion so fierce that it shook him out of hawk-shape into
bruised and naked humanity.

No woman lay there, nor serpent either, but a creature
who was somewhat of both. Roland knew that long pale
face, that colorless hair, that shaved circle of tonsure. Of
the monk's robe he saw nothing. The naked body was hairless, sexless, not a woman's nor yet a man's. Faintly on its
sides he caught the glimmer of scales.

With a deep shudder he recoiled. Ganelon's servant was
dead. His—its neck was broken. But that alone had not
killed it. On its smooth and nippleless chest was a raw red
wound. It was as if a coal had burned through flesh and
bone to the living heart.

The amulet was hot against Roland's skin—not hot
enough to burn, not quite, but very close. He clasped it with
a hand that could not stop trembling. Its song was as clear
as he had ever heard it, a high sweet singing like the music
that drove the spheres of heaven. White magic, high magic.
It had protected him; saved him.

Even high magic could not save him from the truth.
Ganelon knew, if not yet what Roland was, then certainly

that he was a danger. And he had killed one of Ganelon's servants. He would pay for that, and dearly.

He would have paid with his life if he had not killed first. He gathered his garments, his weapons, everything that could betray him. He blurred and scattered the human footprints that he had left, and laid a wolf's trail far into the wood. Then he buried the body, digging the grave deep beneath the roots of an oak. The tree shuddered at the presence of so ill a thing, but it was old and it was strong. It would render the flesh into earth and the bones into stone, and dissipate the darkness within them.

Ganelon would miss his servant soon, if he had not already. But Roland prayed that it would be long before he discovered what had become of the creature.

CHAPTER 8

⚌ ⚌ ⚌

The hour before sunset found Roland at the king's table, seated in a place of honor at Charles' right hand. He was scrubbed clean of black earth and serpent's blood, and dizzy with the simple pleasure of living and breathing and walking free under the sky. Even when he caught sight of Ganelon far down among the priests, his heart barely stopped. He was safe, for the moment. And when this feast was over, he would speak to Charles. He would warn the king.

He took his determination with him well into the night. The feast went late. Charles drank little, nor did he encourage his men to drink themselves into a fine Frankish stupor, but he was caught up in a disputation between a pair of priestly philosophers. Charles loved such contests, though his Companions tended to find them stupefying. Roland, who had no earthly interest in the precise order and ranking of the angels, nodded off where he sat.

When he woke with a start, it was deep night. Charles was gone—to bed, no doubt, and wisely, too. There were no few snoring bodies amid the remnants of the feast. Roland had drunk little, but he had eaten less. His head ached abominably; his stomach snarled at him.

There was still half a loaf of good white bread near his hand, and a bit of roast duck. He ate what he could, a few grimly determined bites of each, and drank from the cup he had been mostly ignoring. The wine was well watered. It steadied him well enough.

As he sat sipping the last of it, gathering will to rise and seek his proper bed, a small sleek shape wove among the snoring bodies. His belly knotted, then eased as he saw what it was.

A grey cat leaped into his lap, curled there with the utter insouciance of its kind, and began to knead his thigh, purring raucously. Its claws were wickedly sharp.

He had seen this cat among the Saracen tents, the night he went there as bodyguard to the king. It was fey as all cats are, but still, he thought in the clarity of very late night, this one was more fey than most.

Its purring rose to a crescendo. He plucked it from his stinging knee, tucked it under his arm, and went out into the night.

It was almost dawn. He could smell the morning. The cat was quiet under his arm, purring still, tail flicking gently in rhythm with his stride. It had about it an air of considerable satisfaction.

Roland could refuse to let a cat rule him so, but he sensed no evil in it, though he searched wide and deep, and by every way he knew. This was no serpent come to slay him. But neither was it a simple mortal cat.

Its purring soothed him. The part of him that twitched to run to the king, wake him, warn him, subsided somewhat. His steps slowed. His senses opened as they had seldom done since he was a boy in the wood of Broceliande. The tent-city was beginning to wake. Men were yawning, stirring, rousing out of dreams. Monks and priests were up and praying, some in the slow roll of chanting, others in a shimmering silence.

The darkness was like a canker, small as yet but already deep. It had Pepin, held him fast. It stretched—yes: toward the queen and the child within her. It did not touch Charles. He was too well guarded.

Roland paused in an aisle of tents. If he slipped down this way, then turned to the right, he would come to Ganelon's tent. Durandal was close by his hand. One swift blow and he would end it.

Oh, surely, he thought with grim irony, it would be as

easy as that. Ganelon had lived for thousands of years. Others must have thought the same, and tried it, too; and he was alive and they, Roland could be sure, were long dead.

Ganelon did not seem to be guarding himself, or concealing what he was from one who could see. That was not innocence, not at all, nor carelessness either. Roland had used that same sleight in battle. It drew the enemy in, lulled him into complacence, and closed him in a deadly trap.

It was very hard to turn away from that path, even knowing that he would surely fail. Yet as the grey light grew about him, he took the opposite way. The cat slipped free of his arm, climbed to his shoulder, and draped itself about his neck. Its claws, he could not help but observe, were perilously close to his throat.

He was being ridden like a horse. Rather oddly, he did not mind. It was like the old days, when Merlin sent small servants, wise beasts or minor spirits of earth or air, to teach him this lesson or that. For an instant he wondered—

Merlin had no such power, not so far from Broceliande. This—spirit? Yes. This spirit in cat-shape was nothing of Merlin's doing. It was its own master, he suspected, or near enough; and it had something that it wished him to do.

It was purring again. The purr guided him through the waking morning. It led him past the king's tent and Roland's own nearby, then through those of the king's court to the closely guarded enclave in which dwelt the king's women, his children, and their servants.

Roland did not often go there. The women had their own kingdom. He, who had neither mother nor sister nor wife, had little occasion to enter into their world. Sometimes he went with Olivier to visit Olivier's sister Aude, who was a nun in the service of the king's sister, the Abbess Gisela, but he had never gone without an escort. It made him strangely shy.

The cat's claws had tightened. It wanted him to walk in among those tents. The voices there were higher, but not always softer. Somewhere nearby, a woman was cursing a servant's laziness in devastating detail.

It was quieter by the queen's tent: a murmur of voices, low and urgent; a child's cry, quickly cut off. The cat saw to

it that Roland stopped not far from the entrance, which
was closed. There was no guard in front of it.

There was darkness here. It was not as deep as it was
about Ganelon's tent, but it was distinct, with the same odd
dryness to it, like the rustle of a serpent's scales.

The cat slipped from Roland's neck and leaped lightly to
the ground. It vanished beneath the flap of the tent.

Roland could not follow. He knew what was inside, what
it must be: the enemy reaching for the queen, perhaps to
take the child she carried. But what could he do? He could
not wield the sword here. He knew nothing of women's
magic.

A woman slipped out of the tent nearly as gracefully as
the cat had slipped in. She carried a water jar. There was a
satchel slung over her shoulder, heavy for its size, but she
bore it easily.

He gaped like a raw boy. He had not realized that she
was tall. Her eyes were nearly level with his, her back
straight, her steps light but firm. She could dance, he
thought out of nowhere at all, as well as she could ride a
horse. And . . . heal a queen?

Her face was troubled, those wonderful eyes downcast.
It was not going well within.

He must have made a sound. She looked up, startled,
and their eyes met. She was not as appalled this time as she
had been before. She was not visibly delighted, either.
"You have a message?" she asked him.

He blinked. From the king, she must have meant. He
shook his head. As ridiculous as it sounded, he said,
"The cat—"

"Tarik? Tarik brought you here?"

Indeed: the cat was weaving between them. Its purr was
a low rumble. It sprang into Roland's arms and grinned a
fanged cat-grin.

Sarissa glared at the creature. "Yes? And what can
he do?"

"Nothing," Roland said. "I shouldn't be here. I didn't
mean—"

"Didn't you?" She was still glaring at the cat. "He cannot," she said as if it had spoken.

The cat hissed. Its tail lashed.

"This is a women's thing," Sarissa said.

"Indeed," said Roland. He turned on his heel to escape, but the cat's claws sank into his arm, holding him fast.

"This creature thinks," said Sarissa, tight and angry, "that you can be of some help here."

"And why would it think that?"

"God knows," she said. "What can you do for a woman whose child is sought after by something dark?"

"I know little of women," Roland said. "But—"

He regretted that word as soon as he had uttered it. Her eyes fixed on him. "But?"

"But surely you can have a priest exorcise the evil."

"We have had holy women raising walls of prayer about her," said Sarissa. "This is stronger than they. Stronger than a priest, too."

"Then what do you think a plain fighting man can do?"

"It's not what I think," she said. "It's what Tarik thinks. He says that you are more than a soldier."

"I do not want to be," Roland said in a kind of despair.

The cat's claws sank deeper. It was, in its way, dragging him toward the tent, toward that nest of whispering women.

There were things that Merlin had taught him. Defenses against dark things. Walls of air. Their like had imprisoned the enchanter in the wood; but in lesser strength they could protect a man—or a woman—beset by ill magic.

For an instant Roland's hands remembered the not-quite-human softness of a demon's skin, and heard the hiss as the serpent-creature sucked the breath from him. He was as dizzy as he had been then, weak, swaying, heart pounding, gasping for air. Pain brought him back, sharp-clawed and merciless. He was not to escape this. Not unless he wanted to lose a portion of his hide.

He did consider it. But he was not so great a coward after all. Nor did he need to go into the tent for this. He had simply to know what the boundaries were, and sense where the queen was, with the child enfolded in her.

True magic was quiet, a thing of the spirit. It had no need for extravagant displays. He spoke the words softly, without drums or trumpets, magical gestures or sleights of the magician's art. He raised the walls as Merlin had taught him, secured them with bars of light, and bound them with

the chains of the earth. He delved deep in his strength for
that, but there was enough. He even kept his feet after,
bowed to Sarissa without falling over, and walked away.
The cat, for a wonder, let him go.

CHAPTER 9

❈ ❈ ❈

Sarissa stood flat-footed, taken for once completely aback. When she could begin to think, her first thought was pure white anger. The nerve, the sheer gall of the man, to come here, raise the powers, leave—and hardly a useful word spoken.

And oh, dear forgotten gods, the strength of him, to do it with such ease, as if it were no more complicated than the simplest of fire-spells. There was no gap in the wall he had raised, no weakness. When she went inside the tent, Queen Hildegarde was sleeping peacefully, and once again there was color in her cheeks. Sarissa had not been able to do that, not so easily or so strongly. And she was a healer and more. She was strong herself, strong enough to bring down a mountain or raise a fortress of living light.

"The only way," she said to Tarik when they could be alone, "the *only* way he could have done it was by knowing where the darkness came from. That has been hidden from me. But he knows."

Then, Tarik's tail-flip said, she should ask the enchanter who it was. Tarik was singularly unaffected by Sarissa's outrage, or by the cause of it, either.

"Suppose that he is part of it," Sarissa said. "You've seen him. He's a devil's get. It's written in his face. And that power he has—that's not plain human strength. He's no mortal man, whatever he may be pretending."

You should ask, Tarik said, as close to mere words as he ever came.

Sarissa was not about to do that. She should offer thanks, for now truly the queen was safe; but she could not bring herself to do that, either.

Pride was a sin. Yet she could not overcome it, nor truly want to. She could well convince herself that he had warded the queen so easily because the whole was his doing: darkness as well as escape from darkness. Devils thrived on confusion.

Tarik was disgusted. He stalked away with his tail stiffly erect. Just before the corner of a tent would have hidden him, he vanished. A raven spread broad black wings, climbing into the sky.

The Abbess Gisela, who had been born a king's daughter, heard Mass each morning with the other holy women who attended the queens, and with such of the others as were minded to attend. This morning Sarissa was so minded. She put on a gown like a Frankish woman, and a dark mantle, and slipped in among the faithful. She knelt and stood and crossed herself with the rest, lifted her voice in the responses, and prayed when prayer was fitting.

She had been recognized. Whispers spread. She was careful not to listen too closely. The Mass had its own power, raised its own citadel of light. For a little while she rested in it.

When it was over, the abbess happened to pass Sarissa making her slow way back to the tents. They walked side by side, with the abbess' women trailing at some distance. They took the long way about, which gave them ample time for conversation.

Abbess Gisela seemed in no haste to begin it. Sarissa walked in silence. She was aware of the abbess' eyes on her. Young eyes, and bright; curious. "Were you mocking us?" Gisela asked at last.

"I am not a Muslim," Sarissa said.

The white-fair brows rose toward the black veil. "Truly? But you let everyone think—"

"People may think as they please," Sarissa said.

"And so betray themselves?"

The corner of Sarissa's mouth twitched. Not all Franks, she thought, were innocents, though this one seemed as wide-eyed as the worst of them.

"Tell me what you need of me," said Gisela.

That was a Frank beyond doubt: direct, to the point, and no graceful dancing about the truth. "Tell me of the man who won the sword," Sarissa said.

"Ah," said Gisela. "He's pretty, isn't he? Shy with women, tongue-tied to a terrible degree, and quiet enough among the men, too. But he's the best fighter in Francia."

"That I know from watching him," Sarissa said. "I need to know more. Who he is. *Why* he is."

"And whether you can trust him?"

Sarissa nodded.

Gisela looked as if she might have offered her own opinion as to that, but instead she said, raising her voice slightly, "Sister Aude! Lady, come; walk with us."

One of the sisters stepped forward from among the rest. She was a tall, robust creature, with a curl of coppery hair escaping from her veil, and milk-white skin richly freckled. Her body was ripe in her habit, full-breasted, deep-hipped. Sarissa would have expected to find her beside some great bear of a man, with half a dozen of his children at her feet, and yet another swelling her belly.

And yet she was consecrated to the Christian God, forbidden man's touch, and all that richness shut away from the world. It was a great sacrifice, Sarissa supposed. She could hope that it was worth the price.

"Aude," said Gisela, "attend this lady, if you please. Tell her such things as she wishes to know."

Aude bowed as an obedient nun should. Her eyes were alert under the veil. She did not have the look of one wholly given up to submission.

She was skilled, too, in leading without seeming to lead, taking Sarissa away to the courtyard formed by the walls of the queens' tents. It was a lovely greensward, with a little stand of trees, and a canopy under which one could sit and ply one's needle.

This Aude proceeded to do, taking up the work that had lain folded on the bench. She had the air that nuns cultivated, of sublime patience. And yet Sarissa noticed that the garment she was embroidering was a man's tunic, and a fine one, too, of scarlet silk. She threaded a needle with gold and continued the embroidery of the hem.

Sarissa sat on a bench opposite her, regretting for a moment that her own hands were empty. She had brought no needlework with her from Spain, nor was there any laid out for her as there had been for Aude. It would have been welcome now, to occupy her fingers. She laced them in her lap, tilted her head toward the tunic, and inquired, "For your father?"

"My brother," Aude said. She shook her head and smiled a little wryly. "Not that I expect him to keep it clean for more than a moment, once he puts it on. But he does need something that's fit to wear at festivals."

"I don't suppose your brother is the Count Roland."

Aude laughed. She held up the tunic. It would have covered two of Roland. "Oh, no! My brother is Olivier—his friend, the king's Companion."

"And do you approve of that friendship?"

Aude's mirth retreated to her eyes and to the corners of her mouth. "I swore vows," she said, "but if God had not had me first, you can be sure I'd be flinging myself at that lovely creature."

"The abbess says he's shy of women," Sarissa said.

"Very shy," Aude agreed, "but charming, and bold enough once you've persuaded him to trust you. It's quite like taming a wolfcub."

"Wolfcubs grow into wolves," Sarissa muttered.

If Aude heard that, she did not acknowledge it. "He was half-wild when he came to court. His mother died when he was born, poor thing. His father fostered him with a seneschal, then died in battle when Roland was still a child. He was brought up all anyhow, and he knew nothing of women at all. Not one thing."

"But he knew how to fight."

"Oh, yes," said Aude in a slow exhalation of breath. "Yes, indeed. And courts, too, and the ways of kings—those he knew."

"Indeed? A count's seneschal could teach him such a thing?"

"Well," said Aude, "no." She stitched at her border for a moment, finishing the curve of a golden vine. "Brittany is . . . strange," she said at length. "Its people are still pagan, mostly. The Marcher Counts have never so much ruled it as kept it from being a thorn in the king's side. Nor have they always succeeded in that."

"Roland is not a Breton?"

"Roland is half a Breton," said Aude. "His father was a Frank. His mother was of the old people. Very old. There are whispers, stories—one never knows what to make of them."

"That he has devil's blood?"

Aude crossed herself quickly. "He's not evil! Truly he is not."

"And yet his forebears were not all human men."

"Is that why you came?" Aude asked her. "To hunt him down? To see him condemned?"

There was no mirth in this lady now, and no friendship, either. If she had had a sword, Sarissa did not doubt that it would have been in her hand, angled toward Sarissa's heart.

Sarissa spoke carefully, not in fear—she was not afraid of any mortal thing—but to be sure that she was not misunderstood. "I will hunt down evil wherever it is. That I am sworn to. If he has no evil in him, he's safe from me. I only want to know."

"Because he won your sword?"

"How did you know it was mine?"

"I could see," said Aude, "when you gave it to him. You weren't happy that he won it, were you? Did you want to keep it?"

"It was meant for the king."

"So I've heard." Aude sighed. "Very well. But if you use this knowledge ill, or turn it against him, I will see that you pay for your treachery. So will every one of the king's Companions, and every other Frank in this place who has cause to love the Breton Count."

Sarissa inclined her head. "Has he no enemies, then?"

"Every man has enemies," Aude said. "Count Roland has fewer than most. He is loved here. Remember that."

"I will remember," said Sarissa.

Then at last Aude seemed satisfied, or close enough. She nodded; she stitched at her embroidery. She said in a soft slow voice, "He never speaks of this. But some things people can know, and one is an old story. It's said that in Brittany, in the forest of Broceliande, is a hidden fastness, a prison built strong and high. In it one lies bound. He has been confined so for years out of count, and will be bound till the moon dies. He does not die, they say, because his blood is not human. He is the child without a father, the forgotten enchanter. He is the hunting hawk of the gods.

"His guardians are also his children. They are a line of enchantresses, it's said, witches of great power. The old gods' blood is in them, devils' blood, but their magic is white and their power of the light. Roland is their child. Or so," said Aude, "it is said."

Sarissa sat still. Very, very still. She had been thinking slantwise, slipping round this truth. She did not want it to be so. That he should be a child of *that* one. That ancient evil, that enemy of all she was sworn to.

It did make a great deal clear. Even why the sword had chosen him. There was great power in him—for the light as well as the dark. But the dark was there, coiled in him. It had created him, at great remove: it had sired his forefather.

"I thank you," she said. Her voice sounded far away in her own ears.

"Mind you," said Aude as she stitched at her brother's tunic, "these are all tales and rumors. They may be nothing more than that. And if he is a devil's get, it's marked little but his face. He's a good man. I'd trust my life to him."

"And your soul?"

Aude never hesitated. "And my soul," she said.

CHAPTER 10

✠ ✠ ✠

"It is here."

Pepin regarded Ganelon in astonishment. Passion was altogether alien to that cold quiet man, but something very like it was in his voice as he paced the confines of his tent. The two monks who were his servants had effaced themselves by the walls. The third had gone out a day or two before and not come back.

Ganelon stopped in the tent's center, spun on his heel, and hissed at them all. "It is *here!* And not a one of you was aware of it."

"What, my lord?"

That was not wise at all, but Pepin was still somewhat less than adept at curbing his tongue.

Ganelon turned on him in a blaze of white-faced fury. For an instant Pepin saw his death in those black eyes. But Ganelon eased abruptly, with a faint twist of the lips that dismissed Pepin as any sort of threat. It would have been galling if Pepin had been able to feel anything but shock. "Blood of the Grail," he said, as if that answered Pepin's question.

Pepin stared blankly at him.

Ganelon had already forgotten him. "There is blood of the Grail in this place. It raised a great warding in the queens' camp. And Borel is gone. Gone utterly. Do you understand?"

The two monks bowed to the floor. "Borel is dead," said one. He had a soft voice, almost too soft to hear, full of the hiss of breath.

"And why is Borel dead? What killed him?"

"Blood of the Grail," said the hissing voice. There was no emotion in it at all.

"Did you know? Did you shrink from telling me?"

"Lord," said the monk. "Lord and master. He went to be certain, before he sought you out. It was hidden so well, warded so strongly—it could have been nothing. A memory; a dream."

"Dreams do not destroy your kind," Ganelon said. "Great power destroys them. Power great enough to stand against us. Power of the Grail." He knelt beside his prostrate servants. His voice dropped to a hiss, colder and far more deeply disturbing than theirs. "If it knows—if it has discovered what we are doing—"

"We are warded, master," said the monk. "And we know now that it is here. We can—"

"We can do nothing," Ganelon said, "until we know its face."

"Master," said the second monk, even more softly than the first, "the sword that the Saracen gave—is it a mortal sword?"

Ganelon's back stiffened. "You know it is not."

"The one who presented it—did you see her?"

"I saw a woman of the Saracens," said Ganelon.

"Her name," said the monk, "is Sarissa."

Ganelon sat on his heels as if he had been struck a blow. He stayed so for a long moment. Then he said, "Ah, so. It has been too long—too long in the dark, too long in forgetfulness. I've forgotten all I knew. To have failed to perceive that one of *that* kind was here, and that one of them all—to take her for no more than she seemed to be—indeed I have grown blind."

"She may not know of us," the second monk said. "The Frankish king is a great beacon in the night of this world, a great center of prophecy. Might not the Grail have come seeking him, too, master? As we did?"

"It would be astonishing if it had not," said Ganelon. His servants rose, bowed deeply, slipped away.

*   *   *

"Will they kill the woman?" Pepin asked.

Ganelon was silent for so long that Pepin reckoned himself ignored once more. Then he said, "What purpose would that serve?"

"She's an enemy. She killed Borel."

"If she killed Borel," said Ganelon, "then she will pay. There are worse punishments than death."

Pepin wanted to ask what they were, but another question struck him with more urgency. "What is blood of the Grail?"

"Much too high a thing for your understanding," Ganelon answered.

"Teach me, then," said Pepin.

"No," Ganelon said.

Ganelon would say no more, not for pleading, not for threats. He went back to his endless ink and parchment. Pepin went off to sulk.

Too high for him, was it? Too lofty for him to understand? He could see well enough that Ganelon was angry, and maybe even a little afraid. Whatever this Grail was, it must be very powerful and very terrible to incite Ganelon's enmity. It had killed Borel, which could not be an easy thing to accomplish. Pepin knew already that Ganelon's monks were something other than men.

Pepin went hunting the Grail's servant. On his way he paused where some of the young men were at practice with swords. That practice had a purpose to it now, to prepare for war in Spain; they were even more exuberant than usual, leaping and whirling and making a great deal of noise.

Roland was with them. He had the sword. The beautiful sword that made Pepin's heart ache when he looked at it.

She had brought it to Francia. That, he understood. Had this Grail made it, then? Or laid a magic on it? It shimmered as Roland wielded it, and sang a high sweet song.

Roland was as beautiful as the sword, dancing in the sun, bareheaded and dressed in a leather tunic, with his black hair flying as he spun. His back was straight, his steps light. As Pepin paused, Roland paused also, blade hovering, poised to fall and cleave a lesser blade in two. His face was rapt.

It was not the straight back or the breathless grace or

even the sword that woke Pepin to a pure and perfect hate.
It was that face as it stared through him, the yellow eyes
clear and focused and yet utterly remote, the mouth smiling ever so faintly. The world belonged to Roland, and well
he knew it. Whatever he touched turned to gold.

Pepin, whose father was a king, struggled for every gift
that was given him. Roland stretched out his hand and
took whatever he pleased. Roland the Breton, the witch's
child. Before he came to court, Pepin told himself, people
had noticed Pepin; had cared what he thought of them.
Then Roland came, and everyone ran after him, fell in love
with him, hung on his every word.

Part of Pepin knew perfectly well that he was being un-
reasonable. But there was no denying that Roland had
been a favorite from the moment he walked into the king's
presence, with his quick wits and his wild beauty. No one
ever loved Pepin at first glance. Pity was more likely, or ill-
suppressed revulsion.

Pepin was hunting another quarry now. But he would have
Roland, too. When he had mastered magic, he would teach
that young upstart the meaning of pain. He would twist
that so-straight back and mar that handsome face. He
would take away all its arts of war and the dance, and the
sword, too. He would have them all. And Roland would be
left with nothing.

Pepin went on in dark satisfaction, though somewhat
weakened by the knowledge that he had, as yet, scarcely
even seen magic, let alone wrought it.

She had been among the women, but had left, one of the
queen's maids said, on some errand of her own. Pepin paid
the maid with a silver ring—a high price, but she would not
speak to him for less—and when he tried to snatch a kiss,
she slipped lithely away. "For that you pay gold," she said.

Pepin would not give her the pleasure of seeing him
angry. He smiled, which made her stare, and sauntered off
with every appearance of ease. She too, he thought. When
he was a great mage, she would pay, too. They would all
pay, every human creature who had ever mocked or
slighted or pitied him. "Better honest scorn," he said to the
air, "than pity."

He went hunting where the maid directed him, into the

wood that stretched upward along the mountain's slopes. He regretted somewhat that he had not paused to commandeer a horse, but the woman had been on foot, he had been assured. Surely he could catch a lone unmounted woman, even if she were something that had Ganelon alarmed. Ganelon was old, and he was slow. Pepin was young and strong and quick enough on his feet, however crooked his back might be.

He found the marks of her feet soon enough, slender and light, moving without haste but without tarrying, either. She had an assignation, he thought. They would not be the first lovers to tryst in those woods. It was safe enough: no bandits dared raid so close to the king's tent-city, and the more dangerous beasts had been hunted out long since. There had even been an aurochs, whose kind some had thought vanished from the world. Roland had slain it, of course. Who else would have dared?

Gnawing on the seeds of his bitterness, almost reveling in them, Pepin wound among the tree-boles. The way was steep for a while, but then it leveled. Birds were singing. Once something small darted through the undergrowth. A fox perhaps. Pepin paused at a stream to slake his thirst, and to regret that he had not brought somewhat with him to eat. The day was warm and growing warmer. The trail went on and on. Sometimes he thought he glimpsed her, but she flitted out of sight again.

He knew he had been tricked when he realized that he had seen the same cluster of five beeches before, their slender boles like the splayed fingers of a hand. The trail led on, the light tread of narrow delicate feet in the leaves of years, but he stopped.

The sun was distinctly lower than it had been the last time he looked. He had no weapon but the knife at his belt, no food, nothing at all useful for either finding his way home again or camping for the night in the forest. If he had thought to bring a bow, or a loaf of bread . . .

The clouds came with evening. The rain began at nightfall. Pepin found shelter in a thicket of trees, dug like a rabbit in the leafmold and nursed his misery until morning.

He was not cold. Oh, not at all. His anger warmed him wonderfully.

*   *   *

The worst of it, the very worst, was that it was Roland who found him. He emerged blinking and shivering in a grey morning. The rain had stopped but the clouds hung low. His tracks were all washed away. He could only go downward off the mountain, and follow the rain-swollen streams as they leaped and tumbled toward the lowland.

Roland and Olivier came on him when the clouds had begun to break. They carried hunting-bows, and Olivier had a brace of hounds on lead. Roland had his great horn slung on a baldric, flaunting it as he always did, splendid prize and rich royal gift that it was. They strode together with the ease of long companionship, and Olivier was chattering of somewhat or other—a woman, probably; that was all Olivier ever thought of.

Pepin wavered between two base impulses: to fling himself at their feet, weeping with relief, or to hide from them till they were past. The hounds settled it for him. They sprang baying toward him. One slipped its lead and bolted, bowling Pepin over. The other dragged Olivier through the thicket till he stumbled over Pepin's body.

When the tangle had sorted itself out, Pepin was on his feet and Olivier was fussing over him like a great ungainly girl. Roland had caught and leashed the hound. He stood back with his air of lordly arrogance, letting Olivier play the fool.

At long last Olivier's tongue stopped rattling on for a breath's span. In the interval, Roland said, "You look as if you were out all night. Were you lost?"

No doubt he meant to sound properly concerned. To Pepin he only sounded disdainful.

Pepin lifted his chin as a prince might, and said haughtily, "Take me back to Paderborn."

Roland bowed. Insolent, thought Pepin.

It was a bare hour's walk back to Paderborn, down off the mountain and along a stream that led to the river. Pepin dismissed his escort in sight of the tent-city. "Go back to your hunt," he said. He did not thank them. Gratitude would have been a lie. They began laughing, he was sure, as soon as he was out of earshot. Pepin the child, Pepin the fool, lost in the woods almost in sight of his father's city.

He would not tell Ganelon of this. Ganelon had the Grail and the Grail's blood, and the woman who had brought the sword. Roland was Pepin's enemy. He belonged to Pepin. When the time came to destroy him, Pepin would do it. And no one else.

He slunk home in humiliation, but it appeared that no one had even noticed he was gone. That for once he was glad of. And when he came to Ganelon, presenting himself as he did each day, for the first time there was something in the tent that had not been there before.

It was a silver basin, very plain. There was nothing in it but clean pure water. When Pepin slipped through the tentflap, Ganelon said without greeting, "Sit here."

Pepin sat as he was told. The basin lay on the table between them. The light of lamps gleamed on its polished sides.

Ganelon breathed on the water. It quivered and went still. "Tell me what you see," he said.

Pepin bent over the basin. "I see water," he said. "I see silver. I see—" His breath caught.

"Tell me," Ganelon said.

Pepin's heart was hammering. He could see. God help him, he could see. "I see a woman. I see *her*."

"What is she doing? Tell me. Tell me everything."

Pepin did not dare take his eyes from the water that had turned as it were to a glass, reflecting things that were never in this tent at all. But he could ask, "You can't see?"

"The Grail and its works are hidden from me. But you they do not know. You can see what I am forbidden."

"Yes," Pepin said. "Oh, yes."

"Tell me."

It was splendid to have such power, and now of all times, too, when his heart most needed it. He thought for a moment of concealing some of what he saw, but there was no profit in that. Later, when he knew more, understood more, he could keep a portion for himself.

Today he told the master everything. "I see her standing on a pavement of stone. There is a tower above her. The walls fall far and far away below. A grey cat sits at her feet. There is a man beside her. He sits in an ivory chair. He is wrapped in a mantle, round and round about. He seems cold. He looks . . . old. Not in the face. Not really. His beard is still black. His cheeks are smooth, like a young man's. But his eyes have seen everything there is to see. I think he may be dying."

"Yes," breathed Ganelon. "Yes."

Pepin smiled to himself. His eyes were riveted on the water. "She has a cup in her hands. The cup is full of blood. She holds it to the man's lips, but he turns his face away. She seems sad, and angry. But he refuses to drink. She walks away from him, very fast. So fast, she spins the world away. And when it stops, she stands . . . here. In this place. With a sword in her hands."

"We knew that," Ganelon said. "Look again. Keep in your mind the man's image, and the tower beside him."

Pepin tried, but all he saw was the woman and the sword. She was holding it out. If he stretched out his hand, he would have it. He would have won the sword.

At his touch the image shattered. The water was colder than ice, colder even than Ganelon's heart. He recoiled. It was only water again, quivering in a silver basin.

"No matter," Ganelon said with remarkable equanimity. "I only wished to be certain. Now I know."

"Was that it?" Pepin asked. "Was that what it is? Blood of the Grail?"

Ganelon did not answer. But Pepin did not need to hear the word to know it was true. The cup of blood, the dying man, the woman—he had seen them. He, and not Ganelon. He knew them now. In time he would come to understand them.

CHAPTER 11

✠ ✠ ✠

In the handful of days that followed the death of Ganelon's servant, it almost seemed as if Roland was prevented from approaching the king. He could swear that it was chance, that the preparations for war were engrossing them all, and that the king had little enough time for idle chatter. But whatever the cause of it, Charles continued to see Ganelon as they all saw him, all but Roland: a holy priest, a loyal servant of God and of the king, and tutor to the king's eldest son.

The day after Roland and Olivier found Pepin wandering lost in the forest an hour outside of Paderborn, Roland caught the king at last. Charles was just out of bed, washing before he dressed. As Roland had hoped, Charles was all but alone. There was a soft and scented presence behind the curtain that concealed the king's bed, but Roland sensed no danger there. The servants were of long standing and famously discreet.

Charles grinned at Roland as he stepped through the tentflap, and said, "Good! I was missing some company this morning."

Roland helped the servants dress the king. There was not overmuch to do but hold this garment or that till he was ready to put it on, and be companionable. As Roland helped him into his silk-bordered tunic, Charles said, "Tell me. Are you pleased with your new sword?"

Roland flushed and looked down. "I know, sire, it was meant for you. If—"

"Stop that," said Charles. "You won it fairly. God meant it for you. You'll do great things with it in Spain, in God's name."

"I do intend to," Roland said, "but if it belongs to you—"

"It is yours. Shall I belt it on you, as a king may? Will that convince you?"

"Your word is enough," Roland said faintly.

"Good," Charles said. "Good, indeed. The assembly will disperse tomorrow, and all the lords and the fighting men go home to prepare for the war in Spain. We'll travel across Francia ourselves, and secure the kingdom. Then early in the new year, we'll stand at the gates of the Pyrenees."

"Yes," Roland said. His mind's eye could see it. The great army; the bright banners. The mountains like a wall rising to the sky.

Charles smiled as if he understood. "Will you forgive me if I don't release you to return to Brittany? I'll send good men to administer your domain there. I've a mind to keep you near me: you and your sword."

Roland's heart swelled. Of course it was the sword, but it was a great honor. And more than that, it was what he had been praying for. He did not want to leave Charles alone, unprotected, within Ganelon's reach. Even to fly free in the wood for a little while. Even—even to see Merlin.

Aloud he said, "I'm honored, sire. I'll gladly stay and serve you."

"What, you don't mind? I know how you love your country. And . . . your kin there."

Charles' eyes met Roland's. He knew, but like the Companions, he never spoke of it. "My kin will understand, sire," Roland said. "Now more than ever."

Charles looked hard at him, caught perhaps by a change in his tone, or by a nuance of expression that he had not even been aware of. "Why, sir, you're afraid for me. Why?"

There, thought Roland. Now. He drew a breath. "Sire, I hear your son has a new tutor."

Charles' brows rose. "You fear *him*? The man is elderly. He asked leave to rest from his travels. He is old, he said; he grows weary."

"Then he will stay behind, safe in a monastery, when we travel through Francia?"

"Of course not," said Charles. "He'll travel in comfort with the priests and instruct my son. He's a wise man, and holy."

Roland bit his tongue on what he might have said to that. Ganelon left behind could work great evil in Charles' absence. Ganelon in the court . . .

Ganelon in the court was under Roland's eye. The king himself had made sure of that. "Sire," Roland said. "Do you truly trust him? Do you know who he is, or where he was born?"

"He was born in Apulia," said Charles, "of an old family there. He was ordained by Pope Gregory and sent into Francia in the train of the papal legate. He's been here since; he loves this country, he tells me, as if he had been born in it."

It was a very plausible story. More plausible than Roland's own, if he paused to consider. And yet he had to try to warn the king. "My lord," he said, "I know that he lies. He was never born in Apulia. Where he was born, I think even he may not remember. He's old, sire, as old as mountains. The Devil is his master. He's been corrupting kings since before the Flood."

Charles was not an easy man to astonish. He knew who Roland was, and what. He had known since Roland came to him, because Roland could not serve a king who did not know the truth. Still, his eyes, wide and round by nature, had grown wider yet. "You . . . have proof of this?"

Roland shook his head. "I know, my lord. I know because—he wrought Merlin. In his way he's my grandfather."

"And he knows you?"

"God willing, no," Roland said, crossing himself. "Merlin turned against him, and was bound forever for it. I'm Merlin's child. Do you think he'll wish me well at all?"

Charles frowned. "And yet, sir, you have no proof. I have what I see, which is a man of impeccable loyalty and great sanctity. I would believe that the old enemy still lives, if Merlin himself is alive; but that it is this man? Not without proof. You could be deceived. Your enemy could be anyone, anywhere. He could be mocking you with this delusion."

"No delusion," Roland said. "I know. In my very bones I know. This is the ancient serpent."

But Charles did not believe the evidence of Roland's bones. It was nothing a man could see or understand—that much Roland had learned long since. Men born without magic had no comprehension of it.

"Roland," said his king, "I believe that you believe this. But until there is proof, I can do nothing."

"Trial," Roland said at once. "By combat. I'll challenge him. He won't fight; he never in his life has. But one of his servants may. These servants are nothing human. If you can see—if I defeat him—"

"On what grounds? What has he done to you? Has he murdered your kin? Seized your lands? Done one perceptible thing to betray his king?"

"He will," said Roland.

"I can't know that," Charles said. "No trial, sir. No challenge. If it will comfort you, I'll keep Archbishop Turpin near me when you can't be hovering and fretting and fondling your sword. Unless he too is some ancient demon?"

"Turpin is as mortal as the grass of the field," Roland said, "and as pure in spirit."

"There, you see? He'll look after me as well as you could ever wish." Charles clapped Roland on the shoulder. "Here, boy. Stop fretting. We've a war to win."

"And if that one won't let you win it?"

"If he makes a hostile move," Charles said, "or threatens me in any way at all, I'll give you leave to question him. But until then, nothing changes. Do you understand?"

"When he moves will be too late," said Roland.

"Do you understand?"

The king's voice was mild, his expression calm, but Roland heard the thunder beneath. He had no choice but to bow and obey.

He had won a little, at least. Turpin would guard Charles, and Roland would look after the rest. And Charles knew now what Ganelon was, and would be more wary. It was not enough, by any means, but it was a beginning.

CHAPTER 12

✠ ✠ ✠

When the gathering of the Franks dispersed to the year's tasks of governing, tilling the land, and raising armies for the war, the emir Al-Arabi departed with his escort for Spain. But Sarissa remained behind. The queen asked it. Sarissa would have stayed even without that, but it gave her a place, rank of sorts, and a reason to keep watch over the royal ladies. Queen Hildegarde was still not entirely well. Nor would she be, Sarissa thought, until the darkness was removed from the court.

Sarissa was notably less than pleased to discover that when the lords scattered to their domains, Count Roland did not go. One of the king's counselors went instead, armed with authority to act in his name. That was not usual, she gathered. Roland was most attentive to all his duties, in his domain as well as before the king.

They said that the king wished to keep him close because of Durandal, to serve as a banner for the war that was beginning. Sarissa could believe that. She wondered if Roland chafed at his king's command—if it galled him that he could not run home to his master Merlin.

The king rode away from Paderborn, leaving behind him the makers and builders, the city guard, and the freemen who would farm the land to feed them all. Their women had begun to arrive already as the court departed, so that it was a large and mingled company that gathered to see

him go. Already the armed camp was transmuting into a
town. It would be a city when next the king saw it, its walls
raised, its citadel built, and its houses filled with people.

Charles for his part, with the great train of his court and
kin, continued the long round of the royal year. His
palatium, his palace, was no single edifice or city but the
king's own presence attended by his clerks and servants.
That went with him wherever he traveled, traversing the
whole of his realm from year to year.

This year he kept mostly to the north, but directing his
path into the west and south, so that at Christmas he would
approach the marches of Spain. The kingdom was alive
with news of the war. There was no word of aiding an infidel caliph in putting down a rebellion. Every man seemed
to believe that the king intended to take Spain away from
the infidels.

The king made no effort to alter this belief, any more than
he had before the assembly at Paderborn. Even when the
word of crusade swelled to a roar, he let it go on. It brought
the young men to the practice-fields where they might not
otherwise have gone in the heat of summer or the labor of the
harvest. It set the smiths to forging weapons with a fiercer
will, and the priests to blessing any who pursued the king's
cause. It roused the kingdom as nothing else had, not since
his grandfather drove the Saracens back from the very walls
of Toulouse.

That was an old enmity, but Sarissa had found another
and stronger one: war for the souls of the king and his kin,
and most of all for his unborn child.

In Gisela's abbey of Chelles outside the city of Paris, the
king's train paused. Queen Hildegarde was brought to bed
there, far too early, and delivered of a daughter who drew
a breath, loosed a faint whimpering cry, and died. The tiny
body was baptized and laid to rest in the nuns' graveyard,
in a grave without marking or remembrance, for the life
had been too brief and the child too small to bear the
weight of a name.

The queen had lost children before. It was the lot of
every woman, and God's fortune that she did not lose her
own life as well. But the grief was never less, nor the pain
of loss. "If I had been stronger—if I could have—"

Sarissa comforted her as she could, and saw that she

rested, that she healed. She was free of the darkness now. Having failed to capture her child alive, it had abandoned her.

It was not Sarissa's task to take word to the king. Sister Aude did that, sorrowfully, but not, Sarissa noticed, in fear. Charles was known as a fair man. He would not slay a messenger who brought him such news.

For men it was not the same. A child lost so young was a lesser grief to them, if it was grief at all. A man who had sons in plenty would hardly feel the loss of another daughter.

He had the grace at least not to demand that the queen depart when the court was ready to go on. It was she who insisted, who climbed into the wagon and refused to be lifted out again. "You will keep me whole," she said to Sarissa. "I have a need to be away from here. To breathe air that is free. To be outside of walls. To be—to be with my husband and my children who are alive."

"What killed your child," Sarissa said bluntly, "is in the court. It could strike again."

The queen would not listen. She would go. That was her will. There was no choice but to obey it.

The ride from Chelles was almost distressingly lovely. It was a fine day of late summer, no rain to mar it, no mists or fogs to dim its clarity. The sky was clear cloudless blue. Some of the young men were singing, if softly. One clear voice was so sweet and its song so poignant that Sarissa's breath caught in her throat. It was not a sad song, at all, although it was in a minor key. The words were in a language she did not know, yet they seemed to be words of healing and of peace.

The queen was listening. She had had a maid tie back the curtain of her wagon so that she could hear the song. She lay in her banks of cushions, her body at ease for the first time since Sarissa had known her. For a little while, maybe, she forgot her sorrows.

Sarissa beckoned to one of the maids. "Find that singer," she whispered. "Bring him to us. If he can soothe her majesty . . ."

The woman nodded. Her cheeks were wet with tears, so strongly had the song affected her. She dashed them away as she dragged her mule about and sent it protesting in search of the singer.

She was gone for some little while. The song ended and did not resume. The queen sighed, slipping back visibly into melancholy.

Then came the mule with its rider, and another behind her, mounted on a splendid young grey. Sarissa regarded him in something that wanted very much to be hatred.

Roland did not seem to notice her at all. He rode up beside the queen's wagon, bowed low over his saddlebow, took her thin white hand and kissed it. "My lady," he said. "Oh, my lady. I am sorry."

For a man who claimed to know nothing of women, he had a fine gift with this one. She clung to his hand, though the cart's rocking and his horse's gait made it difficult. "Please," she said. "Sing to me."

He sang to her all that day. Songs of Brittany, songs of Francia. Hymns and canticles. Love-songs, of which he seemed to know an amazing number. He sang for her ear and not for anyone else's, which saved his voice, but still, by evening it was a whisper. Then at last she let him go, sending him back to his world of men and war.

Sarissa could have escaped at any moment. The king's train was long, and the queen was near the beginning of it. It was a penance of sorts that kept her there, listening, watching, alert for any hint of danger. There was none, but she did not trust that. A sorcerer of the power she suspected in him would be adept at concealing himself.

If he was the one, she thought—if he was, this day's charity was a cruel thing. And yet to the eye and to every sense she had, he was utterly gentle. Had he been anyone else, of any other blood, she would have reckoned him compassionate.

For that, and in defiance of her suspicions, she brought him honey mead with herbs to soothe his throat, no less than three times as the day lengthened. The first time he barely acknowledged her, except with a nod. The second, she fancied that a flush stained his pale cheeks. The third, she knew it. He was noticing her after all, and striving mightily not to show it.

She was all in confusion. Every tale she had heard of Merlin and his works bade her walk wary of this man. But her heart and her body were captivated. If he could know how she loved a sweet singer—if he could—

If she had been thinking clearly, she would have stayed by the queen that evening when they stopped for the night. They had hoped to reach one of the royal estates, but their advance was slow, to spare the queen; therefore they paused instead at a small lordly holding. Its lord was away, but his lady was in residence. She put on a brave face at sight of the king's whole court and retinue, and gave up her house to the king and the queen and their chief attendants, but the rest had to camp in the fields.

Sarissa's belongings were in the manor with the queen and her maids, but she was stifling in the closeness of that small and crowded house. The queen was safe under the queen mother's eye. Sarissa went in search of air.

Or so she told herself. She did not admit that she had decided after she noticed the absence of a certain face among the king's attendants. Some of the Companions, it seemed, had gone to settle the men and to assure that the horses were well tended.

Sarissa's horse came and went as he pleased, which was somewhat difficult to explain. She had asked him to stay in that shape when they were traveling, though if they paused long enough to turn horses out to pasture, he was free to take whatever semblance suited him best. Most often it was a cat.

Tarik was grazing on a tether in the war-stallions' line. The master of horse insisted that he belonged there; lady's mount or no, he was entire, and he had no place in the proximity of mares. Sarissa could hardly inform that profoundly practical Frank that her horse was not a horse, and that he was quite able to control himself in the face of temptation. It was true enough that he might not choose to do that; he might find it greatly diverting to play the stallion in all respects.

He was quiet enough this evening, gleaming in the long golden light, playing his part perfectly. "I must admit," she said to him, leaning against his moon-white shoulder and smoothing his long waving mane, "that I like this shape best of all."

Tarik switched his tail. He was most fond of his cat-shape. It was small, sleek, fast, and wicked—the perfect embodiment of his self.

"But you are a beautiful stallion," she said. "All the king's warriors covet you. Count Ascelin asked me just today if I would consider putting you to a few of his mares. I didn't decline. Though he might find the results . . . interesting."

Tarik stamped and snapped at a fly. He would happily sire a herd of changeling foals. Some of them might even prefer to be cats.

"I prefer horses," said Sarissa, which won her a wet and eloquent snort.

It was chance, purely, that one other was among the stallions, tightening tethers, seeing that they were fed, watered, in comfort. It was not the master of horse, though he was horseman enough. His own grey stallion had a place not far from Tarik.

If Sarissa had looked for him to betray himself, to find him off guard, she was disappointed. He did seem startled to see her, but the spirit in him was bright with innocence. If his eyes had been properly human, there would have been no indication at all of his darker blood.

Her heart wanted that to be the truth. She greeted him politely, and suppressed a smile at the quick flush of his cheeks. "You sing beautifully," she said. "The queen is visibly better tonight because of it."

He was like a shy boy, not knowing where to look. "I am glad her majesty is better," he said. "It's a hard thing to lose a child."

"Not many men would understand that," Sarissa said.

That brought his eyes up, reminding her forcibly that this was not a simple man. "Maybe not in Spain," he said.

"There is more to Spain than you may know," said Sarissa.

"I know little of it," he conceded. "Only what one can read and hear of. Old tales. Rome was there once. It was Christian; then the Saracens came. And we," he said, "are going to take it back. Or so people believe."

"Do you?"

"Does it matter?"

"Your possession of that," she said, tilting her head toward his sword, "says that it does."

"You are not a Muslim," he said. "You should be delighted that this war has been turned into a crusade."

"It is good that your king comes into Spain," she said. "For whatever reason."

"Even the wrong one?"

"If it raises the army he needs, it is right."

"The Caliph in Baghdad might not agree with you."

Sarissa felt her brow arch. "It seems to me that the Caliph wants his rebellion put down by whatever means he finds closest to hand."

"Minds are subtle in Baghdad," said Roland.

"And not in Francia?"

"We're the world's innocents," Roland said. "And also its strong arm. We're very good at it."

"Is that what you would like to be? Simple brawn?"

"Sometimes I think it would be more comfortable," he said with a touch of wryness.

"*More* comfortable? And what would be less?"

"Many things." He soothed a restless horse, stroking the sleek neck, murmuring in the twitching ear.

"You aren't simple," she said. Dangerously, maybe, but the words were out of her before she could catch them.

"Mostly we aren't," he said. "We try to tell the truth, most times. That makes less . . . blunt people think we can't see all the ways around a thought."

"Do you always tell the truth?"

If he sensed that this was a trap, he did not show it. He shrugged a little, spread his hands. "I try."

"And if you can't?"

"I choose silence."

"Always?"

His black brows rose. Fine straight brows they were, too, and his face so open and fair, but those eyes . . . "And what lie might you think I have told?"

"None at all," she said.

"Good," he said. She could not tell if he was angry, or troubled, or amused. "It's a great insult in this country to call a man a liar. Even a lady of rank might be wary of it, for fear of making enemies."

"Are you my enemy?"

He met her stare. "No, lady. Are you mine?"

"I should not like to be," she heard herself say.

"Good," he said again.

There was a silence. Not silence with a falsehood in it,

she hoped. Her hand had a terrible, almost irresistible desire to take his. They were close enough for that, standing side by side among the horses. She clenched her fist and set it firmly behind her. "Tell me one thing," she said.

"If I can," he said. He sounded wary.

"If you were offered a throne, would you take it?"

"Not from my king," he said promptly. "Not ever from my king."

"And yet you took the sword."

"The sword took me."

That was manifestly true. He did not say it with great joy, either.

"And if a throne took you? Would you accept?"

"Are you offering me one?"

"Not this moment," she said.

"I will not betray my king," he said. "Never. Do you understand? Never."

"I understand," she said. And maybe she did, if her heart was to be trusted, and not her head. It was her heart that said, "The sword has chosen a man of honor. Spain will be more than glad of him." Spain, she thought, and more than Spain. But he was not ready yet to know of that.

PART TWO

✠ ✠ ✠

SARAGOSSA

CHAPTER 13

❖ ❖ ❖

Siege-engines crashed against the walls of Saragossa. The thundering boom had become a part of the world, so that one barely heard it, except when it stopped. It even went on during the singing of the Mass. The priests had learned to modulate their voices in time with it, a sinuous rise and fall that was strangely beautiful and oddly terrible.

On the feast of Peter and Paul, King Charles heard Mass in the bitter-bright morning. The heat was already rising. Any man with sense went about stripped to his tunic. But no fighting man had any sense. This was war; and in war, one wore mail. Even in the blazing sun of Spain.

As with the pounding of the engines, one grew inured to it, after a fashion. The army of the Franks had been in Spain since the early spring; they had grown into the heat, more or less. They would never come to love it, or to love this country, either.

"God-cursed Spaniards," Olivier muttered after the Mass had ended.

The king had withdrawn to his usual vantage in the siege, a rise of ground within sight of the locked and guarded city. A canopy shaded him. He had learned on this campaign to cultivate a luxury of the infidels: a servant with a fan, which cooled him as best it could in the heat of the day. If there was a wind, that same servant would wet a blanket in water from the great slow river that flowed past the city, and hang it to catch the breeze. That cooled him, too, and rather remarkably well.

People found excuses to call on the king, to catch a breath of that coolness. Some of the men in the lines had found ways to mimic it with spears and cloaks, so that sometimes the whole windward side of a line would be a wall of woolen mantles.

This morning Olivier and Roland were attending the king. Turpin had come up from the field where he had been singing the Mass, clad in a mail-coat over a linen habit—as practical an expedient as Roland could imagine, and probably more comfortable than linen tunic under leather coat under mail. Turpin took his wonted place on Roland's left hand, as Olivier stood on the right; they rode so, hunted so, fought so. It was a deeply comfortable place to be, Roland thought, in war or anywhere else.

Olivier went on cursing the whole race of Spain, while the king busied himself with matters of the siege. Roland listened to each with half an ear.

"Curse them all, Christian, Muslim, or pagan. Lying, deceitful, treacherous, slippery, contentious, perfidious—"

"One would think," observed Turpin, "that you didn't like the Spaniards."

Olivier growled under his breath. "What, you love them? They seduced us. They lured us here with promises. Lies! Not even the Christians want us. The cities we were promised, the wealth, the oaths of allegiance— look where that has brought us." His hand slashed toward Saragossa. "This was supposed to be the crown of our kingdom. And what did we find when we came here? Gates shut and barred. Promises broken. Oaths cast in our faces. We've fought our way across Spain, and every man here, Christian, rebel, or Caliph's servant, has turned against us. We came because they asked us. Now that we've come, not only do they not want us, they're doing their best to drive us out with fire and sword."

"Well," said Turpin, "you did liken Spain to a woman. A woman changes her mind."

"She could have done it before we mustered the greatest army that ever marched out of Francia."

"What, and deprive us of that glory?"

"Glorious heat. Glorious dust. Glorious flies. Glorious plagues of Spain. Who'd want to rule it even if we won it? If there's a more pestilential pit of a country, I've never heard tell of it."

"I do like a cooler air myself," Turpin admitted, "and a friendlier populace."

"At least with the Saxons, we knew from the beginning that they hated us. That was an honest war. This is rank confusion."

"Then victory will be all the sweeter," Turpin said, "once we win it. They say Saragossa is beautiful within those walls."

"Francia is beautiful. Saragossa is loot." Olivier looked ready to spit, but the king's presence forestalled him. "God, I hate this country."

Truly, thought Roland, it was not going well, if even Olivier's sunny disposition was so clouded. Few of the Franks were in the least surprised by the Saracens' perfidy. That was the way of infidels, they told one another. But the Christians of Spain should have welcomed them with open arms, hailed them as saviors, and rallied to their banners. Instead, every Christian man, without fail, had taken arms with his infidel conquerors. Every one.

One of them, captured in the fall of his recalcitrant little town, had explained for them all. "You would make us into Franks, and make us bow to Frankish lords. The infidels let us be."

"You bow to Saracen lords," Charles had said to the man, as baffled as the rest of them.

The man shrugged. "They're not Franks."

That was the essence of it. The Caliph's people had grown frightened when they saw the size of the army raised in their cause, protesting that it was too large, too unwieldy, and far too likely to turn on them and destroy them. The rebels had never been in any doubt as their own enmity. And the Christians fought on both sides, but never on that of the Franks.

Now Charles besieged Saragossa, which should have given itself to him when he rode up to its gates. He had a grim look about him these days, a deep and abiding anger that sat strangely on his open face and equable disposition. Charles was a fair man, and kind as kings went, but of all things he could not abide, treachery was the worst.

He still would not believe that his son's tutor wished him ill. He persisted in seeing only the harmless and holy priest. Therefore Pepin continued under Ganelon's tutelage. Roland could find no proof, nothing to tie the man to any ill thing. It was still no more than a feeling in his bones.

A stir caught Roland's attention. Something was coming through the ranks. Nothing evil, not at all; men were smiling, moods were lightening. Good news? Roland wondered. God knew, they had had little enough of that, of late.

She came riding as she had come into Paderborn a year past: mounted on her white Spanish stallion and dressed for riding in the Saracen mode, in light flowing robes. But she was not concealing her sex now, or her name either. They all knew her. "The queen's healer! The queen's healer has come from Francia!"

She rode up to the king's pavilion. Charles by then had left his maps and charts and plots of war and stood just out of the sun, frowning as she approached—the only man in Roland's sight who was not smiling or laughing.

His frown deepened as she slipped from the saddle. Her knees buckled as they could if one had been riding overlong. Roland had moved with no thought at all, to catch and steady her before she fell. He barely touched her, but his hand felt as if it had clasped a fistful of fire.

She did not acknowledge him even with a glance. She was smiling a beautiful, a marvelous smile, full into the king's eyes. Charles blinked, dazzled. "My lord," she said in her clear voice, "you are the father of sons."

"I should hope so," Charles said, evidently without thinking. Then it struck him, what she must mean. "Are you telling me—has she—is it—?"

Sarissa laughed. "Oh, yes, my lord! Queen Hildegarde was brought to bed of twin sons. They were born early, but they thrive. All the omens promise, my lord: one of them at least will be a king."

Charles smote his hands together in joy. But he was not ready yet to let go of his temper. "You left her alone?"

"She is safe," Sarissa assured him, "with the good sisters in Chelles. She bids you win a great victory, then come swiftly back to her."

"It seems she has won a victory of her own," Charles said. "But you—"

"It was time I left Francia," Sarissa said. "My task there was done. I am a healer, after all, and armies have great need of such. Or would it discomfit you to set a woman in that office?"

"Not at all," Charles said with better humor than he had shown since he found the gates closed at Saragossa. "You are very welcome here. Roland, of your courtesy, look after her. Find her a place in the camp, and see that she has all she needs for her comfort."

Roland opened his mouth to protest. But Charles had already turned away, summoned by a messenger with word from the siege-engines. He was, after all, waging a war. He did concede to the joy of the news with a swift command as he went, to turn the daymeal into a feast of celebration for the birth of princes.

Roland, meanwhile, had no choice but to obey his king's command. It was rather bleak consolation that Sarissa seemed less happy than he, and even less able to object. Her dislike of him, it seemed, had lessened not at all with time or distance.

He set himself to be a courtier: coolly cordial, undismayed by enmity. He found a place for her tent and baggage among the few women whom the king had brought with him on this march: a mistress or two and their maid-servants, and a small company of nuns whose duty and occupation was to pray for the king's soul. Sarissa fit somewhere between the two, though Roland suspected that she would have been happier as a nun than as a royal paramour. Her escort was much simpler to place: a small company of queen's guards, and a pair of wide-eyed and very young nuns from Chelles.

Those two, unlike Sarissa, seemed delighted with the guide whom the king had inflicted upon them. Their names, they made sure he discovered, were Rotruda and Emma. Sister Emma was taller and thinner. Sister Rotruda was smaller, rounder, and fairer, with a look about her that said she might have chosen another life if anyone had thought to ask her. She drank in the Spanish air, heat, dust, flies, and all, as if it had been fine wine. "Oh!" she said. "Oh, it's a marvel to be free about the world!"

Sister Emma hissed at her to be quiet, but she took not the slightest notice. "My lord, have you fought bravely? Has your sword drunk rivers of pagan blood? Is that it, that you carry? Is that really Durandal?"

After a year, such eagerness had grown rare. Roland had passed from shyness through annoyance to wry acceptance. Now he found it rather amusing. "Yes, Sister. That is Durandal."

"Does it sing when you fight? Is that true?"

"Every sword has its song," Roland said. "Hers is sweeter than most."

"*Hers?* Durandal is a woman?"

"She does seem to be," said Roland. He smiled impartially at the little round woman, still wearing the courtier's face. With some dismay, he realized the effect of that simple attempt at courtesy: the flush on the plump white cheeks, the hint of a swoon. If she had been some lady's wanton maidservant, that would have been a prelude to delight. But this was a nun from Chelles, however unwilling she might be to accept the vocation her family had forced on her.

A moment more and she would make an excuse to droop toward him and cling. He eluded her, deftly he thought, and let Sister Emma interpose her taller, stiffer, and visibly disapproving self. "Sisters," he said, "if you will look yonder, that tent belongs to the king's holy ladies. They'll be delighted to welcome you among them."

"Oh, no," said Sister Rotruda, "we'd crowd them out. We'll stay with Lady Sarissa, will we not?"

"You will not," Sarissa said, clear, amiable, but unshakably firm. "Now, Sisters, go where my lord bids you."

"But—" Rotruda began.

Sister Emma cut her off with a sharp word and a sharper tug on her arm. She yelped indecorously and scrambled to keep her feet as Emma dragged her toward the nuns' tent.

Roland would have fallen back against a wall if there had been one. He did manage a sigh of relief. From the

midst of it, his eye caught Sarissa's. Her expression astonished him. There was no disapproval in it, and no dislike, either. It was full of laughter.

Her mirth was infectious. It blew like a clean cold wind
through his spirit and left him standing in the harsh sunlight, grinning like a fool. "Oh, lady!" he said. "God and the
saints be thanked for Sister Emma."

"Amen," Sarissa said, still laughing. She shook her head.
"That child. Abbess Gisela thought the journey might
teach her the beginnings of discipline."

"Did it?" Roland asked.

"Indeed," said Sarissa, "I believe it did. But very, very
small beginnings. Now she's here, and a whole army to
yearn after . . . *Ai!*"

"There now," Roland said. "Put your heart at rest. I sent
her exactly where the good abbess knew she would go.
She's in Sister Dhuoda's hands now. Sister Dhuoda," he
said with no little relish, "is the sword of the Lord. Strong
men quail before her."

Sarissa eyed him warily. "You're making fun of me."

"By God and His holy Mother," Roland assured her, "I
am not. Your headstrong little Sister will find she's met her
match."

"I do hope so," Sarissa said with the fervor of a long
journey made even longer by that difficult companion.

Roland should go. Her tent was up; the servants had
pitched it while they contended with Sister Rotruda. Her
belongings were in it. There was a basin coming at the
king's order, a bath and rest for her travel-weary bones.
But he could not seem to tear himself away.

The last he had seen of her, she was standing with the
rest of the queens' women before the gates of Chelles,
watching the king ride off to the muster. He had put her
resolutely out of his mind. She was nothing to him, nor he
to her. She was no part of his world.

And yet she had come all unlooked for to this untidy
tangle of a war, and for no reason at all, he was glad. It was
as if—how odd; as if, now she had come, this land of Spain
had become less hateful. He had never cursed it as Olivier
had, but he did not love it, either. Now she was here, and
he was somewhat less inclined to despise it.

Poor lady, she was swaying on her feet. She had traveled

far and fast to bring Charles the first good news he had had
since he marched into Spain. With as little thought as when
he had steadied her before the king, he swept her up and
carried her into the tent.

CHAPTER 14

※ ※ ※

Sarissa was dizzy, as if she had been drinking a great deal of unwatered wine. But she had drunk nothing but the king's cup of welcome. Nor, despite what this arrogant creature seemed to think, had she taxed her strength unduly on the journey. Sister Rotruda had been a constant irritation, to be sure, but Sarissa had endured worse.

She tried to tell Roland that. He, of course, was not listening. He carried her into the tent as if she had been an invalid, laid her on the cot that the king's marvelously efficient servants had set up for her, and stood over her until she had eaten a sop of bread in watered wine and honey. He even, curse him, greeted Tarik, who sauntered in with grey cat-tail at its most insouciant angle, and said to that spirit of mischief, "Look after your lady, sir, and keep her safe."

Insufferable. The Spanish war had done nothing to teach him humility. Nor—and that was maddening—had it in any way marred or faded his striking, half-inhuman beauty. She had let herself forget just how odd he was, and how strongly he could shake her composure.

As soon as he took himself away, her strength remembered itself. She settled her belongings to her satisfaction under Tarik's ironic yellow eye. She ascertained that her two young charges were indeed welcomed by the nuns, and that Sister Dhuoda was if anything more formidable than

Roland had foretold. Rotruda was already looking some-what quenched—and that was a holy miracle.

The war was going poorly. She had known that since she ascended the wall of the Pyrenees and came down past Pamplona. The Frankish king's great triumphant crusade had shrunk and weakened till it was hardly more than the surrender of a few towns and a siege mounted against a city that had promised in the beginning to submit to him.

Neither Franks nor Spaniards were at all enamored of one another. The Franks had not the art the infidels had of conquering gracefully. Even Charles, for all his charm and easy manner, was more at ease with a sword than with the soft words of diplomacy.

It was still an impressive army. It maintained discipline in the face of a land and a climate that were altogether alien to it. The camp was remarkably clean as siege-camps went—the king's influence, that—and the men were not permitted to languish in boredom. Companies that did not man the engines or maintain the camp were detailed to supply duty, or else to keep the land clear of rebels, whether Christian or Muslim.

Sarissa traced the borders of the army, walking wide of the siege-lines and the recalcitrant walls. There were banners from all over the kingdom of the Franks—even half-pagan Saxons, rebel Lombards and Bavarians, and companies of men from Italy, quite like in their dark wiry smallness to the people of Spain. It was marvelous to see so many nations brought together under one king. Small wonder that he dreamed of adding Spain to it—and had leaped at the chance when it was offered.

As she walked the borders of the camp, she took the measure of the spirits within. There was anger in plenty, frustration, outrage. And a dark thing in the heart of it, that fed on ill will.

There was darkness enough in the world, but this was the one she had come to find. Twice now the spirit in her had led her to the royal court of the Franks. Durandal had taken substance there—and so, it seemed, had the power against which it had been made. Both the light and the dark were in this place, in the circle of souls about Charles the king.

Both light and dark could be incarnated in the same

man—the man whom Durandal had chosen to wield it. The nagging of doubt had lessened not at all since the army left Francia. The long quiet months with the queen had nurtured it. There was no threat to that lady or the new lives she had conceived as soon as might be after the loss of her daughter. That shadow had marched away with the king.

As Sarissa circled the camp, she laid down wards. If any dark thing passed them, coming or going, she would know. She would find the master, the enemy. And the second war, the greater war, would begin.

Nine ladies stood round a table of stone, nine enchantresses clad in white. Light poured down upon them through the high dome of a roof. The air was full of singing: a song as pure and high and unearthly as the stars' own music.

The chief of the enchantresses approached the table, an altar of dawn-grey stone unadorned. One thing only lay upon it: a silver shrine. Four fierce winged creatures upheld it, that seemed wrought of silver and gold and gems, until the light caught one wild golden eye. Then it seemed that they lived, but stilled to stone.

The lady in white bowed low before the shrine. The light streamed over her, seeming tangible as water. With great reverence she opened the silver doors.

Light flooded from them, and music so piercing sweet that the nine ladies gasped in unison. All their senses were overwhelmed, inundated, drowned in supernal sweetness. It was beyond mortal bearing; but they were somewhat more than mortal.

She who had opened the shrine lifted from it the source of all that splendor. It was an utterly simple, utterly earthly thing: a wooden cup without elegance or adornment. Its shape was pleasing to the hand, but there was little about it to delight the eye. All its beauty, all its glory, was in what it was, not in what it seemed to be.

She sang the Mass in that shrine of light, but the deity to whom she sang it was Mother and Goddess. The faith she professed, the words with which she professed it, were older far than the cult of Rome.

This, like Rome's rite, was blood-rite: blood of a god, caught in the cup that was called the Grail. The sun bowed before it. The moon paused in its sphere. The earth lay still, drinking in its blessing.

Sarissa woke slowly. The dream of the Grail slipped away. The last of it was the body's memory: the smooth roundness of the cup in her hands, the light weight, the substance of it, plain olivewood, carved by a poor man for a poor man's supper. Yet it was imbued with the power of heaven.

She sighed and stretched and lay blinking in the dimness of her tent. If she closed her eyes, she could see another place altogether: a high and airy chamber with a window on the sky. That room was empty now, waiting for her to come back.

The edge of homesickness was not as sharp as it had been. Crossing the mountains, she had thought herself likely to die of it; but here on the threshold of the plain, she knew that she would live. And every day that she endured brought her closer to her return.

As she rose and dressed, combed and plaited her hair, she felt out the wards on the camp as if they had been limbs of her body. Small things had come and gone in the night, but nothing strong enough to rouse her. The darkness was still within, nested like a worm in an apple. In the handful of days since she came here it had been quiescent, but this morning it seemed to be stirring. Responding at last to the presence of her wards? Or was it waking for reasons of its own?

She would watch and wait, and attend the king as he had requested, between his morning toilet and his daily swim in the river.

Priests were singing Mass in the camp, if she had been minded to attend. This morning she was not. That other rite, even in dream, had nourished her soul as nothing else could. The strength it brought her, the deep joy even in her yearning to be home again, went with her into the king's presence.

He was seated outside his tent, taking the morning air. The usual flock of attendants surrounded him, though not as many as there would be later in the day. He greeted Sarissa with a vivid blue glance and the sudden brightness of a smile. "Lady!" he cried. "You look splendid this morning. Glorious—beautiful! Is it good news? Fine weather? A friend?"

Sarissa matched his smile with a smile. "A dream," she said, "no more. But a very pleasant one."

"Ah," said Charles. "You're blessed then. Will it come true?"

"I do hope so, my lord," she said.

"Good," he said. "Splendid! Come, sit beside me, and indulge me with patience while I settle a matter or two."

Sarissa could hardly mistake the several meanings of that. Charles had a famous eye for women. In his queen's presence he kept it in check, confining himself to his mistresses and the occasional willing maid, and of course her majesty if she was not with child. On the march, when the queen was left behind, he indulged himself freely. But never without consent. That, every tale agreed. The king would have only a willing woman—and women nearly always were, with Charles.

Maybe Sarissa would accept the tacit invitation. Maybe she would not. That was not why he had summoned her this morning, though tonight, or another night, might be a different matter. She sat by him in the place of honor while he settled a dispute between a pair of freemen, and sent one of his Companions out with an armed company to replenish the stores of meat and grain, and read over a capitulary that he had had a clerk copy to be sent to Francia. Not even the smallest detail escaped him: a man ill with coughing fever, a need for new privies, an inequity in the distribution of arrows between one wing of the army and another.

Somewhere between the capitulary and the privies, the king's guard changed. The new captain slipped smoothly into the place of the old, just behind the king's chair on his right hand. That happened to be almost directly in back of Sarissa.

She could feel him like a fire on her skin. Perhaps it was the dream of the Grail. Perhaps that reminder of who she was had made her more intensely aware of the power that was in him. Maybe he was stronger himself. He had had a year to hone his strength; and he had Durandal. The sword was wrought of magic, was magic. It could only have heightened what was in him already.

She had done a very dangerous thing in bringing that sword to this man. How dangerous, she had not allowed herself to think. Now she had to think it. She had to consider what it meant, and what would come of it. She had to try—

"Lady," Charles said, startling her out of her reverie. "I beg your pardon for keeping you about so long. Can you forgive me?"

"Easily, my lord," Sarissa said, recovering her wits quickly, wrenching her thoughts away from the man behind her. Where, she could not help but reflect, he could with utter ease slip a dagger between her ribs.

Not that one. He would destroy her with magic or cut her down in fair fight. Roland was not a man for the knife in the back.

"My lady," said Charles, "I have a favor to ask of you. You may refuse it freely. But if you will, I have an offer of alliance. The man who offers it is an infidel emir who professes loyalty to Baghdad. One of his wives is Christian, and comes from Saragossa. I'm sending a man to him with suitably noble escort. It would please me greatly if you rode with them. You speak the languages of this country— none better, I'm told—and better yet, you can speak with the emir's wife as lady to wellborn lady. She has considerable influence with the emir, it's said."

Sarissa inclined her head. "I'll be honored, sire."

"Excellent!" said Charles. "It's not much more than half a day's ride to the estate where he's promised to meet my envoy. You'll leave before noon, and be there with the sunset. My chamberlain will fetch whatever you need for the journey."

Sarissa glanced at the sun. There was precious little time to prepare. But if anyone was hoping that she would refuse on that account, he was disappointed. She bowed, smiled, was dismissed with a blessing on her head.

CHAPTER 15

❖ ❖ ❖

"You have all the luck," Olivier said.

Roland looked up from the last of his packing. "Luck? What? You could come, too."

"Not likely," said Olivier. "Turpin's going to speak for the king, you're going to look fierce and wave your pretty sword about. Someone has to stay here and look after the king.

"Besides," he added, flinging himself on Roland's cot and propping his chin on his fist, "I'm not talking about playing ambassador. I'm talking about *her*."

"I wouldn't call that luck," Roland said dryly.

"Have you looked at her? She's extraordinary. That skin, those eyes ..." Olivier sighed. His mood, Roland noticed, had improved remarkably since Sarissa had come to Saragossa.

"So go in my place," said Roland.

Olivier looked ready to leap at the chance, but after an instant his face fell. "You know I can't do that. The king wants you to brandish your sword. Mine is a good blade, but it's not the famous Durandal."

He spoke without rancor. Olivier did not bear grudges. Roland shook his head. "My dear friend, I would happily trade places with you. But I can't trade swords."

"No." Olivier sighed. "Honestly, you don't think she's beautiful? She's like honey and cream."

"I'd have said pepper and nettles myself," Roland muttered. "She seems to dislike me intensely."

"Don't believe it," said Olivier from his vast fund of experience—considerably vaster and more varied than Roland's. "Women act like that when they can't take their eyes off you—and they can't forgive themselves for it. She's captivated. I'd wager gold on it."

"One of those gold armlets you won in Pamplona?"

"Done!" said Olivier. "If you'll put up the ruby you snatched before I could get my hands on it."

"I did not—" Roland caught sight of Olivier's grin. He broke off. "I'll have the ruby set in the armlet after I've won it."

"What a marvelous idea!" Olivier declared. "And what a perfectly suitable wedding gift for the two of you."

"*That* will never happen," Roland said.

"Why not? Nobody quite talks about it, but she's noble born. Maybe royal. It's in everything she does. That's no common woman, nor ever was."

"She doesn't want me," said Roland.

Olivier snorted. "Get on with you. They'll be waiting."

So they were, though not quite ready yet to leave without him. The company he was to lead was drawn up, armed and mounted. Archbishop Turpin was just bidding farewell to the king. Roland received an embrace of his own, a kiss of farewell, and a murmur in his ear: "Take care of the lady. Bring her back safe."

Aha, thought Roland with an odd twisting in the stomach. It was that way with the king. And with her?

There was no telling. She was as aloof as ever, sitting astride her splendid stallion. Roland had to pass by them to reach his own Veillantif. As he did it, his eye caught the white stallion's. His step caught for the fraction of a breath. He knew those eyes. He knew that bright wickedness. The last time he had seen it, it had gleamed out of a cat's face.

One shapeshifter knew another. He saluted Tarik with a tilt of the head. Tarik snorted softly in response.

Veillantif was safely, peaceably unmagical, a simple mortal horse. Roland paused for a moment to rub his shoulder before springing into the saddle.

He was the last to mount. They rode out with a flourish of banners and trumpets, perhaps a little too glad to be free of the siege, but they made a handsome show.

Once they were away from the army, they settled to a more reasonable pace. Roland's men were a picked company, Franks of the king's own guard, who had served together since before Roland came to court. They never seemed to mind taking orders from the Breton Count; they had taught him most of what he knew of guardroom songs, willing maids, and the fine art of profanity.

Turpin's presence would not have deterred them in the slightest from running through every scurrilous ditty they knew, but before Sarissa they were remarkably circumspect. Roland could have sworn that even Benno Scarface was abashed, as smitten with that odd beauty as any other man in the king's army. For her sake they chose only the most decorous songs, and curbed their tongues, too.

Roland wondered if she even began to appreciate the effort. She was riding with Turpin, conversing quietly. He was telling her of the man they were riding to visit. "His grandfather was among the conquerors of Spain. They were princes before that, in the court at Baghdad, and they've always been loyal to the Caliph there. His name is Musa. They call him Nur al-Din, Light of the Faith."

"And his wife?" Sarissa asked.

"He has three," Turpin answered, "and, it's rumored, three dozen concubines. But the ruler of them all, though but the third wife in age and rank, is the lady Leila. She was given that name when Musa took her to wife. Her baptismal name is Julia. She comes from an old family in Saragossa, that goes back to the Romans. Saint James himself is said to have preached the Gospel to her ancestors, and converted them to the true faith."

"They seem to have made the best of this conquest," Sarissa observed.

"It's said she's won her husband's consent to teach her children the faith of Rome."

"Indeed," said Sarissa.

Roland could not tell what she meant by that. For that

matter, who or what was she? No one had ever made that quite clear. People assumed that she must be from Barcelona or Gerona, since she had first come to the king with the emir Al-Arabi. Or maybe she was from Saragossa, though she had made no effort to enter that city.

What rank she had, who her kin were—Roland could not recall that anyone had ever said. She had come riding into Paderborn on that day of late spring, dressed as a young man of the Saracens, and allowing people to think what they liked of who she was, where she had come from, and why she was there. Whatever they thought or said of her, she went on apparently untroubled.

She was not a Muslim. He was sure of that. She appeared to be a Christian. She was possessed of magic. Even without the rest of it, Tarik proved that. In Britain, Merlin had taught him long ago, they called such a creature a *puca*, a spirit of mischief that ran now in the likeness of a horse, now in that of a cat; and sometimes too a black dog or a wolf or a raven, or whatever other shape suited its fancy. And how had a Spanish woman—if she was of Spain at all—come by a *puca*? And not only come by it, but bound it to her as a servant?

He regretted that he had not found a way after all to return to Brittany before he rode to Spain, to ask Merlin's counsel. Once in a great while the enchanter came to him in dreams, but Roland could not seek him out, nor call on him through the walls of his prison. And that, just now, drove him nigh to distraction. Merlin would know what this woman was.

Roland had only such knowledge as Merlin had already taught him, and what scraps and fragments he had learned for himself. He was a very young enchanter, as he knew too well; but he'd not felt quite so young in a long while.

He watched her as she rode, aware in his skin of the road as it passed underfoot, and the sky overhead, and the country they rode through, barren to his forest-bred eye, burned brown by the heat of summer. No travelers met them. Armed Franks were a thing to walk well shy of here; even pilgrims making their way to this shrine or that had chosen another road rather than cross paths with Archbishop Turpin's embassy.

The birds of the air did not care what banner men rode under. The beasts of the field fled anything human, for it might be hunting them. The wind sang impartially, whether it plucked at Frankish mantle or Spanish cape or Saracen robes.

Sarissa, who was none of those things, had fallen silent, composed, complete in herself. Turpin was immersed in his prayers as he liked to do on the march, knee hooked over saddlebow, book in hand, brown beard nodding on his breast as he murmured the holy words. Roland slid easily into the quiet watchfulness of the guard. It was like wearing the world on his skin, aware of everything that passed on or over it. But his eyes kept wandering to Sarissa and fixing there. The straightness of her back, the lift of her chin, the delicate arch of her profile against the rise of brown hills . . .

He turned Veillantif abruptly and rode down to the end of the line, where the ranks of broad mailed backs and steel helmets hid her from sight. No one snickered. Maybe he had not been obvious about it, after all. He preferred to take the rear; it was most vulnerable to attack, and most vital to defend. It had been more remarkable that he kept to the front for so long, mooning like a raw boy after a woman who hardly cared that he existed.

Musa's holding was an old Roman villa set on a hill, ringed in vineyards. It had an olive grove and a water mill, and a village round a squat little church. The cross had been struck off the dome, and a minaret put up, converting it to the infidel.

The muezzin was calling the faithful to prayer as they rode up in the evening, the high rhythmic wail that was the daily music of this country. Franks professed to hate it. Roland would never confess that he found in it a sort of beauty. He had asked once what it meant—if there were words in it. Indeed, he was told: words of power and holiness.

God is great! God is great! There is no god but God, and Muhammad is the Prophet of God!

*Come to prayer! Come to prayer! Come to prosperity!
Come to prosperity!*

God is great! God is great!

Allahu akhbar! the muezzin sang. One or two of the men
signed the Cross, as if to assure themselves that they were
still Christian.

Men were praying in the villages and in the fields, white-
clad figures kneeling and standing and bowing toward the
east. They ignored the Franks riding past in a clatter of
hooves and a jingle of mail.

The gate to the villa was open, turbaned guards on either
side of it, their prayer just finished and their eyes glittering
in the dusk, by the still-wan light of torches. They bowed
Turpin and his escort through.

Servants in the courtyard took charge of the horses and
baggage. As the riders stood in the growing darkness, the
master of the house emerged from the colonnade. He was
robed in white, a cap on his shaven head, and a white smile
gleaming in his dark face. That blood had come up from
Africa, that skin as black as the night sky, those features cut
blunt and broad and strong. His voice was soft, a cultured
gentleman's voice, his bow and his words graceful, wel-
coming them, inviting them into his house.

Sarissa was taken away by soft-footed womenservants.
That was as they had expected, but Roland was oddly
moved to object.

He held his tongue. He would have preferred the guardroom for himself, but he was a person of rank; he was given
a small but airy room with a tiled floor, and a mute servant
who made himself clear with signs and glances.

There were baths in this house, in the Roman style: lamplit pools and a room filled with clouds of steam. The hot
pool bubbled up out of the ground, a spring that gave this
place its name, Agua Caliente.

Turpin shared the baths with him. Musa had left them a
message: they should take their leisure; then when they
were done, they would dine with him, partake of bread and
salt, and seal, if not alliance, then a truce while they remained in this holding.

Roland lay in the hot pool till the flesh seemed ready to
bake from his bones. Turpin, scarlet and sweating, had long
since retreated to the cold pool. "You're half salamander,"

he said as he fled. "I'm but poor clay. I'll crack if I stay longer."

The heat of the water made the heat of this country somehow more bearable. Roland emerged reluctantly, face to face with a sleek grey cat. It blinked, smiling at him. He smiled back. The *puca* followed him to the cold pool, sat on its rim and bathed itself in cat-fashion, with its tongue, while Roland plunged into water that seemed doubly icy after the heat before.

Turpin floated on his back, beard jutting toward the vaulted ceiling, broad bear's chest lapped with water. He seemed asleep. Roland considered the uses of wickedness. He was on the verge of resisting temptation when Turpin said, "Don't even think about it."

Roland grinned, poised, leaped.

Turpin won, just. He was heavier, and Roland was laughing too hard to breathe sensibly. He could barely gasp out his surrender, lying on the cool tiles by the pool, with Turpin sitting on him, dripping water in his face. They were both as slippery as eels.

Roland got his breath back, as much as he could with that massive weight on his middle. Turpin shifted, preparing to rise. Roland pitched him back into the pool, rose with as much insouciance as he could muster, and went in search of cloths to dry them both.

The emir Musa regarded their clean and freshly robed selves with evident pleasure. The bread and salt that he offered them had ample accompaniment: stewed lamb, roast fowl, a great bowl of golden rice with bits of fruit scattered in it, a sallet of greens and onions, and a sweet subtle wine to wash it all down.

Turpin bowed to the quality of the wine. "And yet," he said, "I thought men of your faith did not . . . ?"

"I do not indulge," Musa said, saluting with his cup of sherbet, "but my Christian servants do; and this holding has been a vineyard since Caesar's day. Mostly now, of course, the grapes are eaten from the vine, or dried into raisins such as you see yonder in the rice. But a few still go into the vats for old times' sake."

"I'm glad of that," Turpin said, "for it's as good as any wine I've drunk, and I've sampled the great Falernian."

"Ah! In Italy itself?"

Turpin nodded. "Not a healthy country for our people—its fevers are infamous—but its wine and olive oil are the best we know of."

"That's the memory of old Rome," Musa said. "We all live in her shadow—all of us in these latter days."

"There is a saying in Francia," said Turpin, "that while a dwarf may be little in himself, if he stands on the shoulders of giants, he can see farther than any of them."

Musa smiled. "Indeed? Now that is clever."

"And true," Turpin said. "If we could restore Rome, we would have all that they had, and, one hopes, more. More wisdom. Clearer sight. A longer view, if you will."

"Is that what you aim to do? Bring back Rome's empire?"

"Not I," said Turpin, "but my king dreams of it."

"A man may dream," said Musa.

"And you?" Turpin asked. "What does your Caliph dream of?"

"Insofar as I may presume to guess at the dreams of God's beloved," Musa said, "I would say that he dreams of peace."

"The peace of Allah?"

"Even so."

"Well," said Turpin, "God is God. And peace is peace, one might suppose. My king is your Caliph's ally, and some would say his friend. They do seem to be amazingly like-minded, when all is considered."

"So it's said," said Musa. "You will remain with us for a day or two, yes? I should like to see what manner of man the Defender of the Faith calls friend."

"For that," Turpin said, "you would wish to meet the king himself."

"In time," said Musa, "perhaps. One can tell much about a lord from his followers. Both those who choose him, and those whom he chooses to work his will."

Roland had been silent, listening. When Musa spoke of followers, Roland fancied for a moment that the dark glance had flickered toward him. If it had done so, it flicked away almost at once, returning to Turpin's far more solidly human face.

Muslims knew a great deal of magic, it was said. Perhaps they also knew enchanters.

Roland sensed no danger here, not of that sort. This man was not an enemy, if not precisely an ally. If he felt himself betrayed, he would kill without compunction, but he would not kill for lack of cause, either. As long as they dealt with him honorably, they were safe enough.

CHAPTER 16

✖ ✖ ✖

Sarissa knew that the men had met and begun conversations with the master of the house, but the ladies let her be until morning. She was taken to a room in the harem, waited on by maids with demure faces and downcast eyes, bathed and given a soft robe and fed a fine meal with wine, but with only herself for company.

They were watching her. She could feel eyes on her, prickling her spine. She was careful therefore to do nothing that they might find odd. She ate and drank lightly, and went direct to the cool sweet-scented bed.

Tarik joined her there, a small and ordinary-seeming grey cat. He curled in the curve of her knees and lulled her with his purr. He had found no evil thing in or about this house. Its spirit was clean, and the place itself empty of threat.

"We brought nothing with us?" she asked him in the softest of whispers.

Not a thing, his purr said. Not a single thing.

"But that one—the Breton—"

Tarik was asleep. Conspicuously so. Sarissa considered shaking him awake, but where was the use in that? She sought sleep herself. If there were dreams, she chose not to remember them.

* * *

The emir Musa's third wife was younger than Sarissa had expected. She was barely come to woman's years, but had already given her husband a son, a beautiful child with limpid black eyes and an enchanting smile. But for the darkness of his skin, he looked very like his mother.

In the morning she had Sarissa brought to her. She sat in an exquisite bit of garden, canopied by an arbor of roses, crimson and white. Her garments were chosen to match them: crimson gown, snow-white veil over her dark curling hair. A ruby hung between her wide black eyes, suspended from a golden fillet.

She looked as regal as a queen, and yet as Sarissa approached, she rose and bowed to the ground. Her maids did the same, graceful as a field of flowers.

Sarissa raised her, though she came up reluctantly. "Lady," she said. "O great lady. That you should honor us with your presence—"

"You know me?" Sarissa inquired.

"Oh, yes, lady," said Leila, whose father had named her Julia. "You come from—"

Sarissa laid a finger on the trembling lips. "Let us not speak that name here," she said.

Leila nearly went down again, but Sarissa prevented her. "Lady, I am sorry! I—"

"Lady!" Sarissa spoke sharply. "Stand up. Lift your head. Remember your rank. And mine—as anyone here may be permitted to know it."

Leila was not so overwhelmed that she had lost her wits altogether. She stiffened her spine and did as Sarissa bade her. "And here you are . . . ?" she asked with admirable steadiness.

"I'm a Spanish woman of unknown but evidently noble rank," Sarissa answered, "a healer and a sometime follower of the Frankish king."

"Kings should follow you, lady," Leila said.

"I may choose to serve a king," said Sarissa.

"That one?"

"He is a great man, a great king, and will be greater as his years ripen. Time will make him an emperor."

"Not here," Leila said. Her voice was gentle, but there was no yielding in it.

"Yet you accept the infidels."

"God has willed that we do so," said Leila. "Did you come to tell us that He also wills this?"

Sarissa shook her head. "God I have not spoken to. Charles would be glad of your help against the rebels from Cordoba."

"Only against the rebels?"

"That was why he came," said Sarissa.

"It is said that he came in order to conquer this country."

"Many things are said," Sarissa said. "The Caliph in Baghdad begged him to do this. He is doing it as best he can, against the Caliph's people as well as the rebels."

Leila coaxed Sarissa onto the bench she herself had vacated, and sat like a servant at her feet—nor would she be dissuaded. Sarissa sighed and endured it. Worship was not a thing she had ever grown accustomed to. For the most part she had avoided it, passing unknown through Spain and Francia. But this daughter of the Iulii of Saragossa, whose family had known Sarissa's kin and kind since the Romans ruled in Spain, was not to be deceived.

"Can you be sure," Leila asked her, "that this Frank is honorable? That he will allow us our own rule and our own ways, and not force his Frankish ways upon us?"

"This king is in command of his people," Sarissa said. "If he gives his word, he will keep it."

Leila nodded slowly. "My husband thinks that this king is honorable, and open-minded for a Frank. Is he not the Caliph's friend? But the rest of the Franks are another matter. They turned this war into a crusade; and that makes us uneasy. Holy war too quickly turns ugly."

"It was holy war that won Spain for Allah," Sarissa pointed out.

"Indeed, and one such war is enough. We're not willing to endure another."

"King Charles understands," said Sarissa.

"I can hope he does, lady." Leila paused, frowning, pondering some thought that did not entirely delight her. After a little while she said, "It's coming, isn't it? The other war. Is he the champion? Is that why you ride with him?"

She was touching on matters that perhaps she had no right to. Still, she was what she was, and this place had no evil in it. Sarissa said, "The champion rides with him. Or rather . . . the one who was chosen. Whom the power chose."

"Not you?"

"I serve the power," Sarissa said. "It does as it wills."

"Ah," said Leila with a child's wisdom. "Is it someone very unexpected?"

"Very," said Sarissa. And perhaps not wisely at all: "Have you seen the king's envoys?"

"Oh, yes," Leila said. "The archbishop is very large. The captain of his guard is very—"

"Odd?"

"Beautiful," Leila said.

"That is no guardsman," said Sarissa. "That is a lord of the king's court."

"And *he* is . . . ?"

Sarissa nodded.

"Oh," said Leila. "Oh, my."

"All the women say that," Sarissa said with more ill temper than strict good sense.

Leila's eyes danced. "I can imagine! He's wonderful. Has he conversation?"

"Do you intend to discover that for yourself? What would your husband say?"

"My husband would say that I can look, but I can't touch. He trusts me, lady."

Sarissa was unwontedly abashed. "I never meant—"

"I'm sure you didn't," Leila said. "Well? Can he talk? Or is he no more than a pretty face?"

"He's very shy with women, they say. And quiet with men. But he can sing."

"Oh!" said Leila, clapping her hands. "That's even better. I'll have him sing to me."

"He'll capture your heart and carry it away to Francia."

"He can't do that. My husband already has it, safe in his hand. But I do love a sweet singer. Would he learn our songs, do you think? Could he?"

"He has a very good ear," said Sarissa, "and many languages."

"Good, then," said the emir's wife. "I shall do it. Only tell me one more thing."

Sarissa raised her brows and waited.

"Does the Frankish king know? What you are, what you came for?"

"No," said Sarissa. "Not yet."

"And he, the champion. Does he?"

"Not before his king," Sarissa said.

"You should tell him," said Leila, "before too much time passes."

"He will be told when it is proper for him to know."

Leila looked as if she might have said more, perhaps protested, but her awe of Sarissa was too strong. Instead she said, "Lady, will you bathe with me? Then break our fast. And hear the singer from Francia."

Sarissa could decline; Leila would not dare be offended. But she nodded, and bowed slightly. She would put herself at this lady's disposal. After all she was the Frankish king's emissary, and she had a task to perform.

The Breton Count seemed not too terribly abashed to be summoned to an audience with the emir's third wife. She received him from behind an intricately carved screen, which let her see him, but of her he could see only a shadow. Sarissa, between them, had a clear view of both.

Leila was delighted with him—both his beauty and his strangeness. It seemed he had ample conversation with wedded ladies; he was as gentle with this one as he had been with Charles' queen. She did not speak to him of anything of consequence, or ask to see his sword. Nor, and that surprised Sarissa, did she command him to sing. She simply wanted to look at him, and hear his voice. It was a pleasant voice, Sarissa admitted, both deep and sweet.

When after a while Leila let him go, Sarissa prepared to go with him. Leila called her back. Her maid was taking down the screen, and she had put aside her veil. Her eyes were sparkling. "He is marvelous," she said. "Delightful. And the magic in him! He shimmers with it."

"You can see—?"

Leila nodded. "I have none of my own, which used to be a great grief to me, but I've learned to accept it. But there is one thing I can do. I can see magic."

"He is brimming with it," Sarissa said, a little flatly.

Leila seemed not to hear the tone, only the words. "Yes! He's a fire in the dark."

"And dark in the heart of him."

"No, lady," Leila said. "No darkness. Not anywhere."

Sarissa did not know why that made her angry. "Do you know what he is? Can you begin to guess? He's the enemy's child. The hawk of the gods. Merlin's get."

Leila neither blanched nor recoiled. "I always did wonder," she said, "about that one. Remember who his pupils were, and what he taught them."

"Only to turn on them and betray them."

"Of course you would know that, lady," said Leila, "since you are what you are. But there's no evil in this child of his. It seems to me the sword chose wisely."

"It was supposed to do that," Sarissa said.

She left then, rather rudely maybe, but Leila did not seem to mind. Sarissa needed to think. And that was difficult, when it was Roland she must think of.

The men were preparing to hunt. They carried swords and spears and bows for whatever quarry they might meet, man or beast, but they would hunt first and foremost with falcons. Musa was a great lover of the art, and Turpin had a little skill in it. Roland went, of course, as captain of the archbishop's guard. Sarissa suspected that he knew falconry well—as both man and hawk.

Today he rode as a man, as did Sarissa. A young soldier of the emir's guard slept a sleep full of dreams while she rode his horse, carried his weapons, wore his clothes. The falcon on her fist had Tarik's eyes. His wickedness delighted in such ruses as this.

She was fonder of them herself than perhaps she should have been. She slipped through the ranks as they rode out through the vineyards, until she was close behind Roland. He was watching the emir and the archbishop, quietly, alertly, as a good captain of guards should. He had been offered a falcon, but he had refused. He was here to guard the archbishop, his manner said, and not to entertain himself.

He was aware of her presence. Her skin felt the prickle of it. He would know where every man in this riding was, what he did there, what threat he posed to the man Roland guarded.

She did her best to radiate harmlessness. She was a very

young man of the Saracens, wide-eyed with curiosity, captivated by the Frankish strangers.

It seemed he believed it. He did not turn to unmask her. He rode hunting as they all did, in innocence of her presence among them.

It was a good hunt. The prey was plentiful: doves above the vineyard, rabbits running beneath the woven and terraced vines. Turpin and Musa waged a contest. Turpin won with two dozen doves, but Musa came within a dove of matching him. There would be a feast tonight.

"I know," said Musa as they came to the vineyard's edge, "where a bull has run wild, menacing the villages. Are you bold enough for that, my lord?"

"I've hunted the last of the aurochs in the forests of Germania," Turpin said. "Are your bulls as great as that?"

"They are smaller," Musa admitted, "but they are deadly. As to how we hunt them—this you may be intrigued to see. Will you ride with us?"

"Gladly," Turpin said.

The bull was alone, a rogue. He raided farmsteads and trampled the cattle-pens, stole cows and gutted the dogs sent after him—and, Musa said as they rode, he had acquired a taste for manflesh.

"The young men of a village went hunting him with nothing but rakes and pruning-hooks, and met his horns. It's said he gored six of them, gutting them as neatly as he had gutted the dogs. But when he came to the seventh, he tore out the boy's throat."

"He sounds like a very devil," Turpin said.

"Indeed he is possessed of Shaitan," said Musa.

Turpin laughed. "Then I'm your man, sir! For exorcisms are my stock in trade."

They were very well agreed, just then. Side by side, with their men riding before and behind, they went in search of the bull.

They found his track not far from a huddled scrap of village: a few houses, a flock of goats, and not a cow to be seen. Where perhaps one or two had been, was a broken wall and a confusion of trampled earth.

They followed his spoor from there, along a path that seemed made by goats, up the slope of a ridge and into a maze of tumbled hills. Small wonder that the bull had yet to be caught, if he could take refuge here.

Musa had with him a man who professed to know this country well. This man led. The rest followed as they could, often singly in steep defiles and down sudden drops. It was admirable country for an ambush, if anyone had been minded to lay one. Sarissa spread her senses wide, but nothing human stalked them. They were alone in the waste, except for the birds of the air and the small creatures that crept and crawled on the earth. And, ahead of them, the black bull.

Her horse had elected to follow close behind Roland's grey stallion, sometimes nose to tail. Roland might have been riding down a clear road in Francia. His back was erect, his seat light in the saddle.

On a brief level, Tarik left his perch on Sarissa's saddle-bow and settled on Roland's. She thought she caught a flash of a smile. Those two, she thought rather sourly, seemed to have formed a fast friendship.

They found the bull, or the bull found them, in a circle of sand and stones rimmed by low hills. The bull was trotting purposefully toward the edge of the valley, where the hills opened on a glimmer of greenery. Sarissa's senses, still at full stretch, caught the scent of grass and water.

There was his lair, she thought. There was his safe place. At Musa's swift command, a company of his men set off at the gallop, sweeping around the bull, aiming to cut off his escape.

He was as startlingly fast as his kind could be, but he could not outrun the swift Berber horses. He stopped in a spray of sand and wheeled snorting, shaking his heavy head and his long wicked horns. His back was a mass of scars; one ear was a tatter. No peaceful cattle, this. He was a fighting bull, with a taste for human blood.

Roland's Franks were ready to run baying to the kill, but he held them back. "Wait," he said. "Watch."

They growled but obeyed. Those who had bows had strung them. The rest had loosened swords in sheaths and unslung lances, balancing them for use.

Roland sat quiet though his stallion was fretting, roused by the sight and smell of the bull. Spanish horses had been fighting his kind since long before Rome. Veillantif might never have done so, but his bones knew this for an old, old enemy.

Musa and a handful of his men closed in on the bull. They were mounted, all of them, on Veillantif's kin, sturdy ram-nosed stallions with tails that brushed the ground. For all their thickness of body, their massive necks and deep barrels, they were as quick on their feet as cats.

The bull lowered its head and pawed. The horses circled, dancing. One of the riders darted in suddenly, lance uplifted, striking down into the bull's hump.

The bull wheeled away. The lance fell useless. The rider poised, off guard. His horse half-reared. The bull snorted explosively. The horse shied and veered and bolted.

The rider rolled as he fell, eluding the trampling hooves and the bull's charge. He should have escaped, but the bull went after him. Heedless of lances that stabbed but failed, bodies of horses reeling out of his way, men shouting in confusion, he went for the downed man, swift as a storm in summer, relentless as a wave of the sea.

Sarissa sent her mount leaping forward. There was another beside her: grey horse, white-faced man, fierce high song of a sword. He with sword, she with lance, fell on the bull from either side. She felt her lance bite flesh, grate on bone. The bull's recoil twisted it painfully from her hand. Her horse scrambled away from the deadly horns.

There was a man on the bull's back, riding the surge and heave of it. One hand gripped a horn, twisting the head back. The other swept the bright blade of a sword across the thick throat.

Blood sprang, flooding the dun earth. The bull's bellow died in a bubbling sigh. It stumbled and fell to its knees. Roland leaped free. The bull swung its horns in one last fading arc, tongue lolling, eyes glazing over. It was dead before it struck the ground.

Sarissa hardly noticed. She had fallen to her knees beside Roland. He was covered in blood.

It was all bull's blood. None was his own. He looked into her face with clear recognition and an utter lack of surprise. He sat up, rising, moving past her, bending over another huddled figure in the sand.

Musa's man was alive. His leg was broken, caught by the

bull's hoof as it wheeled to meet its new attackers. Otherwise he was bruised and winded but well enough.

"The lady who rode with us is a healer," Turpin said to Musa. "I can send a man to fetch her."

Sarissa opened her mouth to reveal herself, but Roland said, "I have a few arts. I'll do what I can. Then we can carry him back to the lady's more capable hands."

He had more than a few arts, damn him. He set the leg and splinted it with swords wrapped in cloaks, had the men fashion a litter of spears and cloaks, and saw that the wounded man was borne safely back to Musa's holding. The bull came behind: his head, his tail, his hide and the meat of his bones. The rest they left for the vultures.

They would feast on the bull's flesh tonight, and once more Roland would sit in the place of honor. It seemed that Sarissa, or rather the man whose semblance she wore, would be expected to sit beside him; and yet they would be looking for her to tend the wounded man.

"Feed him a sleeping potion and leave him in the care of his friends," Roland said as they rode. She had said not one word to him of what she was thinking, but he knew. Just as he knew what face she wore in truth.

"You should have let me speak," she said.

Roland lifted a brow. "And let them all know what you can do if you choose?"

"I can protect myself," she said stiffly.

"Here, you can," he said. "But my people have no love for such arts. Devil's sleights, they call them. You could be harmed if they knew."

"They know what you are," she said.

That gave him pause, but not for long. "I belong to them. You—"

"I am a foreigner," she said, but she shook her head. "They can turn on you, too. Maybe worse, because they've loved you."

"Not today," he said. "Not soon, if God is kind. You would not have that grace."

Little as she liked it, that was true enough. She set her lips together and rode beside him in silence. He seemed content with that. Smug, insufferable man. There was a spatter of bull's blood on his cheek, drying dark against the white skin. She caught herself just short of reaching to wipe it away.

It struck her as she rode through those brown hills. It was not the king she wanted. It was this one—this man whom she neither liked nor trusted. But her body sang when it was near him, and her heart paid no heed at all to doubts or suspicions. It envied Tarik, who in hawk-shape could perch on his armored shoulder and bask in the warmth of his presence.

Even the champion's sword, even Durandal, had fallen before him. Was it so astonishing that her heart had, too?

CHAPTER 17

✠ ✠ ✠

Pepin had been biding his time. He studied; he learned whatever he was taught. He waited upon his moment.

Now his enemies were gone on the king's embassy, and Pepin's time had come. He had discovered by degrees, by asking among the tale-tellers in the camp, what the Grail was. It was a weapon, a thing of power, so strong that he who held it could rule the world. Ganelon had nearly had it once, but been cheated of it. This time he meant to have the victory.

But first he had to find it. Sarissa was the key to that. Ganelon had bidden Pepin gaze into the basin a dozen times since she came to Saragossa. Pepin had never seen anything useful. The tower and the dying king were the same as they had always been. Other things that Ganelon bade him look for were not forthcoming.

Still, Ganelon persisted. This morning Pepin had seen the lady in a house he had not seen before, eating grapes and soft white cheese. It was pleasant to watch her; she was very beautiful, and she wore a light robe that revealed the shape of her body. But Ganelon did not want to hear of that. "Is anyone with her?" he demanded.

"No one," Pepin had to answer.

Ganelon sent him away after that. "Go. Be a boy for once. Do whatever boys do. Leave me in peace."

Pepin escaped in a kind of guilty delight. No letters to

copy today. No endless pages of spells, either, in languages that made his head ache, but Ganelon had made it clear: if he wished to learn magic, he had to learn the words that made the magic.

He was free, and for once could do as he pleased. The light of day felt odd on his face, so seldom had he been out in it. His eyes blinked and watered.

The siege was accomplishing as little as ever. Even with all the king's ruses to keep the men busy, there were still clots of idlers, soldiers with no fighting to do. They hung about, played endless games of knucklebones, and passed round such drink and women as they managed to find.

One such gathering hovered just on the edge of a quarrel. Most were Franks, but there were a few Bretons, slender black-haired men like their Count, save that their eyes were human as his were not. The Bretons had a fighting cock, which as Pepin paused, had just finished ripping apart the Franks' feathered champion.

"And I say," snarled the foremost of the Franks, "that it was not a fair fight. That's a basilisk's chick. It looked our bird in the eye, and he froze. We all saw it. It laid its spell on him and killed him."

The leader of the Bretons, a tough and wiry man of no age in particular, laughed in the Frank's face. "Your bird was a coward. He saw our bold warrior and went stark with fear."

"He was bewitched. We saw it!"

"You oxen see witches everywhere," the Breton said. "Especially when you're getting your arses whipped."

The Frank growled like a dog. Pepin stepped in front of him before he could leap. "There now," he said. "There. What's this?"

One small advantage he had found in his deformity: everyone knew him on sight. The Frank backed away quickly. The Bretons, insolent dogs that they all were, stood about grinning. One had the fighting cock under his arm. It was a black cock, and its eyes were a striking, fiery gold.

Those eyes inspired Pepin to do what he did. "Tell me now. Is it true? Is there witchcraft here?"

"Not likely," the Breton captain said. And after a small but significant pause: "Lord prince."

"That's a lie!" the Frank declared. "They're all witches

where he comes from, everybody knows that. And that's a witch he's got under his arm, or a witch's familiar. It killed our bird before he even struck a blow."

"It is an unusual bird," Pepin observed, peering at the cock. "Does it come from Brittany?"

"We found it in Pamplona, lord," the Breton said. "We won it in a game."

"You conjured it," said the Frank. "You made it to win fights for you."

"It looks very fierce," Pepin said. "And . . . it's odd. But—"

They all waited. He let them. It was a pleasure of rank, that men hung on his words.

At length he said it. "Isn't it strange, how . . . Breton it looks? After all? Or rather, how much it looks like your Count?"

The Breton nodded and grinned as if he had no care in the world. "Yes, doesn't it? We thought so when we won it. Mahon over there, he calls it Count Roland. It's as great a fighter as the man it's named for. But," he added, "there's no witchcraft in it. No more than there is in—"

"As to that," Pepin said, "there are those who whisper— but no, that's just rumors. He's a great champion, your Count. Odd to look at, a bit, but when did that ever stop a man from being a good fighter? He's never the Devil's get, of course. That's womanish nonsense. Have you ever heard his sword sing?"

The men looked at one another. Pepin laughed inside. Oh, he had done it. They had forgotten their quarrel, and found something else to think of.

They would keep on thinking, he thought. And wondering. And suspecting even the innocent, as they suspected the black cock. It was a simple earthly bird, for all the oddity of its looks—like Roland, as far as Pepin could tell. But he had those eyes, and others had spread whispers before Pepin, telling tales that could serve him very well indeed.

He walked through the army as a prince might, favoring the common folk with his presence. It was remarkable how often he could stop, work his way into a game or a gathering, and bring the conversation round to the one he hated. People loved to talk of that damnable man. Everyone had a story: a battle he had won when no one else could, a hunt he had excelled in, a heart he had touched, so that the man grew all misty and foolish in remembering it. They were all in awe of the sword, how it sang, how it shone when he drew it.

"God has blessed him," Pepin would say, and they would all sigh and agree. Then he would add, "Unless you believe people who say it's not only God's doing."

He had to be careful. People loved Roland, or claimed to. They could grow angry if they heard ill of him.

But they loved to tell stories, and some of the stories were more than useful for Pepin's purposes. There was one—a man of the king's guard told it, and he was well enough gone in wine that the king would be most unhappy if he knew. "I saw once," he said, slurring the words, but they were clear enough. "I saw him out riding by himself. You know how he likes to do that; he's a wild thing, and solitary, if he's allowed to be. He went away out of sight, but I was following, because I was tracking a deer. It was a doe, and when I found her she had a stag, a dark stag, almost black, and his eyes were almost gold. And the Count was nowhere I could see."

"Did you shoot the deer?" someone asked.

"I loosed an arrow," the man said, "but they were gone before it struck. Vanished like a wind in the trees."

"Deer do that," the other man said. "You're not telling us the stag was—"

"Well," the king's guardsman said, "I'm not saying it and I'm not *not* saying it. But I found his horse in a clearing, and no rider, and his clothes packed away in its saddlebag. That horn of his, that he always carries, was slung over his saddlebow. And the only tracks there, except for the horse's, were the tracks of a stag."

Pepin could have hugged himself with glee. People did not believe the man, of course. They called him a liar and a drunkard. But the words were said. No one could unsay them. The seeds were planted. He had but to watch them grow.

And what, he wondered, if after all they were true? What if Roland was more than Pepin had taken him for? Ganelon did not consider him worth noticing, except that he had the sword. He was mortal, the old man declared. He had no magic in him.

Magic could conceal itself from Ganelon. Pepin would

not have been gazing into basins else, and telling the old man what he saw.

Pepin knew the words now, and the way of it. He could not get hold of the basin—he had already tried that. If Ganelon himself was not in the tent, guarding its contents both visible and hidden, one of his servants was there, silent and formidable.

Pepin had a thought, a wicked thought, but one that so excited him, he could not but follow where it led. There was a silver chalice. He had seen it raised in the Mass: striking, and memorable, because so many chalices were of gold and heavily ornamented, but this was a simple bowl of pure silver, kept polished till it gleamed.

Pepin did not think Archbishop Turpin would miss the thing, since he was away on the king's embassy. Water from the river was a simple matter. Solitude was harder, but there was the archbishop's tent, conveniently and comfortably deserted. Turpin kept no more state than was required of him as the king's servant. His bed was a simple cot, his belongings few and poor enough, except for the silver chalice.

It was exhilarating to work sorcery in surroundings so priestly. Pepin set the chalice on the lid of the chest in which he had found it. He had had to bring in lamps, since Turpin only had one, and there was no oil in it. That had taken a little time and a deal of stealth, but Pepin managed.

Now the lamps were arranged and lit. He poured the water into the cup, murmuring the words exactly as Ganelon did. Words and accent, timbre and cadence, were vital to the spell. Pepin had a good ear. It served him well in this.

He nearly laughed aloud when the water stirred and shimmered, just as it did when Ganelon spoke the spell. Pepin firmed his will as he had been taught, and fixed his mind on the one he wished to see.

Water shimmered in the water, an expanse of lake or river, rippling like silver. A sword rose up out of it. He knew the blade, like ice made steel, and the hilt with its white stone. A falcon descended, small and swift: a merlin. It perched on the hilt and spread its wings. Pepin could only see, not hear, but he fancied that it loosed a high fierce cry.

The image shifted and changed. Pepin held his breath. There at last he saw Roland. The Breton Count was standing in a wood, alert, intent on something that came toward him through the trees. His eyes were the hawk's eyes, golden and wild.

Again the image altered. The wood was the same, but Roland lay in the leafmold. A woman's body writhed over his. There was no doubt at all as to what they were doing.

At first Pepin thought it was *she*, but this was a black-haired woman, with skin like olives rather than dusky cream. She was as supple as a snake. Roland seemed passive, until suddenly he blurred and—changed. The merlin shot up from beneath her. It seemed intent only on escape, but at the height of its ascent it paused. It clapped wings to its sides. It plummeted.

The woman shrank into a snake, a black-and-silver serpent. They fought, they two. The hawk slew the serpent. And when the creature was dead, its throes ended, Roland stood again in man's form, gazing down at—

Borel. Ganelon's servant Borel. Pepin could not mistake him. He was not human; but Pepin had realized that some while since of the two who were yet alive. One could see a shimmer of scales on those gaunt cheeks, if the light was just so; and he had never seen even the hint of a beard on either of them.

Roland had killed Borel. Not the lady of the Grail. And if the vision was true, he had done it as only an enchanter could. An enchanter strong enough to destroy Borel and deceive Ganelon—who knew what else he might prove to be?

Pepin danced in Turpin's tent, a dance of pure savage glee. He had Roland now. He *had* him.

He would have to tell Ganelon. But when he did it, and how, he would have to think on. This was such knowledge as men would kill for.

Maybe he would tell the king. Or maybe . . .

So many choices. So many delightful decisions. Pepin had never felt so powerful before. A prince held men's lives in his hands, ruled them, and if their fate so decreed, ended them. But never such a life as this. Never a man he had chosen to hate with a perfect hate.

CHAPTER 18

❈ ❈ ❈

Sarissa tossed in her bed. When on occasion she dozed, her dreams woke her gasping, her body throbbing.

She had not felt so in long years. Not since—

Memory helped her not at all. Nor did Tarik. He had retreated to a far corner of the bed to escape her thrashing. Now that she was fully awake, he stalked off with clear intent. He was going to find another body to warm him in the night. A fine body, a handsome body. And above all, a quiet one.

Sarissa sprang to her feet. She wrapped a robe about herself, the first that came to hand, and went hunting in Tarik's wake.

Roland appeared to be asleep. The lamp burned low. His room had a window, which was fastened open. The night wind blew through it, rippling the gauzy draperies about his bed. He was lying on his face, head buried in his arms, black hair tangled on his neck and shoulders. They were wide, those shoulders, and his hips narrow, his legs long and strong, with an elegant turn of ankle. There was not a slack or a superfluous line in him, from head to heel.

Sarissa glided closer, till she was standing over him. His skin was smooth and white as moon on marble. There were scars, old ones and new, though not as many, she would have wagered, as there were on his front.

She made no effort to resist temptation. She lifted the draperies softly and let them fall behind her. Lightly, gently, she traced the furrow of his spine with her finger.

He shivered in pleasure. She felt him wake, like a brush of wind across her skin, a sharpening of awareness in her center.

He rolled onto his back. No garment covered him, no ornament but the coin of the Grail on its chain, gleaming on his breast.

He must think he was dreaming still: there was none of the shyness she had expected. There were indeed more scars on his front than on his back. But she was not counting them.

He opened his eyes and smiled drowsily, as if he had been expecting her—as if he welcomed her. He must not know he was awake. If she forgot all her doubts and her fears, if she saw only what the heart saw, she could smile the truest smile that was in her. He blinked as if dazzled, and laughed in astonishment and—delight?

Her robe was hardly more substantial than the gauze of the curtains, and she was forgetting to wrap it about her. Her hair streamed loose over her shoulders and her breast: half-bared white shoulders, white breasts, smooth white belly and gold-brown curls concealing her sex. That was aching, a sweet and almost unbearable pain.

By the old gods, she wanted this man. He was so full of magic that he brimmed and ran over; and he was as splendid a young thing as she had seen in long years.

He reached to take her hands and draw her down. His eyes were as soft as falcon-eyes could be. She half-knelt, half-sat beside him, her slender fingers wound in his long strong ones. A small part of her observed that she was trapped; that he was stronger than she in body, a trained fighting man, honed to a keen edge. He could seize her, fling her down, have his will of her.

If he had intended to do that, he would have done it already. She bent and brushed his lips with hers. A spark leaped between them, a small but potent shock.

He did not recoil, though his eyes went wide. His hands tightened painfully, then let her go. She caught them before they escaped. "I'm not asleep!" he said, startled.

"Now you notice," she said.

"Lady," he said, blushing furiously. "Lady, I never meant—"

"I came to you," she said. "So: you dream of me."

He did not know where to look. She took his burning face in her hands and held it, meeting his eyes. Words came to her tongue, but she did not speak them. She kissed him again, deeper this time, slow and sweet. At first he resisted, struggling; but she held him fast.

He surrendered all at once, as a wise man should to the inevitable. She drew back softly. He reached for her in protest. She smiled. She traced with her hands the lines of his body, shoulders and breast, belly and flanks, and at last, with wicked delight, the exuberant thing between his legs. He gasped as her fingers closed about it. She soothed him, stroking him, till he calmed in spite of himself.

Lovely, lovely man. If she let her heart think for her, see for her, all doubts vanished. She saw only the light in him, and the Grail's protection about him, embodied in its token. No ill thing could touch him, within or without.

His hands ran lightly, almost timidly down her back. She purred at the touch. It grew stronger, surer of itself. She half expected him to leap on her then and take her as young men were wont to take women, but instead he began to play her like a harp. He found each note and sounded it, one by one. He made of them a melody, and then a song.

It was as if he could not help himself. She laughed inside herself, half incredulous, half delighted. She could play this music as well as he, match his rhythm, his notes; from melody make harmony. It almost did not matter when, or whether, he entered her. They were bound, body to body, heartbeat to heartbeat, breath to breath. She came to crescendo an instant before him; then he was with her, his song in her ear, a clear, sustained note.

It died away slowly. She lay on her back, remembering how to breathe. He lay on his face. She thought him asleep, until he turned on his side, head on folded arm, and regarded her with a steady golden stare.

She stared back. For the first time she allowed herself to look at him—look her fill, and not turn away. Nor did he retreat or blush or try to hide his face. He was studying her as carefully as she studied him. She wondered what he saw.

Not simply the lines of her features, color of hair, eyes, skin, shape of nose, but the rest, the spirit beneath.

She saw light. Sunlight, starlight, moon on water. She saw a hawk in the blue heaven and a stag in the wood. She saw a young warrior in the Frankish king's army.

He wore that mask with ease and grace. But his face would never be a plain Frankish face, or plain Breton, either. The old god's blood had marked him too strongly.

Here, set apart from horror, fear, suspicion, she allowed herself to see the beauty. It was god, not demon, who had sired his forebear; that she knew in her heart as she looked at him, though every tale told otherwise. An air-god, a sky-god, a god of wind and sunlight. Roland, she would wager, had that god's very face. But there was human warmth behind it. Gods were cold strange creatures. This was a man, however great the power that was in him.

She kissed him for the simple pleasure of it. He blinked, surprised, but responded willingly enough. She smiled. "I do think," she said, "I've fallen in love with you."

"I thought you hated me."

"Did you now?" She laid her palm against his cheek. It pricked a little: what beard he had, he kept shaven, but for the upper lip. That, in Frankish fashion, he let be. It suited him. Her thumb smoothed the soft black hair across his lip and down round the corner of his mouth. His eyes closed.

"I did—almost—hate you," she said. "But my heart kept getting in the way."

"It will do that," he said with a touch of wryness.

"And you? Do I appall you?"

"Not in the slightest," he said.

"Not even a little?"

"Do you want me to be?"

"No," she said. And like a fool, like a woman who knew no better: "Do you love me?"

"Yes," he said. Just that. Just the word.

"I could be your worst enemy," she said. "I could be sent to destroy you."

"Yes."

"And still you think you love me?"

"I know it," he said.

"Do you say this to every woman you lie with?"

He did not seem offended, though his eyes narrowed a fraction. "No," he said.

Another man would heap words on words. This one was not so much shy, Sarissa thought, as unable to see the use in idle chatter.

"You hardly know me," she said to him.

"The heart knows," he said.

Exasperating man. Stubborn, headstrong— "Arrogant," she said.

"It's arrogance to speak the truth?"

"Is that what you were taught? I'd have thought you'd be more subtle."

"More treacherous?"

Her cheeks flushed. "More like a courtier."

Roland smiled thinly. "I never had that gift, lady."

"Or the desire to cultivate it?"

He shrugged. His hair slid over his shoulder. Her hand followed it, altogether of its own accord. The muscles were tight under the smooth skin. She stroked the tension from them. He sighed and lay on his face, much as he had been when she first came there. Slowly, thoroughly, she worked the tautness out of him. Her own body eased as she did it, sitting astride him, digging into the knotted muscles, kneading them till they loosened and flowed.

He turned on his back. He was ready for her again, taking her so swiftly that she gasped. She arched and let her head fall back, giving herself up to it. Never, she thought with what little wits were left to her. Never, with any man, had she been so utterly, so perfectly, so completely overcome. She had always ruled in this dance. Always. Men did not rule her. No man—ever—

"It's not a battle," he whispered in her ear. "No victor, no vanquished. Only—always—delight."

And love, she thought but had no breath to say. *For us, at the least, love.*

CHAPTER 19

✠ ✠ ✠

She fell asleep in Roland's arms, folded close against him. Her hair trailed across his breast. He smoothed the brown-gold curls, stroking them away from her face. She slept as deep and limp as a child—startling in a woman so very self-possessed and so very determined that the world should go as she would have it.

He had coveted her beauty and lusted after her body. He had never expected her to come to him so, still less to give herself to him. Nor had he ever looked to fall in love with her. The surprise with which she confessed to it herself—he had felt the same. Surprise and dismay, and a white, mad joy.

"Beware the love of a woman," Merlin had told him. "It can snare you, destroy you. But ah," the old man had sighed, and his eyes had gone mellow gold with memory, "what sweet entrapment! For all that it cost me, I would never wish it undone."

Roland had heard without understanding. He had only known that love was perilous; that it could turn to poison. "I'll never succumb," he had declared. "I'm forewarned. No woman will bind me."

He had been angry then, because Merlin laughed at him. "Never say never," the old man said.

Now Roland understood. It had come on so fast, was so complete. No warning could have prepared him. No songs, no learned treatises made it clear how very swift it was. A touch, a glance—he was lost.

It was the magic in her. Power called to power. Coupling with mortal women—the body found it pleasant; sometimes mind would meet mind and find kinship. But she was enchantress to his enchanter. When their bodies met, their souls met likewise, and the fire of magic in them mingled.

This, Merlin had found in Nimue. Even if this lady turned traitor, too, Roland did not care. It would come when it would come. For this while at least, he would have joy, and a spirit that for once in the world was like his.

She was gone when he woke. His arms were empty, his bed cold. He rose slowly, creaking a bit, gusting laughter at the myriad small pains and half-pleasurable aches. His rod stiffened as he washed in the basin by the bed. The touch of the cloth made him gasp. His spirit sought refuge in hawk-shape, in the fierce small mind and deep-folded sex.

He shook free of that temptation, forcing himself back to man-shape. His rod spent itself so suddenly, so strongly, that he sank to his knees.

At least there was no servant to witness his ignominy. He cleaned himself, made such order as he could of scattered wits and pride, and dressed not in the flowing robes of a Saracen but in Frankish shirt and drawers, tunic, hose, and boots. Each garment was armor of a sort, protection against his body's rebellion.

If Olivier had been there, he would have known at once what Roland had been doing in the night. Turpin was not one to notice such things, or to betray that he noticed; and the men kept their own counsel. Roland could play the guard in peace.

The emir Musa was gracefully determined not to come to the point of the embassy. This day he entertained his guests with a more formal version of the dancing of the bull. A great press of people gathered in the theater that the Romans had built, to watch a succession of battles between bulls and men. It was high art, Roland gathered, and a matter of great seriousness, with much laying of wagers.

Musa's captain of guards grinned at him and offered by signs to lay a handful of silver on one of the mounted fighters. Roland smiled and shook his head. The man persisted. The bull was enormous and strong; his heart was as black as his hide. Roland should wager; he would win much silver.

"But," said Roland in Arabic, "my bones tell me the man is quick and he is skilled, and the bull is too big to be agile. I'll keep my silver, sir, if you don't mind."

The man gaped as if the bull himself had opened his mouth and addressed him in the language of the Prophet. Roland smiled sweetly. It was not his way to startle people so, not if he could help it; but today his mood was odd and wild. Sarissa had not come out for the bullfighting. He had not seen her at all since he fell asleep with her in his arms.

Well, he thought. Men loved and left women often enough. Why should not a woman leave a man, for once?

If he had been younger he would have wanted to weep, and then to hit something. He was a man now. Having astonished an emir's guardsman with the gift of tongues, he accepted a different wager, on how quickly the fighter would defeat the bull.

While he did that, the emir was explaining the rite of battle to Turpin. "The *corrida* is a ritual, a ceremony of honor. The bull is the worthy enemy, the honored foe. The man fights him by strict laws of combat. The bull can win—and often does. The man who enters this place knows that it could be his life spilled on the sand, and not that of the bull."

"I've heard tell," Turpin said, "that this is a very old spectacle. It goes back to Rome, yes?"

"Before Rome," said Musa. "Long before it. It was a rite of pagan gods once, before it became a test of manly courage and fighting skill."

"Horsemanship, too," said Turpin. "I know nothing of fighting bulls, but riding I know, a little; I'm a Frank, after all. And that, I say, is a truly fine horseman."

"Oh, yes," said Musa. "Diego is one of the great riders of this part of Spain. It's a privilege that he agreed to fight here, and on his marvelous Diamante, too. Diamante is fully as famous as his master."

"And no wonder," Turpin said as the black horse leaped and curvetted on the sand. The reins were on his neck. His rider was fully occupied with the wielding of spear and sword.

The man slew the bull, who had indeed proved too slow for the man and his marvel of a horse. He was given the ears and the tail—great honors, those; but after he had bowed to the emir, he paused. His eye sought and found another face. He called out, "My lord! Is it true what I heard? Is there one here who slew the bull in the old way, the holy way? Who rode the bull, and poured his blood on the sand?"

Roland did his best to be inconspicuous, but it seemed that everyone knew him and what he had done. Men stared, fingers pointed. Hands drew him out from behind Turpin.

Diego the slayer of bulls looked him up and down, a long, raking stare. Roland hoped that he was not too unprepossessing an object.

"I bow to you, sir Frank," Diego said. "Had you slain a bull before?"

"Not of that kind, sir Spaniard," said Roland. "I slew an aurochs once."

"Did you indeed?" said Diego. "I see that you are a great champion of the Franks. Please, of your courtesy, accept the honor of the bull."

Roland had been braced for a challenge. Instead he found himself presented with the ears and tail of the bull, still warm, still dripping blood: grisly trophies, but great in honor. The people's roar deafened him. He acknowledged it as he had been trained to do, and endured until it was done—until a new bull and a new fighter freed him from the weight of so many eyes.

"Memories here are long," said Musa. "The way in which you slew the bull—when Rome ruled here, that was a great rite of the soldiers' cult."

Roland nodded. "The cult of Mithras. Yes."

"So," said Musa, eyes glinting. "You are an educated man. Then you know what you did."

"It was the best way to kill the bull," said Roland.

"Indeed," said Musa.

Roland sat in the emir's receiving-room and endured that stare as he had endured it a thousandfold in the theater. He was aware of the curtain at Musa's back that seemed to cover a wall, but the sound of soft breathing came from behind it. There was someone there. A woman: he caught the scent of perfume, rich and sweet.

He had scented that perfume before, when Musa's third wife asked to speak to him. She was there, then, watching and listening. That gave this meeting rather more significance than the simple desire of a host to inquire after his guest's comfort.

A servant brought sherbet and offered wine, but Roland was content with the cold sour-sweetness. He sipped slowly from the cup of blue glass, savoring the taste, and the smoothness of the cup in his hands.

Musa spoke at last, in some bemusement. "You are a . . . surprising man," he said.

Roland raised his brow. "Because I know of Mithras?"

"Among other things," said Musa.

"Ah," said Roland. "I'm young. I'm a Frank. I'm a fighting man. I should not be anything else."

Musa laughed—startling himself, maybe; which made him laugh the harder. Roland waited him out. At length he said, "My lord, I beg your pardon! I don't mean to offend. And yet—"

"I am a surprising person," Roland said.

"Yes," said Musa, wiping away the tears of laughter. "Yes. Though one would expect—knowing the sword—"

"You know Durandal?"

"I know what it is," Musa said. "And you, it seems, know what it meant that you slew the bull in the way of sacrifice, as Mithras himself did, and as men here still recall. It makes you more than a Frank or a warrior. It makes you something that the people will remember."

"As one who committed sacrilege?"

"No," said Musa. "They'll remember you as—a champion, I suppose you would call it. One who defends them against their enemies and fights battles on their behalf, as you slew the bull that was slaying men in the villages."

"Even though I am a Frank?"

"Even so," Musa said.

Roland set down his empty cup. The servant moved quickly to fill it, but he left it where it was. "Will this help my king in his war?"

Musa sighed. "What you do, what you are, has nothing to

do with your king. You slew the bull for these people, not
for him."

"But my king is—"

"You are not your king," Musa said.

"I am here in his service."

"People here care little for that."

"You're not going to aid him, are you?"

Musa shook his head, though not in reply to Roland's
question. "I see," he said, "why you were not sent to speak
for him."

"Maybe I should not have been sent to guard his ambassador, either," Roland said.

"The bull would be alive still," Musa said, "and still trampling down walls and murdering children."

"You would have slain him yourself," said Roland. "Or
someone would have. I did nothing that another man
could not have done."

"That is a matter of opinion," said Musa. He shifted,
straightened. "My lord, we owe you a debt of gratitude. My
people have asked that I pay it for them."

"I need no payment," Roland said, "nor any gratitude."

"Nevertheless," said Musa, "you will receive it. They
have no gold to give, but they know that you would not
take it. The honor of the bull, you have. What they wished
to give you—"

He nodded to the servant. The servant bowed and
opened the curtain behind Musa.

Two veiled ladies sat there in an alcove with a high grate
of window. One was young and slender. The other was
shrouded in black, all but the pale gnarled hands and the
bird-bright eyes.

Roland knew better than to stare at either of them. It
was a great honor, and great trust, that a Muslim of rank allowed a stranger to look on one of his wives. The other,
Roland doubted was kin to either of them, but she did not
have the manner or bearing of a peasant, either.

"This," said the younger woman in a low and lovely
voice, "is Sibella. Her family is very old, from before the
Romans. She holds in her heart the memory of her kin. She
asks, in thanks for your sacrifice of the bull, to tell you a
story."

Whatever Roland had expected, it had not been that. He could think of no response; could only sit in silence.

His surprise must have shown on his face. The old woman let fall her veil. Her face was as pale as her hands, wrinkled and folded like a dried apple. Her smile illuminated it. "Child," she said, "don't look so startled. Hasn't anybody told you a story before?"

"Yes, lady," he said. "But not—"

"Not as payment for a debt." Her eyes danced on him. For an instant he saw what she must have been in youth: not a beauty, maybe, but spirited, and utterly fearless. "We owe you more than you may know, my lord. Our people have lived in this land for time out of mind. They remember stories from long and long ago, when the gods were young, and the bull did not die in the dance, though the dancers sometimes did."

"Before Babylon," said Roland, remembering: Merlin's face, and his voice, and stories that he had told. "Before Ur of the Chaldees."

"Yes," Sibella said. "Though my story does not go back so far. But first, tell me something. Are you the hawk of the gods?"

It was a plain question, simply asked, but Roland felt the weight and the force of it. He could have refused to answer, or answered sidewise. He chose not to do that. He said, "Not he, but his seed."

She nodded. She was not surprised or appalled. She seemed almost pleased. "Good," she said, but not to him; her eyes were on the emir's wife. "This is the one," she said.

The emir's wife nodded. "I thought so," she said.

"Your eyes are as clear as ever," said Sibella. She turned back to Roland. "Tell me, child. One more thing. Have you heard of the Grail?"

Roland's teeth clicked together. "The—"

"The Grail," Sibella said. "The cup of the Lord's Supper. Have you heard of it?"

"Yes," said Roland. "Yes, certainly. How—"

"Good," said Sibella. "Now listen. I will tell this story once. If you understand, that's well. If not, then not. This gift comes from my people to you; from the old kindred to the champion of the sword, who slew the black bull."

Roland did not have Durandal with him; not here, in his

host's presence, where no guest should in honor go armed. It lay safe in his chamber, wrapped and hidden. And yet he could have sworn that he heard its song, sweet and high and deadly.

The amulet on his breast, the silver coin that he had worn since Paderborn, was suddenly heavy, and warm as if he had held it in a flame. His heart quickened beneath it.

"Sword and spear," the old woman said. "Cup and coin." And as he sat rigid, remembering the dream in which Merlin had spoken those words, she told him the story as she had promised.

"Far away and long ago," she said, "there was a kingdom in the mountains. Part of it was in the world we know, and part lay in the realm of the gods. Its people could walk on mortal earth, then between step and step, find themselves under another sun, on grass that never dies. The gods would come to visit them, and creatures out of legend lived on their crags and in their deep valleys.

"Not so long ago, but still long lives of men, a man came to them. He bore a great gift and a terrible burden. He had fled a terrible war, the destruction of his people, and the pursuit of implacable enemies. He sought rest and peace, and a place in which his burden might be safe.

"This kingdom in two worlds opened its gates to him and took him in. Its king accepted the task of guarding the thing he brought with him. Nine ladies swore themselves in service to it. Nine enchantresses built a great castle and shrine, and there kept it safe through long years.

"But at last its great enemy came seeking it, and nearly won it. He came close to destroying the king and his son. The nine ladies stood against him, and a hundred knights, and with them the king's successor, who had come from the world without. At great cost in lives and blood, they cast down the enemy and so preserved their treasure."

"I know that story," Roland said. "That is the story of the Grail. Nine enchantresses guard and serve it. The kingdom is called Montsalvat. A king rules it. His castle is sometimes called Montsalvat, and sometimes Carbonek. Great magic raised it, and the power of the Grail preserves it. It's said that it will endure until the end of the world."

"Unless an enemy rises to destroy it," Sibella said. "There are prophecies, as there always are round great things of power. One foretold the coming of the enemy and the maiming of the king, and the wise fool who healed him. Another tells of a dying king, and again the enemy, and a war greater than he waged before. A vast army marches on the hidden kingdom, breaks down its walls and its defenses, and besieges the stronghold of the Grail. If that stronghold is broken, the darkness will fall; nor shall it be lifted for a thousand years."

Roland shivered. He could see it as she spoke: the castle on the crag, the army of shadows, the wide wing of darkness stretching across the sky. He even, for a moment, glimpsed the face of the dark angel: a beauty too potent to endure; a splendor to break the heart.

"How," he whispered, catching his voice before it failed. "How can it be prevented?"

"By great courage and sacrifice," she said. "With sword and spear, cup and coin. So the seers foretold."

Merlin's words. Was this Merlin's prophecy? It had a flavor of him. And yet he had never told Roland of it, only of Parsifal and the maimed king.

Sibella was done. Her hands were folded, her bright eyes suddenly weary. She must be very, very old. Her smile was sweet and vague and elderly, not at all like the clarity of a moment before. "That is the story I was given to give you," she said. "Remember it."

Roland bowed to her. His mind was full of questions, but he saw no answers in her face. She had given him all she had to give. He accepted dismissal in silence, and went away to ponder tales and prophecies, power and terror. Somehow, his bones knew, the tale would come to him. He would be a part of it.

CHAPTER 20

✠ ✠ ✠

Roland came to bed late. He had been sitting up with Turpin, sharing a jar of wine and telling old stories. It was the first Turpin had heard of the Grail; he had needed to hear it all, and it was long—most of the jar's worth.

Roland seldom spoke so many words together, though he could sing a night away; but tonight his heart was too full to endure. Turpin he trusted as he trusted himself—and the man was wise, and learned, though he seemed mere brute muscle.

Roland's throat was burning when he was done. He soothed it with the last of the wine.

Turpin peered into the jar, found nothing but the lees. He sighed, shrugged. His mind, clearly, was not on the wine, or the lack of it. "That is a striking, a wondrous tale. The cup of the Last Supper? Truly?"

"As true as I sit here," Roland said.

"God in heaven," said Turpin. His hand sought the silver cross he wore on his breast. "There are churches that claim to keep such a relic. Byzantium—"

"There is only one cup," Roland said. "It rests in Carbonek. The light of the world is in it."

"You know this."

Roland nodded.

"In your bones. Your magical, not-quite-human bones."

That was the wine speaking. Roland took no offense. It was true, after all.

"The cup," Turpin murmured. "*The* cup. And mortal men can look on it?"

"Men pure of heart and devoted to its service. And women. My master told me so. The Church would hate to know it, he said, but this is not the Church's domain."

"If the Church knew—" said the Archbishop of Rheims.

"Only men pure of heart," Roland said. "None other may find it, still less look on it."

"Ah," said Turpin. "You wound me to the heart. Which I doubt is pure enough; priest or no, I'm distressingly human."

"You'll do," said Roland. He stretched, yawned. His head was light and buzzing with wine. His body seemed dim and far away. He was a pair of eyes, a babble of thoughts, a voice speaking soft and slow. "Maybe we should go questing, after this war is done."

"What, the two of us? Or the whole army?"

"The king might object to that."

"Unless he went questing with us." Turpin grinned at the thought. "Imagine. Tearing him away from his court, his *palatium*, his whole kingdom, taking the band of his Companions, and riding away to find the Lord's Grail. Just like that. Just—*like*—that."

"He could be King of the Grail," Roland said. "The latest of them must be very old. Older than mortal span. The one from whom he took the kingship—he was born when Rome was young. The Grail nourishes the body and the spirit. A man can live a thousand years, and die in bliss, wrapped in the light of heaven."

Turpin returned no answer. The wine had caught up with him at last. He was snoring softly, sitting upright in his chair.

Roland smiled a little wryly. It was as well, perhaps, that Turpin had not heard Roland's foolishness. Charles as Grail-king? Oh, indeed; what glory, what splendor. Maybe he would do it. Maybe that was his destiny. But it was presumptuous of Roland to propose it.

Turpin was by no means awake to reprimand him. He heaved up the heavy body and tipped it into bed, pulling off the shoes, straightening the limbs, pausing for a moment to peer down at the sleeping face. "Not pure enough of heart?" he said. "Then no man is. Whereas I—" He shook his head. "You know what I am. You don't care—not you, blessed man. But the Grail, it would. It would care very much indeed."

That was as it was. He drew the draperies about the bed, stretched again till his bones cracked, and went in search of his own bed.

She was in it, as if the day between had never been: fair face, brown-gold hair, glimpse of round white breast above the coverlet. She, unlike Turpin, did not snore. Nor was there any scent of wine about her.

Roland stood in the doorway. He did not know, at all, what his heart was saying as it pounded beneath his breastbone. All that day he had done his best not to think of her. He had said nothing to Turpin, though he had told a greater secret by far, the secret of the Grail. What she had meant in coming to him, he had not questioned. He had taken it, or let it take him, and drunk deep joy of it. But he had not asked or expected to drink it twice.

Maybe he was a fool for that. Olivier would say so, loudly and at length. "What's love for," he would demand, "if not to grasp and hold with both hands?"

Not this woman. She was not to be held or confined, or possessed by any man.

She had left him to wake alone, but she had come back. He trod softly into the room and sat in the chair beside the bed. It was an ample chair, as if made for a giant of a Frank. He drew up his knees and clasped them, and rested his chin atop them, and watched her sleep.

His eyes must have slipped shut of their own accord. Her voice spoke in darkness, rippling with laughter. "You look," she said, "like a bogle on a hearth."

He blinked at her. She was sitting up, smiling at him, hair tumbling over her shoulders. "What do you know of bogles?" he asked.

"One lived on my hearth," she said.

"In a castle?"

Her brows rose. "How do you know I didn't live in a peasant's hut?"

The answer to that was obvious. He did not trouble to say it.

"I did have a bogle," she said. "It looked—remarkably like you just now."

"A distant cousin, perhaps," Roland said. "With pretensions."

She stared at him, then laughed, as if caught unawares. "And they say you have no humor," she said.

"People say a great deal," said Roland.

"But not you." She smiled at him, her long eyes narrowing and going almost gold, blissful as a cat in the sun. "You keep your counsel while they babble on. Such a stern face you have, and such a somber mouth—no wonder women vie to kiss it."

"Women do not—"

"Don't they? They do battle for a kiss, and boast of a smile."

"But I have no humor."

"Well," she said, "you say so little, and look so haughty. Who's to know?"

"I should talk more? What would I say?"

"Don't do that," she said. She rose, clothed in her hair. He sighed to see her. He had never seen a woman more beautiful.

She drew him to his feet. They were nearly of a height, which was delightfully convenient. He took her face in his hands and kissed her slowly.

When at last he let her go, she melted against him. He lifted her. She was no burden at all after Turpin's dead weight. Her arms linked about his neck; her head came to rest on his shoulder.

He sank back down into the chair. She nestled in his lap. In a little while she did more than that. Frankish garments had not the ease or lightness of Saracen robes, but she managed to rid him of all that mattered.

She was a wild, wanton creature, and she laughed when she was happy. She laughed rich and free this night, first in that rather astonishingly ample chair, then in the bed, with him freed of the rest of his encumbrances.

When he was happy, as when he was angry or afraid, the bonds of flesh and form slipped free. Too late he caught them. Hawk-wings beat against her breast.

She did not recoil or cry out in horror. She was not even surprised. He lay beneath her, stiff and still.

Her palm curved to fit his cheek. She smiled down at him. "Don't tell me you do this with every woman," she said.

His cheek was burning; her palm was cool. It rested lightly against him, but when he tried to turn, to twist away, it was immovable. "I never," he said, "never—"

"Not once?"

"No!"

"I'm honored," she said.

"You knew."

He did not mean to sound so accusing. Her smile widened, then faded. "I sat with you," she said, "after you won Durandal. Your friend the archbishop was quite unhappy that I did so."

"I remember," he said. "I woke and you were there."

She nodded. "I saw the hawk and the wolf and the stag. There are others?"

It was as if she had driven a fist into his belly. He could not breathe. For a long while he could not speak.

She was patient, after a fashion. She kissed wherever she could reach, till he had to hold her off or he would lose what few wits he had left. "You—you saw—"

"I saw what all the Companions know. Are you frightened? Do you trust me?"

"You know what I am," he said. "Can I trust you?"

"If you are to be trusted," she said.

She was laughing at him—but not, perhaps, entirely. "You know far more of me than I of you," he said.

"Do I?"

"Who you are, where you come from, why you came to us—it's never quite been spoken of. You were simply there, with the embassy from Spain. Then you were there with the queen. And the sword. I know your name, that you have arts of healing. That a *puca* is your servant. And . . . that I love you."

"That's not enough?"

He smoothed her hair back from her face. The curling strands of it caught at his fingers, tangling in them. "Only promise me," he said. "You will do my king no harm, nor threaten my kingdom. Swear to it by whatever you hold holy."

She laid her hand on his breast above his heart. The
amulet burned between them. His heart was beating hard.
"I swear," she said, "by the power that rules me. By the
light of the sun over me, and the moon and the stars, and
the vault of heaven."

He shivered in his bones. That was as great an oath as he
had sworn to free Merlin. She swore it without a moment's
hesitation, without flinching or fear.

It was enough. What his heart and his bones knew, what
she had sworn, were all he needed. When she was ready to
tell him more, she would do it. His bones knew that, too,
and his heart was certain of it.

CHAPTER 21

✠ ✠ ✠

They were ten days in Agua Caliente, hunting, riding, being entertained with great honor and courtesy. But for all the pleasure they had of it, not least that of cool bowers, clean beds, and never a clash of battle, they knew soon enough that the embassy had failed. Musa would not give Charles what he asked for through Turpin.

"The Caliph to whom you professed loyalty," Turpin said the day before their departure, "asked that we come into this country to drive out those who rebelled against him. We have had little enough aid from those who claim to be his servants, and much opposition. Is that service to your Caliph, my lord? Is that how you obey his command?"

Musa's eyes glittered. Those were hard words, however gently spoken. He answered in kind, with grace but without softness. "We do what we must for the protection of our kingdom. The Commander of the Faithful is far away. He has not seen the army that came to invade us, or counted its numbers, or heard the songs it sings. The rebels at least are of our faith, and will not impose another upon us. We will contend with them as we may. You we will not help, except to depart as soon as may be. In that I can promise a safe passage and small opposition. That much power I have, and I will wield it."

"You will do no more?" Turpin asked.

"I can do no more." Musa spread his hands. "I give you

as much as I may—more, some of the emirs protest, than I should."

Turpin sighed. They were sitting in the garden near a fountain that sang into its marble bowl. The air was sweet with the scent of blossoms. Tomorrow they would go back to the siege, to dust and heat and flies and the manifold stink of men crowded together.

He could have been tempted to stay in this place. To seize it and keep it, and make himself lord of it, and no matter that he had come under seal of truce.

But he was stronger than temptation—and a fool for it, too, if his darker self were allowed to speak. He smiled as he could, returned courtesy with courtesy, and drank in coolness and sweetness and blessed quiet, for they would have to last him until this war was over.

Musa left him to the garden's peace, professing some duty that could not be avoided. Turpin was glad enough of the solitude. It was given him so seldom.

When he returned to Francia, he thought, he would take himself to a monastery. It was time to remember quiet again, and simplicity. To be a priest, who had been too long a lord of the world.

He prayed for a while, here in this infidel garden, in the sound of water falling. Water was precious beyond imagining in this country. It flowed in rivers, true enough, but it did not rain here as it did in Francia. This was a dry land, a parched land. The sun was like a hammer on the skull, day upon day.

Voices murmured near him, too soft almost to hear. At first he took them for a trick of the fountain's song. Then, as he sat still, he saw figures moving slowly through the garden's greenery. It was not difficult to recognize them. The sun caught the sheen of old gold in a lady's long plaited hair, and the turn of a head beside hers that Turpin knew as well as any among the living.

Ah, he thought with a sensation almost of relief. Olivier had won the wager. Roland walked with Sarissa under flowering branches, arm linked in arm, speaking as lovers do, as if nothing mattered in the world but one another.

Turpin had given that up when he took priest's vows. Not every priest did, whatever he had sworn before God, but Turpin was a man of his word. However sweet the temptation, he set himself to resist it. And there was great temptation for the king's battle-brother. For some women, priestly vows were a challenge. They cared little that Turpin had no beauty. He was a strong man, well made, powerful in battle. Whatever his face lacked, his body made up for it.

As he rose to withdraw, a servant approached him by the path to the colonnade. It was a eunuch, young and shy, with hair the color of new gold, and a fair Saxon face. His Latin was stilted but clear, his message succinct. "Reverend archbishop, the lady Leila would speak with you."

Turpin could not say he was astonished. Was she not a Christian, and was he not a priest? But he had been thinking that if she had not sent for him before this, she would not do it. He had been nine days in her husband's house. There had been ample opportunity to summon him.

Now she had sent for him. The eunuch led him to the colonnade and round, then up into a part of the house that he had not been admitted to before. It was not the chief entrance to the harem, Turpin thought, but a narrow stair and a postern, and a passage almost too small for his breadth and height. It smelled faintly of cats and more distinctly of some cloying scent, flowers or perfume or both.

The eunuch opened a door near the end of the passage, into a room that was small but very bright, with a balcony on the garden. It was warm there, almost too much so, but a fan lessened the heat, with a drowsy child swaying it back and forth.

There was a couch and a table and a pitcher of sherbet, but Turpin stayed on his feet, leaning on the rail of the balcony, drinking in what coolness came from the garden. He could not see the lovers from here, nor hear them, either.

A soft step sounded behind him. He turned as he had learned to do: swift but quiet, not to alarm one who meant well, but quick enough to catch a dagger aimed at his back.

It was a woman in veils, alone. Her eyes were young and bright and rather imperious. She held her head high, as a servant would never permit herself to do.

"My lord archbishop," she said in lovely Latin, easy as if she spoke it every day. "I bid you a belated welcome to this house."

Turpin bowed. She kissed his ring and tilted her head

toward the divan. It was large enough for two, with room between.

He wondered briefly if this was one of those women who were greatly excited by the violation of a twofold vow: that of a priest and that of a married woman. But there was no languor in her look, no suggestion of seduction. For all that he could see, she looked on him simply as a priest from Francia: exotic, interesting, but no more than that.

When they were seated, she sat for a while in silence, gazing not at him but at the light that poured in from the balcony. He let the time shape a prayer, until she said, "I should have spoken with you long since. Can you forgive me?"

"Easily, my lady," Turpin said.

"No," she said. "No, I was a coward. I knew what my husband would have to say to you."

"Do you agree with it?"

She paused. Her fingers smoothed the folds of her mantle. "I . . . can't disagree."

"A woman should be obedient to her husband," Turpin said.

Her eyes flashed up. "Certainly she should. But I speak for myself. I do regret it, my lord archbishop. I would help you if I could."

"I wish I could understand," Turpin said, "why Christians will not help Christians to free their land from the infidel."

"Because, my lord, it's never as simple as that. If it were, this war would be won and you would be lords in Spain."

"Italy is complicated," Turpin said. "Rome is beyond complicated. We've done well enough there."

"There are no Muslims to speak of in Italy."

"That makes a difference?"

She shrugged, tilting her head, turning her hands palm up. "It's different here. Different worlds, different troubles. If anyone frees us from the infidel, it will be one of our own."

There it was, he thought. There was his answer. Christian or no, the Franks were foreigners. The Christians of Spain had suffered invasion enough. They wanted no more of it.

Charles would not be pleased to hear the outcome of Turpin's embassy. Still, Turpin thought, the king was no fool. Nor was he inclined to kill a messenger, however ill the news.

"My lord archbishop," said the emir's wife, "it would be a great pleasure for me if you would sing Mass here before you go."

"Gladly, my lady," Turpin said. That was true. He did not fault her for her honesty, nor would he deny her her soul's comfort.

She bowed her head. "And . . . would you hear my confession?"

He regarded her in some surprise. "You have no chaplain or confessor?"

"My husband allows me the freedom of my faith," she said, "but he prefers not to support a Christian priest in his house. I go to Mass in the old abbey beyond the village. Father Abbot hears my confessions. But, my lord, he is old and deaf and he grows blind, and he hasn't walked in the world in longer than he can remember. He's a good man, a pure spirit. But not—"

Such irony, thought Turpin, that he had spoken to Roland so recently of purity of heart—and concluded that he was not so blessed. The thought made his smile wry, and made him say, "You have a worldly confession, then, and think a more worldly priest would better hear it."

"I don't mean to offend, my lord," she said.

"No, no," said Turpin. "The holy innocents are much beloved of God, but when it comes to matters of the world, they're not always able to advise as well as they might."

"Yes," she said. "Yes, my lord. Though it's simpler than that, maybe. Or so complicated it seems simple. I've broken an oath, after a fashion. It's a great oath and sacred, but what it bound me to—my lord, have you ever questioned the command of your liege lord?"

"On occasion," he said.

Her fingers twisted: a great confession of anxiety in one so composed. "Did you feel that it was an unwise command? That it could do more harm than good?"

"Sometimes, yes."

"Did you act on it? Did you do what you thought was right?"

"Once or twice." Turpin kept his voice deliberately soft. She was in great trouble of mind, however quietly she expressed it.

"I keep a great secret," she said. "My whole family does.

That—that was why I asked my husband to offer your king a chance of truce. He knew that your king would send a wise ambassador. He also knew that the ambassador would have attendants. One of those, I made him ask for."

Turpin did not need to ask which one she meant. "You wanted to see who had won the champion's sword."

"Yes," she said. "Yes, I did want that."

"And the sword means somewhat to you."

She drew a breath, as if to steady herself. "It's not—what he may think it is. What he's been allowed to think. I told him as much as I dared. It may have been too much—or far from enough."

"He's not to be champion for Spain, is he? That's not what it was for."

She paused, eyes fixed on his face, as if she had not seen him before. "You see very clearly," she said.

He shrugged. "It's not difficult. So this is a great secret, and you fear you've betrayed it."

"I fear . . ." she said. "I fear that if I don't betray it, it will be very ill for us all. But if I do, it will be ill for me. And that is cowardly."

"I see," he said, pondering that. "Simple and yet complex. To keep the oath you swore, and do harm; or to break it and pay the consequences. What does your heart tell you?"

"That I haven't said enough," she said, "or broken it far enough. That I should tell more. But if I do, what if that works more harm than good? What if, once he knows, he refuses the task for which he was chosen?"

"Somehow," Turpin said, "I doubt that Roland would ever refuse a duty."

"Even a terrible one? One that could sunder him from all he knows, and bid him do things that he thought never to do, and force him to service that he would never have chosen if it had not been chosen for him?"

"Is it service of evil?"

"No," she said fervently. "Oh, no. Never. But it is service that gives no choices, accepts no refusal. I was bidden to tell him nothing of it, to let others reveal it to him when the time was fitting. But I think they'll wait too long. He should know now. He should have time to understand it, to accept—not be forced into it when it's too late to turn back."

"And do you know why you were bidden tell him nothing?"

"That's why," she said. "So that he can't refuse. They fear that if they give him a choice, he'll choose to walk away."

"They don't know Roland well, then," Turpin said dryly.

"They think they know enough. They don't trust him."

"So they should not, if they ask him to do anything dishonorable. But if there is honor in it, and he was chosen, you can believe that he will accept the burden."

"But if they don't tell him? If that angers him? Is he a man to take revenge for great slights?"

"I've never known him to be vindictive," Turpin said. "Proud, strong-willed, protective of his honor, but he's never been one for hunting down those who offend him."

"This will be worse than offense."

"Is it a very great thing they want him to do? Will it cost him his life?"

The emir's wife lowered her eyes. Her fingers were twisting again, knotting in the folds of her mantle. "He is the champion."

"And champions fight for the cause. Whatever that cause may be."

She nodded.

"I would tell him," Turpin said, "and pray for lenience in the matter of the oath. It seems you know him better than those others, whoever they may be."

"They think he may be part a demon," she said. "That frightens them."

"It is said that his ancestor was a devil's get. But that was long ago."

"It doesn't matter, if the blood is there. It's strong in him—but not the darkness. Only the magic. And the face. That's what they see, and for them it is enough."

"I see," said Turpin. "As, it appears, do you. I can't counsel you—that is for your own heart to do—but I can pray for you, and give you such blessing as in my power to give."

He laid his hands on her bowed head, and spoke words of blessing and of peace. Then in a lovely small chapel not far from the room in which she had met him, he sang Mass for her and for a handful of her maids. She seemed to take great comfort from it. He was glad. She was a good woman, a loyal daughter of the faith. If she was also a loyal daugh-

ter of Spain, that was as it should be, little as he or his king
might wish it.

He would ponder the rest when he was alone, when he
could make sense of the things she had said, and the mystery she had hinted at. He thought he knew what it might
be. If that was so, then it was a great task Roland was given,
indeed. And Turpin could not speak of it. He too was oath-
bound, because he had been told in confession, which was
sacrosanct.

She was clever, was the emir's wife, and protective after
all of her secrets. If she did not tell Roland, then no one
would. In her way she had laid on Turpin the burden that
was laid on her.

Simple, he thought, and complex beyond understanding.
In its way it was a very Frankish dilemma.

CHAPTER 22

✠ ✠ ✠

It was harder to leave Agua Caliente than Roland would have believed possible. Musa in refusing to become Charles' ally had become his enemy, and yet Roland could not help thinking that this had been a place of great joy and friendship. He had found welcome here, gracious manners, praise and admiration, and the arms of a lover.

Now he must return to the siege at Saragossa. He had feared in his heart that Sarissa would not go, but when they readied to ride, Tarik was waiting in his white horse-guise.

Sarissa was not yet in evidence. Roland saw to his men, and greeted Turpin as he came into the courtyard. Musa walked arm in arm with the archbishop, as honored enemies might do: it was a kind of friendship, after all. Musa smiled at Roland and bowed lower than an emir need do to an infidel count. "My lord," he said, "I wish you well."

Roland bowed in return. "And I you, my lord, though we may fight on opposing sides of this war."

"May it not come to that," Musa said.

Roland bowed again. There was a flurry among the horses, an argument between stallions. When that was settled, Musa turned back to converse with Turpin. And Sarissa came out of the house, walking alone, dressed in her Saracen riding clothes.

Very carefully Roland forbore from his heart's desire, which was to sweep her up in his arms and kiss her till they both were dizzy. He bowed to her as he had to Musa. She inclined her head. Tarik, wearing again the white stallion's shape, snorted laughter. Sarissa grandly ignored him, springing into the saddle and waiting with conspicuous patience for the rest to follow suit.

How very interesting, Roland thought, that she had done what a king might do, or a queen: come out last, as one who was entitled to do such a thing. Nor did anyone voice an objection.

Royalty indeed. Lesser rank would not dare this, even in an infidel's house.

They were not to ride out, he discovered, without a full farewell. Musa's servants, his men-at-arms, his kin who were in the house, had all gathered. As the Franks rode through the gate, they found the road lined with people.

Those were for Roland. They chanted his name as he rode past, a long roll of sound that seemed to carry them all down the dusty road to Saragossa. He was moved by it to do a thing he seldom did, for then the whole world knew he was there: he set his aurochs' horn to his lips and winded it. Even as softly as he blew on it, the sound shook the earth and trembled in the sky.

His men were grinning. They did love it when their commander was celebrated—and these were foreigners, infidels, which made it all the sweeter. Roland could not but do it justice: keep his head up, his back straight, and acknowledge the people's acclaim with all the grace that he had.

The crowd thinned as they rode on, until there was nothing but open country ahead. Roland found himself riding side by side with Sarissa. "You're a great favorite hereabouts now," she said.

"Pity it failed to be of any use to my king."

"Yes," she said. "Pity." But she did not seem unduly cast down.

"I half expected," he said, "that you would stay in Agua Caliente."

Her eyes flashed on him. "Did you? Why?"

"It's a pleasant place. You're clearly welcome there."

"I'm welcome among the Franks."

"More than welcome," he said. "But it's a siege. There's nothing pleasant in it."

"You are in it," she said.

Even now he could blush when she spoke so. "You do this for me?"

She nodded. "Can you think of a better reason?"

"Myriads," he said.

Her quick smile warmed him. "O modesty! You are enough. Believe that."

"But when we come there," he said, "how can we continue as we were? Your honor, your good name—"

"Will yours be harmed by association with me?"

"No," he said. "But—"

"My honor is my own," she said. "You can do it no harm."

He slid eyes at her. "That could almost be reckoned an insult."

"What, that you have no power to dishonor me? No man's love can do that."

"You are not . . . of a mind with the rest of the world," he said.

She did not take the bait. She only smiled her most infuriating smile and wandered off to torment someone else.

The siege was much the same as it had been when they left. The engines battered walls and gate. Both were held fast against the Franks.

After so long away, the stink of siege was overpowering. Roland envied Sarissa the Saracen veil that she drew over her mouth and nose as they passed the outer boundaries of the camp. Even coming from upwind, it was a mighty stench. He breathed as shallowly as he could, and tried not to taste the air that he drew in.

He would learn to bear it again. It was not a choice one had in war.

He had expected the stench, and the spread of trampled, barren land outward from its extent of a dozen days past. So too the toll that sieges took on men: boredom, sickness, quarrels and ill humor that could spread like a pestilence from company to company and nation to nation. But there was something else.

He had hardly looked to be welcomed back with shouts and wild cheering, or with such adulation as had seen him off from Agua Caliente. This was Turpin's embassy, not his; he had gone simply as commander of the guard.

Still, as he rode through the lines to the king's vantage, what began as a prickle in the spine grew to a distinct sense of enmity. It was a stench all its own, black and potent. At first he reckoned that there must be enemies in the camp, envoys from Saragossa perhaps; but he caught a man's eye in passing, and it focused on him. That was hate—clear, direct, and no doubt in it. This man hated Roland. Hated and feared him.

The man was not alone. It was a murmur through the ranks, a shadow passing over them, as word of his coming spread. *The witch. The witch is back.*

Roland's shoulders tightened. His skin rippled. If he let go now, he would gratify them all.

He held to his human shape. He rode as he did in battle, as if he knew no doubt, no fear. Those were buried deep. *Never show fear*, Merlin had taught him even before the master-at-arms in his father's house. *Never let them know that they can overcome you.*

He thought he knew who it might be, who had done this. The length of his absence would have been long enough if seeds had already been sown—and he did not doubt that they had. Ganelon had had a year to discover both what Roland was and that Roland had slain his demon servant. He had lain low, tutored the king's son, pretended to be no more than he seemed. Now, perhaps, he had begun to move. What was a year, after all, to a man who measured his life in thousands of them?

For the moment Roland had duties, and no proof that Ganelon had begun the whispers against him. He rode through that fog of hate, denser than the reek of men and dung and cookfires. He armored himself against it as he could, and did his best to be glad of one thing: that he would see his king again.

Charles' welcome was as glad as he could have wished, even though the king knew by then that Turpin brought back no new alliance. He greeted both Roland and Turpin with a broad and altogether unfeigned grin, and embraced them heartily, kissing each on both cheeks. He had, as it were by chance, a barrel of good wine for them, new bread and white cheese, and a haunch of roast ox. It was a coarser feast than they had had in Agua Caliente, but it was their own: their own king, their own camp, their own war.

With the king and the Companions, Roland had come as if to haven. But there was a storm without. It showed in the faces of certain of the pages and servants as they waited on the feasters, and in the eyes of courtiers who happened to be about. People were staring at Roland.

Whatever tales were being told of him, they had spread fast and far. He endured for as long as he could, till he had to slip away or leap out of his skin. Then he did a thing he had never yet done in camp among his own people: he kept his head down and altered his gait and let men think he was someone other than Roland of Brittany.

His own tent was waiting as if he had never left it: his belongings, his armor and weapons, his battle-brother Olivier with a jar of hoarded Frankish ale. The flap was tied back, Olivier sprawled at ease in the shade, grinning lazily as Roland slipped round the tent and dropped beside him.

"You owe me a ruby," Olivier said.

Roland cursed as the hot flush rose to his cheeks. "Pest! Who told you?"

Olivier shrugged. "Everybody knows. But even if they didn't, I would. Her smile is different."

"She never smiled before."

"Yes," said Olivier.

"And they call you a womanizing fool."

"Why not?" Olivier said. "I am." He filled a wooden cup and handed it to Roland. His own was empty, but he let it be.

"Tell me what else everybody knows," Roland said after a swallow of warm brown ale. It was dreadful, but it tasted of home. It comforted him.

Olivier did not try to evade the question. "So you heard it, coming in."

"I felt it," Roland said.

"Fair knocked you down, did it?"

Roland shrugged.

Olivier frowned into the glare of daylight. For once he was not wearing the mask of the amiable idiot. "It began as soon as you left. People started whispering. Stories ran round, rumors—like fire in dry grass."

"But for what? Why, and why just now? I've done nothing but what I always have." Except, Roland thought, for the slaying of the bull. But he had done that elsewhere, days after this would have begun.

"God knows why," Olivier said, "or who started it. Did you do something before you went? Let someone see something he shouldn't?"

"Not a thing," said Roland.

"Maybe," Olivier mused, "it needed your absence, somehow. You've been with the king since Paderborn; you've been away at most a handful of days. Someone must be jealous. Or afraid of you."

"Maybe," Roland said. "But that much hate, that quickly—someone's been telling the truth."

Olivier sat up sharply. "Not one of us. I'd swear it on holy relics."

"I can betray myself well enough," Roland said, "without help from the rest of you."

"Not enough for this," Olivier said. "This is concerted hate. You have an enemy, and he's clever. No one remembers where he first heard the rumors, but everyone has heard them. Everyone's afraid."

"Tell me which stories they're telling," Roland said.

"There are several," said Olivier, "but the meat of them is this: that you come of a long line of Breton witches, that your true father was a devil, and that you can take any shape that suits you. They've been eyeing every creature that runs or flies, and swearing that each of them is you."

"*Ai,*" said Roland.

"Indeed," said Olivier. "And then the whispers get lower, and people say to one another, 'He's so close to the king. What's he doing to the king?' There's the hate, brother. There's the fear. A devil's get is the king's Companion, his champion. Add in envy from the court, and there's a fine brew of poison for a summer's siege."

Roland set down his barely tasted cup of ale, clasped his knees, and rocked as he had done when he was a small feral child. There was comfort in drawing himself in as tightly as possible, as if he could go deeper inside himself and build the walls higher and keep out the world.

The world was calling him. The amulet under his tunic had begun to burn. Durandal was singing, faint but clear.

He unfolded. The sword lay on the cot, sheathed and

wrapped in his war-cloak. He uncovered it, drew it, sat again and laid it across his knees.

Olivier watched him in silence until he had gone still again. Then his battle-brother said, "You don't even look human."

"I don't think I am," Roland said, but distantly. He had, until now, used the sword as a sword: weapon of war, sharp and deadly but simple enough. But Durandal was more than a sword. Great power was in it, high magic.

"I killed a bull," Roland said, "while we were among the infidels."

"I heard," Olivier said. "The Spaniards there were hailing you as a sort of god."

"And here," said Roland, "they curse me for a demon. I need to know why, and why now. What profit is it to anyone to turn the army against me? I have no more power here than I ever have. I've slain no bull for them to marvel at or excoriate me for."

"Personal enmity?" Olivier wondered.

Roland nodded slowly. "It must be. But to prove it . . ."

"Let me do the hunting," Olivier said. "I'm the great ox, the chaser after women. No one will suspect me, or find it odd to see me nosing about. A woman can hide anywhere, after all."

"No," said Roland. "It could be dangerous."

The blue eyes brightened to a distressing degree. "So it could! All the better. As for you, brother, the more ordinary you seem, and the less you stray from your accustomed round, the more likely you'll be to prove the rumors wrong. How perfect a simple soldier can you be?"

"Not very," Roland said with a twist of the lip. "Olivier, I won't have you—"

"It's settled," Olivier said. "Now put the sword away. You look as if you're about to conjure the hosts of heaven with it."

"I should like to," Roland muttered, but Olivier had the right of it. He sheathed and veiled the sword again, drained another cup of the awful ale, and let himself be put to bed though it was barely sunset. Later, he thought, much later, he would slip away. But not while Olivier was awake and watching him.

CHAPTER 23

✠ ✠ ✠

Sarissa heard the whispers, saw the dark stares. She felt in her heart the hate the Franks directed toward Roland. It made her deeply and abidingly angry.

Someone here meant him ill. And no matter that the whispers were not far off her own doubts and fears. She loved him in spite of them. These rough barbarians had no right.

He came to her in the night, creeping softly out of the dark, slipping beneath the wall of her tent. He seemed the simple, eager lover, but there was a tautness in him that even she could not smooth away. It marred the harmony. They were awkward; they struggled, more like warriors than lovers, until Sarissa collapsed in a fit of laughter.

Roland withdrew as far as the tent's compass would allow, drawing into a tight knot, turning his back on her. She bit back the last of her mirth and went softly after him. Just within reach, she stopped. She ran her hand down his spine as she had that first night.

This time he refused to turn. But she persisted. She spread hands across his shoulders, and stroked upward, gathering his thick black hair at his nape. It always seemed to need cutting. It was long enough now to plait, which she did, slowly, lingering over each woven strand.

He had shut her out. She tied off the plait between his

shoulderblades with a bit of fringe from the blanket. Softly she said, "I wasn't laughing at you."

She was astonished when he responded. "I didn't think you were."

"Then why—" She stopped. Of course she knew why.

"I shouldn't have come here," he said. "With what's being said of me, let alone the matter of your honor or your reputation—"

"That matters nothing," she said.

He turned. His face was white and set. "It matters a great deal. I can't ask you to bear the burden of me."

"I already have," she said. "There's no changing it."

He shook his head. "Someone wants my blood, with my name and honor besides. I won't cost you yours as well."

"Let me judge that," she said.

"No." He rose. He found his garments where they lay scattered. He put them on.

She made no effort to stop him. Maybe he thought her vanquished because of it. Well, and let him think so. He had his arrogance, that one.

She let him go, though it tore at her heart to see him so stiff and so very much alone. He needed that, just then. She gave it to him.

When he was gone, she called Tarik. She seldom did that. The *puca* was his own creature; he did not obey orders, though he would serve her of his free will.

He took his time in coming. She had expected that. She used it to wash and dress and plait her hair. Not that he would care, but it settled her mind. It made clear what she must do.

He slipped through the tentflap in a guise he seldom wore, because, he declared, it was anything but elegant. She wondered if this young man-shape had looked so much like Roland before they both met the Breton Count. Maybe it had. They were descended of the same kin and kind, when it came down to it. That too-pale skin, that black-black hair, struck her strangely just now, and those eyes as yellow as a cat's, regarding her with a cat's insouciant stare.

He bowed low, half in reverence, half in mockery. His grace was not human—but it was very like Roland's. "You command, great lady?" he inquired. His voice at least was different: lighter, softer, without the Breton accent.

"I never command you, my friend," she said, "but I do ask. If you can help—"

His lips drew back from sharp cat-teeth. "Help you hunt?"

She nodded.

He laughed silently. "Always, great lady. I will always hunt for you. What are we hunting? Snakes?"

She held him with her stare, though that was not easy. "You know something. Tell me."

"I know," he said, "that snakes hunt *him*." He said it so, with as much reverence as was in him.

"And who is the snakes' master?" Sarissa asked, forbearing for the nonce to remark on a *puca*'s speaking of any man as if he were worthy of respect.

Tarik twitched in his skin, shivering, though his eyes were as bold as ever. "You know," he said.

"I do not."

He shrugged. If she wanted to be a fool, his expression said, then let her.

Snakes, she thought. Serpents—the old serpent. But—

"He was cast down!"

"He rose up," Tarik said.

"Here?"

"Where else would he be? Or you?"

She had been led to this army, this king and his people. And there was darkness among them. She knew that. And Roland was—

"He does not belong to that one," Tarik said flatly.

"He was bred by that one," said Sarissa.

"Even the first of them was no loyal servant." Tarik's grin was full of fangs. "The serpent is here, himself, not his child or his servant. I will hunt him for you."

"How long have you known?" Sarissa asked him.

"Long," said Tarik.

She had not asked, too sure that the darkness came from Roland. Maybe the darkness had fostered that. Was not its master the Father of Lies?

Tarik shrank into his most favored form, the small grey cat. Before she could call him back, he was gone, vanished into the night.

He knew where the serpent was. And he had not told her.

"Great goddess," she whispered. Tarik was going to

hunt the old enemy himself. His powers were not inconsiderable, but he was a very minor demon. He was never a match for the corrupter of kings.

She spun in frustration, a whirling, stamping dance. He had warded himself from her. The fool. He could not die as men died, but he could be destroyed. If the old enemy had restored even a portion of his strength, he could crush the *puca* beneath his foot.

The world she had envisioned even this morning was proved to be a false image. Roland—the more his own people condemned him, the more certain she was that her doubts were folly. Now she faced a truth she was not ready after all to face.

She had come to the Franks in search of a champion. The war in which Roland was to fight was coming as surely as the moon swelled from new to full and shrank to new again. But in her arrogance she had reckoned that the enemy himself would be mustering forces far away, in his stronghold at the edge of the world. She had never stopped to think that he might be doing so here. In Spain. Full in the center of this army that the Franks had mustered to conquer the infidel.

This army. The infidels had seen the size and strength of it and regretted that they had ever begged the Frankish king to aid them against the rebels. It was a very great army—and it was founded on deception. Its men believed that they had come on crusade. But its king knew that he had been summoned as an ally of the infidel. What better weapon for the Father of Lies to take and wield?

She paced, fretting. A great part of her twitched to go out, to join the hunt. But Tarik was a better hunter than she, and far less obtrusive in the night. Come morning she would go after him, but not now.

She mustered her wits, which were far more scattered than they should be. The enemy's influence? Or Roland, shattering the calm of her spirit, laying her open to confusion?

Was there a difference?

No doubts. Not now. She stood still and for a long moment simply breathed. Slowly her heart ceased its hammering. Her thoughts stilled and focused. She found her center again, and the light of magic in it.

It was well aware of the darkness in the camp, as it had been from the beginning. But where that darkness was, or what it was, it knew no better now than it ever had. It could not touch the source or come near it. It could only circle and snarl.

And yet that circle had a center. If she could come to it in the body, she would know. She was sure of that. She would recognize the enemy.

Would she? He had been stripped of everything about him that might be tempting to mortals: beauty, splendor, even the music of his voice. He would seem the most ordinary of men. A lesser lord, perhaps a priest—he had played the part of priests before. Those could come nearer kings than most, and were nearly always trusted.

She slept a little, by main force of will. Her body had need of rest, and it passed the remainder of the night. In the dawn she was up. Tarik had not come back, nor had she expected it.

She dressed for riding, for comfort and to escape the notice that a woman, dressed as a woman, would attract in this camp of war. She walked out calmly.

There was an altar near the king's tent, set under a canopy so that the priests and the king and the highest lords were sheltered from the sun, but the lesser folk could see and hear if they chose. Sarissa held back among them, watching and listening as Turpin celebrated the rite. His acolytes this morning were monks and priests of notable rank, some of them warriors of God as he was, others attached to the king's chancery. The king himself knelt in front of the altar, his silver-fair hair and broad shoulders unmistakable.

Roland's battle-brother was there, the great golden ox whose wits were keener than anyone knew. Olivier was close by the king, guarding him without making a show of it. Sarissa had felt his eyes on her like the touch of both fire and ice: warmth of his recognition, cool reckoning of the danger she might pose to the king.

Beyond him, all but hidden in his shadow, she saw Roland. Her heart stopped, then began to beat very hard. Of course he had come to Mass on this, the first day after his return. He would have been a fool to stay away. Rumors of witchcraft and worse must falter in the face of his calm and faithful presence at the Mass.

Roland did not seem aware of her. He divided his attention between the rite and the king. Nothing else, that she could see, touched upon him. Which was well, she supposed. Her wiser self was glad. The rest was like to weep.

She steadied her mind once more, and made herself face the matter at hand. Between those two, Charles was as safe as he could be. She sensed no darkness in him. He had not been corrupted.

And yet . . .

It was close. Her awareness of it made it seem stronger. She searched the faces of the priests under the canopy. Plain human faces, bearded or shaven clean, pale clerks or ruddy warrior priests. None of them bore the marks of the dark angel. Nor did any cry out to her that he was the ancient enemy.

She slipped away before the Mass was done, tracking the darkness by the shudder in her skin. The trail, to her surprise and dismay, led to Turpin's tent.

It was deserted. Turpin was still at Mass. His servants and his acolytes were attending him. No one else lingered there, not even a guard to protect its contents.

There was little enough to protect. Turpin's armor on its stand; his weapons on their rack. A bed and a chest, a table and a lamp.

She paused on the threshold. Her nostrils twitched. Something here was awry. To the eye it was serene. She scented no fear, caught no stink of death. But her nape prickled.

Something ill had walked here. She tracked it by the flutter in her middle. From entrance to chest, and in the chest a silver chalice. Turpin had been celebrating the Mass with another, more ornate and less purely beautiful. This one he clearly cherished. It was old and full of sanctity. She who had held the Grail in her hands knew this for an earthly image of it, as every chalice was; but this one more than most.

A tarnish of shadow lay on it. She gazed down into it, seeking visions in the silver. They were blurred and scattered, but as she sharpened her eyes, they came clear.

She saw Roland in a wood that she recognized as Saxon.

She saw the attack on him that began as seduction. She knew the face of the creature once it was dead. Yes—yes, that was the old enemy's servant. And Roland had killed it.

The face of the one who had called up the image, she could just barely see. It seemed to be—not Turpin's. She was glad of that, but not so glad of what it seemed to be. The king's?

It was very like his, but younger. The face of a young man, hardly more than a boy. Shadow lay heavy on him.

There, she thought in a kind of sorrow, but in relief, too, that she had not misjudged so very badly after all. Turpin and the king, she would wager, were no part of this. Someone else, someone she barely knew, was the enemy's victim. The enemy himself she could not see, but she had found the way to him.

She bowed to the chalice, wrapped it in its silken shroud and laid it reverently in the chest. She was gone from the tent before Turpin returned to it. No need to speak to him, or to bring him into matters of which he was better left innocent. It was enough that his treasure should have opened the path to the enemy.

The ways of the gods were strange, their humor incalculable. Sarissa saluted it as she went hunting the king's eldest son.

He was easy to find. The last she knew, in Paderborn, he had been a rather fiercely solitary creature; apart from a few servants, he had made his way alone, and seemed content in it.

That had changed. There was a crowd about him now. Most were lesser lords and their attendants, but there were a few men of greater power as well. He held court with a kind of shy triumph, as if it were a distinction lately earned and never truly expected.

Their bond was hate. In most of them indeed it was not so strong. It was mere envy or rankling dislike. But in Pepin it was the pure metal.

Here was the source of the rumors against Roland. But she was not, just then, seeking that. She hunted for another thing, an older, darker, far stronger thing.

As she hovered on the edges of Pepin's newfound court, veiled in anonymity, Tarik's supple cat-form wove about her ankles. The sound that came out of him was not a purr, though it might have seemed so to ears less keen. It was a growl.

She looked where he wished her to look. Priests and monks were common enough near princes. These two in drab robes seemed odd in that flamboyant company. Odder yet was their pallor, and the way they moved and stood, shifting from wooden stiffness to an eerily supple sway.

Three serpents, the old enemy had had. Three servants of the Prince of Darkness, given to him to work his will. One was dead by Roland's doing. These two yet lived.

There was another behind them. Sarissa's breath caught. An ordinary man, a man of no visible distinction: small, pale, thin. A priest of the clerkly sort, not young if not terribly old. He had a cold wise face and long eyes under heavy lids. All his beauty, all his glory, were burned to ashes.

But he had taken this semblance to himself, accepted it, found the power in it—to seem so harmless, to invite men's trust. Now that she had seen him, she knew him, oh, very well indeed. She saw what he had done, how he had chosen this one of the king's children, the crooked one, the one who was vulnerable, and won him with ease that was like contempt.

And she, fool that she was, had never recognized him. She had let herself be blinded by a pair of yellow eyes. She had thought she knew the enemy in the face of his descendant. She had never looked for the old serpent himself.

The war had begun far sooner, and far more subtly than she had looked for, but there was no doubt of it. It stood before her in the Frankish prince's shadow, wearing the face of a priestly counselor.

Tarik's growl was the perfect measure of her thoughts. Had she been younger or more foolish, she would have essayed an attack, however minute her chances of succeeding. But she was too wise and too cold of heart. Even with that, it was all she could do to turn away from the enemy, to efface herself, to slip away.

CHAPTER 24

✠ ✠ ✠

R oland had lived ten days in paradise. Now, for his sins, he languished in hell.

The Companions had drawn in about him. His own men, those who had ridden and fought with him, seemed determined to ignore the tales and rumors. But they were only a few in a large army, and a siege gave men ample compass for idle talk.

Roland had begun to think that he could easily and all too simply run mad. That of course was what they wanted—whoever they were who had turned the army against him. Therefore he clung to sanity, pretended a calm he did not feel, and performed his duty as he could, and when he could, just as he always had.

Always as he went about the king's business, there were eyes on him, stares, whispers. He did his best to ignore them. But one morning a handful of days after he returned from Agua Caliente, he felt so fierce a burning of eyes that he started and spun.

It was not Ganelon or one of the demons who served him. It was a nun in a dark habit. And the fire in her glance was not hate. Not in the slightest. It was fascination.

He remembered her. She was one of the two who had come with Sarissa from Chelles. The younger one, who had been so discontented with her lot. She seemed even more so now. Her round pretty face was pinched and sour. Her flax-flower eyes were narrow.

He had smiled at her. She had taken it too much to heart. Then she had gone off among the women, and he had forgotten her.

He did not smile now. Nor did he speak. He went on his way, as incourteous as that might have been. It would have been worse if he had acknowledged her, he told himself. With what was being said of him now, his attention could only harm her.

He forgot her again once she was out of sight. The long day dragged on. He went early to his tent, looking for rest and a little solitude: Olivier was dining with the king, and the servants had been dismissed.

He undressed in the dim closeness of the tent. The sun had set, but it was still light without. The lamp's glow was wan, the scent of its oil almost overpowering. He banished it with a breath of wind from a snowfield far away. The chill of it made him shiver, but it was a shiver of pleasure.

Unwise, maybe, if anyone could have seen him raising magic—now of all times. But he was alone. On small and wicked impulse, he set the wind to swirling slowly, cooling that place, filling it with the scent of snow.

Tarik appeared on Olivier's cot, stepping neatly out of air. He was purring. When Roland lay on his own cot, the *puca* leaped across, landing with astonishing weight on Roland's middle. He curled there, a warm furred presence in the wonderful, blessed cold.

Roland woke from the first proper sleep in days. The wind was still circling, the tent's air chill. Tarik was gone. Olivier must have come back: a shadow moved across the light.

It was a smaller shadow than Olivier could have made except at high noon. Nor would Olivier have crept in beside him, pressing soft breasts against him, nibbling and licking and kissing him.

He recoiled. Sarissa was never as small or as soft or as importunate as this. Thick fair hair trailed across the coverlet where he had been lying. The plump pink-and-white body lay astonished, dimpled rump uppermost.

"Olivier is not here," Roland said: the first thing he could think of to say, and foolish in the extreme; of course she would know that.

"I don't want Olivier," the woman said—a very young woman, and petulant, glaring at him through the curtain of her hair.

By that glare he knew her. His stomach clenched. This was the nun of Chelles. Sister—Emma? Rotsvit? Rotruda. He could not see her habit at all, nor any other garment, either. He snatched up a cloak, one of Olivier's, and dropped it over her.

She curled in it like a sulky kitten. "This is magic, isn't it? It's cold in here!"

He did not answer. He pulled on shirt and drawers, tunic and hose, and boots for riding. He ran shaking fingers through his hair, making what order he could. He took up the bundle that was the nun from Chelles.

She wriggled out of the cloak and wrapped herself about him, arms locked round his neck. "If you take me out," she said, "I shall scream. And tell them you lured me here with magic and took me by force. And—"

He pried her loose and set her sharply on her feet. He did not look at the ripe young body. He covered it again, more tightly this time, with Olivier's cloak. "What do you want from me?" he demanded.

She straightened, shaking her spun-gold hair out of her face. She was quite lovely in her disheveled way; and she knew it. She let the cloak slip to bare the tip of a rose-pink breast. "Rescue me," she said. "Save me from life in a tomb."

His brows rose in pure astonishment. "You come to *me* for that?"

"Who else?" she shot back. "The stories are true, aren't they? I saw you once. You were playing with the flames in the king's campfire. Do you always do that when you're bored?"

Roland started, and flushed.

She seized on that. She was not the silly fool she had seemed, at all. "Free me," she said. "Turn me into a bird. I should like to be an eagle. Can you make me an eagle?"

"I can't do that," he said flatly.

"Why won't you?"

"I *can't*," he said.

"Of course you can! Sister Beatrice says you can be a stag, a wolf, a hawk—"

"I can't turn you into anything," he said. "I don't have the power."

"So," she said, sharp with temper. "Magic me away instead. You *can* do that. All sorcerers can."

"And what do you know of sorcerers?"

"Everything!"

She was astonishing. She was dangerous, with her lordly kin and her holy vows and her presence here.

His eyes narrowed. "Who sent you here?"

"No one," she said.

"I don't believe you."

She stamped her foot in a passion of frustration. "No one sent me! I want to be free. If you won't let me fly, then marry me. You can send me off to Brittany and forget me, except when you want to make sons. Just get me out of these chains!"

"Do you think," he asked her, "that even if the Church would release you from your vows, your kin would let you marry me of all men? They'd sooner mate you to the Devil."

"If the Devil is rich enough," she said, "and has lands enough, and will repay my dowry to the Church and dower my sister in my place, who is the most mealy-mouthed little saint you ever saw, my kin will happily match me with him."

Roland struggled for calm. "Then you should find yourself a willing man, and persuade him."

"If you say no," she said perfectly reasonably, "I will scream."

"You will not," said Roland.

"Magic me away, then," she said, relentless. "No one will ever guess you did it."

"No," Roland said, flat and hard and well past any pretense of patience.

"Not even for my soul's sake?"

"Your soul is best served by your staying in orders."

Her eyes went perfectly wild. She flung herself toward his weapons. She had Durandal half drawn before he caught her, her small hands on that great hilt, and the blade shimmering in the lamplight.

He spun her about, away from the sword, falling in a tangle to the carpeted floor. She twisted beneath him, tearing at his drawers.

They tumbled up against a pair of booted feet. The voice that spoke above them was not Olivier's. "Good evening," said Sarissa.

Rotruda froze. Roland extricated himself from her softly clinging grip. He had never been more glad to be caught *in flagrante*.

"Sarissa," he said. "Thank God. This woman—"

Rotruda began to sob convulsively. "He—he—he forced—he made me—he—"

"Stop that," Sarissa said. Rotruda gaped at her. "Find your clothes and get out."

"He tried to *force* me!"

"That man," said Sarissa with acid sweetness, "is no more capable of forcing a woman than a holy angel. Now go, before I lay a curse on you."

"You can't do that!"

"I can turn you into a toad," Sarissa said. "Go!"

Rotruda's eyes sharpened. "Can you turn me into an eagle?"

"Not in this lifetime," said Sarissa. "Will you go, or will you not?"

"I won't," Rotruda said. "I want to be free. I'll fly if I can. Or crawl. Or you can magic me away."

"Or?"

"Or I'll tell everybody you're even more of a witch than he is."

Sarissa leaned in close. "You will do nothing," she said. "Say nothing, see nothing, remember nothing." Her hand flicked. Rotruda gasped and crumpled.

Roland caught her without thinking. He stared at Sarissa.

She stared back. "You should have done this," she said. "Why did you not?"

"I didn't think," Roland said.

"No," she said. "You didn't." She took the bare plump body from his arms, with no more ceremony than if it had been a bundle of linen. "I'll see to her."

"And imprison her again?"

"Mother Abbess knows," said Sarissa, "as does Sister

Dhuoda. What can be done for this one, they will do. And if that is to find her a complaisant husband, they will do it."

"Does she know that?"

"I doubt it," Sarissa said. "She's a child. Children only know what they want to know."

"I am glad you came," Roland said after a slight pause.

"I should think so," she said.

She took Rotruda away. Nor did she come back, though Roland waited. She had seemed angry, somehow. He did not know why—or maybe he did not want to know. He had done nothing to offend her, that he knew of; and he had certainly not betrayed her with this child.

She did not come the next night, either, nor the one after that. He saw nothing of her, or of Rotruda, who seemed to have been sequestered among the nuns. Nor did rumor spread of either rape or sorcery. That danger at least they had averted.

The nights were long, and his arms were empty. For he would not go to Sarissa, either. For her name and her safety's sake, he let her be. Whatever rumors clung to him, whatever tales men told, none would attach to her. He would make sure of it.

Duty was his refuge. On a day like every other day of that siege, not long after Sister Rotruda came to him in the night, he stood behind his king while Charles received an embassy under a banner of truce. The leader of the embassy widened eyes round the court. The emir Al-Arabi had been left, they thought, in Barcelona, holding it as best he could, in Charles' name and in the name of the Caliph from Baghdad. And yet here he was riding out of Saragossa, looking as if he had never been a friend to the Franks at all.

Roland paid little heed to the words they spoke. They were the same words that had been spoken over and over again. When Al-Arabi spoke them they were sharper, for he had begun all this. He had been the first ally, the one of them all who had seemed loyal.

Now he too had turned against the king. He had come to demand that the Franks leave Saragossa and depart from Spain.

"It was you who brought us here," Charles said. "What brings you to repent?"

"I acted in haste," Al-Arabi said. "I failed to consult my people. That I regret. We ask you to go, my lord. This is not your war. My fault that I brought you here; my duty, now, to send you away."

"And if we won't go?" Charles inquired.

"As great as your army is," said Al-Arabi, "it's far from its own lands. It's stripped all the forage within a day's ride. Its provisions are beginning to dwindle. There will be none from my domains, and none from those of my allies. Whereas Saragossa is a great city, and strong. It can feed itself for a year and drink from its wells, while you starve outside the walls."

Charles' face betrayed no despair, but others near him were not as strong of will. Surely his lords and counselors had been aware of the truth; but to hear it spoken made it more nearly real. They had but to look to see the city barred to them, the river fouled by their presence, the land stripped bare under the merciless sun.

"If you go now," said Al-Arabi, "you go with some pretense of victory. You came in honor, and fought as you could. Now it is time for you to return to your own country."

"No man commands me." Charles' voice was so low that Roland wondered if anyone else heard it. The easy, amiable semblance was gone. His eyes were fixed on Al-Arabi's face. Roland had seen that color in enchanters' fires, bluer than blue, too bright almost to bear.

When Charles spoke for all to hear, he sounded calm, untroubled. "I thank you, sir. I will think on what you have said."

Al-Arabi bowed. "Think, indeed, lord king. But not too long. This land will not support your army for much longer."

"I will consider that," Charles said civilly.

The emir was dismissed. He went without apparent offense, walking with his retinue down the long silent line of Franks. Not one man spoke. Not one offered either welcome or hostility. They all simply watched him go.

Inside Roland, something took root and grew. The emir's words had sown the seed. The endless, useless siege had nurtured it. Now it bore fruit.

It was not a thing he could act on as yet. He must, like the king, take time to think, and consider all the sides of it. But his heart knew what he had to do. Whatever the cost. Whatever came of it.

He spoke to no one of what he intended. He waited a day, then two and three. Charles also had kept silent, though his counselors pressed him to decide: whether to continue the siege or to break it and go. The engines continued to batter the unyielding walls. Men made sallies now and then, met flights of arrows or streams of boiling water or oil, fell back. Rumor spread that the king was contemplating a full attack, that he would storm the walls with engines and ladders. Yet another rumor whispered that he would win the city by treachery; that somehow an ally within the city would undertake to open a postern and so admit the Franks to the city.

Roland saw no proof of either. He did see men tunneling near the walls, and new engines readied to batter at the stones. Charles had doubled the force of archers. They shot at any who showed his head over the battlements, and had driven all but the most foolhardy enemy into hiding.

This could go on, as Al-Arabi had said, until the army starved. And what had Roland ever done but ride out foraging, accompany an embassy on a charge that failed, and stand guard over the king? Had he been named champion for this? What was Durandal for, then, if not to play a part in the winning of Spain? It had tasted Spanish blood, but precious little of it. Most of this war had been march and siege. There had been few battles, and none with any glory in it.

Enough, he thought.

The day he chose was distinguished from the rest by a drift of cloud in the waking sky, and a whisper of coolness—furnace-hot still by the measure of Francia, but distinct to bodies that had known for so long the true fierce heat of Spain. He took it as an omen. He attended Mass with the king as he had done every morning since he came back to the army. The whispers against him seemed little deterred by that, but he found it comforting. Nor did he ever see Sister Rotruda, nor the other nuns, either. They were keeping to themselves. And that, he thought, was well for them all.

Today he prayed with more than his usual fervor. He heard the words that Turpin chanted, truly listened to them, rather than letting them wash over him in a blessed flood.

Plead my cause, O Lord, with them that strive with me: fight against them that fight against me.

Take hold of shield and buckler, and stand up for mine help.

Draw out thy spear, and stop the way against them that persecute me: say unto my soul, I am thy salvation.

Even the Mass favored him, and the clouds thickening, veiling the sun, softening its strength. He left the king to Olivier's guardianship, murmuring of a need for rest, for he had been at his post since before dawn. Olivier eyed him a bit oddly, but let him go. His heart twinged. He should have shared this with his battle-brother. But if he was going to do it, he must do it alone.

It was no simple matter to arm himself without aid, but he managed. When his armor was all on, shield and spear slung, he drew Durandal from his father's scabbard, which he had never quite got round to discarding. He set the sword before him like a cross, knelt and pressed his brow to the cold smoothness of the blade. It sang to him, soft and clear. It knew what it was for. Was it not time, then, that he used it as it was meant to be used?

The sword's song wove with another. On his breast the amulet burned and sang. The note they wrought between them was as keen as the sword and as ardent as the coin. It brought him to his feet. It made his heart strong, and set fire in his blood.

The sword protested when he sheathed it. It wanted, needed blood. "Soon," he promised it. It was not pleased, but it subsided. He was smiling as he left the tent, his first smile in long days. It was edged with steel, and hungry for blood.

CHAPTER 25

⊠ ⊠ ⊠

In the wake of Al-Arabi's departure, the pounding of the siege-engines had redoubled. There were more riders crossing and recrossing the lines than there had been before, and companies of men moving from place to place, in part to aid the siege, in part to confuse the enemy.

One armored man on a grey horse attracted little enough attention, even when he rode past the king's council behind the rearmost rank of siege-engines, until some marked the device on his shield. The golden hawk had flown high in battle before this. At first a ragged cheer followed him; then men remembered the tales they had heard.

None of them ventured to stand in his way. He was riding toward the walls—to inspect them, perhaps. It was only good sense that he should be armed and in full armor.

But Turpin, watching from amid the king's council, saw Roland and began to be alarmed. Roland had been too quiet of late. Brooding, Turpin thought. Those were ill things that were being said of him; he would have to be made of stone to be impervious to them.

Roland rode past the foremost lines under the hail of missiles, into the no-man's-land beneath the walls. It was not so far from the king as all that—just out of arrow's range—but with the engines between and the enemy's archers on the walls, it might have been the width of a world.

The engines nearest him faltered as men saw him there. A thin rain of arrows fell from above. None found its target, nor did he appear to take notice.

He sat still in the grey stallion's saddle. Veillantif stood motionless. The arrows thinned and ceased their falling. The silence was spreading along the wall. They were all, both Franks and Spaniards, staring at Roland who sat his horse alone where no other man dared go. It looked, thought Turpin, as if he would raise the powers everyone said he had, and smite the wall into rubble.

He moved suddenly, like a flash of lightning: drawing the shimmer of his sword, raising it to catch the sun. Not only Turpin gasped; but the walls did not come tumbling down. His voice rang out, too clear and too strong to be altogether mortal.

He spoke in Arabic, but a soft voice rendered his words in Frankish for the king and for those nearest him to hear. Turpin started like a deer. The Lady Sarissa was standing there, in no perceptible fear for her life. She was dressed and armed as a man, but Turpin could never have mistaken that voice.

Her face in the shadow of a Frankish helmet was still, her voice quiet. And yet somehow, in that calm and that stillness, every bit of Roland's passion blazed like a fire in the dark.

"Saragossa!" he cried. "Saragossa! You skulk in your walls. You cower in your citadel. Have you no champion? Is there no one who will come out to fight for you?"

The walls were silent. Turpin saw no movement there. Wise, that. This could be a trap, after all.

Roland spoke again, clearer and stronger than before. "Saragossa! I am the champion of Spain. I won your emir's test of strength; I carry his sword. I slew the bull in the barren hills. Have you a warrior like me? Would he dare to face me?"

"He's gone mad," one of Charles' counselors said.

They murmured among themselves, with much headshaking and clicking of tongues. But one of them was silent. Turpin might not have noticed, save that he was watching Sarissa, and she had turned her eyes from Roland. She was watching the one who stood somewhat apart, who did not speak. His whole spirit seemed fixed on the rider beneath the walls. Maybe it was the flame of the sword. Maybe it was the sound of that voice, taunting the people of Saragossa in their own tongue, with somewhat of the cadence of the muezzin's cry.

Ganelon had the look of a man in the midst of a revelation. His eyes were as wide as Turpin had ever seen them, strikingly dark in his pale face. It was as if he had never seen Roland before—or never known what he was.

And why would the king's counselor care who or what Roland might be?

It was the same expression, Turpin realized with a small but potent shock, that Roland had worn a year and more ago in Paderborn, the first day Ganelon came back to court. Roland had been appalled by the sight of this man whom he could never have seen before. He had acted strangely, and said strange things; then he had gone away. Turpin had wondered at it for a while, then forgotten it, since he had never had an explanation. Somehow, it was beginning again—whatever was between those two.

Sarissa's eyes flicked from Ganelon's face to the rider beneath the walls. In the same instant, Ganelon's eyes flicked likewise. Roland had fallen silent. Shapes moved on the battlement: heads in helmets, heads in turbans. One bold man stood up so that he could be seen clearly. Turpin recognized the voice.

"My lord Count," Al-Arabi said in his stiff but fluent Latin. "Are you asking me to take back the sword?"

"It is not yours to take back," Roland replied in the same language.

"If you know that," said Al-Arabi, "you know what you are champion of. And this is not—"

"If you have a champion for Saragossa," Roland said, "I will fight him. Victor takes the city. Vanquished cedes the war."

"Did your king send you?" asked Al-Arabi.

Roland did not answer that.

"We have said all that we intend to say," Al-Arabi said. "You are brave, lord Count, and there is no better warrior in Francia. But this war is not to be settled in single combat."

"Coward," Roland said. "You know your man would lose."

"I am not to be provoked," said the emir.

"Is there no brave man in Saragossa?" Roland called out. "Is there no man who will fight for the honor of his city?"

Round about the king, the muttering of counselors had grown louder. "Shall we send someone after him, sire? This is humiliating. This is—"

Turpin stopped listening except to note the king's silence. A smaller gate was opening within the great gate of Saragossa.

There was confusion on the walls, the emir turning, gesticulating, but Roland seemed to have forgotten him. His laughter rang across the ranks of besiegers.

The man who rode out was mounted on a Spanish charger, armored in the fashion of the infidels but not turbaned—he wore a simple helmet, as the Christian Spaniards did. Turpin recognized the splendid black horse even as the rider spoke in a battlefield bellow. "My lord of the Franks! Do you question my courage?"

"Yours, O slayer of bulls," Roland said, "never. Will you fight for Saragossa?"

"I will fight for Spain," said Diego, whom Turpin had last seen in the bullring of Agua Caliente.

"That was to be my task," Roland said.

"Was it?" Diego bowed in the saddle. "You are more than I think you know. But you will not lead the Franks into Saragossa."

"I will defend our honor," Roland said.

"It does break the monotony of the siege," Diego granted him. "As you can well see from the flurry above, I am not here on any lord's behalf. But if you will, we may test one another. Sieges are dull and inglorious enough. Let us lighten this one as we may."

That was adroitly done, Turpin thought. It cost Saragossa nothing if Roland won, but it gave him the fight he was so eager for.

But Roland was not a fool. "I am not here to play at war. I have come to fight or die."

"I am not entitled to take your life, my lord," Diego said. He said it flat and clear. He bowed and withdrew, leaving Roland astonished in the shadow of the wall.

Behind the line of the siege-engines, Charles spoke at last. "Turpin. Fetch him. Preserve his honor as best you may, but get him back to me."

Turpin hardly waited to hear the last of it. He was off at a run. There were others behind him: Olivier, the Lady Sarissa.

The wall was no more than arrow's flight distant, but it seemed an endless way. Roland made no move to ride out of danger. He sat his stallion with his sword on his knee, and waited—to be shot, to be struck down by a flung stone, who knew?

Well before Turpin and the rest reached him, the postern opened again. In the thunder of drums and the braying of trumpets, shrilling their battle-cry, a company of Saracens charged toward the lone horseman.

Roland's laughter sounded above even that, and the clear song of Durandal as he whirled it about his head. Veillantif rocked to his hindlegs and leaped forward. Saracens engulfed them both; but there was no mistaking the rise and fall of the sword.

Turpin barely had breath to speak, but he found it somewhere, roaring across the lines: "Forward! Forward, you sons of whores! *Montjoie! Montjoie!*"

He was unarmed—he had been at Mass, and then in council; he was still in episcopal robes. He snatched a sword out of a soldier's hand and a spear from another, and flung himself into the fight.

That was an army pouring out of Saragossa, giving them battle at last—and not at the orders of the emir, either, or the lord of the city. Those stood together atop the gate. For a while they tried to call their men back, but the warriors of Allah were deaf to them.

It was close quarters, up against the wall, with the siege-engines behind and the bulk of the Franks unready or unable to come to the fight. Charles, like the infidel commanders, was taken aback, but he rallied sooner than they. He called for his horse and his Companions and rode down into the melee.

Roland was in the thick of it. Turpin hacked and stabbed his way through, aware of two strong forces at his back. One was as familiar as his own right arm, Olivier singing a bawdy song as he fought. The other fought with flashing speed and breathtaking skill, wielding a sword as if she had been born to it. It was not, just then, astonishing that Sarissa could fight like a man, who dressed as one more often than perhaps she wanted Turpin to know.

The gate had shut behind the last of the infidels. But there would be people within, surely, waiting to take them back again. Turpin, trapped in the middle of the fight, divided his mind between defending himself and making what headway he could toward the gate. It might at last be vulnerable; it might open if they feigned to be men of the city.

It was a small enough hope, but it was the best they had had since the siege began. Turpin needed Roland for it—or Sarissa. Someone who spoke the infidels' tongue.

The fight was fierce. Many abandoned their horses, or were unhorsed, and grappled hand to hand. Roland kept the saddle by skill and by the flashing power of the sword; he was hard beset, the focus of the strongest attack. They must know that if they took him down, they dealt a stunning blow to the honor and the courage of the Franks.

He was singing as he fought. His sword sang the descant. Between them they wrought a deadly harmony.

Turpin's borrowed sword notched on a Saracen helmet and broke. The spear was lost, he did not remember where. The way back was barred by struggling men. The way ahead was full of flashing steel. He was closer to the gate than he had been, but not enough. And he had only his fists to win his way there.

He saw the blade fall, and veered, whirling, but the fight was too close. He could not escape it.

A second blade caught it and beat it aside. Sarissa struck down the swordsman, swooped, wrenched the sword from his hand. She tossed it toward Turpin.

There was no time for thanks or courtesy, nor even for astonishment. By the fortune of battle, the way to the gate was almost open. Turpin sprang toward it.

A wall of flesh and steel closed in about him. The enemy were falling back, were retreating to the gate. "Break through!" Turpin roared. "Franks! Beat them down! Break into the city!"

They gathered as they could, but the Saracens had drawn back too quickly. They defended the gate with all the strength that was left to them. Those in the rear won their way to it and vanished within. Those just ahead of them followed, and so to the front, like water draining from a broken vessel.

Turpin flung the Franks against the last of them, driving for the gate, but as soon as the last enemy had leaped or fallen within, it slammed shut. Turpin threw himself at it. The gate rocked but held. Bars grated into place.

They had slain a fair number of Saracens, and there were wounded to take captive, but they had gained nothing of substance. They had not broken into Saragossa.

CHAPTER 26

✠ ✠ ✠

"And what," the king demanded, "did you hope to accomplish by that?"

Roland knelt as a penitent at Charles' feet. He had come straight from the battle, covered with dust and blood, limping from a wound or two or three. Only his sword was clean. He had seen to that first of all, as a good swordsman should do.

He was profoundly and quite unreasonably happy. It was difficult to suppress the smile; he hoped he was not grinning too foolishly up at his king.

Charles cuffed him hard enough to make his head ring. "Have you completely lost your wits?"

"Sire," Roland said, "I think I may have."

"It's a wise man who knows his own folly," Charles said. His face was stern, but his eyes had begun to glint. "What were you doing? Getting yourself killed?"

"It would seem so, sire," Roland said.

"You failed," said Charles. He pulled Roland to his feet and examined him thoroughly. "And hardly a scratch on you. God loves you."

"Or hates me," Roland said, but without bitterness. "I gained little enough in the venture. Men are wounded. I—"

"There are no Frankish dead," Charles said, "and a full score of Saracens fallen. Most of those, I'm told, fell at your hand."

"Not all," said Roland, "or even most."

"Let men tell their tales," Charles said. "You go wash. Rest. Come to your senses. I'll speak with you again come morning."

"He let you off light," Olivier said as the servants finished filling the great copper basin that the king had sent. The water was barely warm, but that was not so ill, in this heat.

Roland let himself be stripped rather unceremoniously and tipped into the basin. Olivier, like the king, was not light-handed. He paid little heed to bruises and minor wounds. There were no greater ones. "And that's the good fortune that attends madmen," his battle-brother muttered. "Not that I mind a good fight, at all, but whatever possessed you to ride out there alone?"

"It was a good fight," Roland said. "Wasn't it?"

"It was splendid," Olivier admitted, "once we all got into it. Did you honestly think you could win Saragossa all by yourself?"

"I'm supposed to be a champion," Roland said. "But what have I done to prove it? What am I for, if not to do what I did?"

"To fight for the king, as the king commands," said Olivier, who had never yet refused a fight for any cause.

By accident or intent, his fingers dug deep into the worst of the bruises, the one along Roland's side. Ribs were cracked, Roland thought distantly. Maybe broken. The pain was exquisite.

It cleared his head a little. The dizzy exhilaration of battle had begun at last to fade. "I'm not sorry I did it," he said.

"You probably should be," said Olivier. "Though it seems it didn't hurt you with the army. They're starting to think you're not the Devil's firstborn—maybe only a greater minion."

"That is a good thing," Roland said, sliding down in the water. Once the wounds and scratches had stopped stinging, it was a delicious pleasure. He only needed—

No; he had separated himself from her. For her sake. That had not changed because he had done a mad thing, a thing that Franks could understand.

*   *   *

"So," said Ganelon. "So, indeed."

Pepin had been deep in study of a language so ancient that its name was forgotten in this age of the world, when a clamor drew him blinking and stumbling out of the old man's tent. Men were running, shouting. There was fighting by the city's walls. At first he thought his father had broken the siege at last, but this was a skirmish only.

He had but to follow the fierce fixity of Ganelon's stare to find the center of it. Roland. Of course. Who else would, as Pepin learned a little after, have ridden alone against the whole of that strongly guarded city?

Ganelon watched every moment of that battle with eyes as rigidly intent as a hawk's on its prey.

"Master," Pepin said when it was over, when Roland had been led away and they had gone inside the tent again, "did you make him do it?"

Ganelon spread a clean sheet of parchment for one of the king's endless, niggling letters, and took up a freshly trimmed pen. Pepin held his breath. An answer would come, or it would not. He could never be certain which it would be.

This time Ganelon chose to speak. "He did nothing against his will."

"What did he do, then?"

Ganelon, it seemed, was in a mood to suffer questions, though his replies were never direct. "He proved that I have been blind and a fool."

Pepin widened his eyes. "You, master? You would never—"

"Do not flatter me," Ganelon said, soft and cold. "I am not a king, to be open to such blandishments. I cast my vision elsewhere, and reckoned myself clever. And there was he, full before me, with that of all swords in his hand, and all the tales that have been told of him. Merlin's get. *Merlin's.* And I dismissed him. He has power, boy. Be sure of it. He was able to deceive me."

That, his tone said, was a very rare thing. He was not angry. If anything, he was amused.

Pepin's heart was sinking fast. This was his enemy. Not Ganelon's. Yet Ganelon was claiming Roland for his own.

"Betrayal begotten of betrayal," Ganelon murmured.

"Even the face—such was that other, the child of my spirit, when he was young." He rounded on Pepin, so swift that Pepin gasped. "The basin! Fetch it. I need your eyes."

Pepin's feet dragged, but not too much. He did not dare defy the master. He knew what he would be asked to do. Only his heart could resist it. His eyes had to see what they were commanded to see.

"Borel," Ganelon sighed. "*He* slew Borel. Of course. Oh, I was a fool! So much power, so skillfully warded—he is a true child of his forefather."

"Will you kill him?" Pepin asked.

Ganelon's glance was pure contempt.

But he is mine! Pepin wanted to cry. He bit his tongue till it bled.

Ganelon had forgotten him. The two silent servants were there, though a moment ago they had not been. "Watch the hawk's child," Ganelon commanded them. "Do not harm him; above all do not let him discover your presence."

They bowed low and went to do his bidding. If any fear touched them, any memory of their brother's death, they showed no sign of it.

Ganelon seemed darkly pleased, but restless, too. He paced the confines of the tent, shaken for once out of his stillness. "This is a sign," he said. "The time is coming. The champion, the sword . . . how blind I was! How complacent. How easily duped by a child's magic."

Pepin set his lips together and kept silent.

But Ganelon did not spare him for that. "You did badly to incite the army against him—but it will serve us well enough. They fear him already. In time, when I have his soul in my hand, they will destroy him."

"I did as I saw fit," Pepin said stiffly. Outrage was his refuge against the other thing, the shock that Ganelon had seen everything that he did, and known its intent.

Ganelon's dark eyes pierced him through. "You are young. Your judgment is weak. For that I suffer your folly."

"Do you remember, my master," Pepin said through clenched teeth, "that my father is king here."

Ganelon bowed with deepest irony. "My lord prince, I do not ever forget it."

*   *   *

Roland had not meant to sleep. Once he was bathed and dressed in a clean tunic, he submitted to Olivier's strong arm, and lay on his cot. Olivier refused to go away until he slept. He shut his eyes and feigned the flutter of a snore.

When he opened his eyes again, the light in the tent had shifted. The lamps were lit. The walls were dark. Sarissa sat on her heels beside the cot, still as a stone image.

Roland's whole heart and soul yearned to surge across the space between them and clasp her in his arms. Such sense as he had kept him where he was, lying on his side, drinking in the sight of her. In a moment he must be cold; he must consider her honor. He must send her away. But not quite yet.

She stirred and roused as if from a dream. All at once she was there, the whole of her, focused on him with a fierce, almost angry intensity. "What you did," she said, "was the most profoundly foolish—"

"It was very satisfying," Roland said.

"You're mad."

"Everyone's saying that." He stretched, wincing as his body remembered all its bruises. "I did one thing well. I gave the army a reprieve from boredom."

"It won't matter in the end," she said.

He sat up so abruptly his head spun. "You don't care," he said. "Do you? You don't care if we win or lose this war."

She did not answer him, but she did not deny the accusation, either.

Anger gusted through him. It was no more reasonable than the impulse that had taken him to the walls. It came from the same place inside him. "For a year," he said, as low and level as he could trust his voice to be, "I have carried your sword. I have fought precious few battles with it. I have seen this war—which you helped to instigate—dribble away into nothing. There has been no call for a champion. Why, then? Why trouble at all?"

She did not answer that, either. Somehow he had not expected her to.

"I was never meant to fight for Spain," he said. "Was I? This is something else. I'm meant for another purpose."

Her eyes lowered to her hands. They were quiet on her thighs, her body at ease. But he could feel the tension in her.

"Is there another war?" he asked. "Do you have an enemy? Or have you rejected me because I'm not my king?"

Nothing. Roland was the silent one, the one who spoke only when he must. It was strange to be battering at her with words, but meeting only that wall of stillness. She was as recalcitrant as Saragossa.

Roland hissed in frustration. He would never be so rude as to dismiss a lady, but there was nothing to prevent him from dismissing himself. He left her there without a word, rose and dressed and went out, it little mattered where.

The king was still at dinner. There were dancers tonight, and a troupe of jugglers from Francia—nothing Spanish, nothing Saracen, all pure Frankish, as if to put out of his mind all memory of this intractable country. Roland found a place that was none too conspicuous, found wine, bread, roast meat and pungent cheese.

The men near him were either asleep or oblivious. There was an odd comfort in that, in being unknown for once. This must be what it was to be a plain fighting man of the Franks. It was pleasant, and somewhat disconcerting.

Roland was hungry—starving. He ate till he was sated, washing it down with more wine than he was used to. He could sleep here, he thought. No one would mind, or much notice. By morning surely she would be gone from his tent.

He still loved her. He wanted her—oh, terribly. But he could not endure that silence. Whatever she wanted of him, she should trust him enough to speak.

That was it, he thought. Trust. She did not trust anyone, not even a man she professed to love.

That was her sorrow. He would not make it his own.

CHAPTER 27

✠ ✠ ✠

Sarissa was all too well aware of Roland's anger and frustration. Still she held her tongue, though it caught at her heart to do it. He was a child. He did not know what she knew, nor was he ready to know it.

There were greater things afoot than he could understand. She could feel it in the earth and in the spirits of the men who slept on it. The enemy was awake and beginning to move.

Deep in the night, she sent a messenger. It was not Tarik. Tarik disapproved strongly of her choices. She sent a lesser creature, a spirit of air, swift and, for its kind, diligent. It swore a great oath to convey her message exactly, in the very voice in which she spoke it.

In the morning the king's army woke differently. The skirmish had given them hope again, but the return to the drudgery of siege struck them the harder for the respite. Their mood was dark and turning ugly.

Charles' council was a mirror of his army. "We are not going to break into Saragossa," one said for them all. "Such bravado as we saw yesterday may delight the men, but it gains nothing. Those walls will not fall for aught that we can do."

"We may bring them down in time," said the man beside him. "But Spain is set against us. There is no hope of a clear victory. Shall we abandon Italy and Francia and the Saxon lands to devote ourselves to this conquest? Can we, sire?"

"You advise that I retreat?" Charles asked mildly.

Around the circle, faces blanched. Charles was smiling, but it was not a comfortable smile. Not at all.

They were prudent men, but they were not cowards. "Yes," said the chief of them, "though I would not call it retreat. I would call it a return to lands where we are welcome, and abandonment of allies who abandoned us. We came in good faith. Let us depart in the same spirit."

"Retreat," Charles said.

"Then we stay," said Turpin in the same mild tone as the king. "We shorten our rations. We drive the engines night and day. We break Saragossa. However long it takes. Whatever it costs us."

"Don't mock me," said Charles. "I can see what's in front of my face. There are no good choices here. We needed the Spaniards to succeed. They all deserted us. With even the Governor of Gerona and Barcelona gone over to the enemy, we're alone in hostile country. If we persist, we'll be fighting armies in back of us as well as in the city."

"Then we'll withdraw?" asked a lordly prelate.

"In good order," Charles said, "and at our leisure."

Sarissa, listening on the edges, marked the sigh of relief that ran through the circle. It spread, passed from man to man, till the army itself seemed to stretch and sigh and stand a little straighter.

Good soldiers knew when to withdraw as well as when to advance. They had all seen what had taken the council some while to admit. Once Al-Arabi had gone to the enemy, the war was lost.

And that, she thought, made Roland's gesture even more pointed. He had tried to forge a victory in the only way left. The enemy had refused the challenge.

The Franks had hated Spain before. Now they despised it.

She would wager that Roland had known what would come of his recklessness. Roland was only a fool as far as it suited him.

"You forced my hand," Charles said.

Roland was alone with the king. There were guards in

plenty, attendants in multitudes, but they were on the river's bank. Charles had breasted the current to an islet, a bit of sandy outcropping that sustained a twisted fragment of tree. He reclined there, a cloth that he had brought wrapped about his head.

Roland, who had had no such foresight, perched on a corner of the king's cloth, knees clasped to chest. For no good reason, he remembered what Sarissa had said of him when he sat so. A bogle on a hearth.

The sun was as hot as fire, beating down on his back and shoulders. Charles' fair skin was heavily freckled from days and weeks of it. He lay at ease on his back, hands clasped behind his head, but his words went straight to the heart. "You made me resolve this war."

"Sire—" said Roland.

Charles cut him off. "No excuses. Only tell me why."

"Because it was necessary."

"You are entitled to judge that?"

"Am I not your champion?"

"At my pleasure," the king said.

There was nothing to say to that. Roland set his lips together and gazed out across the river. The far bank, past the walls of Saragossa, had been green and lovely once. The army had stripped it bare.

"There are times," Charles said, "when I wonder. When rumors buzz in my ear—when tales heap one on another, and every man seems to have some account of the strange or the uncanny . . . I wonder then, sir. What shall I believe?"

Roland was very calm. The only marvel had been that Charles had not spoken of this before. "You've always known what I am," he said.

"Have I? Have I truly? All of it?"

"As much as I myself know," Roland said.

Charles looked long and hard at him. Roland bore that scrutiny, which after all he had earned. At length Charles said, "I trust you. You're hardly the most comforting of men: you're wild, you're fey, you raise hackles with a glance—but you've never lied to me. I think you are an honest—whatever you are."

"A man," Roland said.

"Not entirely. Men can't do what you can do."

"Will you cast me out?" Roland asked.

Charles sat up, swept a hand across and cuffed him. "Puppy! What do you take me for?"

"A king," said Roland through the ringing in his ears, "whose people have turned against one of his Companions. If they believe that I've corrupted you—"

"It's far too late for that," Charles said. "I'd be no kind of king if I dismissed a loyal servant because my people are spreading hysteria in his name. Serve me as you've served me since you came to court, be loyal as you've been loyal from the beginning, and I'll keep you by me as I always have. But if you ride out again to challenge a whole nation to single combat—ask my leave first."

"Yes, sire," Roland said faintly. "But the men—"

"The men will see that you have my trust. If they're wise they'll forget their fears. If not . . . they'll have me to face. I will hear no ill of you. And you will do nothing to invite it."

"Yes, sire," Roland said again, more strongly.

"And," said Charles, "I will keep the promise I made when you first came to me. I will not ask you to serve me save as a man may."

"I release you from that promise," said Roland. And as Charles shook his head, stirring to speak again, he said, "Don't bind yourself, sire. You may need more than my good right arm. And now that the men know—"

"The men know nothing but rumors," Charles said.

"They know an enchanter serves you. That may prove useful, sire. As may I."

Charles was a king. He used what came to hand, whatever it might be. Just as he could be a good Christian and still declare friendship with the infidel Caliph in Baghdad, so he could see the wisdom in Roland's words. "You are certain?" he asked.

And that, Roland thought, was why he loved this man. Charles took thought for his people. He asked leave, even where he need not.

Roland nodded. It was half a bow. "I am certain, sire," he said.

"Then I'll remember," said Charles.

CHAPTER 28

⊠ ⊠ ⊠

The day they broke the siege of Saragossa, clouds veiled the sun. The wind blew, if not cold, then less searing hot than it had for so long. The Franks took it as an omen, a remembrance of their cool and rainy country.

The people of the city lined the walls to watch them go. There was no jeering, no mockery. Only silence. The Franks sang as they formed in their long column, mounted, lifted banners, rode away. Behind them they had scoured the earth of every living thing. There would be no harvest for Saragossa.

This was a darker joy than had brought them into Spain, but it was joy nonetheless. They were going home. The war had failed, but their honor was intact. They had done as they agreed to do. The Spaniards had broken their word and so dishonored themselves.

That was the song the Franks sang as they rode: the song of Spain's dishonor. They sang it in all the languages of all their nations. Some even sang in the Spaniards' tongue, and a few in Arabic. It was a soldiers' song, fit to burn delicate ears.

Sarissa, who had heard worse, was glad to be riding in man's clothes on a rather plain Frankish cob—for Tarik refused to carry her while she persisted in what he considered to be her folly of mistrusting Roland. It would have mortified the rough troopers in the line before and behind, if they had known what she was.

She was as glad as they that the siege had ended. Now, she thought, the real war would come. Already in spirit she could see the loom of mountains, feel the cool air streaming down from snowfields that lingered even in summer. If she closed her eyes, she could forget this sun-parched plain and see another landscape altogether.

It happened that she was riding between the Bretons and a company of men from the lands near Paris in Francia. Just ahead of those rode the women, both the king's mistresses and the few nuns who had come with the army. Her erstwhile companions from Chelles were riding there, mute and demure beside the formidable Sister Dhuoda.

Sister Rotruda was clenched upon herself, huddled on the back of her mule. Dhuoda's cold blue eye caught Sarissa's. The elder nun nodded very slightly. It was seen to, that nod said. Rotruda would be looked after.

Sarissa sighed faintly. For a moment she allowed herself to remember the abbey of Chelles: the chilly quiet of the cloister, the echo of sweet high voices in the chapel. She had been almost content there in that house of women. In another world, perhaps, in another life . . .

She shook her head and sighed. Not in this world, and not in any world that touched on it. That God was not her God, that rite not hers. She was born to one older and higher.

The world of men and war closed in about her. The wind was freshening. It bore a scent of rain. The Franks breathed deep and sighed, as if for this little while they had come home.

Roland was riding in the van with the king, rather than commanding the rear as was his wont. He had been close by Charles of late—conveying a message to the army, and guarding the king from the old enemy. The men had taken note of the king's favor. Wise that they were in Charles' ways, they understood what he had done. Rather more seemed to find it acceptable than not.

And that, she sensed, was not to the enemy's liking. Now that she knew who he was, she could feel him like a crawling just under the skin. He could by the force of his magic have turned that whole army against Roland, but he did not choose to do it. He was biding his time.

Or perhaps he was preoccupied with greater matters. She had been aware of things passing in the night, wings against the moon, shadows in starlight. Her own messenger had not returned, nor had there been a response, but that was as she had expected. What she had set in train was begun long before.

She would have been glad of something to do. If Roland had not been such a fool as to turn his back on her—

And need he do that now? Between his own headlong act and the king's clear favor, maybe he would reckon himself safe again. Her bed had been lonely these past nights, her arms empty. She had caught herself dreaming of him even in daylight—she, who was not one to lose her wits over any man.

The rain closed in a little after noon. By nightfall it had diminished to a few sudden squalls and a flurry of clouds streaming away eastward. Though the sun had set some while since, the western sky shimmered still with rose and gold.

The king's army camped on a long hill by a trickle of river. There had been no attacks, though they had seen riders at a distance: scouts or spies, sent no doubt to be certain that the Franks were riding homeward. The king had ordered a war camp, with walls of earth about it and guards set on it. Even so, the mood was as light as it had been since they left Saragossa. The men might even have welcomed an ambush. It would have given them an excuse to strike back against the Spaniards.

It was a strange mingling of joy and anger, gladness and hunger for revenge. Sarissa tasted it as she passed through the camp, sweet, underlaid with a gagging bitterness.

The joy was their own. The anger . . . was it stronger than it should have been? Was it darker?

That was one of the enemy's arts and ancient skills. He had never created anything. Like his master of the darkness, he could only misshape and destroy. Whatever he wrought, he wrought of what he found before him. He could use this anger, could twist it to his own ends.

As she walked, a shadow in shadow, she cupped light in

her hands: some from the last gleam of sunset, some from stars and moon, some from firelight and men's hearts. She gathered it all together and sowed it like seed. Where it fell, anger faded. Darkness brightened. The air was cleaner, and not only from the rain.

Roland had gone to the tent far sooner than Olivier, as she had known he would. It wore at him to be stared at, as he still was, though no longer with such open hatred.

The lamp was lit. He was lying on his side, arm crooked under head. Tarik's grey cat-shape curled in the warmth of his middle.

They regarded her with the same flat yellow stare. She would have expected it of Tarik; he was a *puca*, a creature not remarkably susceptible to either logic or reason. Neither was a man, for the matter of that, but she could not think of anything that she had done to Roland to deserve such coldness.

"A fair evening," she said with determined sweetness, "and a fine greeting to you, my lord of Brittany."

Roland's lips tightened. His habit of courtesy, like that of solitude, was well ingrained. "Good evening, lady," he said without warmth.

She sat on Olivier's cot, tucking up her feet, smiling brightly. "Were you glad of the rain today, my lord? A good omen, the men were saying. A promise of a safe and fair return to Francia."

Roland crossed himself. "I pray it may be so," he said.

"So it should be, if you ride straight and swift, and offer no threat to this country," she said.

"You are in great haste to be rid of us," he said. "Was it only a game, then? Were we no more than trained bears dancing to your drumming? 'Let us test the Franks' simplemindedness,' you said to one another. 'Let us see how unwieldy an army they will raise, and how futile a war they will fight, for a cause they are too lackwitted to understand. Then let us cast them back again, and send them home no wiser and no richer; but we have been much diverted by the game.'"

He was as bitter as the worst of the darkness that had lain on the camp, as angry as the angriest of the men she had passed. Her seeds of light had not touched him. He had old blood, wild blood. His magic made him stronger than any mortal man, but it was his weakness, too. The enemy could touch him through it, could lay hold of his spirit.

The gust of his anger rocked her where she sat. "You can't trust me, can you?" he demanded of her. "You'll always wonder. You'll always doubt. You won't ever believe that I'm just as you see me."

"You aren't," she said. It always disconcerted her that he could do that; that he could read her so terribly easily.

And could that be, her heart asked, because he trusted her, and did not doubt her?

He had turned his back on her. She astonished herself with pain. It was only a boy's temper, but it was a cold, lonely thing to be the object of it.

She could not help either her heart or her head. He would learn to see it, or he would not. And that was a cold and lonely thing, too, but it was what she was.

For all of that, she did not have to let him shut her out. She stared down the *puca* until he flattened his ears and hissed, but took his leave. When he was well and thoroughly gone, she slipped off her garments, softly, and fitted herself to Roland's back. He was rigid against her. Her hand moved down over his breast and belly to the proof that one part of him at least would welcome her. He must be aching with it.

He gasped as her fingers closed about it, but he did not ease or turn. She kissed his nape and the curve of neck and shoulder, nibbling, nipping. He flinched but held silent. She slid round to the front of him. His face was set. She kissed his lips. They were stiff and cold. "Do you hate me?" she asked him.

He shook his head once, sharply.

"Then love me," she said.

His whole body clenched like a fist. All at once it let go. She gasped with the force of it, and laughed, opening to take him in.

His own gasp was half a sob. He buried his face in her breasts, and held her till she thought she would faint for want of air. Then they found it again as if they had never lost it: the old harmony, the perfect match of body and body, heart and heart, spirit and spirit.

They lay together in the aftermath, warm flesh on warm

flesh. He was all loosed as before he had been taut, lying in her arms. Little by little his breathing quieted.

"Are you still angry with me?" she asked him.

"Yes," he said.

She kissed the parting of his hair. "Do you love me?"

"With my heart and soul."

"Then I'm content," she said.

"Even though you don't trust me?"

"I do love you," she said.

"But I have no honor in your heart."

"You have all honor," she said.

"And no trust."

"That is earned," she said.

"And love is not?"

"Love simply is," she said.

He sighed. "I'll never understand you," he said.

"No one understands me better than you," she said.

"Then you are truly incomprehensible."

She laughed softly. "I'm a woman. That's ineffable enough, as any man will tell you."

"It is true," he said, "that I know nothing of women. But even what little I have seen—there's none like you."

"There are many like me," she said.

"None," he insisted.

"So strong-willed a child," she said.

He lifted himself abruptly, raising his face over her. For the first time in a long while, she caught her breath, taken aback by the oddity of his eyes. He saw: they narrowed. But his mind was on another thing. "Tell me how old you are," he said.

She blinked. Somehow she had not expected that question. "Do I look ancient?" she asked.

"Sometimes," he said.

"All women do."

He shook his head. "No, don't. Tell me."

"Someday," she said, "I will."

He thrust himself up and away. "I," he said tightly, "have one-and-twenty summers. I keep count. It matters, Merlin told me, when one is young. He stopped counting for long years. Then I came, and he reckoned the years again."

"By that count," she said with the flicker of a smile, "I

was born a year ago, in the spring, in the magic of wood and water."

"I could almost believe that," he said. "Except . . ."

"Except?" she asked.

"You never limned your life in memories of me."

"Are you sure of that?"

Roland did not trouble with answers that she already knew. He was closing her out again. He would not be content, she knew, until he had all her secrets.

In time, if the goddess was kind, he would.

She stormed his walls now, won him back with kisses. When she had him in her arms again, she said, "Don't go away from me."

He looked as if he would speak, but thought better of it. He closed the embrace, sighed and was silent.

It was answer enough, if she would take it so.

PART THREE

✠ ✠ ✠

MONTSALVAT

CHAPTER 29

⊠ ⊠ ⊠

The joy that had brought the Franks out of Saragossa was seared and faded by long days of marching in the sun. The anger that had lain beneath it began to wear through. Mild quarrels sharpened to blows; small frustrations led to drawn steel.

They sacked Pamplona. They had won it as they came down from the mountains, taken and held it in the first bright fire of the crusade. Now, in the bitter ashes, they had no desire to keep it. They rode through its gates as conquerors. The people saw them pass in sullen silence.

What began it, no one knew. The king gave no signal. One moment they were marching through the narrow dusty streets toward the citadel. The next, they had scattered, whooping, striking, pillaging.

Charles made no move to stop them. His mood was as strange as theirs, his anger, if anything, deeper. He rode through to the citadel, broke down its gate which had been too hastily secured against him, and waited in its hall for his men to have their fill of looting and worse.

Roland's place was beside the king. But he had felt a shock in his body just before the men broke loose—as if something outside of him had plucked at his spirit. He had walls and wards against such things, and still he had come close to running wild; and these were plain mortal men. That power from without was playing them like a harp.

He could not find Sarissa. She had lain with him in the night, as she had every night since she came to him outside of Saragossa. In the morning, as every morning, she had been gone. He had not seen her riding in her wonted place near the rest of the women.

They were secure in the citadel, well shut away from the madness without. She was not with them. Nor did he see her near the king.

He asked no one's leave, and spoke to no one. He went out into the city.

The force that had loosed the army's anger was gone. Like a spear in the vitals, once it had struck, it need do no more. They themselves completed what it had begun.

The Franks rampaged through the streets, stormed into houses, broke down doors and walls. Everything that could be seized or carried, they took away. Men who opposed them, they stripped and beat senseless. Women suffered worse.

Roland's armor and the shimmer of his sword gave him passage. He beat men off from struggling, shrieking women; but none of them was ever Sarissa. None would be. His heart knew that. She was not in Pamplona. She was not anywhere that he could see, in his heart or with his eyes.

Still he hunted, if not for her, then for something that he could not set a name to. Charles had made it clear: none of his Companions was to hinder the sack.

But he had not forbidden Roland to fling aside a mob of men who had caught a young woman—a child—and thrown her down and wrenched her legs apart. The first had his trews down and his great red rod erect, thrusting at her, when Roland heaved him up and wielded him like a club, smiting down the lot of them.

They fled like the dogs they were. The child lay stark with terror. When Roland stooped over her, she shuddered to the bone. Her eyes were blank. There was no thought, no reason there.

His heart wept for her. He called such power as he had, gathered it in his hand, and poured it out over her small stiff body. He hoped that it brought her peace.

As he gathered to rise, he paused. The sack went on about him. He was an island in it, a small space of stillness.

Beyond it, men robbed and raped and looted. There was no sin here, no guilt, no awareness of good or evil. Only the raw desire.

It could touch him if he let it. He could run wilder than any of them. The temptation was potent, almost irresistible. It had a slither in it, a slide of serpent's scales.

He neither turned nor raised his head. The corners of his eyes, the tightening of his shoulders, caught the shadow in shadow, the inhuman thing that watched him.

He felt his lips curve in a smile. There was no mirth in it. It had an edge, like a sword. Calmly, steadily, he rose.

The way he chose passed near the shadow. He took great care to seem oblivious.

The force of the shadow's temptation was stronger, the closer he came to it. His smile widened of its own accord, baring his teeth. He drew his sword, his bright Durandal. He felt in his middle the serpent's laughter.

Just as he drew level with the shadow, he dropped his wards. He let the madness in, the wild lust for blood. He leaped, whirled, stamped. Durandal bit deep in the demon's heart.

He met those flat and lidless eyes. There was laughter in them still, but turned upon itself. And no fear. He had sent it to nothingness, not to damnation. For an instant he seemed to see . . . relief?

The creature's long pale hands clasped the blade. Its mouth opened as if to draw in air. Softly, suddenly, and without a sound, it collapsed upon itself. A pallid serpent coiled about the sword.

Durandal thrummed in Roland's hand. Its song was high and fierce and exultant. The serpent melted into air.

Roland stood in an empty street with his sword in his hand. Of the demon there was no sign, no scent, no track in the dust.

Roland laughed, sharp and short. Two of the three ancient servants were gone, and at his hand. Ganelon would have even less cause to love him now.

Durandal's victory song had quieted. It submitted to its sheath. Roland turned about slowly. The tide of the sack had washed away from him. He was alone. The child was gone, the dead and wounded taken away.

Down the empty street, from sunlight to shade and back

to sunlight again, came walking a small grey cat. No lady followed it, maddening or otherwise.

Tarik wove about Roland's ankles, purring raucously. Higher praise he had never given. He sprang lightly to Roland's shoulder, shifted and shimmered and gripped with a hawk's talons, riding that armored perch back to the citadel.

Pepin should have been attending his father. But he eluded the would-be nursemaids who came to take him in hand, gathered as many young rakehells as he could find, and went rampaging through the city. It was pure blood-red joy to sweep up one narrow twisting street and down another, driving shrieking infidels before him. His sword drank blood and tears. He plowed a Saracen furrow or two, or maybe three; he was not counting. He was simply living.

The tides of pillage washed him up on the steps of a church not far from the citadel. He had found a hoard of gold in a small mean house with a small mean man in it—a miser if he had ever seen one. The miser had not lived to mourn his lost gold. Pepin was wearing the best of it: a massive torque, armlets as heavy as the sword he had broken over the miser's turbaned head, and a belt of gold and great green stones. The rest he had cast into the street, laughing as men scrambled and fought over it.

Weighted with gold, dizzy with wine he had liberated from a tavern, with his twisted back aching as it always did, he sat on the steps and watched the city's fall. There were people inside the church, cowering and shrieking, and a priest's drone struggling to rise above the racket. He took little notice of them.

The knot of tension in his middle was gone. In the wrack and terror of the city's fall, amid the roil of anger and fear, hate and blood-red lust, Pepin had found the key that had eluded him for so long. This darkest face of war had shown him the core of his strength, the heart of his magic.

He had magic. After all, he had it. He amused himself as he sat there, striking sparks from the wood of the church door. With them he spelled a name in one of Ganelon's long-dead languages, then a name beneath it in another, and so a third. The door groaned. Such names were never meant to be written in a holy place. Pepin grinned and tapped the door with a finger. It crumbled to dust. Its iron nails, and the bolts that had held it shut, fell clattering to the threshold.

Eyes rolled at him from within. A cloud of incense gagged him. It came to him that he should have chosen a mosque; that these were Christians. Yet had not the Christians of Spain turned against the Franks and all the crusade? They had earned whatever he did to them.

He gestured grandly. He meant but to dismiss them with princely hauteur, but the magic was still in his hands, crackling from his fingertips. It traced a pattern of fire in the air, gathered it together and flung it full in the midst of the huddled people.

The church went up like a torch. Pepin was flung wide, his face and hands seared by the fire, and all the breath struck out of him. He slid to the foot of a wall and lay there, sure in his belly that he was dead.

His breath came back too slowly, but it left no doubt that he was alive. Nothing lived in the church—nothing could live in that holocaust of fire.

He stared at his hands. They were the same as ever, broad white hands with strong fingers, the image of his father's. They grasped a sword reasonably well. They wielded a pen with more than ordinary skill—and that, his father had never been able to do, though he spoke now and again of learning to do it. But this, his father had not even dreamed of. To raise fire with a gesture. To kill.

What need of a sword, or even an army, if he could do this? Such power he had been given, that he had not even known he had—kings would fall at his feet. Emperors. Prelates and popes. The whole world would bow before him.

He sought the fire again. He went down to his center, but found only embers. His head reeled. It was a long while before he could stand, and longer before he could walk. If he had squandered it all, not even knowing—

It was coming back already, growing slowly, but he could have no doubt of it. He had spent it for the moment, that was all. It would grow again, as seed grew in his manly parts. Had not Ganelon told him that magic had a price? It took somewhat from the wielder: some part of his spirit, his body, his strength or his youth.

It was little enough to pay for such splendor. He pulled himself up, clinging to the wall. Once his knees had straightened, they held him not too badly. After a while he could walk.

The sack had gone on past him. He had no desire, just then, to go on with it. He turned instead and walked back to the citadel, a walk that lightened as his strength returned, until he was striding as proudly as a prince should.

He had learned in his lessons to find Ganelon with something other than eyes. That prickle in the skin led him up through the citadel, past guards who stared at him with envy—though not for his sorcery; he was still laden with looted gold.

Past the region of guards, deep in the citadel, he found the clerks' nest. Ganelon laired past even that, high up in a tower. The ascent to it was steep and dark, but Pepin had eyes for that now, and strength enough, though hardly more. The door at the top was unbarred, though he knew from times before that if anyone was not welcome, not heaven itself could gain him entrance. Especially not heaven itself.

He stopped in the door, to breathe and to take in what he saw there. Ganelon was standing in the room's center. Light fell on him, but no sun had ever cast it. A shape lay huddled at his feet. After a moment Pepin recognized one of Ganelon's not-quite-human servants.

In a voice so soft it was barely audible, but strong enough to shiver Pepin's bones, Ganelon said, "Tell me Timozel is not dead."

The creature at Ganelon's feet—who must be Siglorel, the silent one—was true to himself: he returned no answer.

"And who slew him?" Ganelon asked, soft and oh, so gentle. "Whose sword smote him into nothingness? What folly was on him, O my servant? Had he run mad?"

Still, silence.

Ganelon swooped down and hauled the creature to his feet. Siglorel came up bonelessly, as a serpent might. His eyes had forgotten their human semblance. They were round and yellow, lidless and cold, and their pupils were slits in the otherworldly light. His voice was a long chill hiss, and his tongue was forked. "It was his time," he said.

"That power was given me," Ganelon said.

"All power is not yours," said Siglorel.

Ganelon's fingers locked about the pale throat. "You are mine," he said. "You belong to me. By the pact we made long ago, in that name which no mortal dare speak, I seal your power to mine."

Siglorel could not blink. His stare was flat. His tongue flicked, tasting air.

"You will slay that one," Ganelon said. "You will do it now, tonight. You will take his soul and bear it down below, and chain it for everlasting."

The serpent-creature hissed. Pepin realized that he was laughing. "What, are you bidding me follow my brothers into the void? Gladly would I do that, but it will avail you nothing against that one."

Ganelon's fingers tightened. The creature's cheeks had gone somewhat dusky, but his expression never changed. "That is a child," Ganelon said. "A boy. A mortal man's son. How can you fear him?"

"No fear," said Siglorel, a bare breath of sound. "Go, look, see him with your eyes. See what he is."

"I know what he is," Ganelon gritted.

The hairless head shook. "Go and see," said Siglorel.

With a hiss of disgust, Ganelon let the creature fall. Siglorel dropped bonelessly, and lay like a dead thing. Ganelon stepped over him, seemed to forget him, left him unheeded behind.

Pepin followed the sorcerer. It was a fool's act, or a madman's, but he was full of himself still. He was strong. He was invincible. Not even Roland could touch him.

Roland was with the king, flaunting the royal favor in that way he had, as if it mattered nothing to him at all. Ganelon slipped in among the clerks, silent, all but invisible. Pepin, who had no such fortune—there was never any hiding his hump, or the face so like the king's—chose to hide in plain sight, in a clutter of courtiers. If he stood just so, and wore his face just so, he could make it seem that he had been there from the beginning. Pepin the cripple, Pepin the fool, could never have been sacking cities or burning churches. Oh, no, not Pepin.

He watched Ganelon watch Roland. The sorcerer's face was as opaque as a wall of stone, but Pepin had learned to read stone. He saw how the long eyes narrowed, how the thin mouth tightened. The white fingers wove strands of air, mingling light and shadow under cover of his robe. He flung them like a net, invisible except to eyes that could see.

Roland did not seem to move, but the net slipped past him, never touching him. For an instant Pepin saw no man at all but a figure of light, and on its breast a living star.

He covered his eyes against the power of it. The fire he had raised was nothing to what lived in that shape of almost-mortal flesh.

When Pepin could see again, he looked for Ganelon. He was almost surprised to find him. The sorcerer stood as if rooted. He had seen it, Pepin thought: the thing that Siglo-rel had willed him to see. What he thought of it, what he would do, Pepin could not tell. But he would learn. He was Ganelon's eyes, and sometimes, now, his hands. Ganelon would use him again against Roland.

It was not the revenge he had looked for. But it was better than none at all.

CHAPTER 30

⚙ ⚙ ⚙

The sack of Pamplona was the Franks' farewell to Spain.
Laden with its wealth and sated with its suffering, they
rode into the mountains. Already their hearts were in Francia. If they could have flown, they would have done it, the
sooner to be back again.

Roland, who could fly if he chose, chose to be earthbound, to be human. He was the commander of the rearguard, protecting the king's back. Charles had little fear of
attack; Spain was as glad to be rid of him as he was to be
rid of it. But they posted guards in the nights and sent out
scouts by day, as an army should.

The flat brown plain was far behind them. The mountains rose like a wall. Deep valleys plunged down beneath
the mountains, dark and shadowed with trees. The road
wound from ridge to forest and back again, from high
harsh sunlight to green shade.

When Roland had come down this way into Spain, he
had ridden in joyous anticipation. Now, in what was not defeat but was not victory either, it seemed to him that the
woods were full of eyes.

Not all the eyes were hostile, but by no means all were
friendly. Roland's back tightened as he rode, last of all that
long column. Nothing stirred behind, but his bones knew
that there were watchers hidden in the trees and in the
tumbled rocks of the peaks. The amulet on his breast was

strangely heavy, and warmer than his skin, though not quite burning.

This country was made for ambush. But whoever they were who watched the army, they were hidden from him.

He wondered often if one pair of those eyes belonged to Sarissa. He had not seen her since the night before they sacked Pamplona. Tarik came and went as he pleased, but he answered no questions, nor offered explanations. His presence reassured Roland in an odd way. It was as if she had left the *puca* as a gift and a promise. Wherever she had gone, she had gone of her own free will. She had some duty, some task which she must perform. When it was done, she would come back.

In the evening of the fifth day of the march into the mountains, when they camped in a valley somewhat broader and somewhat less densely wooded than the rest, Roland made his way through the trees to the center, where the king had pitched his tent. Charles was in council when Roland came, settling matters of the kingdom as he did every evening on the march. Roland settled quietly on the edges, watching and listening, doing nothing to attract notice.

Ganelon sat close by the king. Roland did not recall that that had been so before this march. The counsel that he gave was wise enough, as far as it went: dispositions of lands and benefices, assessment of taxes and tribute, and the army's dispersal once they came to Francia.

But as Roland listened, knowing what Ganelon was, it seemed that he heard more than simple goodwill in those soft sage words. There was something in the way he spoke, in the pattern of lands and taxes and fighting men—as if he were gathering them. As if—

It might be illusion. Ganelon had been the king's emissary in the west and south, and particularly in Gascony. It was well within his purview to advise the king on matters of that domain.

"Spain may be well pleased to be rid of us," he said in his soft cold voice, "but it may also wish to assure that we never return. Gascony has been . . . difficult before. If it should ally with certain forces in Spain, there may be rebellion on your borders."

"You have sure knowledge of this?" Turpin asked.

Ganelon's expression did not change, but he managed to

convey a clear sense of patience with the foolishness of children. "The Gascons are ever ready to cast off the Frankish yoke. Therefore, sire, I would advise, with due respect, that once you come over the mountains, you consider diverting a portion of your army thence."

"A clear victory would not sit ill with the people," observed Riquier, who had been Ganelon's fellow emissary among the Gascons.

Charles nodded. "Yes, I see that. But if I keep the men in arms once we enter Francia, after I promised them a return to their lands and their wives—"

"So they will," said Ganelon, "but with the pride of victory and the booty of the Gascons. Who, whispers say, are very wealthy of late, enriched with infidel gold. It may be that you find them waiting when you come out of the mountains."

"If they're waiting for me," Charles said, "I'll meet them gladly."

Ganelon inclined his head. He seemed pleased.

And why, Roland wondered, should that be? What did Ganelon have to gain from a Gascon war? Charles' heart? His spirit? Or more—the strength of Francia?

And there were eyes in the wood, and watchers on the mountaintops. What Roland had not felt in Spain, he felt here. Imminence. Danger, and the cold touch of death.

His amulet had warmed to burning. Death, if that was what it was, passed over him like a gust of wind. In the moment after its passing, he raised his eyes full into Ganelon's black and bottomless stare. It was like deep water. He could drown in it, if he had not been armored in light.

Ganelon knew him. All of him. It came as no surprise, and roused no fear. It had been inevitable from the moment the old serpent entered the royal camp in Paderborn.

Roland inclined his head the merest fraction. Ganelon moved not at all. And yet Roland knew that the lines were drawn. It had always been war between the old enemy and Merlin's children. Now there would be battle—if not this moment, then soon.

The council went on about lesser matters, without a decision as to the Gascons. Nor did Ganelon press for one. He could be patient; there were days of marching yet before the army descended into Francia.

Roland left a little while before Charles dismissed the council. The sun had set; the swift night was falling. The king's servants had prepared his bath, which he must have even in this remote place. Roland dismissed all of them.

Charles came to his tent while the water was still steaming hot. He greeted Roland with a swift smile and a raised brow. Roland matched the smile, and bowed. "Your bath, sire," he said.

If ever one wanted to betray this man, Roland thought as he bathed the king, he could do it all too easily with the lure of water and cleanliness. Charles naked, alone, unarmed, all at ease in the basin, could die with a single stroke to the heart, and never know what had felled him.

But then, thought Roland, Charles was never a fool. This was great trust he gave his Companion, such trust as he gave seldom. Roland returned it by refraining from vexing the king while he luxuriated in his bath. When he emerged from it, scrubbed clean and wrapped in a robe of fine silk, he said, "Come, share the luxury. The water's still warm. I'll be your servant as you were mine."

This was not a choice. It was a test of sorts. Roland acquiesced to it.

He stripped and stepped into the basin. Charles was a surprisingly good bodyservant: quick, thorough, and not too heavy-handed. Roland let himself melt into the water, and for a little while be all at ease, trusting utterly this man to whom he had sworn his life.

He might have fallen asleep, had Charles not caught him by the hair and drawn his head back. There was a razor at his throat, light and cold. He smiled into the round blue eyes. So unlike Ganelon's, those; so clear, and so full of light.

Charles shaved him adeptly enough, then laid the razor aside. He had drawn no blood. He folded his arms on the basin's rim and inspected Roland critically. After a moment he nodded. "You'll do. I'll lend you a shirt—yours isn't fit for a dog to roll in."

"I'll be swimming in it," Roland said drowsily.

"And wouldn't it be splendid if we could swim in truth?" said Charles. "Do you know, when I've settled the kingdoms, I've in mind to find myself a city with baths in it. Roman baths. Or a hot spring, or better yet, both. I'll make that my city, and live there as much as I can. And every day I'll swim in the baths."

"Aachen," said Roland.

Charles blinked. "What?"

"Aachen," Roland said. "It's in the east of Francia. It has baths, and a hot spring. The water is wonderful for the skin, Sister Aude told me once."

"I know Aachen," Charles said. "It's a pleasant place. And the baths—yes. I remember them. They're half a ruin now, but they were splendid once."

"And can be again," said Roland.

"Are you making prophecies?"

Roland shrugged. The water was cooling fast, but he was too lazy to climb out of it.

"If I asked, would you?" Charles asked him.

"Are you asking?"

Charles paused for a moment as if in thought. Then he said, "No. I think it's best I not know."

"Wise," said Roland.

"Not wise," the king said. "Cowardly. If I knew the worst, I might never lift my head again."

"Not you," Roland said.

"No," Charles said. "After all, no. I'd thrash like a gaffed fish, and whatever ill is to come, I'd make it infinitely worse." He peered into Roland's face. Whatever he read there did not disturb him unduly. "You didn't come here to share a bath. Tell me."

Roland roused with an effort. He pulled himself out of the water. Charles, still playing the servant, dried him in spite of his protests, for after all it was hardly fitting that a count be waited on by a king.

"I choose to," Charles said. "Now stop wriggling and talk. What brings you away from your post?"

"Suspicions," Roland said as he submitted to the king's ministrations. "We're being watched."

Charles nodded. "There are people in these mountains—ancient and secret. Basques, they're called. They'll let us pass if we hold to the straight road and offer no threat."

"Not Basques," Roland said, "or not only Basques. There's something else out there."

"An ill thing?"

"Something I don't like," Roland said. "And here in this army—sire, you don't want to hear it, but there is one who is no friend to you."

"That good old man? Still?"

Charles was more amused than not. Roland was not amused at all. "Consider, sire, why he counsels that the men stay in arms."

"The Gascons—"

"Certainly the Gascons, sire. But what I know of this one who wears the face of a man . . . he bends kings to his will, and seduces their sons. He has a use for this army. What it is, I don't know. I only know that it will be a weapon in his hand."

"That," said Charles, "is a great leap of unfaith."

"It may be nothing," Roland said. "He may be content with small evils and tiny corruptions. He has a prince in his power—maybe he intends to wield that power long years from now. But he wants this army in Gascony. I would ask why. What use does he think to make of it?"

"To put down rebels," Charles said. "To secure my western borders before I cross the heart of Francia."

Roland shook his head. He needed words of power and terror, but none would come to him. There was no proof, nothing to point to and say, "This. This is his doing."

"I'll post sentries," Charles said, "and send out scouts when we march. This country is made for ambush. We'll avoid it as we can."

Roland bowed. "And the other?" he asked, not wisely, but he could not help himself.

"Find me proof," said Charles, "and I'll act on it."

That was no more than Roland had ever had, but at least it was no less. Dressed in the borrowed tunic, which fit him not so badly after all—it must have been made for one of the king's servants—he returned to his post.

The night was quiet. The watchers had withdrawn, though Roland sensed them still, waiting out the darkness as the army itself did.

It struck him as he walked, that Charles had said nothing of another stranger who was other than she seemed. Roland's arms were empty, his heart cold. Sarissa had abandoned him without even a word of farewell. Because of that, he had not wanted to speak of her; it hurt too much.

No one else had spoken of her, either. It was as if they had forgotten her existence. And that was strange. Very strange, amid so many odd things.

Yet unlike Ganelon, she bore no ancient evil in her. Roland would have staked his soul on that. Whoever she was, wherever she had gone, she was no servant of the Prince of Darkness.

CHAPTER 31

✠ ✠ ✠

Pepin was not given to listening at tent walls. But he had seen the king's servants bring in the basin and the water and then depart, and he had seen Roland slip into the tent. With difficulty he extricated himself from a clinging mob of hangers-on. Time was, he thought, when he could slip away whenever he pleased; when no one cared what he did or where he went. He had grown past that, become more princely.

Prince or no, he could still, when he chose, make himself invisible. He crouched in the shadows and heard what there was to hear. It was not much, but its import struck him as large enough. The king played servant to the Breton count. Roland had Charles in his power—had won him, seduced him.

Pepin would see to it that the men knew. They had quieted overmuch since Saragossa; there had been too little hatred in them for one of their own, when they had all of Spain to hate.

Tomorrow Pepin would spread rumors again, stronger ones, words honed to a bitter edge. It did not matter what Ganelon said, or what he had commanded. Roland would not escape this time. This would begin his downfall, and the end of his power over the king.

The prospect made Pepin smile. But tonight he had another errand. Ganelon needed his eyes once more, and perhaps more than that.

It was nearing midnight. Most of the army slept, all but the sentries walking the edges, slipping like shadows among the trees. Ganelon's tent was pitched in the dark away from firelight. It was strange, rather, that on this march Ganelon set himself full in the light before the king, but set his tent as far from it as he could.

Pepin found his way as he had been taught, with other senses than eyes: by the feeling in his bones, and by a scent like hot iron, that was the scent of sorcery. When he stretched out his hand, he touched the flap of a tent. He lifted it, releasing a shaft of sudden light.

Before his eyes had recovered from their dazzlement, he stood within. He blinked through tears of pain.

Slowly his sight cleared. The rest of his senses were reeling. Fragrance of surpassing sweetness, music beyond earthly beauty, air softer than silk, a taste on his tongue more potent than honey. Petals drifted about him, stroking his cheeks like soft fingers.

This was the garden he had seen before he came under Ganelon's tutelage, the magic he had yearned for since first he happened upon it. The close confines of the tent were gone. Lush greenery and great glowing banks of flowers lay all about him. Down paths of perfect smoothness he glimpsed blue distances, broad expanses of plain and forest, mountain and sky.

Close by was a greensward ringed in blossoming trees. A fountain played in its center, a marble extravagance such as he had seen in Rome: a dance of nymphs about a broad clear pool. They were painted as the old Roman images still sometimes were, given the hues and the texture of life. It even seemed that they breathed, their white breasts rising and falling, their eyes gleaming on him, promising rare delights.

Pepin yearned toward them, but Ganelon stood in his way. In this place he was never the plain old man whom Pepin had known. He was not young, but neither was he old. He was ageless, beyond years, honed and strong. And beautiful. The beauty of the swordblade as it drinks blood, of the wolf's fang as it sinks into the throat of its prey. So must the dark angel be, the Son of the Morning whose pride cast him into the pit.

Pepin was a king's son of the Franks. He did not bow to fallen angels. A prince of the hosts of heaven, perhaps. But not a prince who was cast down. And certainly not to a man who served such a creature, however ancient, however powerful he might be.

"Pride was the first sin," Ganelon said, "greatest and most terrible."

Even his voice was changed here: stronger, more beautiful. But his eyes were the same. He could not conceal those, no matter what shape he wore.

Pepin kept his head up and his gaze level. "Master," he said. "You have need of me?"

"Attend me," Ganelon said. "Say nothing except to me. If there is a question, I will answer it. If there is need of words, I will speak them. Do you understand?"

Pepin was not sure he did, but he nodded brusquely.

Ganelon saw through him; the dark eyes narrowed, perhaps with amusement, perhaps with contempt. But the sorcerer said nothing. He merely turned and walked down one of the paths that rayed out from the greensward like the spokes of a wheel.

They walked from blinding daylight into blind night. It was all Pepin could do not to stumble and fall. He had, ignominiously, to clutch at Ganelon's mantle, and so be guided through the darkness like a child at its mother's skirts.

Firelight glimmered at the end of the long path. Wind shrilled in stony heights. It was keen and rather cold.

They stood in a camp, but it was not that of the Franks. There were no trees here, only wind and stones. A rise of cliff sheltered ranks of tents that marched away into the gloom. Most of the fires were banked. One burned strongly in front of a tent no larger or more splendid than the others, but it was set as near the center as Pepin could tell. From the shadows beside it men emerged, armed and armored, clearly on guard.

Pepin's eyes widened at sight of them. He knew Gascon faces, and Gascon armor, too. These men bowed as Ganelon emerged into the light, bowed to the ground, and lifted the tent's flap for him.

There was a gathering of men within, half a dozen dark, sharp-faced sons of Gascony. Ganelon before them kept somewhat of the power and beauty he had had in the garden. He wore wisdom like a mantle.

It was a pleasure to see the master in glory, accepting the Gascons' worship as his due. Pepin they seemed not to notice—which piqued him, for he was a prince, but pleased him somewhat, too. Everyone in Francia knew Pepin Crookback. Here, he was nothing to remark on; he was simply there. It was not a sensation he had known before.

Ganelon was given the place of honor, and offered food and drink, which he declined. Pepin would have welcomed a cup or two of wine, but a guardsman was not expected to suffer hunger or thirst.

He played the part because he had been asked, and because he was curious. For a while it seemed they would speak of nothing in particular, but that was the way of such gatherings. In time the chief of the Gascons said, "My lord, all is ready. Will you stay until morning, to see?"

"No need," said Ganelon. "I have seen."

"Then, my lord—if I may ask—"

"You may not," said Ganelon, "but I will answer. I have no doubt that you will do as we agreed. I come to ask another thing."

The Gascons leaned forward. There was a hungry air to them, like wolves in winter.

"When you do what we have agreed," Ganelon said, "there is one whom I would have. Take him alive, but confine him closely. And beware! He has more arts and skills than the run of men."

"Magic?" the chief of them asked.

Ganelon inclined his head. "He may not choose to be taken as a man. A stag, a wolf, a falcon—he may be any or all of those."

"We'll net him like a fish, my lord," said the Gascon.

"A net would do well," Ganelon said. "He leads the rearguard—remember. There is a golden hawk on his shield. His horse is grey. His eyes, when you come close, are not a man's eyes."

"Ah," said the Gascon, nodding. "The Count of the Breton Marches. Yes, we know that one. We'll catch him for you."

"That is well," said Ganelon.

It was not well for Pepin, but he kept his tongue between his teeth. Ganelon did nothing on a whim. He had made Pepin privy to this for a reason. What it was, Pepin was not exactly sure. It was larger than Roland, he could tell that, but Roland was a notable part of it.

The Gascons glanced at one another. They were afraid of Ganelon: they shied from him, somewhat. Only their captain seemed brave enough to speak. "Lord," he said, "the men ask a thing—not in return, but for their souls' sakes. They ask for protection—a prayer, a talisman, some simple thing—against the allies that will be called forth."

Ganelon's brow rose. "You told them of that?"

The man blanched, but he held his ground. "My men fight with open eyes. They know the cause and the cost. They accept it. They only ask—"

"I will ward them," Ganelon said, "when the time comes. Only let them do their part."

"They will do it," the Gascon said.

"Tell me you're not going to destroy my father," Pepin said.

"And why would you think that?" Ganelon asked him.

They had returned through the bright garden to the tent that Pepin had known, walking down a path that rounded a corner into that small and priestly space. It seemed all the smaller and all the darker for the splendor that had been contained in it.

Pepin had learned much since Paderborn. He could summon his wits together, and think on what he must think on. He was stronger, he thought, for all those hours and days of scraping parchment, writing letters, learning languages that had long vanished from the earth. He had learned patience.

He had not learned to be less than proud, and he did not intend to. "Whatever you purpose," he said, "it means ill to one of my father's favorites. That ill is to be done by a nation whom you yourself have called rebel. You are subtle, master, and that is a great gift. Will this grand design of yours bring harm to my father?"

"Your father has little to do with it," Ganelon said.

"And I? What is my part in this?"

Ganelon did not smile. It was not his way. Yet he seemed amused. "You are my pupil," he said.

"Why?"

"Because you wished to learn."

Pepin bit his lip. Had he not called Ganelon subtle? This was the truth. Yet it could not be all of the truth. "You need my eyes," he said. "Tonight you needed my presence. What more will you need of me?"

"That will come with time," Ganelon said.

"I will not harm my father," said Pepin.

"You will not be asked for such a thing," Ganelon said. "He has his own destiny. What you are, what I need of you—you know, and will know. You will give yourself freely, as you always have. There will be no compulsion laid upon you."

"Will you swear oath as to that?"

Pepin's heart beat hard. He trod very close to the edge of the unacceptable. But he was royal. He could ask such a thing, and be granted it.

Ganelon inclined his head, both regal and humble. The humility, Pepin thought, was a mask. The royalty was truth. "I swear," he said, "that you will act of your own free will, whatever is required of you."

Pepin was not satisfied, somehow, but that was all Ganelon would give him. He had to be content with it.

CHAPTER 32

❊ ❊ ❊

The king's scouts, sent ahead of the army into the ever-ascending valleys, found nothing. The passes were clear, they said, and the mountains empty of enemies. They had come across a village of Basques, fierce secret people who spoke a tongue like none in the world; but those expressed no interest in the army marching past their borders.

Still Roland was ill at ease. On the second morning after Charles played the servant, he rode for a while with the king. Charles looked him over critically and said, "You're as twitchy as a cat."

Roland shrugged. He was irritable, too, and that was not like him. This ran deeper than plain threat of ambush in the mountains. Forces moved just below his awareness. Things were in train that he could not quite grasp. His dreams, when he could sleep at all, were of drowning in deep water, and of reaching perpetually for a thing that eluded him: sometimes fruit on a tree, sometimes a sword suspended in air.

"We'll be out of the mountains soon," Charles said, breaking in on his maundering. "There's the pass of Roncesvalles ahead of us, steep and narrow as it is. Past that the road grows easier. And then at last we'll be in Francia."

"And possibly in a Gascon rebellion," Roland said.

"If so," said Charles, "we're prepared for it."

Roland nodded—more of a twitch, if truth be told. "I don't like the pass," he said. "It's narrow and steep, and the trees are thick clear to the top of its walls. We can't go round it, we can't go up it. We'll be rats in a trap."

"Well then," Charles said, not quite as if he indulged a fit of folly, "take the Companions and such of the others as you trust, and guard the rear. I'll see to the van. The quicker we're through, the better."

"My thanks, sire," Roland said.

"Listen, now," said Charles, leaning over to tap the horn that Roland always carried at his saddlebow, the horn of the great aurochs, the last perhaps that had been in the world. "If you're in need, wind that. The sound will carry in these mountains. I'll hear it and come running."

Roland bowed to that. Charles clapped him on the shoulder.

It was a dismissal. The Companions, who had been listening shamelessly, were already turning back toward the rear. Some of the others caught Roland's eye: a raised brow here, a quick grin there. They were not mocking him or reckoning him a fool. If they thought at all on the rumor of sorcery and worse, they did not let it trouble them.

Their regard warmed him even in his confusion of mind. They trusted him. They would fight for him if they were called to it.

He followed them back along the line. The rearguard was still in the remnants of the night's camp, as the baggage-train finished forming and began to move out. Oxen lowed and mules brayed. The drovers cursed: their morning song.

Olivier lounged in the saddle, finishing a breakfast of cheese and roast ox rolled in last night's bread. He broke it in thirds as Turpin rode up with Roland behind, and passed a portion to each. "That's a fair troop of champions the king's sent back with you. Who'd you leave to look after him?"

"The whole vanguard," said Roland. And, he thought, Ganelon was well back toward the rear with the rest of the clerks—just ahead of the baggage. Roland could keep him in sight, and track him by the crawling under the skin.

"I expect," said Turpin, "that if there is an attack, it will go for the baggage. Every bandit in the Pyrenees must know by now that we're carrying Pamplona's gold."

Olivier downed the last of his truncated breakfast and eyed the portion half-forgotten in Roland's hand. Roland passed it over with some relief. He was in no mood for breakfast, just then.

"Don't look so grim," Olivier said. "The king must be safe enough if you've let him send his Companions back here. We'll make short work of any robber who tries to take the king's treasury."

"A fight would be a pleasant diversion," said Thibaut. He loosened his sword in its sheath and thumped his cousin Milun on the helmet. "Chin up, boy! We're moving out."

Easily, lightly, laughing and mock-squabbling, they fell in behind the last of the rearguard. The troops were grinning. They found the Companions greatly entertaining.

Roland was glad that they could be so light of heart. It did not lessen their vigilance; and that was what mattered.

He rode last but for a pair of scouts that he had sent to range the rear and along the slopes as much as could be. That was not much, the farther they went. The way was steep, the valley dark, the mountains looming high above it.

The trees closed in. The road narrowed. The pack-mules scrambled up it well enough, but the wagons lurched and lumbered. A day never passed without at least one broken wheel, but today had a curse on it. The way was too narrow for a broken wagon to draw aside; if one failed, they all had to halt till it could be mended.

Some considerable distance up toward the pass, where many of the men had dismounted to clamber beside their horses, a wagon lurched over a stony ledge, caught and held. The drover urged the oxen forward. They threw themselves into the traces. The wagon groaned. The oxen lowed with the effort. The whip cracked over their heads. They scrambled on the hard stony ground overlaid with leafmold, slippery as ice in winter. One ox slipped and went to its knees. In the same instant, its yokemate surged forward.

The yoke twisted and snapped. The wagon wheel gave way. The heavy wagon overbalanced and slid down the slope, dragging the oxen with it.

The wagons behind had nowhere to go. Those directly in back of the fallen one caught and slid. "Brace! *Brace*, you sons of whores!" roared Olivier, nearest and quickest of wit. The rearmost wagons lumbered to a halt. Such as could turn broadside, made haste to do it, making a wall of sorts against the tangle of wagons and oxen.

It all ground to a halt somewhat short of the rearguard. Wheels were locked together, oxen down and caught in traces. Somewhere in the midst of it, a man was screaming.

Roland left Veillantif with the rearguard and pushed his way on foot to the edge of the confusion. Olivier had it in hand. Roland pulled a man out of the ranks. "Run ahead," he said. "Bid the rest of the army wait. We'll be some little time unknotting this."

The man nodded. He swung off his horse and struck upward through the trees, making his way doggedly along the slope.

Roland would have to hope that one messenger would be enough. There was a great deal to do here: wagons to untangle, oxen to sort out, wounded to tend. Of that last there were few, thank God. Worse was the damage to the wagons, and two oxen so badly hurt that they had to be destroyed.

"Roast ox for dinner again tonight," said Olivier, smacking his lips, as he helped with the butchering and flaying.

The sun had lifted over the peaks by the time the column was in order again: a good part of the morning gone, and still the pass to ascend. At least, thought Roland, they would have honest daylight to do it in, however briefly, before the valley's walls cut off the sun again.

The baggage could move no faster than the oxen's slow and labored plod. No word came back from the center; Roland's messenger did not return. The scouts had not come back, either.

He caught himself wishing for Tarik, who could fly as a hawk and bear word to the king; but the *puca* was nowhere in evidence. Nor was Roland willing yet to spread his own wings. Not for a prickling between the shoulderblades. The wagon had fallen by sheer unhappy chance. No art or magic had caused it.

Had it? He had searched with more than eyes and ears,

found nothing. But there were powers that could conceal themselves from him.

He put the thought aside. What he could do, he had done. Both Companions and rearguard were watchful, weapons at the ready. They had all put on their helmets, though the sun beat into the deep cleft, reminding them fiercely that it was summer in Spain.

The great aurochs' horn shifted on his saddlebow, and he steadied it. He seldom blew it: it could smite men down with its power. If he raised its voice in these passes, not only Charles in the van would hear it. The great archangel at the gates of heaven might take umbrage, thinking that a mere mortal man had dared to call the dead to judgment.

Roland's lips twitched. It was a poor jest, and Turpin was not near enough to share it. But it lifted his spirits a little.

CHAPTER 33

✠ ✠ ✠

Sarissa watched from the peaks as the Frankish army ascended the pass. Charles rode in the van, unmistakable even from this distance: he wore a golden helmet that flashed in the sun. The long train of his soldiers and servants wound behind him, down into the deep valley.

The scouts that he had sent ahead slept in the shadow of a stone, lost in dreams of joy and peace. Tarik crouched by them in cat-shape, ruffled and surly. There was a wishing on him, the first compulsion that she had ever laid on that fierce free spirit. But need knew no mercy. Set free, he would have vanished on swift wings, bearing word to Roland of what she did here. The time for that was not yet—though it was close.

A man climbed toward her summit, a wiry Basque born to these mountains, light and agile on the sheer and treacherous slopes. "It's ready, high one," he said in his ancient tongue.

That same tongue came easily enough to her, though she did not doubt that her accent was abominable. "Wait on the signal," she said.

The Basque inclined his head. That, for his kind, was deep obeisance indeed. After a moment he said, "Others may not wait."

Sarissa did not speak her first thought, which was that

his men would obey or know the consequences. They were in position, obedient to her will. "Others?" she said.

"Down below," he said. "Gascons. They stink of brimstone."

What she felt was not surprise. It was a kind of relief. "Where? Show me."

"They're not to be seen," said the Basque. "We smell them. We trust they're not yours."

"Not in this world," she said.

"We wager they're doing the same as we. I don't suppose we'll make common cause with them?"

"Not likely," she said through set teeth. "Send a small company of your men, those with the keenest noses and the strongest minds, and bid them find these Gascons. Let them not be found themselves, but send word back, and wait. Let the Gascons move first. We'll judge our course by what we see."

The Basque looked as if he might have had somewhat to say of that, but he bent his head again, turned and made his way back down the slope.

Sarissa stayed where she was. Her own men were no more visible than the Gascons—and those belonged to the old enemy, she was as certain as she was of the sun beating on her head and the wind whipping her cheeks. She could hope that they had had no inkling of the forces above them. Ambush upon ambush. What it did to all her plans, she could not yet tell.

She kept fear at bay, and kept her mind clear, her spirit strong. In that state of pellucid calm, she saw the line crumble far to the rear as the king reached the summit of the pass. He went on in ignorance of the confusion behind him. The center drew away from the rear, likewise unaware.

That was accident, but accident shaped into design. A glint drew her eye. In the same instant, one of the younger Basques bounded up the slope, light as a mountain goat. He was red-faced when he came level with her, perhaps with exertion; or perhaps it was a furious blush. He spoke clearly, at least. "High one, my cousin Ioan says, the Gascons move."

She could see the movement for herself, distinct from above, invisible no doubt from below. Men were creeping through the deep wood, closing in on the column.

"Tell Ioan," she said to the boy: "to arms, and swiftly. But quietly! We'll ambush the ambush."

As he bounded back down the mountain, she set Tarik free. The grey cat vanished without so much as a glance. A falcon sped on swift wings toward the rearguard so far below, and so far apart now from the rest of the army.

Her own forces were well up in the pass. They streamed down along it, silent as shadows. The army passed oblivious.

She left her vantage, making her way along the ridge. It was rough going, the wood thick, tangled with undergrowth. Once she was in among the trees, she could see nothing. Nor was there anything to hear. The birds had fled the coming of so many armed men. Not even a squirrel stirred in the trees.

She kept her hand to the hilt of the Roman shortsword that she had had since she was as young as she looked. It was smooth and hard and familiar. It had drunk deep of Gascon blood before the lurker in the trees was even aware of her existence. He never saw her face; when she saw his, his eyes were glazed in death.

She paused for a moment to clean her sword on his breeches. He was armed with bow and sword and spear, but wore no armor, only a light helmet. His breast was bare—sensible enough in the heat of this day. He wore something about his neck, a small object on a string of leather.

She was careful not to touch it. Unlike the Basques, she did not smell brimstone, but she saw darkness lingering yet about him, the serpent's tooth sunk deep in his spirit. The talisman that he wore sealed him to powers that she knew too well, and shielded him from others that woke her to heightened wariness.

She went on more quickly but with greater caution. The wards that she had laid on her men were holding, though she felt the strain about their edges. There was no sound of battle, nothing to alert or alarm the Franks in the pass.

At length the trees opened on a bare stretch of stony hillside. Men were fighting on it: her Basques in leather and steel, the Gascons in light armor or none. It was a fierce fight, but nearly silent. Neither side, just then, seemed stronger than the other.

A great blow struck the wards and flung her to her knees. Her skull rang with the force of it. Fool, she thought. Fool and fool. The enemy was older, stronger, and far more devious than she. He had lulled her into complacency, lured her forces out of hiding, and provided them with this thoroughly mortal diversion.

The battle itself was elsewhere, raging over the heads of the Franks—and directing its strongest blow to the rear. Desperate it might be, and dangerous, but she left her body lying in the shelter of the trees and opened wide the eyes of the spirit. Dark wings spread over the Frankish army. What waited beyond the pass was such a thing as she had not seen in long years. To men's eyes it would be nothing more than a mist in the mountains. To she who was more than man, it was a wall and a gate, and beyond it a darkness she had no desire to plumb.

Powers waited on her command. Forces gathered in the heights. The gate cast them into confusion.

Her lovely plan of battle was all in ruins. Her Basques were prevailing over the Gascons, but they mattered little in the face of that gate. Already the Frankish van was coming near to it, breasting the summit of the pass and beginning the descent into shadows and mist.

She left her body altogether and sent her spirit winging aloft. Chains of flesh dragged at her. Dark sapped her strength. It was aware of her. It laughed at her.

She blocked out the laughter and gathered all such strength as she had. She summoned the powers from the heavens and from the mountaintops. She forged of them a shield and a spear, and smote the gate asunder.

Men saw lightning out of blue heaven, and swift melting of the mist: strong enough portents, but nothing that they would understand. The darkness reeled. Its mockery had died a merciless death.

But there was laughter in it still, and a stab of triumph. She hurtled into the bonds of flesh, snapped together, rolled, caught the stab of swordblade down the length of her arm. The pain sealed her to her body. The man who would have cloven her asunder fell dead. The Basque chieftain had already turned away to strike down another of the Gascons.

She barely took notice. As she plummeted into her body,

she had seen the broader shape of the enemy's design. The van and center of the Frankish army were escaping, safe from that dark gate. But the rear, the baggage, the Companions and the king's picked troops, and last of all the Count of the Breton Marches, fought a bitter battle in the defile of Roncesvalles.

She yearned with all her heart for wings. That gift was not given her. She had her feet, and a glimmer of magic still, that lengthened her stride and lightened her step. It was slow, too terribly slow. An army had fallen on the rearguard, men and creatures other than men. They were cutting it to pieces.

All the powers of air were scattered in the fall of the gate. What other forces she had were farther away than she herself was, cut off like the king of the Franks, oblivious to the great need behind them.

As little as was left of her, as hopeless as it might be, she made all speed she could. She gathered men as she ran. The diversion had nearly played itself out: most of the enemy were down, dead or wounded. "No prisoners!" she cried. "Kill and go. There's worse below."

They ran for life and for the fate of kingdoms. She ran for all that, and for the commander of the rearguard, the king's Companion, Merlin's pupil, Roland whom she loved. She knew with terrible certainty that he was the focus of that divided attack; that the others had been meant to pass through the gate, but Roland was the enemy's personal, special prey.

Not, by all the long-dead gods, if she could help it. She stretched her stride, bounding down the steep hillside, spending strength and magic without care for the cost. She would pay it later, when the battle was ended. When Roland was safe. She made of that a prayer, ringing in her heart as she ran.

CHAPTER 34

⌘ ⌘ ⌘

The ambush burst upon the rearguard as the last of it ascended into the pass. There were hundreds, thousands of the enemy. Nor were all or even most of them human, though they were man-sized, roughly man-shaped, and ran more or less as men ran. But no man wore the face of wolf or bear or leopard, or raked flesh with great curved claws, or bit out throats with long sharp fangs.

The Franks were strong and seasoned men of war, even the servants in the baggage-train, but against such enemies they were utterly out of their reckoning. Brave men shrieked and cowered and fled from creatures out of nightmare. Weak men simply died of terror where they fell.

The rearguard held as best it could, but horses were never meant to stand against such horrors as this. Far too many went mad, flung their riders to the ground and bolted.

The twelve Companions held to their saddles, which for some was a war in itself. Roland's Veillantif kept his head, but barely; he snorted and plunged but did not run.

This was not a battle. It was a massacre. They were trapped in the narrow defile, with enemies swarming from above, from before and behind. The guards on the baggage died swiftly. The rearguard fought in close ranks, drawn up afoot. The Companions, among the few still mounted, defended the edges as they could.

The enemy converged on them, driving direct for them, drawn by the horses and the wealth of their armor: finely woven mail, blazoned shields, bright helmets, and weapons of rare quality. Roland above all, with Durandal singing her sweet eerie song, was drowned in attackers both human and not. They swarmed on him like wolves on a stag, leaping, snapping, tearing at whatever they could reach.

Olivier on his right, Turpin on his left beat off those whom Durandal did not touch. Thibaut and Milun fought beyond them, and Ogier the Dane roaring with Berserker fury; Gerin and Gerer, twinned and inseparable, fierce Anseis and Otker the valiant, and Ascelin of Gascony who saw his countrymen among the enemy, but fought for the Frankish king. Twelve paladins, twelve great warriors bound as brothers. They laughed as they fought, and sang as they slew.

Roland sang strongest of them all. When the ambush broke upon them, he woke to a white, mad joy. He counted the numbers against them, reckoned the ranks drawn up from hell, and laughed.

Durandal drank heart's blood from a thing with a wolf's jaws and an owl's great round eyes. A half-naked Gascon leaped yelling in the thing's wake. He fell with his head nigh cloven from his shoulders. There was another behind him, and another, and another, a swarm of fangs and blades and claws.

Milun was down, Thibaut standing over him, howling like a wolf. Anseis had fallen. Gerin and Gerer he could not see at all.

The enemy were innumerable, inexhaustible. The wall of them drove the Companions together, those who were left.

Veillantif shrieked in mortal agony, reared and fell thrashing. Roland tumbled free. Limbs tangled, blades clashed. Something smote him between the shoulders, but his mail-coat held. He dropped, rolled, staggered up. Claws raked his face. Durandal hewed the demon down.

Behind him a stallion screamed. He whipped about. A snow-white shoulder thrust against him. Long white mane streamed, catching his free hand. Tarik all but flung him onto the broad white back, no saddle, no bridle, but the *puca* needed none. His sorrow rang in Roland's skull, made fiery with anger. He had come as swiftly as he could, but he was sore hindered. Demons—no kin of his, by the old gods—had barred his way.

It did not matter. He had come; he fought with more than mortal strength. He carried Roland among the Companions, those grievous few who still stood: Olivier, Turpin, Ogier bloodied to the eyes, and Ascelin the Gascon fighting with grim and loyal ferocity.

There was no end to this battle, no respite. No moment to rest, to breathe, to bind one another's wounds. They could not take up the dead, nor mourn them, either. They could only fight for their lives and their souls' sakes.

Three fanged wolf-things together pulled Ogier down and gnawed his throat. Ascelin shrieked something appallingly profane and flung himself at them. A mob of Gascons, of his own people, fell on him and hewed him in pieces.

Tarik lunged. Roland glimpsed fangs—no blunt horse-teeth in that gaping mouth. Durandal whirled of her own accord, cleaving, hacking, killing.

He saw Olivier sway, with half a dozen men and devils gathered to pull him down. Roland caught him with mad strength and heaved him up on Tarik's back. Tarik barely staggered under the more than doubled weight.

Olivier's arms closed about Roland's middle. His voice rumbled in Roland's ear. "I don't suppose this beast has wings?"

Roland did not trouble to answer that. "Turpin. Where—"

"Down," said Olivier, brief for once.

Roland would weep. Later. For them all, all the paladins, and his beloved Veillantif who had been so valiant.

"You might," said Olivier, "blow your horn. The king probably doesn't know—"

"Lost it," Roland said, with little breath to spare amid a storm of fangs and steel.

Something thrust against Roland's free hand. He almost batted it away, but his eye caught the shape of it. It was the aurochs' horn. "Hold it for me," he said.

"I'd rather you winded it," Olivier said. "Remember what he said. If there is need—"

Roland could not fight and talk and lift the horn, not all

at once. Olivier was leaning heavily against him. He had to take the horn or let it fall. His battle-brother's breath was loud in his ear, thick and labored. He did not want to hear what he heard in it: the bubble of blood.

"Wake the hosts of heaven," Olivier said, faint now but determinedly light. "Let the mountains ring. Blow the horn!"

The hosts of heaven, thought Roland. Except for Olivier, he was all alone in that swarm of hellspawn. No mortal men here, no simple human faces. They were all demons. He could not see the army at all, nor the baggage. Only the seething mass of devils.

It was rout, it was slaughter. It was, he knew with perfect clarity, all for him—for Merlin's child, the last and least of his blood.

He prayed to God and to His holy mother that the king was safe, that the greater part of the army had escaped; that only the rearguard had been so beset. It was a forlorn hope and perhaps a vain prayer, but it gave him a little strength. It let him fight a few moments longer.

Olivier had stopped even trying to defend himself. Roland protected him as he could. He fought his way to a little rise of ground, a low hill on which he could make a stand. There, for a miracle—or perhaps for a mockery—he was given a few moments' pause.

Olivier slid from Tarik's back. Roland had no strength to catch him. He crumpled at the *puca*'s feet. His body was a mass of wounds, his helmet lost, his face white and far too still.

He could not be dead. No, not Olivier. They had made a pact. They would live to a great old age, and then they would die together in the same woman's bed, in the same moment, neither before or after the other.

Roland flung himself down, heedless of the hordes that circled the hill. He took Olivier in his arms, cradling the big fair head. The blue eyes were open. They were empty. There was a faint frown on his brow.

A great wail rose in Roland's throat. He did not let it go. Instead he did as Olivier had bidden him, the last words he ever spoke. He lifted the great ivory horn to his lips, filled his lungs and blew.

No man, even Roland who was other than mortal, could

have made such a sound. It rose up and up, higher and
higher, clearer and ever clearer, till heaven itself rang with
the strength of it.

And as that long note died, he sounded a second, clearer
and even stronger than the first. His ears were ringing, his
lungs burning. But he found breath in them for a third
great blast, with all his heart and soul in it. So strong was it,
so powerful the force of it, that his sight grew red with
blood, and blood trickled from his ears. The horn burst
asunder in his hands.

The shards fell. He all but fell with them, blind, deafened, reft of breath and strength. But not of will. Somehow,
with arms that shook as if with palsy, he raised Durandal,
and steadied his feet as best he could. He stood against the
tide that poised to overwhelm him.

The horn's cry was ringing still, echoing in the deep valley, resounding among the peaks. As hell's children
swarmed upon him, he saw heaven split asunder. A host
rode forth in armor of light. And at their head—

He laughed, there on the border of death, for surely he
was dreaming. Sarissa rode foremost on the back of a great
white swan, and on her head a crown, and in her hands a
cup brimming over with blood. She was beautiful beyond
mortal measure, shining with power, splendid, glorious.

And she was too late. The Companions were dead. The
rearguard was gone—cut down, vanished, he did not know.
Roland would die before she came to him.

Still he laughed, for she was beautiful, and he was not
afraid to die. Durandal's song was faint and thin after the
horn's great cry, but it was wonderfully sweet. The sword
was insatiable in her hunger for demon's blood. He was
more than glad to feed her.

CHAPTER 35

Death was a swift fall of dark and a slow return of light: cool white light and a breath of wind scented with snow. There was pain—dim, distant, but startling; had he not left the body behind?

It would seem he had not. The wind blew unhindered across it. There was stone beneath it, cold but not unpleasantly so. All about him was sweet unearthly singing.

Voices of angels. Angels bent over him, nine ladies clad in white. And foremost, as beautiful as he ever remembered, but higher and stronger and far more powerful, stood his beloved, his lover, Sarissa.

She lifted his head in the curve of her arm. Her warmth was human, and her strength, but her face was unreachably remote. She set a cup to his lips. He sipped blood-red wine, or wine that was blood, or blood that was fire. Or it was all of those things. It seared his throat. It coursed through his veins. It drowned him in light.

Death in darkness, death in light. His third death was silence and walls of stone, and Turpin sitting near him, chin on breast, snoring softly.

It was just as it had been so often before: waking from a long sleep or a wound, to find himself in a soft bed, with his friend watching over him. Roland lifted a hand that felt and looked like his own, and touched a face that surely was his, though there was an oddity to one cheek: a faint interruption, as of healed scars. A dim memory dawned, of battle and blood and the rake of claws. Would his beauty be marred, then, though this was heaven?

Truly he seemed to be in his body, with a new count of scars, but all old, all healed. He was not weak as he should have been; once dizziness had passed, he felt hale enough. He could stand, walk. His bare feet trod carpets of Eastern richness, woven in the colors of heaven: red and blue and purple and gold.

This seemed to be a room in a palace, or perhaps a castle. It had a window, set deep in the stone of the wall. He leaned into it and looked out across infinite space. Clouds drifted below, tattering on the jagged teeth of mountains.

"This is not the heaven I expected," he said.

The voice that answered him was not Turpin's, though the archbishop's snoring had stopped some little while since. "Not heaven, though not earth, either. This is the castle of Carbonek, in the kingdom of Montsalvat."

The names rang like bells. Roland turned. Turpin was awake indeed, but silent. And Sarissa was standing just within the door.

Here in what must be her own place, she was more beautiful than ever, more truly and splendidly herself. Roland, naked and chilled and confused, stood as straight as he could. When he spoke, it was not to her. "Turpin. I thought you had died. Are the others—is Olivier—?"

Turpin's face was stark. "Olivier died at Roncesvalles. Thibaut, Milun, Ogier, the rest—gone. Anselm and Eggihard from the king's own household fell beside them. I was left for dead, but these kind folk found me and brought me here."

Roland swayed against the wall. It was cold against his back, and hard, and as grimly real as the truth Turpin had spoken. Dead, all dead but they two. "And the king? The army?"

"The king is safe in Francia," said Turpin. "He heard your horn; he came back. It was too late by far for any of us, but he took vengeance on those rebels whom he found, gathered the dead and marched over the mountains. All the baggage was lost, all the gold and treasure of Spain."

"But we are not—"

"You were brought here," Sarissa said, "before you

could be killed. I grieve for Olivier and for the others. We came as swift as we could, but we were too slow."

Roland pressed his hands to his forehead. His head was throbbing. "We should be in Francia or laid in tombs. Why are we here? How did we come here?"

Sarissa beckoned. Servants entered, laden with a copper basin and jars of water and the rest of the accoutrements of a bath. They were men, mortal enough to look at, dark and slight and sharp-featured like Romans or Spaniards. Their long tunics were of linen undyed, their mantles of deep clear blue, each held at the shoulder by a brooch in the shape of silver swan.

They bowed low before Roland, set down the basin and filled it, and gently but irresistibly coaxed him into it. He could not but remember the last time he had had such service, in the king's tent before the ascent to Roncesvalles. He nearly broke down and wept; but he would not do that in front of these strangers.

They washed him with an air almost of ritual, moving in unison, without a word spoken or a glance exchanged. When he was clean, his body dry, his hair damp on his shoulders, they clothed him in a long white garment like a monk's habit, then took the bath and went away, as silent as they had come.

New servants came behind them, bearing cups and bowls and jars: a light feast, with wine and new bread, cheese and fruit and lentils stewed in spices, but no meat. He began to wonder if this was an abbey that he had come to, though she called it a castle—Carbonek, in the kingdom of the Grail.

He could not eat, though his stomach growled. Sarissa sat by the bed, poured a cup of wine, gave it to Turpin. The archbishop seemed at ease; he smiled at her. She smiled in return. One would think, thought Roland, that they were friends of long standing.

"Tell me," he said. "What must I be strong enough to know? What is worse than the death of all my friends but one, and my king's bitter defeat?"

"Nothing," she said. "Your king is safe in his own kingdom—I promised you that, and I kept my promise."

"Did you?" Roland set his back against the wall again, as if it could protect him from he knew not what. Grief was darkening in him, turning to anger. *Olivier,* his heart mourned. *O my brother!*

"You asked me," she said, "whose champion you had been chosen to be. This is the answer I could not give you then. You are the champion of Montsalvat."

Time was when Roland's heart would have swelled to hear such a thing; when he would have been dizzy with joy and pride. But he had fought in the slaughter of Roncesvalles. He had seen those he loved cut down one by one. When he closed his eyes, he could see that battle still, and the hordes of devils swarming down upon his people.

"Was there need for that?" he demanded of Sarissa. "Was it necessary that so many die? They were aimed at me. They struck for me. Because they knew what I was. If I had known—"

"You were not their only purpose," she said. "Our enemy—your enemy, my lord—sought to seize the Frankish army and twist it to his own ends. That, we were able to prevent. We saved the great bulk of your king's army, so that it was free to escape. The rearguard . . ." She paused. "Come," she said abruptly. "Come with me."

He might have refused, but she had seized his hand. He could not break free.

He could walk, or he could be dragged. He chose to walk. She drew him out of that room, down a long winding stair in what must be a tower, along a passage lit with lamps that burned with a pale and steady light, and across a courtyard open to the aching blue of the sky.

The wall that bounded the far edge of that courtyard was the outer wall of the castle. Twin towers warded its gate. Sarissa led him to the summit of that on the right hand, and stood with him on the battlement, looking down into a fair green valley.

It was beautiful, that valley. Yet he hardly saw it. His eyes were caught and held by what lay just below the walls.

A camp was pitched there, tents enough and fires enough for a fair army. There were horselines, though most of the horses grazed at liberty in wide pastures. Men watched over them, and tended campfires, and practiced exercises both mounted and afoot. He saw no idlers, though there were men sitting still, fletching arrows or mending shields.

He knew those men, those tents and that order of encampment. The rearguard of Charles' army camped below the walls of Carbonek. From the count of tents, the full ten thousand of them must have come through the battle in the pass, or near enough to make no matter.

"This is not possible," he said, leaning on the parapet, gripping it till his fingers ached. "I saw what came against us. It was red slaughter."

"That was all for you," said Sarissa. "The others, he wanted for himself. Those forces of his were only sent to kill you. For the rest, they were herdsmen. These men were to pass through the gates of hell, and so be enslaved."

He heard the ring of truth in her words. And yet his anger made his sight far too clear. It showed him another thing, a thing that set his heart in stone. "You, too. You wanted my king's army—and my king—to fight for you in whatever war you see before you. He escaped, didn't he? You didn't let him go. The enemy confounded you, even as you confounded him. You only won the rearguard because I was in it. He wanted me dead. You needed me alive. You sacrificed the van and the center, but won this much. Ten thousand Franks, mourned for dead. And still you let the Companions die. Why? Why could they not have lived, too?"

"We came too late," she said. It sounded as if she honestly grieved—but he would not believe honesty of her. Not any longer. "We made all speed we could. First we had to shut the hellgate. And when we had done that—"

"That's why you couldn't tell me, isn't it? Because you needed the army. Not to conquer Spain. To come here. If you had needed me alone, you could have persuaded me to come. But to bring so many of my king's men—all of them, if you could—that needed a degree of treachery. Of deceit. Of—"

"You see clearly," she said, "but your understanding is clouded."

"What is there to understand but that you conspired to steal an army? If you had asked—if you had even begun to trust either me or my king—"

"We dared not," she said. "The stakes were too high."

"So high that you risked losing all at the last? Men are not children, my lady, nor animals, to do as they are told without regard for their will or their wishes. You should have spoken with my king. You should have asked. He would have given himself gladly, if he had reckoned the cause just."

"And if he had not?"

"He rode into Spain at the behest of an infidel Caliph. Do you honestly believe that he would refuse to aid your kingdom?"

"We could not take that risk," she said. "We had to be certain. To take, and not to ask."

"Then you are fools," he said. "Arrogant, and fools."

He turned his back on her. Anger built a wall between them, raised it high and guarded it well. Olivier was dead. Ten thousand Franks snatched away into captivity were no recompense. No, not even a hellgate broken and a king escaped. Olivier was dead.

He abandoned it all—grief, rage, even the bonds of flesh. In falcon's form, with falcon's spirit, he hurtled into the sun.

CHAPTER 36

✠ ✠ ✠

"**Y**ou should have told him," Turpin said mildly.

Sarissa unknotted her fists. Her palms ached and stung where the nails had pierced flesh. Her throat was tight. Still she managed to get the words out. "And have him do what he just did, before we had brought him here?"

"Olivier would have been a useful ally," Turpin said. "It's an ill thing for you that he died."

"We can't bring him back," she said.

"Did I ask that?" He shook his head. He looked weary suddenly, worn with his own grief. "I know how close to death I was when I was brought here, and how far I had to come before I walked again in the daylight. Roland came farther still. The third of us had gone over the river. I would that I had gone in his place—for your sake and for Roland's."

"No," she said. "It was meant to be so. As ill as it seems, as grievous as it is, this is the gods' will."

He raised a brow at her mention of gods, but did not question it, just then. "Suppose you tell me precisely what you need of Roland. Why you had to steal a royal army, and snatch it away by means both magical and secret."

She leaned on the parapet. Her eyes looked out across the wide valley of Montsalvat, but they barely saw its green rolling fields or its deep woodlands. Trust came hard. He was an outlander and a Christian; and though the Grail had belonged to his Christ, it was not a Christian thing. But she had failed once in failing to trust. "Come," she said.

She led him through the castle. Rather deliberately, she took the long way about. He was no fool: he could well encompass the size and strength of the fortress, and the richness of its appointments. People of rank were few this day; most were out and about, performing duties and preparing for the war. Still there were servants enough, quiet and rather shy in the presence of a stranger, but watching him closely under cover of sweeping or scrubbing or standing guard. Many had never seen an unfamiliar face, still less a Frankish one. There was much chatter in the servants' quarters, she was sure, and she did not doubt that many of those she saw had no pressing need to be where they were just then.

She pretended not to see any of them. At length she came round to the long dim hall with its lofty vault. Shafts of sun slanted through the high louvered windows, casting bars of light upon the floor. Artisans out of Byzantium had laid that pavement long ago, a mosaic of wondrous work, glimmering with gold. Gold gleamed on the pillars and in the mosaics of the vault, images of glory and splendor: all the earth spread out on the floor, rising in trunks of trees and golden vines, up to the blue dome of heaven with its myriad stars.

Turpin's step faltered. His breath caught. Sarissa, who had known this hall for years out of count, paused to taste of his wonder. It was beautiful indeed. But they had not come to marvel at the great hall of Carbonek. She passed through it with him trailing slowly behind her.

He stopped again before the dais on which stood the throne. It was rather startling amid such splendor: a simple chair of wood that had gone dark with age. No jewel, no carving adorned it. All its beauty was its simplicity.

She opened the door behind the dais. The chamber beyond was empty, but its lamps were lit. The passage that led from it was deserted but illuminated, waiting for them to pass. It ended in another door and a stair winding steeply upward.

There was nothing here for Turpin to stare at, no beauty, no richness, only the bare plain stone. Yet for her there was more awe in this stark unornamented tower than in any work of mortal hands. The great high singing thing before her was reaching, seeking, drawing her to itself.

She did not enter into its presence, but halted in the antechamber. Even there, its power thrummed in her bones.

This room had been bare once, a simple space for waiting, or for testing initiates before they came into the presence. Now it was furbished as a monk's cell, with narrow hard bed and wooden stool.

Nieve was attending the man on the bed. Sarissa breathed somewhat of a sigh of relief. Of the nine, Nieve was the eldest. Her sweetness and her calm strength had comforted Sarissa often and often; and so it did now, as she looked up smiling. "He sleeps," she said in her gentle voice, "but he'll wake soon."

Sarissa nodded. She would have loved to rest here, to know a few moments' peace, but there would be none of that until the war was over.

Nieve withdrew to the inner chamber—fortunate, to take that nourishment, to renew her body and spirit. Sarissa sat in the chair that she had left, and took the hand that lay slack upon the coverlet.

He had declined even in the day since she had taken her turn on watch. His hand was thinner, his skin more transparent. The bones of his face were stark, his eyes sunk deep. Yet there was no pain that she could see, and neither fear nor sorrow, only a deep peace.

Turpin's broad shadow fell across her. Beside the sleeper he seemed heavier and more bearish than ever. And yet, she thought, his eyes were clear and full of compassion. "Is that . . . ?" he asked softly.

She nodded.

He sank to one knee, half for comfort, half for awe. "He looks so young," he said, "even so close to death. He looks—like—"

"Roland's foremother was his sister," she said.

She watched Turpin understand the meaning of that. "So that's why—"

"Yes," she said.

"But has he no sons—grandsons? No heirs?"

"Only one can be chosen," she said.

Turpin tugged at his beard, frowning. She let him ponder at his leisure. He might mourn Olivier's absence and insist that only Olivier could make Roland see reason, but she could well see why the gods had taken that one of the three, and left this big shambling man with his clear eyes and his swift mind.

The hand in hers did not move, but it changed slightly. Life had come into it, a little. She met the calm grey eyes of her king, and bowed her head in greeting and respect.

He smiled at her. "Little one," he said, his voice the merest thread of a whisper—the old jest, the old endearment. "Why so troubled? He'll come back."

"Are you sure of that?" she asked him.

He nodded. His hand tightened for a moment on hers. His gaze had shifted to Turpin. Turpin met it without fear. "My lord archbishop," said the king of the Grail.

"My lord king," said Turpin.

"You are welcome in Montsalvat," Parsifal said.

"It is a great honor," Turpin said, "and a great wonder, to wake from death into this kingdom."

Parsifal's smile was almost wry. "So I said once, when I was young. Do you wish to see the Grail?"

Turpin blinked as if taken aback. Sarissa, who was accustomed to her king's directness, was somewhat disconcerted herself.

"I . . . doubt that I am worthy," Turpin said after a moment.

"You may doubt," said Parsifal. "The Grail cares nothing. Little one?"

Sarissa kissed his hand, laid it on the coverlet and rose. Turpin seemed astonished when she raised him to his feet. He was trembling. "I truly am not worthy," he said.

"Do you fear that it will blast you for your sins?" She drew him forward. He did not want to come, but she saw to it that he could not resist her.

There was no great gate before them, no fanfare of trumpets. Only the stair and the door, and the white chamber beyond, round like the tower it was built in. There was the altar in its circle of clear light, and the shrine with its four winged guardians. Their eyes glittered as Sarissa entered with Turpin.

The Grail was singing softly in its shrine. Nieve knelt before it, deep in contemplation. Their presence disturbed her not at all.

Turpin had fallen to his knees just within the door. The trembling had left him. He looked as he must in battle, stern and still, but with a fierce light in his eyes.

Sarissa bowed before the shrine. Here always, all trouble left her, all doubts and fears. There was only the light and the singing, and the high white power of the Grail.

She opened the silver doors. The Grail was wrapped in its cloth that had been a Roman legionary's cloak: heavy wool well woven, red as blood. She lifted the cup from its wrappings, cradling it in her palms. It was as light as air and as heavy as the world, as it had always been. Sometimes it brimmed with blood, sometimes with light. Today it was full of blood-red wine, the sweet Falernian, wafting its scent through the gleaming air.

Turpin was rapt before the Grail. She brought the cup to him and set it to his lips. He drank as if in a dream. The Grail's singing was supernally sweet.

She did not drink from it herself. All the nourishment it could give, it gave her by its simple presence. She could feel it in her blood, in her flesh and bone. The burden of years slipped away. The weariness of grief, anger, guilt, all shrank and faded. The Grail brought healing; that was its gift and its power.

It healed her as it healed Turpin; as it had healed Roland, who had been near death. As it had lost power to heal Parsifal.

"I refuse it," he said.

She had laid the Grail back in its shrine, and left Turpin kneeling there near Nieve, lost as she was in holy trance. Parsifal was awake still, drifting half in a dream, but rousing to Sarissa's presence.

"It's time for me to go," he said. "The Grail would hold me to this life for a thousand years; but I was born and raised a mortal man. I was never meant to live the life of a god."

"Is it a curse?" she asked, not precisely of him. "Amfortas also denied the Grail—though his cause was guilt and great shame, for the sin that he committed, and his betrayal of the oath that he had sworn. Are all the Grail-kings doomed to turn their backs on the power they serve?"

"There is a doom on us," said Parsifal, "but so is there on all kings. With great power comes a great price."

"That I know," said Sarissa who was the chief of the ladies of the Grail. And who was older than this man, too, though perhaps not wiser. If she had been wise, she would not have lost Roland.

"Nothing is ever lost," Parsifal said. He read her as easily as Roland had. Perhaps it was a gift of that blood. "When the archbishop comes out, gather your courage. Tell him the truth. It will armor him when the champion comes back—when we all face the consequences of your choice."

Sarissa bore the rebuke in silence, as she should. "Shall I tell him everything, then? All of it?"

"All," said the Grail-king.

"And if he rises up in revolt?"

"Then that is God's will," said Parsifal. "Little one, you cannot make choices for all the gods. Sometimes they're bound to make their own."

That was difficult. Sarissa was not certain she believed in it. But he was wiser than she. He always had been, even when he was a simple fool. She stooped and kissed his brow, pressed his hand to her heart, and left him to guard what strength he had.

CHAPTER 37

✠ ✠ ✠

Roland flew high and far. He little cared where he went, save that it be away from fear, away from anger: clear into the blue heaven, with all his will and spirit gathered into a single bright spark, the mind of a hawk.

As a hawk he hunted and flew. As a hawk he slept when the night came, and took wing when the sun rose again, with the memory of humanity shrinking smaller, the longer he wore those swift wings.

This was rich land, green land, teeming with prey. Other falcons flew in it, and eagles in the jagged heights, and things that his hawk-spirit did not know, winged with darkness or flame; and some wore the bodies of furred beasts but flew as the eagle did, and others were scaled like serpents, trailing a scent of fire.

The hawk flew well away from those. He was fierce and he brooked no rival, but he had a little prudence. They hunted greater prey than his, nor troubled his hunting while he forbore to trouble theirs.

Once a vast dark thing swooped over him, shutting out the sky. It passed without taking notice of him, but he was far too wary after that to linger in the air. Night was falling, true night unmarred by alien wings. He sheltered as he could in a wood of tall dark trees, deep in among the branches. Their scent was strong with resin, clear and pungent. Their needles whispered in the wind.

He had flown far and wide of men's places. Those were not so common here by the dark wood, but there were small huddles of houses scattered along the wood's edges. None dared settle within, though a few pressed up against the shadow of the trees.

Some deep spark of memory stirred at that—remembrance of a place that was not this one, but had been very like, once, long ago. Fair green country, windy moors, rings of stones heavy with old power; and in the heart of it the wood.

Wisdom would have taken him away. There were gentler lands within sight and scent of these, better hunting, sweeter quarry, but the niggle of memory kept him close to the wood and the villages. One village in particular fascinated him, though what there was about it, he could not have told. There was a warren of rabbits nearby, and a flock of doves, but any village might have offered as much. The people mattered nothing to him. They watched him— he caught the gleam of eyes in flat pale faces—but none threatened him with stone or dart.

This was a larger village than some. It stood on a road that ran along the wood's edge, then wound away into the misty green country. There was a deep clear spring on its eastern edge, and a mother tree to which the women came with gifts of wool and bread and bits of honeycomb, and which the children garlanded with flowers.

He took to roosting in the tree's branches, resting there at night and pausing between hunts in the day. From there he could see the thatched roofs of the village, and the road, and the inn that stood beside it. People came to tarry in the inn for a night or an evening, and drink strong yeasty ale and eat fresh-baked bread and chatter as human people chattered.

He had been human once. He had no particular desire to wear that shape again, awkward earthbound thing with its voice like a dog's barking. Far sweeter to be a falcon, swiftest of things that flew, with fierce talons and beak that could rend the life out of tender prey.

Dawn came one morning in a grey gust of rain, but the sun put to flight the clouds and wet. He shook the last of the damp from his wings and spread them to begin his morning hunt. But even with the sharp gnawing of hunger in his middle, he paused. The sun was bright. The clouds were blowing away to the east. Droplets of wet sparkled on leaf and stone. There was no darkness in this world, no shadow, though the wood loomed close.

And yet within him something had been stirring since he saw the dark thing beyond the wood. In this bright morning, in the clear light of the sun, that something stirred and thrashed and woke.

Memory. Fear. Anger, and a gust of sorrow. A rabbit, young and foolish, hopped from its burrow full beneath him and began to nibble on a bit of weed by the pool. His hawk-senses leaped to the alert, but he did not stoop to the kill. On the feathers of his breast, a thing moved, familiar though long unheeded. It was warm, like a spark of the sun. It drew him inexorably to earth.

The rabbit fled in terror. He had no talons to catch and hold it. The air was cold on skin bare of feathers. Arms sprawled on leafmold, fingers scrabbling, forgetful of their purpose. No wings, no claws. No sweet taste of blood. He lay in the fallen leaves and wept, though what tears were, or what they were for, he did not clearly remember.

Marric had been watching the hawk since it took up residence in the Lady's tree. That it chose to rest there, and hunted so close to it, spoke to him of things that he had half forgotten: tales told, visions, dreams in the night. None of them came clear enough to grasp, but he was patient. The gods moved in their own time. When they were ready, they would reveal their purpose.

He had nearly forsaken patience on the day when, glancing sidewise at the bird as he passed by the tree and the spring, he had seen something odd: something hanging at the feathered breast, a gleam of metal where one hardly expected to find it. Further inspection, with care lest the hawk take flight, discovered a silver chain about the neck, and a disk of silver suspended from it. Marric could never come close enough to see what was written on the disk, if anything was; but that it was a thing of power, he could well see.

On the morning after a night of rain, in clear damp sunlight, he woke to a sharp awareness of something different. The village was quiet. No one else had paid much heed to

the hawk. That was Marric's duty, to fret over matters beyond the round of daily things. The rest of them were content to live as they had for time out of mind, tending their
houses, herding their flocks, looking after the visitors who
came to Gemma's inn by the Woodsedge road.

But when he passed the last of the houses and approached the Lady's tree, he saw a cluster of children
standing wide-eyed and silent, staring at something under
the tree. That something was larger than a hawk—much
larger. It had white skin and very black hair, long and tangled, and it clutched at the tree's roots and wept.

Marric stepped through the ring of children and touched
the trembling shoulder. The stranger whipped about,
nearly sweeping Marric from his feet. But Marric was
rooted in earth, and even in utter startlement he was not to
be overset. He stared into a face that had nothing human
in it at all, though the shape of it was more human than
not. The eyes that blazed on him were as yellow as a
hawk's, and wild, and quite empty of reason. On the creature's breast swung the silver talisman. It caught the sun
and flamed, all but blinding him.

"Well," said Marric, without fear though not without surprise. "Well and well. So She called you here. She has an
odd humor, does our Lady."

The man who had been a hawk did not answer. But he
did not strike, either, and Marric took that as an omen.
"Off with you, children," he said to the audience, who had
drawn back in respect for a manifest madman, but in no
more fear than Marric had. "Fetch Gemma and her boys.
Tell them the Lady's brought us a gift and a charge, and
we'll need the fowling net, and maybe the roc's cage, too."

"Oh, no," said the smallest of the children, who had the
largest eyes and the clearest sight of them all. "Not the
roc's cage. But the net, you'll need."

"Just the net, then," said Marric. The children ran to do
his bidding—far more obedient than they were usually inclined to be, but then this was the most remarkable thing
they had seen in most of their short lives. They would
reckon that the sooner they had run their errand, the
sooner they could be back again, staring at the stranger
with the hawk's mad eyes.

He crouched against the tree's bole, sitting oddly, as if he had forgotten how a man's limbs bent and flexed. His toes curled as if to clutch a branch; his shoulders hunched, arms drawn in like a hawk's wings. Tears were drying on his cheeks, glistening in a sparse growth of beard.

Marric settled in to wait while the children fetched Gemma and her pack of burly sons. And, he reminded himself, the net. He was not at all certain that it had been wise to omit the cage, but small Brigid had a clear sight for such things. If she did not reckon it wise to cage this wanderer, then no doubt the net would suffice.

In the event, it did—barely. The stranger was awkward in this shape, but strong, and grimly determined not to be confined. But Gemma's sons overcame him, rolled him in the net and carried him, by then stiffly quiescent, down to the inn. Marric had had in mind to take the stranger to his own house, but he was overruled.

"We have a room with a lock on the door," Gemma said, "and no windows to let a winged thing out. And you laid the guard-spells yourself. He'll be safer here."

Marric was not exactly sure of that, but he shrugged and let the innkeeper take command. Time enough later to win that battle. For the moment he saw one advantage in surrender: the innkeeper could see to taming the stranger enough to wash the sharp animal reek from him, though she was no such fool as to approach him with razor or cutting blade.

He seemed to have exhausted his struggles once the net fell on him. Biding his time, Marric thought. He suffered through a bath and a lengthy combing, much more lengthy than it need have been—for all the emptiness of his face and the madness in his eyes, he was a handsome thing, and very well made. He only struggled once after he was netted: when Gemma tried to touch the amulet about his neck. She escaped with a bruise and a scratch or two, and a greater respect for his strength and quickness.

Gemma took rather too much pleasure in making him as presentable as she could, plaiting his hair and, with visible regret, covering that fine white body in a tunic that fit him passably well: some lord's left-behind, all fine linen and silken borders.

"And right noble you look in it, too," she said to him, stroking his hair that she had labored so long to clean and comb smooth. He endured the touch as he had the rest, without acknowledging her at all.

"Poor thing," she said. "No wits in you, and such a face to go with it." And not only the face, Marric could see her thinking.

While she fussed over him and plied him with dainties which he ignored, Marric sat in the corner and watched, pondering a number of things. Not least was the amulet, and the protection that it granted. Whatever manner of man this was, if indeed he was a man, he was or had been in the favor of great powers. Had he run from them, from some task that they had imposed? Or had they reft his wits from him in punishment for a great sin?

When the Lady was ready, no doubt she would reveal the truth. For the moment, Marric sensed no evil in this man. Danger—yes, he could be thrumming with it. But of darkness Marric could find nothing.

Word of the stranger had spread. The inn was remarkably full for so early in the day. When Marric lengthened an ear to listen, he discovered that they had invented a history for the stranger, as solid as if it had been true. He had come out of the wood, they said. He was cursed—or blessed—by the Lady, and he was mute as well as mad. They had also decided that he was either a beggar or a prince, and that a maiden's kiss would cure him. One or two maidens, and several who Marric knew had not been maidens in some time, hung about the entrance to Gemma's wine-cellar, where the stranger was confined.

None of them had magic enough to pass the wards on the door, and Marric was on the other side of it, making sure that the wardings held. When Gemma came and went, which she did often, attempts to slip past her failed. Still one of them was determined enough to set off the wards; her screech pierced Marric's heightened senses, and brought the stranger flailing to his feet.

He fell at once in a tangle of limbs, thrashing until Marric feared he would harm himself. Marric caught the thin wrists, hissing at the strength in them, and spoke a Word. The stranger stiffened, staring, yellow eyes fixed on Marric's face. Did he see? Could he understand? Marric found no answer there, only walls and shuttered windows.

The woman had made herself scarce. The stranger eased

slowly. His eyes had not left Marric's face. Marric suppressed a shiver. "There," he said for lack of anything more sensible. "There."

The sound of Marric's voice seemed to calm the stranger. His wild eyes closed. He turned his face away. After some little while Marric let him go. He stayed where Marric left him, as if there were no will in him, no wits and no memory.

And yet somewhere, Marric was certain, however deeply buried, was a mind and a spirit. Marric was a mender of things that were broken. That was what he was for. He would find the spirit trapped in that witless body. He would bring it out. And then the Lady would do with them both as she pleased; and that was as it should be.

CHAPTER 38

✠ ✠ ✠

He woke slowly from his long winged dream. Little by little he learned to walk as a man, and not to stretch his arms as if they could grip the air and lift on the breast of it. He grew, if not resigned, then accustomed to skin without feathers, mouth without sharp tearing beak. He learned to eat as men ate, forsaking the hot sweetness of blood, the quiver of meat still faintly, pulsingly alive.

At first he lived in the damp dim room with its door that hissed and crackled with odd lightnings. But when he grew calmer and stopped fighting against this strangeness that had fallen over him, the brown man led him out into the wider world and let him taste the sunlight again. He never tried to run, though sometimes he did his best to fly. The earth bound him as always, and this unyielding flesh.

Speech did not come to him. That the sounds men made had meaning, he understood well enough; with the passage of nights and days, he learned enough to please the woman with the wild red hair, and even the brown man, who watched him nearly always and seldom left him. But there was no desire in him to speak as they spoke. He made no sound at all, even when he stumbled and fell and burned his hands in the fire. The woman made a great deal of noise then, and others who were there clamored like a flock of jackdaws, but he crouched silent, with tears of pain running down his cheeks.

The woman wept, too, after she had roundly beaten the man who, she seemed to think, had tripped him onto the hearth. But he needed no help to stumble; he was still unsteady on his feet, and inclined to forget that his wings were gone.

The pain went away soon enough. The brown man took it, and much of the burning and scarring, too. The rest healed without a mark. The woman made even more noise over that, as if it could matter whether he carried scars or no. She called him her poor beautiful idiot, and her lovely witling, and stroked him as she did her smug red cat. But she did not kiss the cat, or comb and plait its hair as often as she could catch it, or dress it in odd and sometimes uncomfortable garments from an inexhaustible store.

The woman had a name, a word that bound her spirit: Gemma. The brown man was Marric. The others too were possessed of names, some of which he troubled to remember, and some not.

He had no name. There was none in him when he went looking, and no one saw fit to give him one. He was the witling or the idiot or the mad one. Sometimes a stranger called him Yelloweyes, but that was not his name. He never answered to it.

Women were not made as he was made. They were determined to teach him the ways of it, catching him when the brown man was not looking, sliding hands up his tunic to clasp the dangling thing that hung between his legs. They had soft heavy breasts where he had none, and rounded bellies, and nothing below but thickets of curling hair.

One of them was teaching him a new thing one day, pressing his hand to her breast and slipping the other beneath her skirts, into a hot moist cleft that throbbed against his fingers. She moaned as he worked them into it, and arched her back. Her nipple was hard under his hand.

All at once she was gone, and Gemma was belaboring her about the head and shoulders with the wooden laundry-paddle. He stood blinking, baffled, with an ache between his legs, and the stiff rod thrusting beneath his tunic.

"Ah, lad," said the brown man's voice behind him, dry as old leaves, "what I'd give for the women to be fighting over me."

It was a battle royal. Gemma won it, returning battered

and bruised but grimly triumphant. She caught the witling by the hand and drew him unprotesting into the inn.

But when she tried to lead him to the corner where he spent his evenings, watching people in the inn and staying out of the way, he stiffened his knees and refused. Her breast was larger and softer than the other's, and her secret place was hotter and moister, and her lips were fierce on his. She taught him then what the stiff and aching rod was for. It slid home like—

Sword to scabbard.

Man to woman.

Soul to—

Memory tugged at him, slipping away when he tried to grasp it. This thing, this dance of flesh, he knew—he understood. It had its rhythms and its cadences. Now fast, now slow. Now deep and strong, now soft and purringly languid. When the release came, it nigh felled him. But he remembered. He saw—

Gemma's face, slack with pleasure, and the flame-bright cloud of her hair. Her strong freckled arms held him close. Her sturdy legs clasped about his middle. He kissed her lips and her cheeks and her forehead, licking the salt sweetness of sweat.

Tears were salt, too, but bitter. She did not shed many of those. She caught his face in her hands, stroking fingers through his beard. "My dear and lovely simpleton," she said, both rough and sweet, "if you lay hand on another woman after this, I'll geld you with a blunt knife."

She would not. But he had no words to say so. He kissed her instead, and would have done more, but she pushed him away. "Not now," she said irritably. "Away with you, you randy thing, and earn your keep. We need wood for the fire. Find Kyllan, he'll show you how to cut it."

Kyllan was her eldest son, the one who looked most like her, with his shock of fiery hair and his quick temper. But he was patient with the witling, and he understood without need of words. He taught the witling to wield the axe, and to cut and split the logs, and to carry them in and heap them just so, laid ready beside the hearth.

He would have cut wood all day and half the night, if there had been enough of it. It was like lying with a woman. The heft of the axe in his hands, the flex and surge of muscles as he lifted it high and let it fall with force enough to cleave the heavy log, woke memories he had not known he had.

He was sorry when the last log was split and cut and set atop the pile. His arms wanted to lift the axe again, but Gemma had come out to take it away from him. She led him in to a bath and a combing and, tonight, the shaving of his beard. He was not sorry to lose that, but when she advanced on his upper lip, he stopped her. She shrugged, yielded, laid the razor away in its box.

Every night before this, he had slept in his corner by the hearth, curled in a heap of furs and tanned skins. This night she led him past that to her own shuttered box of a room. A bed nearly filled it, and the scent of her was rich in it. He reeled dizzily, tumbling with her into the soft featherbed. She laughed and wriggled and slid until he was secure inside her, and then he was laughing, too, but silently, with the pleasure of this thing that she had taught him.

She slept quickly, once she had her fill of him. He lay awake. He did not want to be a hawk any longer. He was not altogether content to be a man, either, but if it gave him woodcutting, and this, then he could bear it.

The woman rolled away from him, murmuring in her sleep. He let her go. His hand rose to his face, tracing the shape of the shaven chin, and tugging lightly at the mustaches. He wondered then what people saw when they looked at that face. Women seemed greatly pleased with it. Men were a good deal less so, but they did not recoil, either.

Gemma had a mirror, a disk of polished bronze. He had seen her peering into it, one morning when he wandered innocently in. That was before he knew what women were. She had chased him out with much noise but little force, and forbidden him to enter again unless she let him in. Which now she had done, and he was glad.

He found the mirror where it had been that morning, facedown on the chest by the bed. The slant of moonlight was bright enough for his eyes to see by. He held the mirror up between his palms, and stared at the face reflected darkly in it. A shift of his hands cast moon-silver across the bronze, brightening the image to an almost daylight sheen.

He did not look like the people here. His skin was whiter

than theirs, he had known that already, and none of them had hair so black. His face was sharper, his nose longer. One cheek was marked with thin parallel scars. His eyes were wide and yellow as the coins that Gemma took out sometimes to fondle and to marvel at. Gold was precious. Gold was richer than any other metal. His eyes were gold.

He turned the mirror facedown again and laid it on the chest, and sat in the patch of moonlight, staring into the dark with his eyes like golden coins. Gemma snored softly in the bed. His rod rose at the thought of her. He stroked it idly, for the pleasure of it, but his mind was not on it. Was this beauty, then, that he had? Did it matter?

To her it did, and the other women. To him . . . no. She mattered. The weight of the axe in his hands, and the strength of his arms as he swung it up. The pleasure mounting in his middle, bursting hot and wet—that mattered. But a face, what was that?

His lips felt odd. He was smiling. He was being absurd, and he knew it; and that made him smile the wider.

He lay with Gemma, breast to her smooth naked back, and cupped her big soft breasts in his hands, and buried his face in the exuberance of her hair. It smelled of ale and smoke and woman. She murmured but did not wake, nor did she pull away. He sighed—yes, content—and let sleep take him.

CHAPTER 39

✠ ✠ ✠

Witling or no, it seemed the stranger knew how to please a woman. Gemma had won him, and held him against all comers. He seemed content with that, though the women of the village were not even slightly pleased to have lost him.

Marric watched with wry detachment. The boy cleaned up well, particularly once Gemma stopped dressing him like a painted poppet and gave him clothes fit for hewing wood and drawing water. He might grace her bed, but she had determined that he would earn his keep in more seemly fashion. He proved a strong hand with the axe, and a capable one with the horses: the old slow gelding who carried Gemma and her sons about on errands too far or too pressing for simple feet, and Marric's brown pony that he kept at the inn, and the occasional patron's mount.

Then in the evenings he would sit in a corner of the common room by the fire, and though he never spoke, he seemed to listen to whatever people said. They took to talking to him, men and women alike, telling him their stories, sharing their secrets. His silence was like an open door. He seemed to understand: he never laughed or smiled, but his eyes would fix on their faces, and his expression shift subtly with the shifts of the story.

Marric had long since reached certain conclusions about this stranger. He took his time in confirming them. When

one day he caught the witling in the stable, he met steady
golden eyes that had learned to smile, and lifted the unre-
sisting hands. His thumb ran along ridged calluses, traced
old scars. How strong those arms were, those shoulders and
thighs, he knew already. He lifted a foot as if the boy had
been a horse. As filthy as those soles were, barefoot in the
stableyard, they were never as thickened or as hard as if he
had spent his life afoot.

This was a horseman and a swordsman, marked with
scars of battle—many battles, from the look of him. He suffered Marric's handling without resentment, though the
smile had faded from his eyes. The black brows had drawn
together in puzzlement.

Marric put on a smile, which was real enough, and pat-
ted him until the frown smoothed away. "Good lad," he
said then. The witling smiled a little, baffled still, but seeming comforted.

Marric wished that he could have said the same. It was
no good omen to find a man of war here, where lord did
not go to battle against lord, and no man raised hand
against another. The young lords learned to fight because
it was required of them, because they were guardians and
defenders; but those who tested themselves in battle, did so
far away among the kingdoms of the world. Never here,
never in this realm, where the peace of the Grail had held
for time out of mind.

Not long after that, Lord Huon's messenger rode into
the village. He was one of the lord's heralds in fine though
travelworn livery, with a squire to bear his arms, and in his
hand as he rode, a spear with a blood-red pennon.

Everyone in the village who could walk or run or crawl
had come to follow him. He halted before the inn, where
the road was wide and clear, and people could gather to
hear his proclamation. It was brief, and it struck hard.
"War," he said in his ringing voice. "War has come. Your
lord bids you to the muster. Any man or woman who fails
of obedience, let him pay the penalty."

Marric stood apart from the tumult that rose in the wake
of that, searching faces, weighing hearts. None of these
children had ever been called to the muster, not in all their
years. Nor had their elders, or any of mortal blood. Most of

them were grinning, dancing, laughing, as if war were a grand lark. A handful of idiot boys tumbled together in mock battle.

The herald called the muster that day, just after the sun passed noon, reckoning the count of each clan and kindred, and choosing the levy from among the young and the able and the eager. His eye was quick and his heart cold. He discarded the strong young woman with her baby at her breast, but chose her husband without a flicker of compunction. If a clan's offerings were too young or too old, he took the penalty in grain or hides or hoarded coin.

Of Gemma's household he chose Gemma and three of her five sons, discarding Madoc with his lame leg and Rhodri who was but twelve summers old. That should have been enough, but the swift cold eye had caught the figure that hovered behind them. The witling had come out with the rest of them; nor had anyone thought to chase him back into the stable where he belonged.

Marric, looking at him, knew a kind of wry relief. His tunic was ancient and filthy. His hair was snarled out of its plait. He must have been cleaning the hayloft: he was covered in dust and cobwebs, his feet spattered with mud and ordure, and a great smudge of soot across his face.

Marric caught Gemma's eye. She met his stare stonily. She must, thought Marric, have devoted a good hour to the disguise. He himself could hardly have done better.

But the herald was well schooled in the arts of doting women, and there was no disguising the breadth of those shoulders. He approached the witling, riding on his tall bay horse, and halted within reach.

Gemma had schooled the witling well. He did not lift those startling eyes. He stood with them lowered, and seemed to remember, rather too late, to hunch his shoulders and make himself smaller.

"That one," said the herald to his squire. "He's young, his back is straight. Add him to the muster."

"My lord," said Gemma. Her voice was tight with the effort of keeping it civil. "That's but a poor idiot with barely wits to lace up his own tunic."

The herald's brow rose. "Indeed?" he said. He lifted from his belt the rod of his office. Without warning he tossed it toward the witling.

The boy caught it in the air, swifter than the eye could see. He stood holding it, still with his eyes fixed on his feet.

"Give it back," the herald said.

The boy's hand blurred. The herald was barely quick enough to catch the rod as it flew. "Wits enough," he said, "to wield a spear in the lord's name. Reckon him with the rest; and see that he comes to the muster."

Gemma looked ready to kill someone—whether the herald or the witling, Marric doubted that even she knew. But against the levy there was no recourse. The herald's squire completed the roll and tally of the village, rolled up the scroll, bound it, and laid it away in his saddlebag. Even as he straightened, the herald was on the road again, spear in hand, riding on with his burden of war.

"This is the great war," said Kyllan in the inn that night. The long low room was crowded to bursting. Most of the men and women who had been called to the muster, and a good number of their kin, had come there well before the sun went down, drinking Gemma's good brown ale and eating every scrap that she could set out for them.

Kyllan was kept running with platters of bread and meat and mugs of ale, but he was an old hand in the ways of inns. He could carry on whole rounds of conversation as he worked, sometimes three or four at once. Tonight there was only one, and it held them all in the same irresistible grip.

"The great war," said Long Meg. "Of course it's the great war. What else would bring war here at all?"

A murmur ran round the room, with the hint of a growl beneath. "So he's come back," said Donal, whose clan farmed the lands to the east of the village. "He wasn't dead; he's risen again."

"*We* knew he didn't die," Kyllan said, filling mugs all round and setting a steaming bowl in front of Long Meg. As she dived into herbs and stewed mutton, Kyllan went on with the grand surety of a man too young to have remembered the last war that had rent the kingdom. "He was cast down, but he's had long years to restore himself. And now, as he swore when he fell, he's come back. This time we'll destroy him forever and aye."

That met with a rousing cheer. When it had died down,

young Rhodri asked, "If there's a war, and the enemy's come back, does that mean the king is well again, to lead us against him? Or is there a new king?"

"There is no new king," said his brother Madoc repressively.

But one of those whom Marric barely knew, a man from Careol coming through with a wagonload of wool for the weavers in Lord Huon's city, looked up from his mug of ale to say, "She's come back, they say—she who went away. She's brought back a great weapon. And, it's said, one who was foretold."

"The new king?" Rhodri breathed.

The wool-merchant shrugged. "Who's to tell? The weapon needs a hand to wield it, after all. And if they've called the muster, they're thinking, surely, that they have strength to face what's coming."

"Or it has come," someone muttered in the shadows, "and they have no choice but to mount a defense."

Marric heard that. No one else seemed to—except, perhaps, the witling in his corner. Marric saw the gleam of eyes there, flicking from face to face, fixing on any who spoke. They held long on the man in shadow. What the boy was thinking, if he thought anything at all, Marric could not tell.

He slipped through the close press of bodies, settling near the witling. The boy saw him: the yellow eyes brushed him with a swift hint of warmth. Marric smiled at it, though his thoughts were anything but light-hearted. The conversation had splintered into fragments, some speaking of the enemy, some of the old king, some of the new; and the rest chewed over such memories of the last war as their forebears had passed down. None of them spoke of the true face of war: blood, wounds, death. It was all glory and trumpets, grand marches and splendid battles, and of course a quick victory.

These innocents would die gladly for their king. Yet if he was dying, and if no successor had come, then victory would be neither swift nor certain. Whereas defeat . . .

Marric sighed. The omen that he had seen in the witling was all the stronger now, a shadow of fear that no light of sun or fire could dispel. A dying king, a kingdom long untested in war, and now a war that none of them could escape. If the champion had come, if there was hope, he would have known it. But no word of such a thing had come to him here on the wood's edge, far away from princes or palaces.

The witling had a confidant again, one of the young women, great with child, whose lover had been chosen for the war. As Marric watched, she burst into tears. The witling gathered her in—looking not quite so witless now, holding her and letting her cry herself out. For an instant Marric thought he saw a glimmer of intelligence in those odd eyes. Then they were empty again, and he was rocking the young woman with mindless gentleness.

CHAPTER 40

�֎ ✖ ✖

People kept talking to him. He did not know why, except that he never spoke, and they seemed compelled to fill the silence. At first their words made little sense, but as he went on, and they went on, he began to understand more of what they said. Their words built the world.

When the tall man came with his red pennon, Gemma dragged the witling away and made him filthy. He decided that he would never understand her, after she had labored so long and so vehemently to keep him clean. Then as she rolled him in the hayloft and smeared his feet with mud from the worst of the midden and slapped soot across his face, she commanded him with terrible urgency never, ever to let the tall man see his eyes. "Don't give him any cause at all to notice you," she said, "or choose you. Do you understand?"

But she had not forbidden him to catch the stick that the man threw. The man chose him for that, whatever he was being chosen for. He drew himself tight inside, so that her anger would hurt less when it came.

To his astonishment, she only looked at him after the man had ridden away, then shook her head and sighed. When she spoke, she sounded tired. "Go get clean," she said. "Then get to work."

He did as she bade, as he always did. There was much to do in the stable and the yard. When it was done, the sun had set. He went to his corner by the fire. She never asked him to run about with mugs and platters as her sons did, though sometimes she bade him turn the spit. His duty was to sit and be quiet, and let people talk to him.

They had a great deal to say tonight. Mostly it was those who had not been chosen, weeping for those who had. And sometimes it was the latter, telling him how frightened they were.

He did not remember what war was. That thought was clear behind his eyes. He should know. He did not remember. All he had was a darkness in his heart, and something that he could not name. It was not fear, nor was it elation. It was a little like both. Glory, he thought, and trumpets. And blood—red tides of blood.

For the first time it troubled him that he had no words to speak. He would have said—something. Of war, of killing. Of what they all were coming to.

He had been chosen to fight. So had Gemma, and Kyllan and Cieran and Peredur. And Long Meg and Gwydion the smith and Donal and Macun and . . .

All those names. And he had none. That troubled him, too. He had not been so troubled before. It was as if the word of war had waked him from a long deep sleep. He stumbled, confused; he had no words; but he was beginning, a little, to rouse from his stupor.

In the night after that long and grueling day, Gemma wanted him with fierce urgency. He would have been gladder simply to sleep, but she was determined to eat him alive. He pleased her as best he could, which seemed to be enough. Mercifully, once she had had her fill of him, she fell headlong into sleep.

He lay awake. Things were stirring inside him. They made him think of an egg in the nest readying to hatch: rocking, swaying, as the fledgling inside struggled to break free.

Did the fledgling try to stop itself? To stay within the egg? Did it yearn for the darkness and the dim quiet, and the awareness of nothing beyond its shell?

He had no more power to stop or even slow this than the fledgling did. He could only let it happen, and hope—or pray, if he knew how—that the world he entered into was one he could live in.

* * *

In three days they marched out of the village that was all he could remember. It seemed perfectly natural that Gemma led them. It also seemed natural to him to walk last. They marched in a column, with the mules in the middle, carrying the gear that the men and women could not carry. Everyone had a coat of boiled leather and a helmet of iron or, sometimes, age-darkened steel, and a pair of spears. Most had knives. One or two had swords, brought out from long keeping and worn proudly by children who had never lifted such a blade even in mock battle.

He had the spears, and a knife that Kyllan had slipped him when Gemma was not looking. Kyllan had a sword—another guest's leavings, it would appear, though that guest must have come and gone long before Gemma's grandfather was born. He did not know how he knew, but the sword was old, very old. It was short and thick and rather heavy, without grace or elegance. It looked like what it was: a tool for killing men.

Kyllan strutted with it, marching close behind his mother. The witling did not strut. He kept his head up, so that he would not shame Gemma or anyone else, but he was closer to the tears of those left behind than to the laughter and song of those who went to the war. They did not know, he thought. Truly they did not know.

When they had passed the last house of the village, with children and dogs running after, a stocky figure on a brown pony fell in beside him. Marric was dressed for riding, and laden saddlebags were slung across his pony's back. More to the point, he had a sword at his side. It was very like the one that Kyllan carried, short and broad-bladed. He did not strut because he had it. He looked as if he had worn it before, and drawn it and used it, and had hoped not to have to again.

The witling was not surprised. Marric had been remarkably silent in past days. Coming to decisions, the witling had thought. Choosing himself as the others had been chosen.

They were all glad to see him. No one tried to send him back. He was not someone who could be sent, the witling thought.

The witling was glad, too. Gladder than he had thought he

might be. The brown man had found him first, and had
borne him company since. He would have been sorry to
leave the brown man behind.

Marching was tedious. At least, as Gemma observed, it
did not rain. The road wound on and on. Villages strung
along it like beads on a string. Columns of the chosen had
marched from those, too, so that the road bristled with
spears. They were all going toward Lord Huon's city, which
was called Caer Sidi.

As he marched, it seemed to the witling that he could see
worlds beneath this world, like visions through clear water.
The country through which he passed was mortal enough
to the body's senses, woods and fields and villages, lakes
and little rivers. The dark line of the wood slipped away
and vanished behind. There was a sense of familiarity
about these lands, as if he had walked in them, or lands like
them, before.

Yet beneath them, sometimes, he saw other things. Sharp
stones and windy heights. A stretch of wind-tossed sea.
Mountains marching on the edges of the world, high and
stark, crowned with snow.

They were both true. Both were part of this country,
though he did not know how, nor precisely why he could
see them. The others did not seem to, except maybe the
brown man. Their eyes were mortal eyes. They saw what
mortals could see.

Which meant that he . . .

That was not a thought he knew how to face, though he
suspected the brown man could. When he was seeing in
that other way, the creature on the pony was not a man at
all. Nor was the pony exactly a pony, either.

The longer he went on, the more he found he could see.
Most of the people on the march were human folk, and
most of those in the villages, too. But some were other than
human, though wearing human guise in the main; the rest
walked on four feet or flew as birds. Those he saw with a
constriction of the heart, and a yearning down to the bone.
That yearning had become a tingle, an awareness that if he
bent his will just so, he could spread wings and soar up
among them.

Yet in that path was deadly danger. He had lost his self

once, nor gained it back except in fragments. If he ventured it again, nameless and scattered of wit as he was, he might never find his human form at all.

What he saw, he began to understand, was magic. It lay on this whole land like a glimmer of mist. It was in the ground they walked on, the air they breathed. It let them walk now on living earth, now in worlds shaped of magic, from mortal sun to one that shone for everlasting.

And all the while he learned to see with more than eyes, he marched in the company from the village of Greenwood, under Gemma's command. Rumors of the war ran with them. When they camped in fields or under the eves of woods, other companies camped beside them, and more of those, the nearer they came to Caer Sidi.

Of all the tales he heard, one thing seemed to be true: that the war was not in Lord Huon's city. It was far away on the edges of the kingdom, where they would go once all their companies had mustered into an army.

The name of Caer Sidi struck him strangely, as if it were a dark thing or sad; but the city was a wonder of white walls and gleaming towers, set on a promontory of stone above a deep swift river. The muster did not ascend to the city; the camp spread along the river's bank, a long swath of tents and fires that could look up to the city on its crag.

Some of the younger folk were audibly disgruntled. "Walls of silver," they muttered. "Streets of gold. And will we ever see either of them?"

"We could go up," Kyllan said.

"Not likely," said Long Meg, who always saw the dark side of things. "They won't let us set our dirty feet on those golden pavements."

"Why not?" Kyllan demanded. "We have as much right to walk there as any other. It's only that we can't *stay* there. There are too many of us."

That was eminently reasonable—too reasonable for Long Meg, who stalked off to nurse her grievances in peace.

The witling thought of following her, for surely she needed someone to listen; but Gemma caught his arm. "We're going up," she said. "They've summoned the commanders."

He hung back, but her grip was too strong to resist. He

was not a commander. He was not even possessed of all
his wits.

She wanted to keep him under her eye. That was it, of
course. No one else was coming, though there were objections. It was odd that none of them spoke of him, not even
with scowls or glances. He was part of Gemma, he supposed. They would expect him to go where she went.

Walls of silver and streets of gold. White walls and
pale golden paving stones, and a green scent of gardens
even in the city's heart. It was clean, that city, and full of
light and singing, though laughter was muted now, overwhelmed by the rumble of war. He walked through it
wide-eyed, flinching somewhat when walls closed in, but
keeping his head up even when he wanted to crouch and
hide.

Far more of these people wore masks of flesh over
bright fires of magic. The city itself was shimmering with it.
Magic bound the stones, held up the walls.

It was strongest of all in the center, high up in the white
citadel. They passed beneath a gate warded by stone dragons, into a courtyard full of light. A bored personage met
them there, mortal but weary as if with long ages of existence, and led them through a maze of passages.

The witling walked without fear. He had no memory of
such places, but his body knew them. After a little while he
saw in surprise that Gemma was drawn tight upon herself.
Even the coppery brilliance of her hair had dimmed. Her
hand gripped his still, but she was not doing it to give him
her strength. She had none.

He tried a smile. It was stiff, but warmed with use. He
brushed her hair lightly with his hand. For a moment she
leaned into his touch; then she stiffened against him.

He did not press her. He had given her what he could.
She stood straighter, walked more steadily. She looked
more like herself again.

The hall to which they were taken was smaller than he
had been expecting—and what would he know, to expect
anything at all? It was a receiving-room, he thought. A
place for lesser audiences. It was full of people like
Gemma: nearly all of them mortal, sturdy and solid, people
of earth and stone. Few of them had any splendor to boast

of. Their garments were plain, their weapons without pretension.

There was a deep and subtle rightness to this gathering. The land embodied itself in these commanders of the villages and towns. Gemma had eased in their company, falling in with people she knew, who knew her inn and her village. They even seemed to know her silent companion. He remembered one, and maybe two: a woman and a man who had spent a night in the inn, and stopped to talk to him in his corner by the fire. Their eyes on him were warm. None of them betrayed either mockery or astonishment that Gemma had brought her idiot to the great war. Indeed the man said, "We'll need every strong arm, I hear."

He tried his new smile. People smiled back at him. That was delightful. Maybe he would try laughter; but not quite yet. And not here.

They were nearly the last to come in. As the murmur of greeting died, the air shifted. The witling's hackles rose. He felt the others turn in the instant after he did.

More than one person had entered through another door, but only one of them mattered. Mortal eyes saw a tall man, pale-skinned, with long dark hair and a handsome, somber face. The eyes that saw beneath the flesh, saw much the same; but that white brow was crowned with the antlers of a stag.

At his coming, all the chatter, all murmuring and laughter, fell silent. Some of the commanders began to bow, but he raised a long thin hand. "No ceremony," he said in a voice that made the witling think of far horns blowing. "There is little enough time as it is. We are needed and sorely, with as much haste as we can make. And prayer, my people; prayer to any gods you worship."

Those were grim words, though spoken without despair. They brought every man and woman to the alert.

He sat in a carved chair, not particularly high or elaborate, but princely enough. Servants went round with wine and ale and platters of bread and sweet cakes. Few refused either. They were soldiers; they ate when they could.

Lord Huon shared the wine and the bread, but his mind was clearly not on it. Soon enough he said, "Listen now, and listen well. I will hear your counsel, and gladly, but first you must know what I know. You will not speak of it to

your men without my leave. If that is not to your liking,
then you may go. No shame shall attach to you, and no
penalty be paid. But you will know only what the army
knows: that there is war in the kingdom. The old enemy has
risen again. He marches against us with a great force of
men and hellspawn."

That much, they all knew. The commanders glanced at
one another. None moved to depart.

Lord Huon sat back. His expression did not change, but it
was clear that he was pleased. When he spoke again, he
spoke with care. "We fight as we have from the old days, for
the Grail and for its king. We defend the great power that
guards us, for which the enemy has lusted since before
Jerusalem's fall. Our faith is strong and our loyalty unshaken.

"But our king is dying. He wills himself to pass beyond
the world's veil into the light. He cannot restore himself
even for this war. On the road that he has taken, there is no
turning back."

The silence was profound. No one spoke, or seemed to
breathe.

Lord Huon bowed his head as if in weariness. When he
lifted it again, his face was drawn. "There are prophecies,"
he said, "and omens and foretellings. A king will come, they
say. A champion will stand forth. The Grail will have its
great defender, as always before.

"Prophecy sent out the lady from the castle, chief of the
enchantresses who guard the shrine. She traveled far from
this kingdom, from the Grail and from her king. She followed the guide, the words and the magic. She found the
champion."

Breath hissed. Someone bit back an exclamation.

But there was no gladness in Lord Huon's face. "The
magic led her to him. The Grail chose him. He won the
sword, the blade in which resides the power of the king.
She found him, and she brought him back to Carbonek.

"And there she lost him. He vanished from the castle.
The enemy has him, we greatly fear. And if the enemy has
him . . . then there is no hope. When the old king dies, no
king will come to take his throne. No champion will rise to
defend the Grail."

Those words struck hard. Even the witling, who knew
nothing, not even his name—even he could understand

what a calamity this was. A dying king, his successor lost, no champion, no strong defense . . .

"My lord." Gemma's voice was clear and rather harsh, and forthright as it always was. "This is evil news. But are we lost yet? He's only one man, however great his power. We're many, and our faith, as you say, is strong. Won't the Grail defend us as we defend it?"

"Surely," said Lord Huon, "and we will fight as strongly as we may. How not? But our greatest weapon is lost."

"Is it, my lord?" Gemma asked. "Can't it be found?"

"They have searched in every way known to men and magic. In the kingdom, beyond it, they have hunted without rest. They have found nothing. It is as if he has vanished from the world."

"Dead?" one of the other commanders asked.

Lord Huon raised his hands. "No one knows. *She* says not. But he is nowhere to be found, in any world."

"So we'll fight without him," Gemma said. "We have the Grail, after all. We have the nine ladies. We have a king, though he's dying. We'll be strong enough, one way and another."

"One may hope so," Lord Huon said. He smiled at her. "And truly, if all our people are as determined as you, we have little to fear."

She shrugged off his praise. "So. What do you need? Advice? What can a village innkeeper tell a great lord of the Grail, that he doesn't know already?"

Lord Huon's smile erupted into laughter. "Why, madam! All manner of things. The disposition of forces, the lines of their supply, the order of march—"

"Ah," she said. "All that. Yes, that's simple enough. Where shall we begin?"

While Lord Huon spoke, the witling had retreated to a corner. He huddled in it, knotted tight. Nobody took any notice of him. Those words—they had no meaning. And yet they smote him like blows. Champion. Sword. King.

Champion.

He was nothing. He had no name. He came from nowhere, he belonged to no one. He had been a hawk; man's shape had been forced upon him. Even that shape was not truly human, the hawk's eyes in the man's face.

He was not the lost one. That would be a man, great and holy, a prince of blood both ancient and royal. Not a half-human halfwit in a borrowed tunic.

He pressed his hands to his ears. Still that clear voice spoke, ringing in his skull, driving the words home. They should not matter to him. They should not. He was nothing. He was no one. He was *nothing*.

CHAPTER 41

✠ ✠ ✠

The camp was a blessed refuge, as solidly human as anything in this kingdom. Gemma had gone with the other commanders to see to some matter of the army. He had slipped away from her, unnoticed and unregarded. If she looked for him, she would find him safe enough, curled inside her tent, with a blanket over his head.

Something tugged at it. He set his teeth and held on. A small solid body insinuated itself beneath a dangling fold, purring raucously.

It was only a cat. Though what a cat was doing in the camp of an army, he hardly had wits to guess. It pressed against his belly, kneading ferociously. Even through the thickness of the leather coat, its claws pricked his skin.

The small pain was almost welcome. It drew him away from the roil in his skull. Lord Huon's words echoed and reechoed till he could hear nothing else. Nothing save the cat's purr.

He was lost in a dark dream. He did not want to wake. Light was terrible, was terrifying. He had no strength to endure it.

The cat crawled up through the blankets to butt its small hard head against his chin. Its tongue rasped his neck. Teeth bit delicately, not quite hard enough for pain.

He worked fingers into soft fur, rubbing places that he

knew without knowing how. Without wanting to know how. This was a door to memory. The cat was a key.

A great part of him wanted to fling the creature away. The rest, which was stronger, let it stay. He was many things, and a coward not the least of them, but even cowardice had its limits.

Once more he heard Lord Huon's voice, heard the tale that he told. A king; an enchantress. A champion. A weapon—a sword. Blade that rippled like water. Hilt of silver unadorned. On the pommel a white stone like the moon. His fingers curved, remembering the shape, the heft of it, the weight and balance—and yes, the way it sang, sweet and high.

He was no champion. He was certainly no king. He was the halfwit from Greenwood, the foundling from the Lady's tree. He had no name. He did not want one.

But memory, once unlocked, would not retreat behind its walls. Little of it was as clear as the sword. Places, faces—a blur of vision, a cacophony of names in tongues too many to count. Two he saw most often: a big fair man, now bareheaded, now crowned with an iron crown; and one even bigger and even fairer, laughing and flinging a heavy arm about his shoulders. That memory smote him with grief so strong that he doubled up gasping.

There was another, too. A woman. Now clad in strange silken garments. Now clad in nothing at all. His body heated at the sight of her. His temper, too—a gust of anger as strong as the grief that had struck before. It was not hate. He was very sure of that. But he was angry—furious. She had betrayed—she had lied—hidden—she had—

The cat sank claws in his shoulder. He hissed with pain. He was back in the world again, such as it was: Gemma's tent with its clutter of belongings, weapons, bits of leather armor and ironmongery. It was as familiar as anything could be. Too familiar. As if he had lived in such tents for long and long, tents of war. The armor—it should be steel, fine woven mail. There should be helmets, bows, quivers of arrows. A horn of some vast creature, carved with intricate artistry. A sword—*the* sword. The champion's blade. Durandal.

His lips shaped the name. He had no voice, nor wanted any. But the word had come to him. It would not let him be.

He was not the champion. He was *not*.

Truly—as he was, he could not be. He was fit to carry a spear in a lord's army, that was all.

But the need—the war. The king was dying.

Behind his eyes he saw a dark-haired man lying on a narrow cot. He wore no crown. His robe was a monk's robe. Yet there could be no doubt that he was royal.

She sat by him, his hand in hers. Were there tears on her cheeks?

Well might there be, after what she had done. Keeping silence. Letting him believe—leading him to think—

Anger wore wings, bore talons. It tugged at him. It lured him back into the dark.

Once more, pain cast him out into the light. The cat crouched on his breast. Its glare was baleful.

He knew this cat. Which was not a cat. Heedless of the threat of claws or teeth, he brushed his finger along its jaw. It stroked fiercely against him, as cats will, to mark and claim him.

"I won't," he said. His voice was raw, rusted with disuse. "I will not."

The cat begged to differ.

It had trapped him. It had wakened memory, put an end to his silence.

He could refuse. He could still do that.

Could he?

Anger was a sin, a deadly one. It had driven him out of himself, reft him of his name, cast him naked and mindless in a strange land. He was a broken thing because of it. And war was coming, led by an enemy both ancient and strong. An enemy whom he knew in his bones, deeper even than he had known the sword. He was bound—he had sworn—

He surged to his feet. The cat rode up on his shoulder, claws locked tight.

He did not know where he was going until he had come there. The brown man was squatting by a campfire, feeding it with bits of sweetly scented wood. Night had fallen without his knowing it. People were eating, drinking, sleeping.

No one kept Marric company. Perhaps because of that, he labored less than usual to seem a human creature. The firelight caught his long pointed nose and his long pointed ears. When he grinned up at the newcomer, he bared long pointed teeth.

"Bogle," said the one who still had not found his name. His voice was not as rusty now, though still far from its polished self. "Bogle on a hearth."

The brown eyes went wide. There was a green gleam in them, as in a cat's. He looked rather alarming, and yet he roused no fear. "So," he said after a stretching moment. "You can talk as well as see."

The other nodded. He squatted beside the bogle. The cat leaped down from his shoulder to purr and preen against the bogle's shin.

"Ah," said Marric. There was a world of understanding in the sound. He did not seem surprised. Rueful, maybe, in the face of the cat's green stare. "You didn't look far enough," he said to it. "And I . . . well, I'm but an earth-spirit with pretensions. Who would have thought She'd send him to me?"

The cat hissed and lashed its tail. It was more angry at itself, perhaps, than at the bogle.

"She has Her ways," Marric said, "and Her reasons. We do tend to forget that."

The nameless one did not understand. "Tell me what to do," he said.

Marric blinked. "You're asking me?"

"Tell me," the other said.

"I'm a bogle on a hearth, such as it is. You are a great deal more than that."

He shook his head sharply. "No. I am nothing. No name, no memory."

"Well," said the bogle, "as to that, if you are what I think you are, and what this *puca*'s presence makes you, you do have a name. That name is Roland."

He reeled, staggered, fell. That name—that sound—it smote him to the ground. The door that he had thought opened wide, showed itself to have been but a chink in a postern gate. The gate itself roared open, loosing a horde of memories. All that he was, all that he had done; the whole world that was encompassed in his name. He was—he *was*—

"By the stars," said the bogle's dry calm voice. "She is not merciful."

He clung to that voice. He made of it a lifeline. He crawled toward it through the flood of remembrance.

He lay in firelight, with Marric bending over him, and a small grey cat perched on his breast. His head ached abominably. He knew where he was, and how he had come there, and above all, who and what he was.

He swallowed. His throat was burning dry. "How long?" he asked.

The cat did not care. The bogle, who had taken an entire village for his hearth, shrugged and said, "Long enough. Time's odd here. Sun and moon travel as they please. Less so over Carbonek, which stands on the edge of the mortals' world, but you were far in, near the Worldwood itself."

Marric liked to babble. "Tell me how long," Roland said.

"Long enough," Marric said again.

Roland sat up carefully, balancing his aching head on its stiffened neck. He steadied it in his hands. The cat slid down into his lap, leaving a stinging trail. "Tarik," he said. He did something, he was not sure what; a flick of the hand, a shift of the eye. The *puca* blurred and shimmered and grew.

A naked youth crouched beside him, glaring with yellow cat-eyes. Roland met that glare with golden hawk-eyes. "Did she send you?"

Tarik hissed. "*I* sent me."

"But she knows."

"I never told her," Tarik said. "She chose badly. She pays for it."

"You are a spiteful thing," Roland said, though not as one who passed judgment.

"I prefer to be a cat," the *puca* said.

"Yes." Roland set his teeth. The throbbing in his skull was worse. It was close to blinding him. But there were things that he must say. "If I may ask this of you—stay here. Don't go back. Keep me secret. Will you do that?"

The *puca* bared sharp white teeth. "Oh, yes! I stay with you. She sheds tears, you know. When she thinks herself alone. She says your name. She dreams, and you are in it."

"Good," said Roland out of the deep well of anger.

"Are you going?" the *puca* asked after a moment. "Or will you stay?"

Roland drew a breath. "I . . ." Only his hands kept his

head from shattering. "I will go. But in my own time. In my own way. I am not her dog or her slave. If what people are saying is true, I am supposed to be rather more than that."

"You are supposed to be a king," the bogle said.

"That, I am not," said Roland. "I don't want it. I won't take it. But if this kingdom needs my sword-arm—if the Grail needs me, even me, to defend it—then I will do what I can."

"And if you have to be king to do it?" asked the bogle.

"I will pray that I do not," Roland said.

CHAPTER 42

✠ ✠ ✠

Roland tumbled headlong into sleep. He woke dazed, with hammering skull, as if he had drunk the night away. But his memory was bitterly, painfully clear. The *puca* had returned to its cat-shape once more, draped heavily over Roland's knees.

He could hear Gemma's voice outside the tent, and the voices of her sons, and others that he knew from the dark time. His heart constricted. Dear saints, what was he to do? The creature they knew, the mute and witless fool, had died under the *puca*'s claws.

Best get it over. He rose and set himself in order, combed and plaited his hair that had grown halfway down his back, dressed and straightened his shoulders and arranged his face, and stepped blinking into the morning light.

Gemma looked up. He had hoped, rather desperately, that she would see no change in him. But her eyes were far too keen for that. They widened, then narrowed. She looked at him as if he had been a stranger.

So he was. He had a name. He had memory. He walked differently, he supposed; his face would have changed. He was not the witling any longer.

Kyllan said what they all must be thinking. "Sun and stars! What happened to you?"

"Remembrance," Roland said.

They all stared. Again Kyllan spoke for them. "You can talk."

"Yes," said Roland.

The bogle was crouched by the fire as he had been in the night, tending a pot that bubbled fragrantly. He handed Roland a cup that proved to be full of ale. Roland downed a good half of it. They stared at that, too.

He stared back, which was not wise at all. He made their eyes drop. All but Gemma's. She measured him as if he had been a stranger in her inn, weighed and balanced him and found him sadly wanting.

He had expected pain. He had not expected it to be so sharp.

He turned on his heel. Her hand caught him. Her grip was not particularly tight, but it held him rooted. "No," she said. "You don't run away. You stand and face us. You tell us your name, and you convince us that you haven't been playing us for fools."

"I have not," he said.

"Easy to say," she said.

"By my heart's blood," he said, "I was exactly as you saw me."

"And now?"

"I remember." He must have betrayed something of what he felt, whether in voice or expression: she blinked twice, hard, and her face went stiff. "My name is Roland," he said.

"What kind of name is that?"

"Frankish," he answered.

"You are no Frank," she said.

"My father was."

"But not your mother."

"No," he said. "Not my mother."

"She let your father name you?"

"She died when I was born."

"That is sad," she said, as if she meant it. She was still holding his wrist. "Is that why you run? Because you never had a mother to teach you sense?"

His lips twitched. "That is as good a reason as any other."

"There are no good reasons for running."

He might have contested her certainty, but his tongue

had run on enough. He set his lips together and took refuge in silence.

She let him go. "You're still under my command," she said. "Mind you remember it."

She left him there, stalking off down the line of tents, the thick coppery plait of her hair swinging to the small of her back. He shook himself. The others were stirring likewise, glancing at one another. Several bit back grins.

Roland did not try to suppress his. Kyllan caught the contagion of it. In a moment they were all laughing like mad things.

When the laughter had passed, he was still a stranger, but they had begun to warm to him. Donal tossed him a loaf fresh from the baking. Macul dipped an extra cup of stew and set it in his hand. Kyllan sat beside him as they all ate, and said, "Don't mind her. She'll calm down soon enough."

"It is a shock," his brother Peredur said. "She doesn't like surprises. And you—you're so different. You look—"

"Alive," Donal said.

"Awake," said Cieran.

"Arrogant," Kyllan said, stopping them all short. "That's what she doesn't like, I'll lay wagers on it. Are you a king's son?"

"No, nor a king either," Roland said, too fiercely perhaps.

"You've got a stiff neck on you for a peasant," Long Meg opined, looking him up and down as she had not presumed to do since Gemma laid claim to him. Now, it seemed, he was fair quarry again.

"He's no peasant," Kyllan said. "Farmers' sons don't walk like that or talk like that, or look like that, either."

"Unless the farmer's wife caught a prince's eye," said Long Meg.

"But he said—" said Peredur.

No one was listening to Peredur, or paying much attention to Roland, either, though he was the subject of their conversation. He emptied the bowl that Marric handed him, eating without appetite but with grim awareness of the need. Some of the boys were playing past Gemma's tent, hacking at one another with unblunted swords. It was a holy miracle that none of them had lopped off a hand or an ear.

He set the bowl down and went to end the melee before it came to bloodshed. Neatly and deftly he plucked a Roman shortsword from one hand and what looked like a Saracen blade from another.

These children stared as everybody else had, except for one young idiot who growled and tried to leap on him and wrest one of the swords from his hand. He caught the boy against him, holding him easily—dear saints, these babes knew nothing of fighting at all. The child snapped and cursed. He clipped the boy's ear, just enough to quiet him.

"If you would fight," he said to the whole goggling pack of them, "you had best learn how."

"I suppose *you* know," sneered a boy whose name, he seemed to recall, was Mabon.

Roland's lips stretched back from his teeth. It was not a smile. The boy blanched, though he held his sneer in place. "I know," said Roland.

"Prove it," Mabon said, predictable as an antiphon in the Mass.

Roland tossed him the longer blade. He caught it clumsily, and dropped it. When he bent down to pick it up, he found the point of the Roman sword at his throat. "And so you die," said Roland.

"That wasn't fair," Mabon said.

"War is not," said Roland. "War is about killing, and about winning. There is nothing fair in it, or just, or even right, most times."

"*This* war is just!" declared a young woman in the crowd.

"I'm sure it is," Roland said mildly. "It won't keep the enemy from killing you, if he knows how to fight, and you don't."

"We know how!" the girl said.

He was still holding the boy who had attacked him. The child was motionless now. Roland set him aside, gentle but firm, and faced the girl with the bright fierce eyes. "Show me," he said.

She did not produce a sword; she snatched a spear from the ground near one of the tents. She held it not too awkwardly, as if it had been a quarterstaff. Someone had taught her that mode of fighting, Roland could see. It might serve her; but it made no allowance for the point of the spear. Or, indeed, for a sword in a skilled hand, that struck the spearhaft lightly aside and came to rest on her shoulder, not quite touching her neck. "Beheaded," he said, "and quickly, too."

She blinked rapidly. Her cheeks had flushed scarlet.

Roland lowered the shortsword. He half thought she might attack with the spear, but she stood motionless, fingers white on the haft, eyes fixed on his face. She hated him.

He smiled, a true smile this time. "Yes, hate me," he said. "Hate is useful. But only if you know how to use it."

"So teach us," she said, haughty as any princess.

He laughed. "If you so command, my lady."

That made her blush even more hotly, and drop those bold eyes, as if suddenly she did not know where to look.

Roland spared her, he hoped, turning somewhat away from her, running his eyes over the baffled young faces. There were many more than he had thought when he first came. Not all of them were so very young, either. No few were older than he, but in war they were infants.

"I can't make great swordsmen of you," he said after a moment, "or skilled warriors, either. That needs training from childhood. But I can teach you to fight, to defend yourselves and your comrades, and maybe to win a battle. If," he added, "you ask it."

"We ask," the girl said. Her chin was up. Her cheeks were as vivid as ever.

"Tell me your name," he said to her.

"Cait," she said, startled maybe, forgetting to be resistant.

"Cait," he said. "And I am Roland. While I teach you, I am commander. You are my second. Choose seconds of your own, and fetch a spear for everyone who needs teaching."

"No swords?" she asked.

"No swords," he said. "Although ..." He frowned, considering choices. "Who hunts with arrows?"

Nigh half of them admitted to that, among them the boy with the Saracen sword.

"Good," said Roland to all of them, but chiefly to the boy. "We have archers. And you are in command of them."

The boy's eyes were wide. He knelt suddenly and laid the sword at Roland's feet.

Roland nodded and took it up. "Bows," he said, "and arrows. Find them. Bring them here. And targets, too, if they're to be had. Is there a field nearby, wide enough to shoot in?"

"Outside the camp," the boy said.

"Then we'll claim it," said Roland. "Spearmen, too. Everybody."

They were quick to do his bidding—eager, as innocents could be. He felt very old, walking behind them, watching as their numbers grew. By the time they came to the field, most of that end of the camp had joined the march, bringing such weapons as they had. Word spread fast in armies.

Whatever they lacked in skill, they made up for in goodwill. Roland had fared worse with raw levies in Francia, barely bearded boys called in from the fields, or Saxon peasants sullen and confused to be fighting for the king who had conquered them.

He had never commanded women before. They were fiercer than the men, he discovered quickly, and less inclined to think of honor when there were lives to be defended. With spears they were quicker if not often as strong. With bows they matched or mastered the men.

It could be a mildly competent army, with time and labor. Labor he had plenty of. Time was sorely lacking.

He would do what he could, and do his best not to curse the lord who had called this muster without ever taking measures to see that his soldiers could fight. "What was he looking to do?" Roland asked of Kyllan and Cait, who happened to be standing by him while a ragged line of archers shot at hastily cobbled targets. "Magic you all into soldiers before the battle?"

"That's what they were talking about last night," Kyllan said, "all the commanders. How to turn us into an army."

"This is how," said Roland.

"You know that," Cait said. "You were a soldier somewhere. We don't do that here. Except people who go away—and most of those don't come back."

Roland shook his head. Peace, he thought, was every Christian's prayer. But a peaceable kingdom was ripe prey for an army honed in war.

He owed this kingdom nothing. Not one thing. But these people had taken him in, fed him, clothed him, been kind to him. For them he would do this. Not for the haughty woman in Carbonek, or her dying king. Not even for the Grail.

CHAPTER 43

✠ ✠ ✠

Roland was aware as he drilled the troops—his troops, he could not help but think of them—that others came, watched, went away again. Some were commanders of the levies. Some stood higher: men or women on horseback.

He did not acknowledge them. If they wanted to punish him for doing what they should have done from the moment the muster was called, then let them. But first he would see to it that these children learned how to stand in ranks, and a little, a very little, of how to fight.

Marric had come, somewhere amid the ordering of ranks, and made himself useful among the archers. He had runners fetching arrows, and a fletcher or two settled in the shade, making and mending new ones. He was no stranger to war, that one.

Sunset surprised them. Roland dismissed the by now somewhat less ragged ranks. Their steps dragged as they left, as much with reluctance as with exhaustion. He would not need to bid them sleep; not tonight. Their own bodies would see to it.

Only Cait and Kyllan lingered, and Marric regarding Roland with a crooked smile. Kyllan was grinning, and trying not to yawn. "We're good," he said. "We're going to be splendid."

"We're going to be barely adequate," said Cait. She did not sound cast down about it. "I could eat a whole ox."

"Save another one for me," said Kyllan.

They went off arm in arm. Roland watched them go.

"You're not a bad armsmaster," a voice said behind him. "For an idiot."

He glanced over his shoulder at Gemma. Marric had wrapped himself in shadow, which a bogle could do if it chose. Gemma's hair caught the fire of sunset. Night's shadow was already in her eyes.

"I suppose," he said, "you've come to haul me off in chains."

Her lips twitched, then tightened. "We did discuss it."

"And?"

"We realized that we need every man. And idiot."

He turned to face her. She did not flinch, but he saw how her eyes narrowed. "I don't bite," he said.

"I don't know you," she said.

That was pain, walled in brusque impatience. He touched her cheek. She ducked away. "Don't," she said.

"Do you dislike me so much?"

"I'm not for the likes of you."

"What is 'the likes of me'?"

She seized his hands, turned them up in the last of the light. The calluses there were older by far than the marks of pitchfork or broom. "Knight," she said. "Lord and prince. Don't shake that head at me! You couldn't pretend to be a commoner if you tried."

"I did just that," he said, "for longer than anyone will let me know."

"You were a very convincing idiot."

"Can't I be a convincing soldier?"

"You just appointed yourself armsmaster to the whole nether half of Lord Huon's muster, and you ask me that? You can't help yourself. Put you in an army, you take command of it. It's in your blood."

There was a terrible truth in what she said. "I am still—mostly—human," he said. "Part of me is still your beloved idiot."

"Not enough of you," she said.

"You are not being reasonable."

"I am being as reasonable as a woman can be. You can have my tent—my lord. I'll bunk in with the boys."

"Gemma—"

"Don't argue. It won't help."

"Gemma!"

"My lord?"

He growled in frustration. No man living had ever got the better of Gemma. Roland, it was too clear, was not about to be the first.

Very well, he thought. So be it. If she wanted a lord, he would be a lord. "Don't speak of this," he said, "or of me, to Lord Huon."

"I won't need to," she said. "He'll know soon what you did, if he doesn't already. You weren't circumspect."

Roland sighed. No, he had not been. Nor had he been thinking of anything but the need of the moment.

She agreed: her glance was full of irony.

He met it full on. "Gemma," he said, "stand with me. Help me. Not for me—for the people. I'd like to bring them back alive if I can. I can only do that if they know how to fight."

"Do you honestly care what becomes of a pack of commoners?"

"Yes!"

"Well," she said after a pause. "If that's the truth, I'll do what I can. But I won't lie about you to Lord Huon."

"I'm not asking you to."

She snorted at that, but she did not argue with it. That was as much assent as he would get from her. It would have to do.

Lord Huon's messenger was waiting for him come morning, sitting by the fire outside the tent that had been Gemma's, eating the bogle's fresh barley bread. It was the same herald who had called the muster in Greenwood.

He recognized Roland: his brow leaped upward as Roland came out of the tent. It leaped even higher when he met Roland's eyes.

Roland stared him down. The messenger looked as if he might have liked to ask a spate of questions, but he held his tongue. He rose somewhat stiffly, and thanked Marric courteously for the bread and ale. Marric responded with equal courtesy.

The messenger did not bow to Roland or grant him respect. "My lord would speak with you," he said.

Roland inclined his head. When he spoke, it was not, at first, to the messenger. He said to Kyllan, who was hanging about, all ears and eyes, "Take charge of the exercises. Same as yesterday, till I come back."

Kyllan nodded happily and ran to gather the troops.

Roland turned then to the lord's messenger. "Lead," he said. "I'll follow."

Clearly the man took a dim view of commoners who ordered him about as if they had been lords; but he was well trained. He led his charge up to the citadel.

Lord Huon was hardly waiting on Roland's pleasure. Roland was set in an anteroom to wait, while servants trotted back and forth, and men and women of greater note were let in upon their arrival. He was not offered food or drink.

He considered anger, but that was hardly useful. Amusement served him much better. A brief hunt uncovered a kitchen, with a cook who was amenable to his best smile and his sweetest words. He won a plate of fine cakes, a jar of wine, and a wedge of good yellow cheese slipped into a new loaf. He brought his booty to the most comfortable corner, arranged a chair and a stool to his satisfaction, and settled at his ease, nibbling cakes, sipping wine, and savoring the cheese melted into the hot fresh bread.

The servants glanced at him as they passed. After a while they began to smile. He smiled back. None would speak to him, of course; that would not have been proper. But they were as amused as he was.

The anteroom had a window high in the wall. The sun climbed up to it, paused at its zenith, began its long descent toward the night.

He finished the bread and cheese. The wine was half gone. There were still a fair number of cakes. He rose, stretched, prowled the room. There was little of interest in it, to the eyes of the body, but the magics that shaped and warded it were intricately wrought. He traced the lines and curves of them with interest, noting the ways in which they wove and interwove. One in particular tempted him to follow it, teasing it out of the rest, straightening it, weaving it in a new and clearer pattern.

Just as he smoothed the edges of it into place, the inner

door opened. It had been doing that all day, releasing clusters of men and women in fine clothes and haughty expressions. This one looked as if it had been dismissed unceremoniously: moving quickly, scowling, muttering, herded by a grand servant in livery of silver and green.

They glared at Roland as they were hastened past. He smiled serenely back.

The servant shut the outer door on the last of them and turned. He clung to his dignity, but his eyes were glinting. "You will come with me," he said.

Lord Huon was alone in the inner room. Roland had expected a chamber like that in which the lord had received the commanders of the muster, but this was more portico than walled chamber. The court beyond was nigh filled with a great shimmering pool. Blossoming trees rimmed it. Fishes danced in it. A small grey cat sat on its edge, eyeing the fish with naked hunger.

Roland's belly knotted. He had not seen Tarik since he woke that morning. And no wonder, if the *puca* had been betraying him to the lord of Caer Sidi.

Lord Huon rose from the chair in which he had been sitting and walked out into the court. Roland followed him. He did not acknowledge the *puca,* who likewise did not acknowledge him, but walked round the opposite side of the pool. There was a bench under an arbor, convenient for watching the fish, and a basket of bread. He tore the bread in pieces and cast it upon the water. The fish leaped and swirled, devouring the offering.

"I do beg your pardon," the lord said at last, "for keeping you waiting so long."

"I was in no discomfort, my lord," Roland said.

Lord Huon looked up from the fish. His eyes, dark like a stag's but lit with strange green lights, took in all of Roland that there was to see. That was not a great deal, but his face, maybe, was enough.

"It was presumptuous of you," Lord Huon said, "to rebuild the wards on my wall."

"They were crooked," said Roland. "There was a weakness there. An enemy could find it, pierce it—"

"Indeed," said Lord Huon a little coldly. "I see you make a habit of mending what you consider to be flawed. Would that happen to encompass the governing of my realm?"

"That seems to be very well done," Roland said.

"I am glad that you think so," said Lord Huon.

Roland supposed that he should be abashed. He could only think of Gemma, and of what she had said: that he could not even pretend to be other than he was. In the world that he had come from, to which he had died through Sarissa's contrivance, he had been this lord's superior in rank.

He was a poor liar and a worse deceiver. And there was Tarik on the pool's other side, drooling over the lord's bright fish.

"I am going to use you," Lord Huon said after a while, "as a weapon in my hand. I care little who or what you are. You are protected of the Grail; that is known to me. What you are, what you are hiding from, matters nothing. Only that you will fight for me, and teach my people how to fight."

"What would you have done without me?" Roland asked him.

"Another weapon would have come to my hand," said the lord of Caer Sidi.

"I will not fight for you," Roland said. "Nor will I swear fealty to you. That is given elsewhere. But for your people I will do all that I can."

"They said that you had a prince's arrogance," Lord Huon said. "I say that you do not. You are as haughty as a king."

"I am not a king," Roland said, as he seemed to be saying to everyone he met.

"That may be," said Lord Huon. "Serve my people and you serve me. I will agree to be content with that."

Roland inclined his head. It was not a bow, but there was considerable respect in it. "I will serve your people with every art and power that I have. So I swear to you."

The air rang like a great bell. "Sworn and witnessed," said the lord of Caer Sidi.

CHAPTER 44

✠ ✠ ✠

Roland had not intended to swear to anything in Lord Huon's citadel, where the magic was strong enough to bind his heart and soul. But he had been tricked into it. Now he was bound.

It was a binding he could bear. These outspoken, fractious, headstrong people had worked their way into his heart. They were afraid of nothing in heaven or earth. And though they acknowledged the power of lords and princes, they never groveled to it.

They almost made him forget his grief, if not his anger. Franks they were not, but they were a free, proud people. Nor did they find him startling, even knowing that his blood was not wholly human. In a country in which a bogle could live unquestioned among mortal villagers, and the lord of a domain sometimes wore the face of the Horned King, Merlin's child was nothing to wonder at.

He went back to the army with Lord Huon's binding on him, and the rank of captain in the army. He had weapons and armor from the armory of the citadel: a bow of horn, its arrows fletched with shimmering blue feathers; a long knife, for he would take no sword; and a coat of mail, the rings wrought of blued steel.

That he would have refused as he had refused a sword, but Lord Huon's armorer would not let him leave without it. "A captain's a target," he said. "Boiled leather's good enough for a soldier, but if you're going to set yourself up to be shot at, best you have a good mail-coat to ward your vitals." He gave Roland a shield, too, a round horseman's shield painted blue and blazoned with a silver swan. It was not Lord Huon's livery—his men bore a silver stag—but it fit well to Roland's hand and arm.

Such a shield needed a horse. Roland was only half a Frank, but that made him all a horseman. He was almost cravenly glad to be informed that he must be mounted; his charge was every raw recruit in the lord's army, and for that he would need to move swiftly through the ranks.

He returned to the camp astride a sturdy bay gelding, with a groom behind him leading a mule laden with weapons and baggage. He rode like a lord, rather against his will: horse, armor, sumpter mule, and groom. The camp received him with broad grins and a ragged cheer. He had not known how tight his back was until he heard that cheer. He nearly slid from the saddle in the limpness of relief.

Gemma's son Cieran took horses and groom in hand. He had been horseboy in the inn until Roland came to free him from it. "It's fate," he said, grinning. He was fierce in driving off any who might have displaced him.

Gemma had emptied her tent of her belongings. There was only the pallet Roland had been sleeping on, a small bundle of clothing, and Marric sitting with his bony knees drawn up. "You need a squire," he said. "Kyllan would do. Or Peredur. Or one of the less inept archers."

"I don't want a squire," Roland said.

"Of course you don't want one," said Marric. "But someone has to see to your armor and weapons, make sure you're fed, look after your tent, pitch it when we camp, take it down when we get ready to march—"

Roland flung up a hand. "Enough! You do it, then. You'll be a better squire-at-arms than any of these children."

Marric sighed vastly. "So I would. But do I want to?"

"It's you or no one."

"Obstinate." Marric was delighted, Roland could see, though he hid it behind a ferocious scowl. "Very well. I'll do it. Now get on with you. I've things to do if this tent is to be livable in."

"It already is—"

"Out!" cried Marric. *"Out!"*

Thus summarily dismissed, Roland had no recourse but to do the chief of his duties, which was to oversee the training of the army. That engrossed him rather perfectly, and kept him preoccupied until well after sundown.

When he stumbled back at last to his tent, he found it transformed. It had a cot and a clothing-chest, a stool and a rug and a rack for his mail-coat. There was bread waiting outside by the fire, still warm from the baking, and a pot bubbling on a tripod over the fire. Marric had even, somehow, procured a jar of moderately acceptable wine.

Kyllan had followed him like a large red dog, and Cait, and one or two of the others. The tent was too small for all of them, but the space in front of it was wide enough. The pot was ample to feed a dozen hungry warriors, and there was a cask of ale to drink when the wine was gone. Marric glowered and grumbled, but he would not have been a bogle if he had done otherwise. He was a good servant and an excellent cook.

While they were eating and drinking, Long Meg wandered in with Gwydion the smith bulking behind her. In a little while Donal had come, and Peredur, and Cieran damp from a washing in the river; but he still, Meg declared, reeked of horses.

"That's a good smell," Cait shot back, slipping in between Cieran and his brother Kyllan, linking an arm through the arm of each. She grinned ferally at Meg.

Meg yawned and stretched. She was a long elegant creature with ruddy brown braids that, unwound from about her head, fell almost to her knees. Her breasts were round and high, and she was proud of them; she wore her tunics somewhat tight, so that there could be no doubt of the shape beneath.

She claimed the place beside Roland and held it against all comers. Clearly she had none of Gemma's scruples, nor her prickly pride, either. But Roland would far rather have seen Gemma there.

None of them lingered overlong. Vast yawns claimed them once they had eaten and drunk. Meg would have liked to stay, but Roland bowed as if she had been a lady of rank, smiled, and withdrew into his tent.

It was a pleasant place to be alone in, lit with a lamp that burned sweet-scented oil. His weapons were cleaned and laid away, his mail-coat arranged tidily on its stand. Roland had thought to grieve for his solitude, but once he had it, he found that he was glad of it.

He dropped his clothes on the chest and stood for a moment, kneading muscles that ached somewhat excessively. He had not sat a horse in too long, nor bent a bow, nor wielded a spear. He had grown soft.

He grinned to himself. Soft—indeed. He had done hard labor in Gemma's inn, but it was not the same as the labor of war. He stretched as high as the tent's peak would allow, rising to his toes, arching, spreading his arms wide. It turned, one way and another, into the step and turn of a dance, constricted by the tent's small space.

Tarik was on the cot when he went to lie there, claiming it as a cat could not but do. Roland fit himself around the small furred body. Tarik began to purr.

"Then I'm forgiven?" Roland said.

Tarik would not go as far as that. But he was here. It was absolution of a sort.

Roland dreamed of Sarissa. He saw her perform what must be a rite of the Grail, standing foremost of nine ladies clad in white. He saw her sit vigil by the king's bed, bent over that gaunt frail body, holding back tears. And he saw her in a room tiled with the colors of the sea. Water shimmered in a pool. She stood on its rim, draped in white. A little dark-haired maid slipped the robe from her shoulders. She stood naked as he too well remembered her, slender but shapely, with her cream-brown skin and her tumble of gold-brown hair.

She slipped smoothly into the pool. The water closed about her, blurring but not concealing her beauty. She swam from end to end of the pool. When she came back, she sat on a ledge beneath the water, while the maid washed her hair. She had let her head fall back. Her breasts arched out of the water.

In his dream he reached to touch her, but his hand had no substance. She did not move or flinch.

When her hair was washed and scented with some sweet herb, she sent the maid away. She sat on the pool's rim, took up an ivory comb, worked it slowly through the thick wet curls. She frowned as she wielded the comb, her hand moving slower and ever slower, till at last it stopped.

Her face twisted suddenly. For an instant he saw raw pain. Then she had smoothed it again, but her voice was rough as if with tears. "O goddess," she said. "O gods and spirits. How I miss that maddening man!"

The water flickered in lamplight. The comb clattered to the tiles. She clasped her arms about herself and rocked. "Roland," she said to the air beyond the light. "Wherever you may be, whatever has become of you, for the gods' sake, for love of the Grail, will you not come back? If not to me, then to the light that needs you?"

Roland was not even air, not even spirit. He could not answer her.

And yet she seemed to hear something, perhaps some glimmer of his thought. "Well I deserve your anger," she said, "but I would do it again, if I had to do it over. I could do no other than I did. Are you strong enough to understand? Can you begin to forgive?"

He was not. He could not. Her words heated his temper again, even when she cried in pure pain, "Oh, gods, I love you! My arms are empty without you."

So they should be, he thought. Let her suffer as she had sown.

"Cold heart," said a voice in the darkness. "Hot head. That's an ill match."

He turned to face the one who stood on this edge of the Otherworld. It was a man more young than old, dark hair, pale skin, keen-drawn face. He wore a monk's robe, but he was not tonsured. Roland knew him very well, though he had never seen the man in living flesh. "Parsifal," he said.

"Roland," said the Grail-king. "Kinsman—and in more than blood, it seems. I was a fool, too. Still am, maybe. Once a fool, always a fool, Merlin used to say to me."

Roland's lips twitched in spite of themselves. "The young know nothing of good sense, he also said to me."

"Not only the young," said Parsifal wryly. He did not move, but the world changed. They stood atop a high tower of Carbonek, raised far above the world. The stars were near enough almost to touch. The moon cast cold light on their faces.

"Look," said Parsifal.

Roland barely needed to be told. His eyes had found the horizon with its jagged teeth of mountains. Through those mountains poured a river of darkness. Walls of light had been raised there, but they were broken down. Their shards lay scattered among the peaks.

Well he knew that darkness, the taste of it, the shudder on his skin. A slither of scales, a serpent's hiss.

"This is nothing I did not know," he said.

The Grail-king nodded. "Surely. But do you understand? Do you care what becomes of us all?"

"Yes," Roland said. "I even know that if he has the victory, and gains the Grail, the world will fall. A thousand years of darkness. A thousand years of pain."

"Yet you refuse the task that is given you."

"Did I say that?" said Roland.

"You fled from us."

"I fled from her." Roland gripped the parapet. The stone was cold, but not as cold as his heart. "To ride, to shoot, to abhor the Lie—so it was said of the old Persians. But it could as well be said of the Franks. She lied; because of the lie, those I loved died."

"But your king lives. Your friend the archbishop, he lives. Ten thousand Franks—"

"Olivier is dead!"

Parsifal let that echo away into silence. Then he said, "Grieve. Mourn. Get it over. But never lay the blame on her. She did not wish his death. The enemy wanted you dead, and cared little who died with you."

"Then it's my fault? I'm to blame?"

"There is no blame," said Parsifal. "There is only what is."

Roland sank down on the paving. It was very real under his knees, hard stone, bruising-hard. Old scars stretched and pulled. Bruises twinged. He was as wholly in his body as he was in the waking world. But Parsifal could not be here in the flesh: his body was dying. This was a vigorous man, hale and strong, standing over him, dark against the stars.

"I think I am too young for this," Roland said.

"You are as old as you need to be," said the Grail-king.

"I can't be—I'm not strong enough."

"What, you admit it? Then you're not young at all!"

Roland snapped erect. Parsifal was laughing at him.

"Kinsman," he said, "blood of my blood, we are none of us strong enough. Not alone. But together . . ."

"With her?"

"With whomever the gods have given us."

Roland scowled. But his temper had died to ashes. Parsifal had cooled it, and deliberately so. Roland could not fan the flames again. "Clever," he said. "Clever and cruel."

"I do what I must," the Grail-king said.

"Don't we all?" Roland pulled himself to his feet.

"Kinsman," Parsifal said, "for whatever cause, for whomever you please, come to us. Come quickly. If you choose then to refuse what's been laid on you . . . so be it. But come."

"I come," Roland said wearily. "It seems I have no choice in the matter."

"Does any of us?"

"I don't know," Roland said. "Oh, God, to be free and innocent again."

"Were you ever either?"

"Long ago," said Roland. "Long and long. Before—"

"Before Merlin."

"Before I knew what magic was." Roland raked his hair out of his face. Parsifal was looking somewhat frayed himself. He was thin about the edges, flickering like an image in clear water. "I will come," Roland said to him. "I give you my word."

CHAPTER 45

⌘ ⌘ ⌘

The Breton Count was dead. He had died in the slaughter of Roncesvalles. His body lay in the earth at the head of the pass, where the king had ordered a shrine to be raised and Masses sung for all those who had died.

He must have died in great pain. Pepin had seen the body when it was brought in, and it was terribly, unrecognizably hacked and mutilated. But there was no mistaking the armor, or the shards of the great aurochs' horn that had been found on its breast. Charles wept long and grievously over Roland, and over the rest of the Companions who were laid down beside him, all slain as he had been, recognizable only by their trappings.

They had not found the sword. Durandal was lost—looted, stolen, like the gold of Spain. Robbers had been stripping the body of armor when the Franks came on it. The thieves were dead, but Durandal was gone.

It was a grim march home to Francia. Men who had cursed the Breton witch in life were hailing him a hero now that he was dead. Already there were songs of him: his prowess in war, his magical sword, his great horn that had nigh brought down the mountains. It had brought the king back too late to save his rearguard.

Pepin was in an ill mood himself. He had been cheated of Roland's blood and kept far away from his death. There was no joy in it, no satisfaction. Only a faceless thing on a bier, and a sour taste in his mouth.

Ganelon was closer to the king's counsels than ever. That his grand plan had failed, his gate of power broken and ten thousand men lost to him, seemed to trouble him little. Roland was dead, and that was well. The rest he could accomplish by other means than an ambush and a hellgate. They were neither as simple nor as easy, but they were certain enough.

Ganelon had made sure that Charles found Gascons among the enemy dead, and fanned the fire of rage against them. But Charles was strangely recalcitrant about leading his army to a new war in Gascony. "In the spring," he said. "By the time we come to Francia, it will be the beginning of autumn. We'll disband the army, send them home to finish the harvest, give them a winter's rest. Come spring they'll be ready to fight again."

Ganelon was as oddly acquiescent to this as to the ambush that had failed. He bowed to the king's will. He did not argue as Pepin would have, that the army was gathered now, ready now, and would be glad to take a swift revenge. He let the king march unhindered out of the mountains and into his own country.

Pepin was powerless to speak if Ganelon would not. The court seemed a paler, duller thing with the Companions gone from it. Charles made no move to gather a second dozen of paladins. The various lords' heirs were granted their new ranks and places, and Rheims had a new archbishop. But the king took none of them to his heart as he had their predecessors.

It was not the sweet victory Pepin had dreamed of. Nor was he initiated into a new and greater order of magic. He was still Ganelon's pupil, still writing letters and studying grimoires and practicing small spells and piddling workings. Ganelon did not need Pepin's eyes any longer, now Roland was dead and the sorceress had vanished.

She was not dead. Pepin looked for her in the silver basin, one day when Ganelon was out of his tent attending the king. He found her in the high castle where he had seen her before, standing on a tower, staring out across the empty peaks. She did not speak or move, though he watched her as long as he dared. Nor could he read her expression at all.

On a night of stars but no moon, when the army had left the marches of Spain behind but before it dispersed to all its various nations, Pepin came late to his tent. He had been tasting the wines of Provence, fresh from the carts of the merchants who had been waiting for the army to descend from the hills.

There was no lamp lit in the tent, no servant waiting to undress him. Yet there was light, pale and strange, and Ganelon sitting in it.

Pepin stopped, reeling slightly, dizzy with wine. It was the wine that made him ask, "Do you need my eyes?"

"I need you," said Ganelon.

"Now?"

Ganelon raised a brow slightly. Pepin's throat constricted in spite of itself. "The king will disperse the army when we reach Toulouse," Ganelon said. "When he does that, you will ask his leave to go. Your soul is troubled, you will tell him. You have in mind a season of prayer and contemplation."

Pepin stared.

Ganelon's expression did not change. "When he asks where you will go, tell him that you go with me, and that we will cloister ourselves among holy monks in an abbey near Toulouse. He should little care which, once he hears my name."

"You'll see to that?"

Ganelon did not answer.

"And we really will do that? There are monks who follow your way?"

"There are monks in plenty, and priests, too," said Ganelon, "and great princes of the Church."

"Popes?"

"Even so," said Ganelon.

At Toulouse the court and *palatium* continued on its round of the kingdom, but the army dispersed into the fields and forests of Francia. Pepin asked for and won his father's leave to go into retreat—more easily than he had expected, for the king was preoccupied. Word had come from the east. The Saxons were rising again. The spring's campaign, Pepin could already see, would march east instead of westward into Gascony.

Charles had dismissed his son almost absently, intent on matters of greater consequence. Once Pepin would have resented that. Now he was too eager, and too curious, to discover what Ganelon had in mind.

They rode out of the walled city on a fair morning of autumn, Pepin and Ganelon and the silent Siglorel. Pepin was not permitted to bring a servant. He went in plain clothing, with only such baggage as his horse could carry. The sorcerer and his servant rode tall Spanish mules, and Siglorel led another laden with bundles, but none of them belonged to Pepin. Nor did Pepin receive an answer when he asked what was in them. He was to be condemned to silence, it seemed.

Very well, then he would be silent. His skin quivered, his heart beat with anticipation of great things. Strong things. Workings of great magic.

That night they sheltered in an abbey, but it was not the one of which Ganelon had spoken. The monks here were ordinary enough, their abbot respectful of the king's counselor but not visibly in awe of him. The place stank of holiness.

Pepin was not pleased to discover that they would be expected to dine with the monks and to attend all the offices, even into the night. Barley bread and sour ale were excessively penitential. Droning through endless psalms came close to torment.

Discipline, he thought. Discipline was the first virtue of a mage. Ganelon had taught him that. He was not perfect in it, but he had learned a little. He set his teeth, ate the hard bread and drank the terrible ale and suffered through the offices. In the morning they would go. Then he would discover what great thing had brought Ganelon out of Toulouse.

In the morning they rose unholy early as the monks did. The skies had closed in with grey cold rain. The first storm of winter lashed the abbey's walls. Damp sank into the stones. Pepin braced himself for another day of monastic discipline. But after the monks had sung their office, as he prepared to retreat to the cell he had been given, the demon Siglorel stopped him. The creature, silent as ever, beckoned him out of the cloister.

The horse and the mules were saddled and waiting, though the rain continued to fall. Ganelon was mounted, wrapped in cloak and hood. Pepin opened his mouth to demand of him why he chose this moment to go. Could he not wait for the sun to come back? But a gust of rain struck his face like a cold slap. He wrapped his own cloak more tightly and scrambled gracelessly into the gelding's saddle.

Ganelon seemed to be in no distress. Did he even feel the rain? Siglorel was a demon; Pepin doubted that anything of earth could touch him. Least of all now that Roland was dead.

Even in death Roland went on vexing Pepin. Pepin huddled into his cloak and wished himself in hell, where the fires at least might keep him warm.

He came to himself with a start. He must have slid into a doze, as improbable as that was. Mist had closed about them. He could just see the rump of Ganelon's mule ahead of him. He heard rather than saw Siglorel with the packmule behind him. Every sound seemed vast: the roaring of breath in his lungs, the hammering of his heart, the slip and clatter of hooves on stone.

The road had grown steep and very narrow. It had no feel of a road in Provence. Had they ridden back to the Spanish March, then? In so little a time?

For a sorcerer, all things were possible. Pepin sat up and gathered his scattered wits. His brown gelding plodded on as if sudden mountains and blinding mist were of no concern.

The mist brightened. Pepin narrowed his eyes against the growing light. All at once he emerged blinking into the sorcerer's garden.

His horse, with a horse's wisdom, lowered its head and began to graze in the blindingly green grass. The air was warm, so warm that Pepin began to shiver convulsively. He slid from the saddle, knees buckling, catching himself against the gelding's shoulder.

Ganelon paid no heed to him. The sorcerer and his demon servant had left their mules to graze as the gelding was doing, and stood over the pool that filled the garden's center.

It was larger, Pepin thought as he gained back somewhat of his senses. He let fall his sodden cloak and hood. His clothes were damp, but drying already. It was almost too warm, and he was dressed for raw cold in furs and leather. He stripped off his tunic and straightened as much as his back would allow, luxuriating in the coolness of his linen undertunic and the warmth of the air—twin wonders, twin marvels after the abbey's discomforts.

He approached the pool, walking steadier now. The water was full of visions that spread outward in spokes like a wheel. The center was this garden, and three figures in it, standing by a pool, in which was reflected . . .

He stopped that before it spun him down into madness, drew his mind back sharply, raised his head and looked at the image from which the shadows came. More paths than ever led out of the garden. Each one, in sunlight or rain, bright day or night's shadow, showed much the same: the camp of an army, or an army marching. Some of them he recognized. His father had sent them home from Toulouse. Now they marched again, with white set faces and eyes lost in the shadows of their helmets.

And others he knew, too, by garb and nation: Gascons, Saracens, Christians of Spain. Still others were strangers, and many not human at all.

He had grown up in camps of war. He knew how to count men and companies. And this was a great army— greater even than his father had mustered against the infidels in Spain. There were thousands of them. Tens of thousands. All bound by the same great spell. All marching toward a single place.

Mountains reared against the sky. He knew those mountains, that sky. He had struggled through them twice, once going to and once coming from the Spanish war. And yet there was something strange, something new or different about them: the light on them, the height of them, the way they reached toward the sky.

They were not earthly mountains. They were rooted in earth, borne up against heaven, but the light that shone on them was not the light of the sun. The moon that waxed and waned over them was higher, whiter, colder than the moon that he knew.

Ganelon's armies were swarming up those jagged slopes. The scope, the vastness of it, left him breathless. They were storming the walls of the world. He saw where gates had been: pillars of earth and stone, shards of light. Dark things poured over them to the lofty summits, and streamed down out of sight.

"How well you see," Ganelon said.

Pepin started like a deer. The sorcerer stood beside him, who an instant before had been long strides away. Ganelon did not betray amusement, but his dark eyes glittered as he said, "You may still refuse to go."

"Go?" Pepin asked stupidly. "Refuse? What do you need me for?"

"Your blood," Ganelon answered. And as Pepin gaped at him: "Blood of kings, or of kings' firstborn sons, has great power. Did I not teach you this?"

"You'll . . . drink . . . my blood?"

Ganelon's lip curled. His teeth were white and sharp. They did not fit his pale wise face at all—they would have been more at home in the jaws of a wolf. "That would be wasteful," he said, "when your soul is so simply won. No, fool; great magic, great sorcery can work through you, through what you are and what you hope to be."

"Even in a twisted body?"

"The Church will take no maimed or misshapen man for a priest," said Ganelon. "My Master is less fastidious. Royal blood is royal blood. He little cares for the shape of the vessel that bears it."

Pepin laughed harshly. "Then I've well chosen my way, haven't I? Will you make me a king? Will you do that, master sorcerer?"

"If you prove yourself well in this war," said Ganelon, "I may consider it."

"Or I may do it without you," Pepin said.

"You may," said Ganelon without expression. "Gather your garments and your horse. Make ready to ride."

Pepin did not take orders well, but for once he was too eager to care. He did as he was bidden, was mounted and ready before either of the others had left the pool. There was nothing to keep them there, surely. Only armies marching and mountains looming toward the sky.

"Come," said Ganelon as Pepin began to lose patience. "Ride."

Pepin did not ask which path to take away from the pool. All were the same, he thought. All led to the same place, to the mountains and the armies. He chose one at random, turned his horse's head toward it. Ganelon followed him without a word.

CHAPTER 46

✠ ✠ ✠

The sorcerer's army gathered on the far side of the mountains, beyond the wall of the world. It stretched far and far away across the bare hills, beneath the jagged crags. Men and beasts, demons and spirits of earth and air, met in companies but did not mingle.

The spirits were bound with chains of air. The demons had sworn mighty oaths to the sorcerer, and so been enslaved. The men lay under a spell.

The Franks thought they were still on the march, still traveling toward their own country. They were awake and aware, but the land they saw did not seem to be the land that met Pepin's eyes. They knew him perfectly well; they bowed to him as the king's son, and some of those who had trailed in his following were minded to do so again. But Ganelon forbade. "No princes' follies here," he said. "No mortal stupidity. This is war, not a royal hunting party."

Pepin snarled and pondered defiance. His blood warded him to a degree. Ganelon needed him too badly to damage him unduly.

But he was far from his father's protection, and he wanted this too much to cast it away. High magic, great sorcery—it was coming to him at last. There could be no working without him. Perhaps there could be no victory.

All that Ganelon had not seen fit to teach Pepin, he

taught him now: arts, castings, spells and dark workings. Pepin's head reeled with all that he had to remember.

And yet he could do it. He was good at it. The more he was asked to do, the more he could do. He had a gift.

Ganelon did not like to admit it, but he could hardly deny it. "It seems you have magic after all," he said, "and not only for the blood that is in you."

Pepin hugged the knowledge to himself. He was a sorcerer. He could raise demons, command spirits. He could bring down the lightning. When he chanted spells, the powers answered.

When the time came, he would need no sorcerer's help to make himself King of the Franks. He had as much power as he needed, and the skill was coming swiftly, day by day.

For the moment he needed Ganelon. The sorcerer had not given him the secret of the garden, nor had he been able to discover it for himself. Without it he could not return to Francia.

Time enough for that when he had learned all that the sorcerer would teach. And, he thought, when the war was won.

War for the Grail. Much of what he learned was directed at that mighty instrument of power: winning it, holding it, mastering it. Ganelon's army would break down the gates of the Grail's kingdom and destroy the men and spirits who defended it. But when that was done, there was still the Grail to take and keep.

For that, Ganelon needed Pepin. He needed a prince of blood royal, whose soul was his own still, who had not sworn himself to the powers of the dark. This was Pepin's power and his protection. As long as Ganelon needed him whole and free, he was safe from the sorcerer's malice, and that of his servants. Some of them might try, but he had learned spells to blast them where they stood.

He took considerable pleasure in the refinements of the spells. Better, he thought, to leave the man alive, but take away his hands, or leave him without feet, or seal his lips and tongue so that he could not speak. Two or three such workings, and the rest bowed before him in awe and fear.

Pepin Crookback was no laughingstock now, no object of pity or scorn. Nor would he ever be again.

*   *   *

There was no counting days here between the worlds. The sun rose and set. The moon was born and died. They seemed to bear no relation to one another, nor were the days of equal length. Sometimes the day was endless, sometimes it flashed past in a moment. One night the moon was full, the next it was a thin sliver of new moon. Time was all strange here. The only constant was the breath in Pepin's lungs, the beat of his heart, and the relentlessness of Ganelon's teaching.

One morning—or so the sun's height told them, and its nearness to rising—the army rose and broke camp and marched toward the shimmer of the horizon. Pepin had had no warning. He woke late and was nearly left behind. He had to scramble his belongings together without benefit of servant. His horse was saddled and waiting, but there was no one to strike his tent.

He stood staring at it. Anger surged up in him. He called the spirits of air. They came in a whirlwind, swift enough almost to take him aback. He knew a moment's flutter in the belly, an instant's fear; but he was stronger than they. "Strike my tent," he commanded them. "Bear it to the baggage-train."

They strained at his will, but he held firm. With a last rebellious wail, they did his bidding.

The army was moving slowly, yet move it did. He mounted. Already the foremost ranks had vanished into a shimmer of mist. He spurred his horse after them.

This was not hell, nor yet purgatory. It was, Ganelon said, a world beyond the world. The mist was the power of the Grail, obscuring their sight and confusing their minds. The earth flung up stones to trip feet and bruise hooves. Rivers snaked across their path, seeming to widen as they approached, and deepen and grow swifter, so that they were hard pressed to ford the roaring torrents. Mountains reared in front of them.

But they pressed on. They camped when it grew too dark to see, whether with cloud or night. Their will did not falter, for it was Ganelon's will. He ruled them all.

This was not such an army as Pepin had known. There were no gatherings of lords and counselors. There was only one general, and that was Ganelon. Captains led at his pleasure. If any showed signs of chafing against the sorcerer's rule, he vanished. Ganelon heard no one's word but his own. His rule was absolute.

Pepin was Frank enough to find that rather uncomfortable. A king could do whatever he pleased—but what if he needed advice? Or more to the point, what if he needed someone to take the blame for his mistakes?

He held his tongue, learned his lessons, felt the power grow inside him. The farther they traveled into this strange dim country, the stronger, rather than weaker, he became. He could see the strain about the army, the bindings fraying. Now and then a demon or a spirit would escape. Some simply vanished. Others ran wild in the army, sowing havoc, until they were caught and either bound again or destroyed.

The Franks were beginning to wake a little. They would look up suddenly, look about, shake their heads. Or one of them would begin to speak, seem to reconsider, fall silent again.

Ganelon himself seemed unmoved. That was a mask: the army was the image of his strength, and it was struggling against the power of the Grail. One morning, evening, it was difficult to tell, he said to Pepin, "The Franks belong to you. Control them."

Pepin stared, struck briefly dumb. Ganelon's eyes were bitter cold. Past startlement, past fear, Pepin knew the first dawning of elation.

Twenty thousand men. Twenty thousand Franks, given to him as if they had been an outworn tunic. "May I do whatever I please with them?" he asked.

"You will make sure that they follow me," said Ganelon, "and that they fight for me when we come to the battle. There will be not one man lost, not one drop of blood shed. They will come whole and obedient to the field. But past that," he said, "you may do as you like."

It was little enough, but there was still great pleasure in the thought of it. Pepin had barely turned away before he let the grin escape.

He knew the spells. He had seen Ganelon work them, and assisted in the chanting. He was sure that he could remember exactly how to raise and hold them. It was easier in any case, because the binding was already made. He had only to strengthen it and turn it toward himself.

It was evening, he decided. The sun was setting. Camp was made. Fires burned, pale in the mist. He was stiff from a long while—day, whatever—in the saddle, but he rode among the Franks, for no good Frankish prince would be seen afoot when he had a horse to carry him.

Men should have been tending campfires and preparing the night's meal. A few of them were doing that, but more were huddled together, muttering, shooting glances at the grey sky, or at the wall of grey cliff against which they had camped.

"Spain," Pepin heard one say. "We're still in Spain."

"Italy," said someone else.

"The marches of the Rhine," said a third.

"So where's the king?" demanded the first. "Where's the lords all high and mighty, riding back and forth? Did they all get killed in the mountains—or did we dream that, too?"

Aiee, thought Pepin. They were awake indeed.

"Maybe we're dead," the second soldier said, "and this is hell."

"I don't remember dying," said the third.

"Would we?" the second asked. "What else can this be? Have you seen what we march beside? I swear I saw a thing with fangs, and another with batwings. They're devils. We're in hell."

"Hell would be a long march to nowhere," muttered the first man.

Pepin had the spell ready to hand, the words on his tongue, the gestures half-begun. But something, some demon perhaps, held him back. He rode in among them.

They barely moved to give space to his horse. They did not look on him in hostility, but neither did they bow to his rank or his name. He had seen such faces among rebels and newly subdued enemies. Never among Franks from the heart of the realm.

He leaned on the saddle's high pommel, looking from face to face. They stared insolently back. He smiled. "You're not dead," he said, "and you're not in Francia, either. How would you like a war? A real war—one you can win."

"Another crusade?" said the first soldier with more than the hint of a sneer.

"No crosses here," Pepin said. "No lies. This war is real. There will be battle. There will be victors and vanquished. One army will stay on the field, bait for the crows. The other will take a great kingdom, great wealth, and a glorious prize."

"Loot?" the first Frank said. His eyes had brightened, but doubt had swiftly dimmed them. "One prize? What's that?"

Pepin paused. He had been a fool to let that slip.

Make the best of it, he thought. "We'll take a castle," he said, "and a king, and nine beautiful ladies."

"Castle," the man sneered. "King. Ladies. What good is that to us mudfoots?"

"Gold in the treasuries," Pepin said, "jewels, treasure uncounted. Women, too. All the loot we lost at Roncesvalles, all the loot we should have won in Spain, would barely fill one treasure-room in these vaults."

That won his argument for him. The lure of gold and the promise of battle swept them all up together.

For the first time Pepin heard men cheer his name, and salute him as commander. It was a heady sensation, glorious, wonderful.

And he had cast no spell at all. The one he did cast, let them see the demons about them as men of sundry nations. Best, after all, that they not know the whole of the truth. They would follow him, and the hope of the Grail, and the promise of treasure. They need not see the faces of all those they marched with, nor understand what master they fought for.

CHAPTER 47

✠ ✠ ✠

Sarissa started awake. Memory of warmth caressed her. She stretched her hand to the one who lay beside her.

There was only cold emptiness and bitter absence.

She had been dreaming of him again, of the sunlit days in Agua Caliente, when no anger lay between them, and the only doubts were hers. She could still remember the shape of him, the salt-sweet taste of his skin, how he loved to trace her breasts and belly with kisses.

A sound escaped her, halfway between laughter and a sob. So brief a time she had had him, in all the years of her life, and those days had swelled to overwhelm the rest.

She had driven him away. Her error, her folly had done it. She had not trusted him, though he proved over and over that he was stronger than his blood.

Only the gods knew where he had gone. People were saying that the enemy had taken and corrupted him. She did not believe it. He had fled by his own will, under his own power. He had vanished from all awareness—save that she would have known, deep in her heart, if he had died.

The enemy was coming. He had breached the outer defenses of the kingdom. He had entered the marches, the grey country between worlds. Men and demons followed him.

"Open the way for him," Nieve said. "Lure him in. Close behind him and destroy him."

The nine ladies gathered in a high chamber. It was in another tower than the shrine of the Grail. That one looked eastward to the sunrise. This looked north, to the winds of winter and the cold still light, and the enemy's ancient stronghold beyond the world's end.

Here was a chamber of guard and watchfulness. Its center was a stone table, and on it a globe of crystal.

They stood round the crystal, nine ladies, tall and short, dark and fair, beautiful and simply pleasant to look on. But to the eyes of the spirit they were all much the same: shining with the splendor of their magic, and bound inextricably to the light.

In the crystal was the orb of the mortal world, blue and white, brown and green, hanging like a jewel in the night. At Nieve's words the vision shifted. The world blurred. The night brightened to twilight, a shimmer of mist and magic, somewhat like falling water, and somewhat like the gleam on the face of a pearl.

Darkness crawled across it. It wore the semblance of a serpent. Its scales were the bodies of men and demons. Its eyes were blind orbs, lit with a pallid light like the moon behind clouds. In its head was set a dark jewel.

There was the enemy, commanding his army of slaves both mortal and otherwise.

"He will break through our defenses," Nieve said in her calm practical voice. "He's too strong for us without the king to anchor our strength. If we let him think he's defeated us before he actually has, he may grow overconfident. Then we may have some hope of driving him back."

"And," said dark Inanna, "if he breaks through in a place of his choosing, he'll ravage our country before he comes to Carbonek. We can offer him our weakness in a corner of the empty lands, and bring him direct here."

None of them took issue with that. They had been together long and long, guarding the Grail. What one thought, another might say, as easy, as unconscious as the drawing of a breath.

Sarissa, who had been apart from them for a year and more, could feel the bonds tugging at her, the weaving closing about her, drawing her into its warp and woof.

She did not want to argue with a plan that was both simple and profoundly sensible. And yet she also did not want to be wholly at one with the rest. She wanted—she knew not what.

Roland.

She thrust that name aside, out of her mind, if never out of her heart. She said, "So let it be done. Let him wander yet a while, and fancy that he tests our defenses. We'll weaken them slowly, open the way to him beyond the field of the standing stones. And when he comes—"

"When he comes," said Inanna, "we face him."

"And vanquish him, one hopes," murmured the usually silent Liu. Her almond eyes were lowered, her ivory face serene.

"We'll do what we can," Nieve said.

"But without a king strong enough to bolster us, what hope do we have?" Freya demanded. "Truly—what hope is there?"

"More than none," said Nieve. "The champion may come back. The sword may do what it was wrought to do."

"Or not." Freya's white hand parted the air. A thing of forged steel took shape above the table. Durandal's white pommel mirrored the eyes of the serpent within the globe of crystal. With a swift, fierce gesture, she thrust it into the globe.

The crystal did not shatter. The sword's blade sank into it as if it had been soft clay. It pierced the heart of the serpent.

"An omen," Clodia said. "May it come to pass."

Freya shook her head, tossing her wheat-fair braids. She turned on her heel and stalked away.

Sarissa stared for a while at the place where she had been. Not so perfect a harmony, then, after all.

The others left one by one. Sarissa, who had thought to escape first, found herself among the last. The sword remained in the crystal. The vision had faded with the breaking of the circle.

Inanna reached to remove the sword. Sarissa stopped her hand. "No. Leave it. We need the reminder."

Inanna shrugged, sighed. When she was gone, Sarissa was alone.

Durandal gleamed in the cold light. Sarissa brushed its

pommel with her finger. She had a sudden, vivid vision of Roland's face. His eyes were on something she could not see. She doubted very much that he was thinking of her.

Alive, she thought. Alive and well. Though where, or what he did there, she was not able to discover.

Turpin was down in the camp among the Franks, as he had been since Roland fled. He had come out of the Grail's shrine with a great stillness on him. He had bowed low to the king, and left the castle without a word.

But in camp among his people, he was as he had always been. He had told them the truth of their presence here, and they had accepted it, because it was he who said it. They had elected him their commander—Franks might do such things, if they were minded.

Sarissa had spent rather more time among these men than might have been reckoned necessary. Many of them she had known since she came to Paderborn. They were at ease with the thought of her, even knowing what she was.

In past days the levies had begun to come in. They camped farther down the long field, toward the green expanse of the valley, on either side of the king's white road. The Franks regarded them with interest—accustomed to fighting in armies with strangers, some of whom might have been enemies only the season before. Though these were stranger than most that they might have fought with. Not all were human, and not all wore human faces.

Sarissa stood with Turpin on a rise above the road, watching another lord of the kingdom bring in his army. This was the Prince of Poictesme, with a great force of mortal archers, and a rallying of wildfolk hopping and slithering and flapping behind them.

"That's nigh all of them, yes?" said Turpin. "Only one or two yet to come."

Sarissa nodded. "Only the lords of the farthest domains: Herne, Gwyn, Huon. Herne is close; he'll reach us before the sun sets. Of the others we're less certain, but they'll come soon."

"And then, the enemy will come."

She looked into those quiet grey eyes. They had not been so calm before he saw the Grail. Nor had they seen so far or so clearly. "Then the enemy comes," she said, "and the war we've all been waiting for."

"I'm ready," he said. He stood easily, feet apart, hand on swordhilt, as warriors learned to stand; but the monk's robe and the tonsure told another truth.

The army of Poictesme camped in its allotted place down the valley. Sarissa saw it settled and its prince sent to the castle to speak with Morgan of the nine, who commanded the armies in the king's incapacity. She went back to the Franks, ate and drank and slept among them. She did not dream of Roland that night. Instead she dreamed of rain, and of rivers running to the sea.

She woke to a cool and misty morning, and a silver sun, and word running through the camps: Herne and Gwyn had come in together. Only Huon was yet to come. And the enemy had found the weakness that the nine had left for him, and pierced it. She felt in her own skin the pain of that violation.

It was necessary. The road would bring him past empty lands and villages long deserted, burned and trampled in the last of his wars. No living place would suffer from his presence. No innocent creature would fall prey to his malice.

She was needed in the castle. But she stayed among the armies. Morgan was a greater general than she, and Nieve far more accomplished in preparing for a siege. Whatever they needed of her, they could provide for themselves.

She was running away—not as suddenly or completely as Roland had, but close enough. She did not care. She could make herself useful here: gathering the commanders, telling them all that was fit for them to know; rallying the troops. They needed her, she told herself, more than the castle did. They needed to see a great one of the Grail walking among them, giving them hope.

CHAPTER 48

✠ ✠ ✠

Lord Huon was late to the muster. It was a long march, and the end of it much beset with storms of rain and sleet. The walls between the worlds had broken. Roland could feel the shards of them grinding in his spirit. The enemy was marching through the Grail's kingdom.

They could travel only as fast as men could walk, and as the earth would let them. Roland struggled to remember a soldier's patience. There was time to teach his pack of raw recruits a little of what they should know; to give them some defenses in the battles that would come.

The closer they came to Carbonek, the more difficult it was to go on. The road buckled and surged under their feet. Winds lashed them. Lightnings battled overhead.

These children of agelong peace were strong of heart, bright and sturdy of spirit, but this was a hard road, with fear upon it and terror at the end of it. Messengers sent ahead brought back word from Carbonek: the enemy was far from it still, on another road than this; and the army had gathered. They were the last.

That, Roland could credit. But that the enemy was far away, he was not so sure of. Sometimes the amulet on his breast would burn like fire. At other times, in the nights particularly, he would wake with a start, and shudder, as if something foul had passed through the tent.

"There's old darkness in the earth," Marric said by the

fire on a night without stars, a day or two out from Car-bonek. "That great thing in the castle, it washes this country with light. But long before it came here, other things walked and burrowed and flew. Those that weren't destroyed, that were only sleeping, will be waking now."

Roland had paused for a cup of heated wine and a loaf of Marric's bread. He shivered in the cool of the night. "I feel them," he said. "They're moving through the earth."

"Are they?" Marric seemed surprised, though he covered it with close attention to his stewpot. "So," he said as if to himself. "It's in your bones."

Roland might have asked him what he meant, but Cait had come into the firelight. Her face was taut with worry. "Bran is sick," she said.

It was not Cait's way to fret over trifles. Roland followed her to her own campfire. He was aware of Marric treading softly behind, but he did not look back. He was equally aware of the rumbling in the earth. Something had roused very close, almost beneath them. He had an instant's awareness of jeweled claws and great gleaming teeth.

Then he was bending over a young man from a village near Caer Sidi. He was a pale and withered thing, lying shivering on a pile of cloaks. His eyes were sunk in his skull.

And yet Roland had seen him only yesterday, practicing with throwing-spears and throwing farther than anyone. He had won a wager with Cieran, a cask of Gemma's ale. He had been a big ruddy creature, strong and proud of it.

"When?" Roland asked Cait, though others were babbling, vying to tell him everything.

Cait knew how to measure her words. "It started this morning," she said. "We thought it was the ale. The rest of them got better. He didn't. When the sun went down, so did he—just all at once, as if something sucked the juice out of him."

"Something did!" said a thin wiry boy with a nose almost as sharp as the bogle's. "I saw it. I did! It was like a bat. It fastened on his neck. I scared it away—I yelled, I think. Nobody heard me. I thought it was a dream. That was last night, when it was still dark, and the sun hadn't come yet. It must have come back when the sun went down again."

"Nursery tales," Cait sneered.

"No," said Marric. "It's real."

They all stared at him, a ring of white scared faces.

"Is he going to die?" a voice asked, faint and frightened, from the back of the crowd.

"Not if I can help it," Roland said grimly. "Cait, send someone to Lord Huon, he needs to know. Marric, put up wards. See if there's anyone who can help you. I'll do what I can, once I'm done here."

"I can do it," Marric said. "Kyllan will help. You look after the boy."

Roland nodded once, then forgot him. Bran was wandering in a black dream, muttering words that made no sense. Darkness was nested in him, feeding on his spirit.

Roland was a warrior, not a healer, but Merlin had taught him much; and somehow, just then, he knew what he should do. He ran hands down the gaunt and shivering body. As he did it, he called the light to him: light of fire, light of stars and moon. Light within, too, through the burning glass of the amulet. What it drew from, he did not know, nor at the moment did he care.

It was as if the moon had come down to fill his hands. He poured it out over the dying man.

Behind him, someone's breath caught. He sat on his heels, rather surprised himself.

What the dark thing had taken, the light restored, slowly at first, then more swiftly. It was like rain on withered grass. The flesh returned to the bones. Awareness returned to the eyes, as Bran opened them, squinting at Roland. His voice was faint, but grew stronger with use. "Sir! Did I fall down? I don't remember—"

"You drank enough ale to drown an ox," Roland said, cuffing him very lightly. "Here, Cait has a posset for you. Drink it and sleep. You should be well enough by the time you wake."

Bran was amenable to that gentle bullying. While they were all intent on him, Roland left them. He passed through Marric's wards as they rose, a tightening on the surface of the skin, a shiver beneath it. He could almost see the shimmer of the wall the bogle had built about the camp.

Lord Huon was sitting by Marric's fire, all alone, dressed plainly and squatting as easily as one of the villagers. He had found a bowl and was eating a helping of stew from the pot. "It's good," he said as Roland squatted beside him and filled another bowl. "What's in it? Rabbit?"

"Mule, I think," Roland said.

Huon choked only slightly, and went on eating. In the dark and firelight, the horns on his brow were almost clear: antlers in velvet, just short of their full growth. His eyes were as large and dark as a stag's. Roland wondered if he would put on the full semblance, come the season, and go rutting after hinds in the wood.

It was not a worthy thought. He put it down and sat on it. Not without a blush, either—for he had run with the deer one autumn, and nearly been killed, too, when he challenged the king of stags. Merlin had sewn him together when he came crawling back, and carefully said nothing of young things' folly.

"The man who was ill," Huon said in the silence. "He'll recover?"

Roland nodded.

"And the wards are up," said Huon. "You took command well, there."

Roland glanced at him. "Did I overstep myself?"

"I don't think you can," Huon said.

"My lord," Roland said. "If I've given offense—"

"No," Huon said. "Tomorrow, late in the day, we'll come to Carbonek. If we're allowed to pass."

Roland raised his brows.

Huon raised his own. "Don't tell me you don't feel it."

"The thing beneath us?"

"Yes. I'm holding it as best I can, but this many men and wildfolk, this close to the Grail—if we pass it, it well may rise up in back of us."

Huon might not understand why Roland laughed, but Roland found the irony rather wonderful. "Give me the rearguard. I'll hold it if it rises."

Huon regarded him for a long moment: weighing, measuring. Roland sat quiet under the scrutiny. He had been judged before. He would pass, or he would not. He ate his bowl of stew and drank a cup of ale.

At last Huon said, "Do it, then. Take the bogle with you. My mages will go, and a company of my own guard."

Roland inclined his head. That was generous. "May I choose the rest of the rearguard?"

"As you will," Huon said.

Roland bowed where he sat, and rose. "I'd best get to it, then. Your mages, your guardsmen—"

"They will obey you," said Huon.

Roland bowed again, a little more deeply, then went where he needed to go.

It was a rather motley company that gathered in the rear come morning: a hundred lordly men of Caer Sidi in silver armor with long green cloaks, mounted on grey horses; seven mages on white mules; and Roland's recruits, his villagers in leather and old iron, with their spears and bows. The former rearguard, seasoned troops from Huon's own lands, regarded them in some disdain, but they kept their chins up and their eyes forward.

Roland might have regretted his choice, seeing how raw these children were, but his heart had chosen for him. If it had chosen badly, he would pay whatever price was laid on him.

They broke camp and rode out just as the sun was rising over mountains that—surely they had not been there before?

If they had, he would not have seen them: they had marched for days in clouds and rain. The sky was clear blue this morning, the peaks distinct, the highest crowned with snow. On one of those foremost was the castle of the Grail. It was barely to be seen, veiled in wards, growing up out of the grey stone, but he knew it. He felt it. It sang to him, sweet beyond bearing, calling him back to it.

He could not let it distract him. The thing beneath the earth was stirring more strongly with the sun's coming. He could feel the quiver underfoot before he mounted. The usually placid gelding skittered and snorted. Roland calmed him with a word and a hand on his neck. "Go on," he said to the rearguard. "March and ride."

They found the order he had given them: recruits first, then guardsmen, and mages scattered among the lot of them, sustaining wards and keeping watch. He brought up the rear, with Marric on his brown pony ambling alongside.

Roland saw Bran marching with the rest of his kin. He glanced at Marric.

"He doesn't remember a thing," Marric said. "We had a

terrible time convincing him he'd been sick for a day—he kept insisting we must be playing a trick on him because he drank more than his share of the ale."

"Did he?" Roland asked.

"He drank enough," said Marric. "No one else was taken ill in the night. The wards held."

"Good," Roland said. "It will get worse, you know, when the enemy comes to Carbonek."

"Then we'll have to keep the wards up. They'll have thought of that in the castle, I'm sure. The people there—they remember the last war. They're not children as these are."

"All of them?" Roland asked after a moment. "They all remember?"

"Most," said Marric.

"And . . . the enchantresses? They, too?"

"All nine," Marric said. He slanted a glance at Roland under the tilt of his brows. "The Grail sustains life far beyond mortal span, and these ladies are its guardians and keepers. They've served it since it came to Montsalvat."

Roland had known that. And yet it was strange, to think of Sarissa as older than Merlin, older than the Grail-king. She seemed so young. She *was* young.

And why should that matter? She had lied to him. She had mistrusted him. He should not care that she had been alive since before the Temple fell in Jerusalem. Or that he, beside her, was less than an infant—he was an insect, the child of a day, born at sunrise and dead of age before the night fell.

The thing below was older far, and it was awake, swimming through earth and stone as if it were water. He thought of a great pike in a northern lake, a spear of bone and gleaming scales, hurtling toward its prey.

The sound of marching feet drew it. The wards barely turned it aside. It had been asleep a long, long time. It was hungry, famished near to death. It smelled their blood, hot and sweet, and the salt tang of their flesh.

"We'll be bait," Roland said to Marric, but loud enough for the rearmost ranks to hear. "Let the bulk of the army draw somewhat ahead. We'll move slowly, but make a great deal of noise. Bring out the drums. Play the trumpets. Sing, shout, laugh."

"That's mad," Kyllan said. But he was grinning. He ran to one of the pack-mules and tugged open its pack, pulling out drums and pipes and a single, surprising small harp. Gwydion the smith took that.

Farther down the line, others did the same, and others past them, in a rippling wave. The lord's guardsmen, between Roland and the villagers, slid eyes at him, but one of those nearest the rear lifted an ivory horn to his lips and blew a long exhilarating blast. Drums rattled and rumbled and boomed. Pipes skirled. Voices of men and women rose in a marching song out of old Rome. There was a strong rhythm in it, and a vaunting arrogance that made some of them laugh even as they sang.

The dragon in the earth lashed its tail. The ground trembled.

Laughter, Roland thought. More than marching feet, more than drums or pipes or horns or song, human merriment drew the thing—lured it, enraged it.

"Slower!" he called. "March slower. Laugh! Taunt this thing. Shower it with scorn."

The lordly guardsmen were affronted. The villagers howled with delight.

The army was some distance away now, ascending a long slope to the summit of a hill. The van had already passed out of sight below. A broad stretch of white road lay open between.

Some of the boys from Greenwood had begun a dance in the grass by the road's edge. It was a very bawdy dance, with much clutching of rears and waggling of anything lengthy that came to hand. One man brandished a sausage as great as a stallion's rod, strutting with it thrust full out before him. As he danced he sang a long wicked paean on the subject of dragons, serpents, and the moistly pulsing caverns of the earth.

The earth swirled and roiled beneath his feet. Jagged knives of crystal flashed within it. Vast jaws snapped shut.

He died laughing. His fellows fled from the great gleaming thing that surged up out of the ground. It snapped, slashed. Some were not fast enough. They vanished in sprays of blood.

Roland's gelding was beside himself with terror. Roland held him by sheer force of will, and drove him forward. The rearguard was holding, save only where the dragon was. And there, most had managed to escape, to dart out of its reach.

Their courage was holding. They fell back in a broad ring, spearmen foremost, archers behind, bows strung and arrows nocked. "Now!" cried Roland.

Fire leaped from his hand and from the hands of the mages scattered round the great circle. The arrows sprang into flame. In a single great swoop, they soared above the spearmen's heads, touched the vault of heaven, bent down upon the dragon.

It was drowsy still, confused by the light, its maw full of still-warm flesh. And yet it was lethally fast. From its sides unfurled wide shimmering wings. The wind of them flattened the spearmen like a field of tall corn. The arrows whirled away.

The dragon struck, swift as a snake. It snatched arrows from the sky and men from the earth. It feasted on blood and fire.

It gleamed with a terrible beauty. It was all silver like the sheen of moon on water. Its eyes were moon-pale, swirling with slow fires. Its wings were the color of mist and smoke.

Claws dug into Roland's shoulder, even through mail. Tarik deafened his ear with a shrill cat-screech.

Roland started violently, and staggered. His strength had drained away, turned all cold by those cold, cold eyes.

Fire burned over his heart. His hand came to rest above the amulet. The heat of it seared his palm, even through linen and leather and mail. He sucked in a breath of sunlit air. It seared his throat and lungs. Fire ran in his veins.

The mages were down or staggering, overcome by the dragon's power. The villagers had drawn back perforce. The lord's guardsmen rallied for the charge, mad and foolhardy and palpably futile, but what else were they to do?

This, Roland thought. He was perfectly calm.

He let the fire go. It left him in a roar of flame, a blaze of light. It fell on the dragon like a great burning mantle. It wrapped the thing close.

Scales of ice melted. Wings of mist vanished into air. Teeth of crystal, claws of diamond fell clattering to suddenly empty earth. And in the center of them all tumbled a coldly gleaming thing, a great white stone that had been the dragon's heart. Fire lived in it, enclosed in it. Of the dragon's body there was no sign, nor of the bodies of the men it had devoured.

Roland sagged on the gelding's neck. His bones hurt. He was empty, scraped dry. Only the dimmest flicker of magic remained in him. Even the amulet was cold.

Victory. And half a dozen lives lost, men and women he had led and trained, who had fought as best they could against an enemy greater than any of them.

There would be many more dead before this war was over. Roland too, maybe, if that was God's will. But not today. Not now. In this first battle of the war, the Grail's people had won.

"May it always be so," he said, or thought, or prayed.

CHAPTER 49

✠ ✠ ✠

Lord Huon's army marched in at evening, last of them all, but first to have met and engaged the enemy. News of the battle had run ahead, and not only through messengers. Sarissa had felt the dragon's rising—felt the Grail wake to defend against it. One of Huon's mages had been the instrument of that defense, said the messenger who paused by her hilltop before riding up to the castle.

That had been a great power—fire so fierce, so strong, that she had felt it in her own heart. She had not known there was such magic in the marches of the kingdom, though there were mages enough, and wildfolk, and creatures of earth and water and air. This was high magic, magic so white and pure and strong that it could wield the Grail itself.

It was not Lord Huon, who rode at the head of his army, resplendent in silver armor. It was none of the mages at his back. Nor certainly was it any of the troops, mounted or afoot, who rode and marched behind him. She did not see it at all, though she would have sworn on the Grail that she would know it if it passed before her.

Was it—could it be—?

No. It could not. He had not known fully what he was, nor had he seen the Grail. And he was long gone.

Still she searched as many faces as she could, as the army marched on past. There were pale faces enough, and straight black hair, and keen profiles—faces of old gods

and heroes, stamped in their children both high and low.
But none had the eyes of a falcon, bright and inhuman gold
in a passably human face.

The rearguard was an odd and rather untidy mingling:
princely horsemen in silver mail, and leather-armored
common folk marching stoutly afoot, armed with spears
and bows. They seemed much at ease with one another:
they were singing as they came, first the footsoldiers, then
the mounted warriors.

It was a contest, she gathered. They were singing a satire
on the dragon's slaying. One wild redheaded boy had a
wicked turn of phrase. One of the armored knights, young
and headlong, almost matched him.

Last of all rode an armored man on a bay gelding, and
a—man?—on a brown pony.

Not a man. A bogle, dressed in well-worn mail and
armed with a Roman shortsword, wearing a thin mask of
human seeming over his quite inhuman self. He was grinning as he rode, taking clear pleasure in the satire. What
his companion thought, she could not see: he was helmeted, and he rode in silence, light and erect in the gelding's saddle.

No, she thought. Oh, no. That was not—but that seat on
a horse, that straightness in the back and shoulders, that lift
and turn of the head, as if in spite of itself, as he passed by
the hill on which she stood—

"Roland." That was not her voice. That was Turpin, forgotten beside her, leaving her side, running down the hill.
"Roland! Roland, you devil's get!"

She thought, with the distant clarity of pure shock, that
he would ride on, oblivious. But he had halted at the hill's
foot. The bogle sat beside him on the shaggy brown pony,
grinning as bogles could, from ear to sharply pointed ear.
It was rather a disconcerting spectacle. The bogle had
very sharp teeth, and there were very many of them.

"Marric," Sarissa said. Not that other name, after all. She
could not bring herself to say it.

The bogle rode up the slope of the hill. His grin had
faded somewhat, but his eyes were wickedly bright. He
paused just below her as she sat on the summit, and bowed
low over his pony's neck. "My lady," he said with courtesy
that he had learned on her hearth, long years ago.

"So," she said. "You brought him back."

"Someone had to," Marric said.

She refused to weep. She dared not rail at the prodigal, whom she had not even looked directly at, yet, though his helmet was off and he was off his horse and Turpin was pounding him thunderously on the back. It was Roland, indeed: white face, long arched nose, yellow eyes. She could never forget that face, not if she lived another thousand years.

She was aware, dimly, that the rearguard had broken ranks. A good number of them were hanging about, staring at the big man in the monk's robe and the finely woven mail. They must be wondering why he was weeping on their captain's shoulder.

He did not do it for long. Were Roland's eyes somewhat damp themselves? Sarissa could not have told. He was expressionless, drawn in tight, betraying nothing.

Wings beat overhead. A grey falcon came to rest on Roland's armored shoulder. Tarik regarded her with a bright insolent stare. There could be no doubt of his opinion in the matter—or of where he had been, either.

He had chosen sides long ago. Sarissa met his stare with one as level and as unbending.

While she tarried on the hilltop, the Franks had come in their companies. They came in some semblance of order, but word had run like fire among them: that the Breton Count was alive and riding to the war.

Lord Huon's villagers were swallowed up by that army of strangers. A surprising number clung to places near Roland. A few had let themselves be removed, pushed up the hill to Sarissa's side. "What are they saying?" they demanded of Marric. "What are all those men saying?"

"That they thought he was dead," Marric answered, "or gone forever. That they're beyond glad he's back. That—"

"Is he their king?" asked a wiry girl-child with fierce eyes.

"Not so high," Marric said. "They're calling him a count."

Breaths hissed. "Is that higher than a lord?" the girl wanted to know.

"Oh, yes," said a redheaded boy in tones of ancient wisdom. "But not as high as a prince."

"If he's what *I* hear he is," one of the others said, "he's higher than anybody."

"Then what was he doing with us?" the girl said. "Wasn't he a drooling idiot in Greenwood?"

Sarissa bit her lip till it bled. The children babbled on, unmindful of her.

"He was mad," the redheaded boy said. "He was all taken out of himself. So for a while he had no wits to speak of. But he got them back. You know that."

"I don't think he wanted people to know who he is," the girl said.

"He slew the dragon," said the boy. "Every mage and enchanter in Montsalvat knows who he is by now."

"He can't help himself," the girl said. She chewed the end of her fair brown braid, frowning at the great crowd of men below. "He just *is,* you know? It's like breathing, for him. He slays dragons. He commands armies. He teaches village children how to fight."

They loved him, Sarissa thought. They were not in awe of him, though they knew what he was. He was theirs. They looked on him with a proprietary air, worried for him, but proud, too, and sure that once he had disposed of all these clamoring strangers, he would come back to them again.

They took no notice of her. But Marric left his pony to graze on the hillside and sat beside her as bogles liked to sit, knees drawn up to chest, sharp chin on them. He was very large for a bogle, as large as a smallish man, and sturdy as bogles went, like a brown tree-root.

"You've prospered," she said to him.

He shrugged. "I get by. And you—you're all worn down with worry. For him?"

"For everything," she said.

"But a great deal for him." Marric sighed faintly. "He can be a terribly worrisome creature."

"Is it true, then?" she asked. "He was mad when he came to you?"

"Completely out of his head," the bogle said. "Lost in the hawk's spirit, and no man left in him at all. You see that woman down there, holding his horse, making sure he doesn't see how she's looking at him? She took him in. She fed him, clothed him. She taught him to be a man again."

Sarissa had not seen the woman until Marric pointed to

her, out of so many. This was not so much a child; she was a woman grown, and ripe with it, with a great deal of fiery hair and a broad, unbeautiful but very comely face. Her eyes on Roland were raw with hunger, and with something like grief.

"Maybe it wasn't wise to tell me this," Sarissa said to the bogle.

"Maybe," Marric said. He did not seem dismayed. "Will you kill her for doing what you were too haughty to do?"

"That was presumptuous," she said.

"Bogles are," he said. "Look at her. She knows he's not for her. She cast him off as soon as she was sure of it. She wounded him, but he'll recover. He's strong again. You know how a broken bone heals—maybe it's thicker, sturdier than before. Maybe his spirit is like that."

"I'll kill *him*," Sarissa said. "For running away. For staying away so long. For—"

"For coming to know this kingdom as few lords would trouble to know it? For taking its land and people to himself? For coming back when he could have run far away and never come near this place—or you—again?"

She thrust aside the pain of that, though it was like a knife cutting her heart. "Why did he come back? Did you force him? Or Tarik?"

"Truth to tell," Marric said, "Lord Huon's man saw the pair of shoulders he has and counted him in the muster, though he was still as witless as a newborn baby. But when he had his mind back, he stayed with us."

"Huon knows?"

Marric tilted his head. "Look at the shield."

It was hanging on the gelding's saddle, uncovered, gleaming in the last of the light. Blue field, silver swan. Her brows rose as high as they would go. "And where did Huon of the Horn get a shield with that device, of all that he must have in his armories?"

"Ah, well, you know," said Marric. "These lords from the old days, they keep any number of things. And maybe some prince of Carbonek left it behind, a long time ago."

"Does *he* know?"

"I don't think so," Marric said. "The common folk aren't likely to know or care, and he doesn't trouble himself with the lords."

"But surely—" Sarissa shook her head. "No, who notices a captain of foot? Or pays attention to what he carries on his shield? It could be livery, after all."

"Lords would do well sometimes," Marric observed, "to lower their noses a bit and see what's passing underfoot."

"Champions and dragons," she said. She had lost sight of Roland. The Franks had taken him away to their camp.

The redheaded woman handed his gelding to one of the villagers who still lingered, though most had gone with Roland and the Franks. She climbed up the hill, wearily, and flung herself on the grass beside Marric. She did not seem to see Sarissa, or if she did, to reckon her worth taking notice of.

"They're going to fight over him," Marric said, "if somebody doesn't do something."

"Not tonight," said the woman. "I made them swear to keep their heads low and their eyes on him. And make sure he sleeps where he belongs."

"With the Franks?"

She shot him a glare. "With his own people."

"But those are—" Sarissa began, startled out of silence.

"We are his people," the woman said in a tone that brooked no argument.

Sarissa carefully refrained from speaking her thoughts, which were too confused in any case to make much sense of. Of all the ways she might have expected Roland to come back, this was one of the last.

And yet it was very like Roland. She sighed and let herself sink back into the grass. The stars were blossoming overhead. The earth was quiet beneath her, secure in the living presence of the Grail.

As was he. As, at last, was he.

CHAPTER 50

✠ ✠ ✠

Roland did not sleep that night. The Franks needed to know that he was there, that he was alive and safe. Then his recruits insisted on their share of him. It was close to dawn before he saw them all bedded down and quiet—they had been full of themselves tonight, of dragonslaying and coming to the castle, and of discovering that he was somewhat more than they had taken him for.

Those brash young things were mercifully unperturbed by it. Once they knew his rank and where he came from, they seemed rather more content than not. They were inclined to strut in front of Lord Huon's veterans, and let it be known that while Huon was only a lord, Roland was a count.

His tent was pitched where it usually was in their camp. There was another for him with the Franks, where Turpin slept now, snoring to wake the dead. If Turpin had been awake he would have gone there, simply to be with that best of friends again. But he elected to settle in neither.

He walked for a long time through the camp. This was not an army yet. It was a gathering of discrete forces, veterans and recruits, lords and commons. It had no one commander, no king or general to stand before it and make of it one single potent weapon against the enemy.

Who would lead it, then? The Grail-king was dying.

There must be a captain among them all, someone to speak for him, stand forth for him, rule in his name.

Roland passed the last line of the camp, which happened to be that of the Franks, and crossed the empty space between camp and castle. The bridge was down over the deep chasm, the portcullis raised. There was no need to close off the stronghold while so many warriors stood between it and attack.

The earth was quiet. Dragons did not sleep there, not so close to the Grail. He paused on the edge of the bridge. The chasm breathed beneath, deep beyond knowledge. The castle loomed above him, gleaming softly against the stars. The Grail was singing.

Its song filled him. Without will, without fear, he crossed the bridge and entered the castle.

He ascended through dim-lit ways. No living creature met him. As he passed doors and passages, he heard or smelled or sensed the people within. They were all asleep or deep in prayer. None came out to see who passed them in the dark before dawn.

Somewhere between the first court and the stair winding up to the tower, he gained a companion. Tarik in cat-shape stalked softly in his wake. That seemed fitting, somehow, and oddly comforting.

He was not ascending to the Grail. The Grail was elsewhere, but close—so close that its singing nigh deafened him to mortal sounds. This was a high tower, its stair steep, spiraling up into the gloom. Gloom, not darkness: there were slits of windows along the ascent, and the light of dawn shone dimly through them.

It brightened slowly as he ascended. The way was long. He was in no way moved to turn back. He must come to the top of the tower. What was there, or why, he cared little. The call was too strong for conscious thought.

He reached the end of the stair at last, and paused, waiting for his breathing to slow, his heartbeat to quiet. His legs ached with the effort of ascending so many steps—hundreds; he had lost count long ago. Tarik, wise thing, had climbed to his shoulder and so traveled in comfort.

As Roland leaned against the wall at the top of the stair, Tarik slithered down the length of Roland's body and butted his head against the iron-bound door. It opened silently.

Within was a high round chamber full of pale blue light. A table stood in its center. On the table lay a globe of crystal. And in the globe, as if grown out of it, was his sword.

He did not remember crossing the room. His hand was on the hilt. He knew a shiver of irony, a memory too old almost to catch: Merlin's face in a shimmer of leaves, and his voice telling a tale of a sword and a stone, and a boy who never knew what he was until he had drawn the sword.

Roland knew what he was. He was the Count of the Breton Marches, and Merlin's pupil, and a captain of soldiers. He belonged to Durandal, or Durandal to him. He had won the sword in fair fight, and with it the name of champion.

Champion of Montsalvat. Which was here—this kingdom, this castle.

If he drew the sword, there was no turning back. He had fled once, all the way into nothingness, no name, no mind, no memory, not even a human form in which to house his spirit. He could not do that again.

The sword and the Grail had called him. They had brought him here. He knew well what they wanted; what they insisted on. Nor did they care if he might object, or find himself unworthy. They were not human, nor vexed with mortal fears.

He was not altogether human, either. He was a dead man—twice, if one reckoned the death of self beside the death of the body. "I did die at Roncesvalles, didn't I?" he said. "The Grail brought me back. It's determined that I do this thing. Fight this war. Oppose this enemy."

"You were born for that."

He did not turn. He would know that voice in any place, living or dead or wandering the lands between.

Sarissa went on, low and steady. "Consider who you are, whose blood is in your veins. Blood of old gods, blood of the Grail. Parsifal is your kin, no more distant than Merlin. You were set on this earth to stand against that one, the enemy of the Grail."

"And I swore," said Roland, "to set Merlin free."

She came to stand somewhat apart from him. She was dressed as he had seen her on the hill the day before: coat of mail, sturdy hose, boots laced to the knee. Her hair was plaited behind her. There was a sword at her side.

She looked paler than he remembered, and thinner. Her face was fine-drawn with strain.

He looked for anger. He found it in plenty, but it would not come to his hand. She had done an ill thing. She had not meant it ill. She had done it out of unwisdom, not out of malice.

Olivier was dead, but not because of her. He faced that, though the pain was almost more than he could bear. Ganelon's treachery had brought about that death. Ganelon had laid the ambush against Roland. Ganelon's servants had destroyed the Companions.

If it was anyone's fault, it was Roland's own. He had killed two of Ganelon's servants. He was Merlin's child. He was Ganelon's enemy from the moment he drew breath.

He was not about to forgive Sarissa. That was not so easy or so quick. But he could lay his anger aside. He could draw the sword out of the stone. He could raise it in salute, then lower it to rest point down against the floor. He had not known that there was an emptiness in him till the sword filled it. But now he knew, he would not willingly let it go again.

Sarissa had gone still. She spoke out of that stillness. "The king would speak with you," she said.

He inclined his head. He too had heard the call. It was a clearer, stronger voice than he would have expected, though strangely distant: a voice of the spirit, all but sundered from flesh.

The Grail-king lay in his bed in the antechamber of the Grail. A single attendant sat with him, a plump woman with grey braids and an air of unassuming modesty. But beneath the skin was a white fire of power.

Roland bowed to them both, king and lady of the Grail. The lady smiled, frankly admiring him. He blushed and looked down, which made her laugh.

The king had no strength of the body for a smile, but his welcome was warm. Roland knelt beside the narrow bed. He still had the sword in his hand; he laid it by the king's side.

Parsifal's hand shifted slightly to rest over the blade. His living voice was faint, scarcely to be heard. "So. You accept the charge."

"Do I have a choice?" Roland asked, but not bitterly. He was past bitterness.

"You could walk away," said Parsifal.

Roland did not see the use in answering that.

Parsifal's lips twitched. "We would have been hellions together when I was young," he said.

He sighed. The grey-haired lady stirred, but Roland had seen what was needed. He lifted the king gently in the curve of his arm, and bolstered him so that he could sit up somewhat and breathe a little more easily. There was little more to him than bone and fragile skin.

The king's thanks were silent but clear enough. "Take it, then," he said. "Take command. Nieve, Sarissa, bear witness. This man speaks with my voice. I give him all power that he requires, to conduct this war, to tend my people. Let no one contest him. Let none refuse him. He stands where I would stand. He commands as I would command."

Both women bowed. Neither seemed inclined to object. Roland had lost the power to do that when he crossed the bridge into the castle.

"Sarissa, look after him," the Grail-king said. "Teach him what he must know. But be swift! The enemy is nearly here."

Roland glanced, perhaps unwisely, at Sarissa. This was a rebuke if she chose to take it as such, and perhaps a punishment.

She did not seem unduly cast down, nor did he sense any anger in her. Like him, maybe, she accepted the duty that was laid on her.

The king sank back as she bowed assent. For an instant Roland's heart stopped, but Parsifal breathed still, if faintly. He clung to life, but his strength was nearly spent.

Roland bent to kiss the bone-thin hand, then after a pause, the smooth cool brow. "Rest," he said. "Sleep. I'll look after your people for you."

They left the king to his rest, and to such restoration as was left him. Sarissa led Roland down from the Grail's tower. She did not speak, nor did he.

The sun had risen while he spoke with the king. The cas-

tle was awake, its people stirring. Sarissa brought him to a
high hall full of sunlight. It looked eastward through many
tall windows, each paned with precious glass. Some of the
panes were grey or clear, but many were jewel-bright, casting shards of blue and green, red and purple and gold, on
the white stone of the floor. White pillars held up the roof.
Tapestries hung on the walls, jeweled marvels, teeming
with figures that seemed to stir and breathe.

Roland might have wandered off to examine the hangings, but there were people waiting in the hall: seven ladies
in white, and a gathering of men and women in the garb of
nobles or warriors, priests or servants. He recognized the
look and the manner of them. These were the rulers of
Carbonek, the high court of its king.

He stood in front of them. Durandal rested naked in the
crook of his arm, for he had yet to find a sheath for her.
God alone knew where her old one was. He was trying not
to feel both young and inept; in this gathering, he was both.

They were all staring at him, measuring him as everybody did in Montsalvat. He could not have been a prepos-
sessing sight. He had left his mail in the Franks' camp. His
leather tunic was worn and stained. His hair had not seen
a comb nor his chin a razor since well before he did battle
with the dragon. His eyes were gritty with sleeplessness.
His mouth was dry.

"Well-watered wine," he said. "Fetch it—enough for all
of us. And something simple to eat. And chairs to sit in."

People obeyed him. He did not let them see surprise. A
commander expected obedience.

While they waited for food and drink and comfort,
Roland set himself to learning names and offices. The
ladies of the Grail he could hardly mistake. The captain of
the king's guard, the steward of his castle, the chancellor in
his gold chain of office, those he could recognize. He
guessed that the handful of men in armor were knights of
the Grail. The rest had duties and offices which he must
learn to remember, and titles, and rank of which some were
very conscious.

It was no worse than being captain of an army. The
clothes were richer and the tempers quicker, that was all.

The wine came, and baskets of bread, and platters of
meats and cheese, fruit and cakes. Roland was glad to sit in

the chair that was set for him, no higher or grander than the others. He laid Durandal across his knees. Tarik, appearing from air as was his way, curled purring in his lap.

It had become an oddly convivial gathering. He could, while he ate and drank, reckon factions and mark lines of battle. Sacred kingdom this might be, but those who ruled it were men and women. They squabbled in human fashion, and made enemies of one another, and eyed the one set over them as if he must choose among them.

Roland would do no such thing. His youth favored him there: he could seem oblivious. He let them eat in peace, but when they had all had their fill, he said, "I've not come to supplant your king. I'm his voice only, and his strong arm. You will continue as he bade you, and conduct this war in his name."

"Indeed," said one of the ladies of the Grail, a tall woman with glossy black hair plaited behind her, and eyes as blue as the heart of a flame. There was a look about her of one more at ease in armor than in the white robe of office. "And shall I continue to command his armies for him?"

Roland paused to draw a breath. "My lady," he said, "there's burden enough for both of us, if you can bear to share it with me."

She looked him up and down. It might have been reckoned insolent, but he did not think she meant to be. She wanted to know him. She measured the strength of him, and his fitness for this thing that the king had laid on him.

She nodded abruptly. "You'll do," she said. "Shall I summon the commanders, or have you done it already?"

"Neither," Roland said. "I'll go down to them. And you with me, if you will."

Her brow went up. "They'll think you're lowering yourself."

"A good number of them knew me when I was a village idiot," Roland said. "This will either amuse or appall them."

"Probably the former," Sarissa said dryly. "Morgan, let be. He's a Frank—they do things this way."

"Half a Frank," Morgan said. "The other half—"

"The other half gives him the right to command in Montsalvat."

Sarissa's tone was fiercer than the words might have warranted. Roland's eyes sharpened.

Morgan laughed like a clash of blades. "Yes, the hawk of the gods and the Grail's own child. If he were a stallion, we'd put him to all our mares."

"If I were a mare, I'd kick you silly," Sarissa muttered.

Roland intervened before matters could grow worse—if that were possible. "Madam!" He did not care which of them he meant. In any event they both turned on him like mares indeed, ears flat, tails switching.

"Fight over me later. We've a sorcerer to destroy."

Neither was chastened, but he had silenced them, at least. Tarik was rolling in his lap, shaking with laughter. He rose, spilling the *puca* to the floor. "Look for me in the camp," he said to them all, "if you have need of me."

CHAPTER 51

✠ ✠ ✠

Roland fled with as much dignity as a man so young could manage under the circumstances. Sarissa glared at Morgan. "That was hardly fair," she said.

Morgan grinned like a she-wolf. "And isn't he lovely when he's mortally embarrassed?"

"Why, do you want him?"

"Do you?"

Sarissa bared her teeth. "With my whole heart and soul."

"So," said Morgan, "go and get him."

Sarissa hardly needed encouragement. Roland was still in the castle, making his way through the maze of halls and courts, with Tarik at his heels.

Tarik had hardly forgiven Sarissa, any more than Roland had, but he was not helping Roland to find his way out of the castle, either. The castle itself had roused in the dim but purposeful way of enchanted stone, and caught him in the hall of mazes. Every arch of the colonnade might be a way out, or it might not. Or an exit might prove only to lead back into the hall itself.

She found Roland in the middle with the cat purring at his feet. He had not given in to panic. He turned at her coming, as if he had expected her. His cheeks were still faintly flushed.

Wordlessly she handed him what she had paused to fetch. He took the worn scabbard in which Durandal had lived since he won her, and slid her softly home. "Thank you," he said.

She bowed slightly.

"So," he said after a moment. "Was there a duel? Am I the prize or the punishment?"

"Which would you rather be?"

"Neither!"

She thought he might turn and run, but he had too many of his wits about him for that. "Morgan has an antic humor," Sarissa said. "And she does love a handsome face."

His face flamed. Sarissa did not even try to stop herself: she cooled his burning cheeks with her palms. He made no effort to pull away. His eyes were wild.

She kissed him softly. He stood like a stone. She kissed his cheeks and his brow and the flutter of his eyelids. She was not thinking at all.

Abruptly he pulled back. "Is this a wager? Will she try it, too?"

"Probably," Sarissa said. Her hands slipped behind his neck and rested there. "You could be more presentable," she said, "for your people."

"So that you can seduce me in the bath?"

"Would that be a terrible thing?"

He did not answer.

She took his hand. It did not return the pressure of her grip, but neither did it elude her. Her heart was beating hard. Her breath came quick. She had not intended any of this until it happened—and time was short. The war was coming with inexorable speed.

The chamber gave them the passage she wanted, and the door into the bath with its shimmer of blue tiles. He started a little as he entered it, with a spark of—recognition?

"I dreamed," he said. "I dreamed—"

"So it was you," she said, "watching me. I felt you. I thought it was a dream of my own."

He shook his head.

She smiled. The water in the warm pool swirled, steaming gently. There were clothes laid out for him, fresh linen, plain tunic and hose in a fashion close enough to the Frankish for his comfort.

She let him undress himself—to his surprise and perhaps annoyance. She sprinkled herbs in the water to sweeten its scent. When she turned, he was naked. There were more scars than there had been before Roncesvalles, but she knew every one of them. She had stood over him while the Grail burned through her, bringing him back from the dark country, healing his body and binding it again to his soul.

He still wore the coin on its chain that had escaped her in Paderborn. It had been a simple enough thing when she had it: remembrance of her own country, and relic of an older time. The blessing of the Grail was on it.

In coming to him, it had grown and changed. It had woven itself into the magic that filled him full of light. It had become both amulet and talisman.

Tarik leaped into the pool. He shifted and blurred in midair, till a silver fish danced in the water. Roland laughed as if he could not help it, and slid in after him.

Sarissa forbore to seduce him—and not only because Tarik was there. She handed him sponge and soap. She scrubbed his hair for him. She shaved him before he cut his own throat. But she was as circumspect as any good servant, except that she was not entirely able to keep her eyes to herself.

She had baffled him. His frown darkened the longer she went on. When he was clean, he stepped out of the cold pool into her hands. She dried him briskly, as if it were nothing to her that it was a man's body she touched so.

Just as she was about to turn away, he caught her hands. "Are you trying to make me strangle you?"

"I'm trying to make you fit to stand in front of your captains," she said.

"I was filthy in front of higher lords than they."

"Yes," she said. "We did appreciate the gesture."

"It was not—"

"Don't lie to yourself," she said. "I don't ask you to forgive me. Only do what we need of you, for the people, for the Grail—it doesn't matter. Just do it."

"But what is it I'm to do?" he demanded. "All of it. All, lady. Not fragments doled out one by one."

Her back tightened. If she lied to him again, or concealed anything from him, he would know—if not now, then soon. And she would lose him. And if she lost him—

"I can't," she said. "I can't tell you. That's for the king, when the time comes."

He lifted his chin. "Ah," he said. "No answer. But truth—that much you give me. Was it so difficult?"

"More than you know," she said.

"Why, do I have to die? Is that what you're keeping from me? You need my blood, and you're afraid I'll run screaming before you can take it?"

"We don't need your death," she said.

He breathed out, perhaps in spite of himself. "What, then? My soul? My bodily strength?"

"No," she said.

She had surprised him: he seemed nonplussed. "So what is it? Do I have to fight a battle? Marry a woman?"

She stiffened at that.

He saw. "That's it? That's what it is? The champion takes a bride, for the strength of the kingdom and the increase of his power against the enemy?"

Ah, gods, he saw clearly. The Grail gave him sight—even if he had not had understanding enough of his own.

"And that bride," he said, "is—" He laughed suddenly, a sound half of astonishment and half of—mirth? He did not sound angry at all. "Is it one of you? Am I to choose, and be judged by my choice? Or do you draw lots? Will you duel, two and two, as we did for Durandal?"

"It was settled long ago," she said with a faint sigh, surrendering to his clarity of vision. "The Grail chose."

"It was you," he said. "You went out. You brought the sword. You thought you were going to a king. And you found a Breton witch, Merlin's get. No wonder you wouldn't tell me! It must have been a terrible blow to your pride."

"No!" He had never heard her raise her voice. It startled him into silence. "What did you think I was doing in Musa's house? Dallying? Lying as men lie to women, to gain myself a few days' pleasure? Do you think I feigned that I loved you?"

"Love is not marriage," he said, far too dispassionate for one as young and hot-blooded as he was. "Pleasure in a fair face is not the bond that unites equals. If I had been Charles of the Franks, you would have been glad to tell me everything—and you would have trusted me to accept what was laid on me.

"But I am Roland of Brittany, and Merlin is my forefather. You'll never forget that. You won't forgive it."

"Forget, no," she said. "Forgive—long ago. You were chosen. You, not Charles—who though he is a great man and a great king, is not the Grail's champion. He is not my champion, whom I love. I never said I was wise. I never pretended to be perfect in my understanding. But when I knew that it was not the one I had thought, after I got over the shock I was glad. Even mistrusting you, even fearing what you might be, I couldn't make myself regret that you and not Charles were the chosen of the Grail."

"You should have told me," he said. That was the young man speaking. It was the other, the clear-eyed seer, who shook his head and sighed. "That's done. It won't be undone. So when was I to be told? Or was I? Would you have pulled me from my bed some early morning, dragged me to the chapel, and bound me before I was awake enough to argue with it?"

"We might have done that," she said, "if we had found it necessary. Will it be?"

He thought about it. He took some little time. He searched her face. He touched his own, rubbing the scars of the demon's claws. At last he said, "Tell me the truth. Are you appalled that you will be bound to me?"

"Are you?"

His eyes narrowed: yellow hawk-eyes under the level black brows. "A man has to marry to get sons. You seem strong. Your rank is sufficient. Your family, I have no doubt, is illustrious. You have no father to negotiate the contract, but then neither do I. And as a dead man, I have no lands to offer you, and no wealth but a sword and a coat of mail, a shield and a helmet, and a horse that was Lord Huon's gift."

"And the castle of Carbonek in the king's name," said Sarissa, "and an army sixty thousand strong, and the wherewithal to keep and command it."

"That is not—"

"It is yours," she said, "for all useful purposes. You are the champion of Montsalvat. Your rank and wealth suffice. For dowry I bring you nothing but my body. And," she said, "the Grail."

"They are enough."

He sounded breathless. Maybe because he was naked and still somewhat damp, and he was chilled. She wrapped her arms about him, the warmth of her white robe and of her body beneath it. He fit precisely in her embrace, the shape, the heft of him, the clean new-washed scent, the smoothness of his skin.

"You can refuse," she said.

A gust of laughter escaped him. "You can stand like this and say that?"

"Not easily," she said. She meant to move back, but found herself pressed close against him, his arms about her. She ran her hands up the long straight line of his spine and across the breadth of his shoulders. She had not done that in—oh, too long. "I missed you. Dear Goddess, I missed you!"

"I suppose it's a sin," he said, "to lust after one's bride."

"Not here," she said. And then: "You will do it?"

"Tell me one thing." He withdrew somewhat, so that he could look into her face. "What is it that we have to do? Is it a great marriage?"

"You know of that?"

"Merlin told me."

She nodded, though she could not help bridling at the name. "It binds you to our circle, and gives you our strength."

"That is a great thing," he said.

"Worth even marriage to me?"

A shadow crossed his face, but he smiled in the wake of it. "If you promise solemnly never to lie to me again."

"By the Grail I swear it."

"Then yes," he said. "Yes, I accept it."

CHAPTER 52

✠ ✠ ✠

The children slept well past dawn, after the night they had had, but Gemma was up as early as ever. She happened by Marric as he tended the fire, waiting for the first recruit to stagger out yawning and demand a loaf of his new-made bread.

"We'll need flour in a day or two," he said, "and more ale."

She nodded. "I'll tell the quartermaster." Clearly she had somewhere else to be, but she paused, squatting beside him. He waited for her to say what was on her mind. "Have you seen Count Roland this morning?"

"Not since last night," Marric said.

"He's not in the Franks' camp. He's not in his tent here. His horse is in the lines. His clothes are in the tent, except what he had on."

Marric's ears quivered, but he kept his expression bland. "You've been looking for him?"

"He's always about. He should be pacing by now, waiting for the children to be up and at arms practice. He's nowhere at all."

"He could be in the castle," Marric said.

Her eyes flashed on him. "Why? Was he summoned?"

"No," said Marric. "But I saw him go in. He hasn't come out. I presume he's safe there."

She shivered, rubbing her arms. It was cool this high in the mountains, but he did not think that chill was of the body. "He was summoned," she said, "if he went there. Every step he takes, he goes higher. He'll go to the Grail, be sure of it."

"Are you afraid for him?"

She shrugged irritably. "I can't get out of the habit of fretting over him. Not that he needs me now, or has for a long time, but I keep remembering. He was such a sweet thing. Everything so new, everything so strange. Those eyes of his were always wide. And no malice in him at all."

"There isn't now," said Marric.

"No, there isn't, is there? But I worry. It's having so many sons—I keep thinking he's another."

"He wasn't exactly a son to you."

"That's over, too," she said. Her voice was flat. "They say the enemy will be here in a handful of days. Maybe sooner."

"I heard that, too," he said, taking the shift in stride.

"Pray we're ready."

She rose. He watched her go and sighed. Gemma was a wise woman, and strong. Surely she would not let Roland become a weakness.

Roland came out near noon. He was on foot, plainly dressed, but clean and fresh-shaven. The *puca* in cat-shape walked at his heel. Sarissa was behind them, as plainly dressed as he.

He was wearing a sword, which he had not done before. And the great gate had opened for him, not the postern through which lesser folk could come and go. He crossed the bridge and walked down the narrow road into the valley.

The army saw him coming. They were all awake, the recruits at practice, the veterans idling about. All but the Franks. They, though veterans all, had elected to follow the recruits' example.

They stopped in a long wave, all down the field, and stared at the two figures walking from the castle. As they drew nearer, Marric saw the hilt and pommel of the sword he bore: plain silver, white stone. The bogle's teeth clicked together.

"So that's why he wouldn't take a sword," Kyllan said. "He left his behind." He unstrung his bow and coiled the string, absently, while Roland drew closer.

Cait made her way from the edge of the line. "I hear all the commanders have been called together. There's someone new in charge. Some new general."

"That must be where he's going." Kyllan slipped his bow into its case and slung it behind him. "Are you coming?"

She was already in motion. So were Cieran and Peredur, and Marric silent behind.

The commanders had gathered in a green hollow somewhat apart from the camp. A ring of trees surrounded it. A broad stone table stood in its center. It had an air of old sanctity, which seemed fitting for the occasion.

They were all there, lords and captains, men and women of rank both high and low. Marric saw Gemma near Lord Huon.

She was watching Roland, who had come in among the last. She did not look as relieved as one might have expected.

No one else took much notice of him. Their glances passed over him and went on. They were all waiting for some prince from the castle.

While they waited, they fell into their factions. Marric watched Roland watch them. He seemed to be idling about, roving the edges, catching snatches of conversation. But Marric thought that his ears were perhaps keener than most men's were.

Marric, whose ears were not even partly human, marked the three strains that ran through the babble of sound. He did not trouble to name those who sang the antiphons; there were so many, it did not matter.

"Do you think," asked a man in the blue and gold of Lyonesse, "that Carbonek can wisely choose a general for us? The king is dying, or for all we know is dead. The ladies in their shrine—they're long sundered from the lands they rule. Surely we're best fit to elect our own commander."

"No, no," said a woman near Lord Huon. "It will be Morgan, or one of the knights of the Grail. They're well fit to lead us."

"Or it will be someone else," said a man of Poictesme. "The champion—"

"There is no champion," his companion said.

"There was."

"He was lost."

"But if he comes back—"

Roland had left the edges and woven though the clusters of conversation. Kyllan and Cait and Peredur had slipped into his shadow, as quiet and almost as subtle about it as the *puca* was.

In the center, by the stone table, Roland stood still for a while. The babble was rising. People were arguing. One substantial faction was set to elect a general, with a handful of contenders for the office. The others looked ready to rise up in revolt.

Roland sprang onto the stone. A few eyes turned to him, but most were caught up in contention. What was he, after all, but an outland captain?

He drew the sword that he had brought out of Carbonek. It sang as he swept it up, a high fierce song. He whirled it flashing about his head and grounded it between his feet, point resting against the stone, cross-hilts gripped in his hands.

The last of the babble died away. His eyes raked their faces. Marric felt the heat of that glance even from the edge of the gathering.

He had not seen Sarissa move through the crowd, nor had he seen Morgan come there at all. Yet there they were, standing on either side of the dolmen.

"My lords," said Roland without raising his voice; yet they all heard him. "Princes and commanders of Montsalvat. I bring you word from Parsifal the king."

The silence was absolute.

"I was chosen," Roland said, "to be the champion of Montsalvat. This is the sword Durandal, which was wrought for that choosing. Now your king bids me speak for him. I will command this army. I will act as he would act, in his name and by his will."

Marric's lips twitched. Elegant that speech was not, but Roland, Marric had noticed, was not one to speak when he could act.

The same could not be said of the lords he faced. But he gave them no chance to raise their voices. "The enemy comes," he said. "He'll pass the borders of Carbonek in a hand of days—perhaps sooner, if he presses the march. There will be guards posted, and scouts in the outlands.

The rest of us will wait for him here. How we wait, what order we take—I give you this day to advise me. But be quick, and be wise. There's no time to waste."

"*Ai*," said Gemma beside Marric. "He's high-handed."

"Maybe it's time someone picked them up and shook them," Marric said.

Her brows went up. "So that's why the champion had to be an outlander. He's not part of any faction. He can say what nobody else will dare to say."

"And he has that," Marric said, tilting his chin toward Durandal.

She nodded. She was frowning, but not with temper. She was watching Roland as she had since he came out of the castle.

Roland stood on the dolmen, staring down either defiance or objections. He had come as a shock to too many of them. They all knew him, or knew of him: Huon's young captain who had insisted that the levies be trained for war.

He should have dressed as a prince, maybe. And maybe not. In plain clothes, with no mark of office but the sunlit shimmer of the sword, he was irrevocably of them, not unreachably high above them.

"Advise me," he said. "Reckon the count of your forces. Tell me what they can best do."

The babble rose to a roar again, voice vying with voice, each striving to out-shout the other. There were again three camps: those who would bring the war to the enemy in the empty lands, those who would take the Grail and retreat to the far reaches of the kingdom, and those who would make a single stand here, at Carbonek.

Roland laid Durandal down on the stone and sat behind the shield of her, knees drawn up, chin on them, watching and listening, waiting them out.

Marric laughed silently. He skipped through the crowd, sprang up onto the stone table, sat exactly as Roland was sitting.

After a moment, Sarissa understood. She grinned, sudden and rather startling, and followed suit. Then Morgan did it; then Cait, and Kyllan, and Kyllan's two brothers; and from nowhere as it seemed, Turpin in his brown habit and his worn mail. That was as many of them as the stone table could hold.

Lord Huon saw them first. He hushed those who were nearest, who would do as he bade. He drew their eyes toward the dolmen. His own were glinting. Only lordly courtesy would be keeping him from laughter.

It took some little time, but at last there was silence, again. Again, they all stared at Roland. He stared back, his eyes as blank as coins.

"It seems," Lord Huon said, "that we have little to offer you."

Roland shook his head. His eyes cleared, focused. He said, "First tell me what our enemy wants."

That did not please many of them: they were muttering of village idiots and outland fools. But Huon answered, "He wants the Grail. He'll devote all his energies to that. He won't care how much of his army he loses, if only it opens the way to the shrine."

"Can the Grail be taken away from Carbonek?"

Eye flashed to eye among the lords, but for a wonder they kept silent. They let Huon speak again for them. "The Grail can live anywhere it pleases. But Carbonek was built by its magic. If Carbonek falls, the Grail loses much of its power."

"But it will still be ours!" cried someone far in the rear.

"If we take the Grail," said Roland, "the enemy will follow us wherever we go. Where the Grail is, there is the war. So tell me. Is there any castle in this kingdom that is stronger than Carbonek?"

"None," said Huon. Even those who objected most strongly to that course were nodding—scowling, but agreeing.

"So then," Roland said. "The Grail will stay in Carbonek. Now advise me. How can we best defend both this castle and the Grail?"

There was more order in it now, more plain courtesy. They spoke one by one, in order of rank, from Gwyn the prince to Gemma the commander of the levy from Greenwood—but Roland heard her with as much respect as he accorded the highest of princes.

Idlers from the army had long since wandered in earshot of the commanders' gathering. From the stone table Marric could see how many had come—an impressive number. Maybe all of them. Faces as far as he could see, and eyes, fixed on Roland.

They settled it before the sun had sunk too far. The bulk of them would defend the castle and the shrine. They would bivouac not on these fields but beneath the castle itself, in a maze of caverns that descended far into the earth and stretched for a great distance under it. Magic of earth and fire were strong there. The light had held it for time out of mind, since even before the Grail came to Montsalvat.

"That is all very well," said the Prince of Poictesme, "but as strong as we may be if we all gather in one place, so much the easier will it be for the enemy to destroy us all in a single stroke."

"If the enemy takes the Grail," Roland said, "nothing else will matter. Everything will belong to him, in this kingdom and every other."

That silenced them all. In the silence he said, "No, we should not make it too simple for him to come to us. You will go, my lord, and my lord of Lyonesse, if you will. Watch the roads against the enemy's coming. Harry him as he comes. Trouble him as much as you may—but not so much that you die of it. Weaken him before he comes to Carbonek."

Gwyn was too much the prince to break out in a grin of delight, but he was visibly pleased with his charge. Roland had hoped that he might be, he and the young lord of Lyonesse. They had the look of men who would prefer battle to the tedium of a siege. And, much more to the point of this war, each of them commanded a strong force of light horsemen and mounted archers.

It was decided, then, and in a remarkable degree of amity. Roland said even less than usual. He played them all like a harp, and with a fine hand, too. When they parted to attend to their various duties and offices, Marric did not think that many of them guessed how much of their free choice was Roland's doing.

"And you reckon yourself a poor courtier."

It was not Marric who said that. It was Huon, pausing when most of the others had left. Those two, Marric thought, got on very well together. Maybe because Huon was not quite human either, and because he had known Roland the longest of all the lords.

Roland was still sitting on the stone table, though his companions had left it and were standing about. Huon leaned on the stone, arms folded atop it, regarding Roland with a crooked smile. "You have a gift," he said.

Roland shrugged, wriggling a little—the hard grey granite must be wearing through his backside. "I did what the king would have wanted."

"You did it well, too," Huon said. "You look like him, you know; you have a feel of him."

"What, the fool whom pity made wise—and none too soon, either?"

"Not quite a fool," said Huon. "Maybe not yet wise, but closer than you were. May I offer a word of counsel?"

Roland opened his eyes a fraction wider, and waited.

"Don't lose that. Don't go all lordly. The people are your strength."

"Will lords follow me if I have too common a touch?"

"Lords will follow power wherever they find it. But the people fight best, and strive most strongly, for the ones they love."

"Any number of lords would say," Roland said, "that the common folk follow whoever is set over them—blindly loyal, because they can do no other."

Huon snorted softly. "They may dream, but when they wake, they find another truth. Remember it, son of the Grail. It may save your soul."

"Have I a soul to save?" But Roland spoke lightly, and not as if he either wanted or needed an answer. He sprang down from the dolmen, stretching till his bones creaked. Shoulder to shoulder, easy with one another, they walked out of the circle.

CHAPTER 53

✠ ✠ ✠

Slowly the grey land changed into one both green and empty. The mists endured, and a slow steady rain that began every morning and drizzled damply until the early nightfall. The road stretched away ahead of them, wide, clear, and completely untraveled. Not even a bird broke the monotony of the sky.

Pepin and his hellions, as they proudly had taken to calling themselves, had the vanguard. He ran scouts ahead because a good commander did, but he was a better scout than they: he could feel the land underfoot, and taste the air that blew past his face. It was all quiet, all empty. Nothing at all either met or threatened them.

"The way is wide open," he said to Ganelon when the army halted. It was perhaps midday. They had come to a wide slow river. The bridge across it was narrow, barely wide enough for the baggage wagons. There was no ambush, not even a troll under the bridge.

Pepin had sent his men on ahead. He sat his horse beside Ganelon, who was riding something more like a horse than not; but claws clicked when it pawed the road, and its scaled tail swung slowly from side to side. Pepin's gelding sweated and trembled but stood its ground. He stroked its neck to soothe it, and went on, "This looks like the gullet of a trap."

"It is." Ganelon's face was turned to the grey and dripping sky. Rain did not touch him; it parted and slid as from a shield of glass.

"You're not afraid," Pepin said.

The sorcerer laughed, a soft cold sound like water under ice. Day by day and night by night as they passed through this country, he had slipped free of the seeming that he had worn in Francia. The elderly priest of no particular distinction was long gone. This was a being of no age at all, ancient beyond the counting of years. His skin was pale and smooth. His cheeks grew no beard. His hair fell long and straight and pale as silver. His eyes were dark and deep.

He had the beauty of a marble angel, though it was anything but insipid. He laughed at Pepin, and there was no pity in him at all, nor any glimmer of compassion. "I go where I most wish to go. They think to lull me, and so overcome me. Fools and children. I will have their Grail, and their souls, too."

Pepin suppressed a shiver. Ganelon needed him, he reminded himself, to take and keep the relic. He was safe until that was done. Afterward, he would find a way to make himself indispensable. Even, maybe, claim some of the power for himself. Would he not have earned it, after all?

"We are close now," Ganelon said through the hum of Pepin's thoughts. "I feel it—Carbonek is near. Are your men suitably prepared?"

"As much as any men can be," Pepin said.

"See that they are," said Ganelon.

All the while they spoke, the army crossed the bridge. Mist had risen on the far side, thicker than before. The vanguard had disappeared into it.

Ganelon was unconcerned. Pepin kept a grip on panic, lest he seem a fool.

They crossed last. Pepin's gelding clattered over the stones. The soft click and pad of Ganelon's mount was just audible. There was only greyness in front of them, a dank wall that had swallowed the whole of the army.

It closed about them. Pepin could still sense the earth underfoot, but it was shifting, heaving like the sea.

He could just see Ganelon in the mist, riding calmly, his pale face gleaming like the moon through cloud. Pepin fixed on that light. His horse plodded peacefully onward. It did not care that the worlds were changing underfoot; that they were entering the realm of the Grail.

Passing through that mist was like being flayed alive and rolled in salt. Pepin clutched the gelding's mane, gasping.

"Ward yourself," said Ganelon's voice, cold and calm in the mist.

Pepin could not. He was blind with pain. It put to flight his wits; it burned away his newborn magic.

Ganelon spoke the words, swift and almost contemptuous, raising the same protection over his faltering pupil that he had raised over the army. The pain vanished. The earth steadied. The mist melted into clear hard sunlight.

Pepin stared blinking at a lofty wall of mountains. The road wound upward through green hills. Clouds wreathed the peaks, but the sun was bright and fierce.

Ganelon beside him raised a hand, sighting along it. "There," he said. "Carbonek."

It needed the sight of an eagle, as yet, but Pepin could just see the gleam atop a summit—lines too straight, too even to be unwrought stone. "They can see us coming," he said. "I feel it."

"There are no surprises here," said Ganelon, "though we may meet an ambush or two, for the game's sake. We all know that this must play itself out."

"They weren't strong enough to stop you."

"They let me come." Ganelon sounded not at all perturbed by that. "Now go. Lead the van. If they begin the war, they will do it here, or close by here. Be vigilant. Bid your men be ready to arms."

Pepin kicked his gelding into a stiff, protesting trot. It was a long way from the rear to the van, past rank on rank of men and demons, all marching with sightless persistence. Ganelon's will drove them—all but the Franks.

After the mute hordes of slaves both human and otherwise, the rowdy mortal clamor of his own people was a relief. They were delighted to hear that there might be battle ahead. "Ambushes!" they declared. "Skirmishes!"

Some had been into the ale again. Pepin had begun to understand his father's objections to drunkenness. But Charles could not do what Pepin could do, which was to lay a spell on the ale. Any man who drank more than his allotted pint would find himself abruptly and massively ill.

Pepin smiled as he took his place in front. The mist was altogether gone. This was a bitter-bright land, all hard edges and sharp colors. It seemed inescapably sunlit, but he noticed how dark the shadows were. They were deep enough indeed, he thought, to hide an ambush.

He had scouts running ahead, and the vanguard spread a little, but not so far that it could not come together quickly to stand against assault. The rearmost ranks marched just ahead of the army's center.

Not all his scouts were flesh and blood. He sent small winged thoughts, eyes of the mind, through the middle airs. That and the spell on the ale taxed him more than he had expected: he swayed in the saddle, but held on. The Grail—it was working on him, weakening him through the defenses Ganelon had raised for him. His stomach felt strange, as if he had drunk too much ale himself.

He was strong enough. He stiffened his back as much as he could, and let his gelding slow to an amble. The first ranks of the vanguard passed him, protecting him with good Frankish steel. He set his spirit free to follow his eyes in the air.

It was dizzying at first to see so many things, shifting and overlapping. He had not sent out this great a number before. He steadied himself as he had been taught, and put down the thought that he was overtaxing his strength.

Green hills, stark teeth of mountains. Deep valleys, sudden silver gleam of rivers. There were no cities here, no towns or villages, no signs of habitation until one came to the castle. Beyond the castle—

It was like a wall of air. He could pass just so far, and no farther. If he pressed, the wall only grew stronger.

The kingdom was beyond the wall. He was not allowed to see it. That was very clear. It was as Ganelon had said: they were being permitted to pass.

He drew back before the wall sucked him in and held him like a fly in amber. With an effort of will he focused on the eyes that were closer in, on the clefts and hollows of this tumbled country.

Movement. An eye nearby the army stopped, hovered. Others converged on it. Down in a valley, moving along beside a dry streambed, were figures in green and brown. If they had stood still, he would not have seen them at all.

The part of him that was flesh, the rider on the brown gelding, snapped out orders. A company of the Frankish foot separated from the rest, advancing toward the valley and the enemy. That it was the enemy, Pepin was sure. Nothing lived or moved here but what the Grail permitted.

The skirmish engaged out of sight and sound of the march. Pepin watched it with as much of himself as he could spare. The green men fought fiercely against the onslaught of Pepin's Franks, but they fell back, overwhelmed by greater numbers.

Pepin smiled at the sight. But after a moment, his smile died. His men were deep in the valley, the green men knotted tight, fighting for their lives. And from the hillsides and from the valley's beginning and ending, as if from the ground underfoot, surged an army of men in bright mail. They swept over Pepin's force that had seemed so large only a moment ago. They crushed it utterly.

Then out of the earth rose a Thing. It was like nothing so much as a great blind worm. Its hide was the white of corpses' flesh. Its vast and eyeless head turned, seeking. And opened—clear to its middle, lined with dripping fangs.

The men of the Grail fled in surprisingly good order. But the worm was swifter than they. It swept through them as a scythe sweeps through ripe grain.

Pepin whirled headlong into his cold and shivering body. He was sick—oh, unto death; gagging and retching over the high pommel of his saddle. His men marched on, oblivious to their fellows' destruction.

There was no strength left in Pepin. His spies were all gone, melted into air. He was no more than mortal now.

The magic would come back. That was the great joy and comfort of it. He need only rest in the protection of his men, and cling to the saddle, and wait for the day's march to end. And pray that no further ambush descended on them.

The land had roused; it was alive that had been empty and silent. It was thrumming with warring powers.

The army marched under Ganelon's protection. Though the earth heaved like the sea, the road under their feet held steady. Winds roared, storms gathered, but the sun shone on the army.

Pepin drew strength from Ganelon's strength, if

slowly. He fell back to Ganelon's side again. Ganelon did not speak to him, which suited him perfectly. The sorcerer was deep in myriad workings. Lightnings crackled about him. Vast voices spoke just below the threshold of hearing. The winds called out to him. He answered in tongues that Pepin had not yet learned, ancient and terrible.

This was war as he had never imagined it, unless the priests spoke of war in heaven. The army that marched on the earth, he began to understand, was little more than diversion. The true war, the deep war, raged beneath the earth and among the powers of air.

There were still men to fight. Men held the Grail. And only a man of royal blood, his soul intact, could take that great instrument of power.

When it came down to it, none of it mattered, except to get Pepin into the castle, and to get his hands on the Grail. He wondered if the enemy knew that. They were not fools, he supposed, and they had fought Ganelon before.

Abruptly he asked, "Who was it? Last time, who was your catspaw?"

He was a little surprised when Ganelon answered. "His name was Medraut. He too was a king's son. He too was an ill-made thing."

"What, a humpback?" Pepin sneered the word.

"His back was straight," Ganelon said. Clearly he did not care what offense he gave. "His spirit was twisted."

"And mine's the reverse?"

"Hardly." The cold voice was already distant, the ancient mind turned again to the great web of power that he had woven through the years.

Pepin was recovered enough to sense the shadow of it. He set aside the pricking of temper, the sharp awareness of insult, for later, when he could exact a price. Carefully, for he was still not particularly strong, he traced the greater strands of the web. Someday he would weave such a thing for himself, to bind the world.

Today he was but a student, and a young one at that. He kept quiet and he studied, and he rode beside the sorcerer to the castle of the Grail.

CHAPTER 54

❈ ❈ ❈

The enemy advanced behind a wall of darkness: shadows and shadowy things, and sleepers waking beneath the earth. One such slew a company of men from Poictesme, who had laid an ambush and been themselves taken by surprise.

It was the second battle of the war, and the first defeat. Word of it came as the castle's defenders broke camp and marched within the walls.

Roland had felt the blindworm's rising. It was too far, too late to warn the company in the valley. Even the Grail could do no more than conceal the few who won free, and close the valley against the creature's escape. But the blindworm had done what it was meant to do. The power that ruled it let it go. It sank back into the earth.

There was nothing Roland could do in this that the ladies of the Grail could not do better than he. It was a hard truth to face. His duty was to command the army; matters of high magic were not within his authority. And yet in the face of Ganelon's power, he itched to do battle with another weapon than earthly steel.

"Patience, lad," Marric said. They were standing over the gate of Carbonek, watching the troops march beneath. Roland had not spoken his thoughts, but the bogle seldom concerned himself with such niceties. "You'll get your chance to hurl lightnings."

Roland glowered at him. He grinned and sat on the parapet, as precarious a perch as Roland could imagine, but he seemed at ease there.

He was still grinning as Turpin climbed up the stair to the gate-tower. The archbishop grinned back, a fine display of broad white teeth. "And a fair morning to you, sir bogle," he said.

"My lord archbishop," said Marric with a mingling of respect and insouciance that Roland admired in spite of himself.

Turpin leaned on the parapet just past the bogle. "Nearly all in," he said. "Our Franks are still refusing to believe that this castle can hold so many."

"It's much larger within than without," said Roland. "Tell them it's magic."

"I already did. They keep on insisting that these walls won't stretch as far as they'll have to. They're all logicians since they were taken out of the world."

"They'll see," Roland said. He sighed and rubbed his eyes. He had slept—days ago? He did not remember. Sarissa had had the night watch over the Grail, which mercifully prevented her from vexing him with commands to rest. Others he could ignore.

Even Turpin, who was fixing him with a look he knew too well. He met it blandly.

Turpin did not speak as Roland had expected. He lifted a brow. The bogle nodded. They struck before Roland could defend himself, caught him and tripped him and flung him over Turpin's shoulder, and carried him off into the depths of Carbonek.

Turpin dropped him onto a bed in a room he had not seen before. It was a large room, for a castle, and handsome, with its carpets and hangings and its wide curtained bed. There was no one else in it. It was a lordly place, fit for a prince.

The bed was too large and too soft. Roland was drowning in it. He scrambled up out of it. "I'm not staying here."

"Until you sleep, you are," Turpin said. "We'll get the men settled. You need to be up and in fighting form when the trap closes."

"On us or on the enemy?" A vast yawn overwhelmed Roland. "At least find me a bed that won't suffocate me before I wake."

"You're clever. You'll learn to swim in it." Marric was hard-hearted, and Turpin was no better.

"We'll chain you to it if we have to," Turpin said.

He was enjoying this much too much. Roland snarled at him. He laughed and abandoned Roland to the mercies of the featherbed.

Roland fully intended to fight his way free and escape to the duties that never relented. But his eyelids were heavy. His body was heavier. Just a moment—just a few breaths' time, to rest, to soothe the burning in his eyes.

He woke in darkness. Warmth pressed against his leg, purring as cats will, or a *puca* wearing the shape of a cat. The Grail's singing filled him.

He had been dreaming, but the dream had fled, except for a memory of sunlight. He sat up amid the coverlets of a wide and lordly bed. He could see a little: dim shapes of hangings, clothing-chest, a figure that drew him half to his feet, heart pounding, until he realized that it was his mail-coat on its stand.

Someone had come in while he slept, moved in his belongings and taken off his clothes. It was cold in the room, a keen mountain chill.

Wrapped in the coverlet, he rose. He was wide awake. He was a little hungry, but bread and cheese in a basket on the clothing-chest did not tempt him.

He had learned the ways of the castle, because a general always knew his ground, either friendly or hostile. This room would be one of those in the king's tower. The Grail was at the top of that, closed in its shrine.

Maybe one did not simply go to it. Maybe one should be taken to it, or summoned. And maybe he was summoned, as he had been to find Durandal.

There was no moon tonight, no stars. Things gibbered against the walls of air, the high magic that protected the castle and the kingdom. He ascended the stair without haste. Somewhere, echoing in the passages, now near and clear, now faint and far away, monks were singing the night office. He recognized Turpin's voice, deep but surprisingly clear.

Deliver me, O Lord, from evil men, preserve me from violent men.

Save me, O Lord, from the hands of the wicked: from the horns of the wild bulls, my wretched life.

Roland was rather startled. He had not perceived this as a Christian place, though it held the greatest of Christian relics.

Well; and there were monks among the Franks, and priests, and an archbishop who sang Mass every day wherever he was. It was fitting that they should raise that chant here, with the Grail's descant running beneath it.

The king slept in the antechamber. Inanna, the dark lady, sat the long vigil beside him. Roland bowed to her, then more deeply to him, though he was not awake to know it. She did not speak or try to turn him back.

The door opened to his touch. He walked into a singing darkness and a faint shimmer of light.

Three of the Grail's guardians knelt about the shrine, each at a corner of the earth. Sarissa had the east, Nieve the south. Pale Freya held the west.

It seemed they had been waiting for him. Without a word, without asking leave, Roland took the station of the north. The floor was stone, cold and hard under his knees. It dawned on him that he was naked but for a blanket.

It did not matter to the Grail. The ladies were deep in trance, raising a tower of light above castle and kingdom. He lifted up a pillar, to bolster them, to spare their strength.

There was great rightness in it, and something better than sleep. The Grail, he thought distantly. It nourished him. It seemed only fair that he stand guard over it and defend its people.

The enemy was close. Tomorrow he would come to the castle. His army was vast, his strength immeasurable. Even the edge of it was strong enough to wring a gasp from Roland, safe though he was in the armor of the Grail.

He would not give way to despair. He would hold, as the others held; as the Grail itself stood fast. It had defied this ancient enemy before. It would do so again.

Morning took him by surprise. Light flooded the high round room. The shrine caught fire with it. Sarissa rose from her knees at the gate of the east and approached the shrine. Nieve and Freya stood also, then Roland, stiff as they had not seemed to be, clutching his blanket about him.

Sarissa opened the shrine and uncovered the Grail. A great part of Roland wanted to fall on his face. But he stood as the others did, rapt in awe before that simple wooden cup.

She brought it to him last. He would not have been surprised if she had passed him by, but her eyes on him were calm, her expression serene. She raised the cup to his lips.

Sweeter than wine, stronger than blood, fiercer than fire. He gasped. His knees buckled. But he kept his feet. She smiled faintly and moved on, returning the cup to its shrine.

He was full of—he was aflame with—

Coolness bathed him. It felt almost like water pouring over him, but it was light, of sun and Grail both, and a whisper of breeze passing through the room. He did sink down then, down to his face. The floor was blessedly cold against his skin.

It was very, very strange. He was not exhausted or reft of strength. He was as strong as he could ever remember. But his knees would not hold him up.

The guard was changing. He could keep watch with these three, too, he supposed. But it was morning. The castle was full of soldiers—his soldiers. And the enemy was coming.

Somehow he got to his feet. He found that he could walk. Liu and Maya and Thais regarded him without surprise, but in some bemusement. He found what he hoped was a smile for them. He walked out of the room, his strides steadier with each step he took.

Sarissa was waiting for him beyond the antechamber. He braced for a blast of rebuke, but she only said, "Don't tell me they took all your clothes away."

He blushed.

She laughed at him and kissed him, which heated him all over again.

"You're not angry," he said.

"Should I be?"

"Everyone is," he said, "when I do something other than sleep."

"That is better than sleep," she said. She slipped her arm about his middle. "Here, I'll help you dress. And eat—you should eat. And—"

"And?"

Were her cheeks ever so faintly tinged with rose?

Oh, no. She never blushed. Not she.

And in any case, there was no time. He could dress, make himself presentable, choke down a little bread, but then he must be among his people.

"Surely," she said when he told her that. They had come quickly to the chamber—which, he thought, might even be the king's own, since he was set in the king's place. He did not like it. He would have it changed. He would—

She backed him against the tapestried wall. The blanket was lost, he hoped not irretrievably.

There was time, after all. All the time in the world. She was bare under the white robe, and fierce with eagerness. Almost too fierce—as if she feared there would be no time later; this was all they had.

He did not believe that. But he would take it, and her, in a kind of wild joy. Maybe Mother Church would be appalled to see them sinning so lustily in the very house of the Grail, but the Grail sang with them. It blessed them. It gave them this gift.

"The great marriage," he said, or she said, or they both did. It hardly mattered.

She clutched him fiercely to her, kissing him until he was dizzy. "It is made," she said, "and made again, from the moment we consented to it. But for the people—"

"For the people," he said, "we need a festival. Though if the enemy is here—"

"What matter if he is? Nieve can say the words, and Father Turpin, for Goddess and God, who are one. Three days, beloved. On the day of the new moon."

That gave him pause. "But isn't that—"

"The Prince of Darkness corrupts all that he touches. Long before he laid his hand on the moon's dark, it was sacred, beloved of the Goddess. We'll remember, my love. We'll make the night clean again."

"He'll be at his strongest. Whereas we—"

"We, too," she said. "And we held the night before him."

He looked into her face. He was supposed to be angry;

to refuse to forgive her. But that was such a small thing, and this between them so great, in so great a war.

He brushed his thumb across her lips, then kissed them softly. She closed her eyes and sighed.

"If we die," he said, "we'll die in the light."

"We won't die," she said.

She believed that. He wanted to, but he had been a soldier too long. He set his lips together and was silent.

CHAPTER 55

✠ ✠ ✠

A black tide of despair ran ahead of the enemy. At first it seemed to be no more than a cloud across the sun, or a passing of fear as word spread of the enemy's coming. The air dimmed. Moods darkened though the morning drew toward noon. Quarrels flared. People squabbled over small things: a loaf of bread, a rent in a cloak.

The Franks seemed inclined to believe, at last, that Carbonek was much larger than it had looked. They had the west tower and the workings beneath it, wide and surprisingly airy chambers lit through deep shafts in the mountain. There was room there and to spare for ten thousand men, their animals, their baggage, and even their complement of camp-followers.

Maybe because most of them were underground, they caught the contagion late; or maybe, being Franks, they were simply inured to fear. Roland's villagers, bivouacked with them, took heart from their lightness of spirit, though not a few muttered about the thickness of the Frankish skull.

"I didn't hear that," Turpin said as he happened past a scowling knot of villagers. He recognized red-headed Kyllan, though he did not see the girl Cait—usually the two were inseparable.

Kyllan's scowl was not as dark as the others'. He seemed relieved by the distraction. Turpin had barely paused; as he went on, Kyllan followed, a bit like a pup in search of a master.

"I was trying to tell them," he said. "It's not us. It's coming from outside of us."

Turpin raised a brow. "You think so?"

"I know so," the boy said. "Some of the others are out trying to convince people, too. But people don't want to be convinced."

"That may be part of the spell," Turpin pointed out.

"Franks must be immune to it," Kyllan said. "And a few of us. Maybe because our skulls are denser than most?"

Turpin laughed.

"I'm glad you can laugh at it," Kyllan said. "It's the first wave, isn't it? The first battle. He's going for our souls."

Turpin's nape prickled, though he kept his smile. "We're not immune," he said. "Just, maybe, better at fighting it. The world's a dangerous place outside of Montsalvat."

"And a dark one," said Kyllan. "Not that we don't have our own dangers. But we've been sheltered for so long—Father Turpin, do you think we can do it? Can we win this war?"

"I think," said Turpin, "that you—we—have the Grail. And that you have us. And yourselves."

"And Count Roland," Kyllan said, "who belongs to all of us."

"And Count Roland," said Turpin.

As if they had invoked him, he was there. The hall was wide, its vaulting high, and he had come in at the far extent of it; but it was as if the sun had come down into the earth. The rumble of discontent faded. Faces, eyes turned toward him.

Turpin felt the light of him, the bright clean presence, with a splendor in it that made him nod suddenly, and almost laugh. Roland had been in the presence of the Grail. He had brought its healing down with him, and poured it out without stinting.

To the eye he was no more or less ordinary than he ever was: a man not small but not particularly tall, slender rather than sturdy, but wide enough in the shoulders. A black-haired man, white-skinned, and young—startlingly so, sometimes. He was plainly dressed as always, with a glint of mail under a leather tunic. From that distance one could not clearly see the oddity, the hawk-yellow eyes in the pale face.

He stood on the stair above them, scanning the hall. Counting faces, Turpin thought. Reckoning mood, judging hearts. Turpin was no enchanter, but he could feel the darkness yearning toward them all, like wings beating against a wall of glass.

"It will get worse," Roland said, not particularly loudly, but the vaulting carried his voice through the hall. "The enemy will try to destroy us in spirit before his armies slaughter our bodies. Things will come—black dreams, nightmares, terrors from the dark regions of the heart. Whatever you fear most, hate most, he will raise up for you. You must be strong, my people. You must hold fast."

"And if we can't?"

Turpin did not recognize the voice, but it spoke for a great number of them.

"You can," Roland said. "Remember what you fight for—and what fights for you. Remember the Grail."

"We've never seen it," the man said. It was a Frank, not particularly prostrate with fear, but not greatly endowed with courage, either. "How do we know it's real?"

"It is more real than anything you ever knew," Roland said. He lifted his hands. "Look!"

Light blazed out of them, sudden, astonishing. Men fell on their faces. Some gasped; some cried out. A few wept.

Turpin kept his feet. The light was blinding, but he could see. He saw the cup of the Grail, suspended above those strong narrow hands.

It was there. Open, unveiled. Turpin thought perhaps he should be outraged, but all that came to him was wonder.

Roland spoke through the glory of it. "Now do you doubt?"

"No, my lord," said the Frank. "No. Never again, my lord."

The light dimmed. Men groaned in protest, but the Grail had taken itself away. Roland stood on the stair, hands at his sides. Turpin wondered if he knew what he had done—what he was. Sometimes Roland just *was*. It seldom seemed to dawn on him that he was anything out of the ordinary.

Beside Turpin, Kyllan let out his breath in a long sigh. "Glory and splendor," he said. "Was that—really—"

"Yes," Turpin said.

"By all the gods," said Kyllan. "And he just reached, and it was there."

"Wait till they hear, up in the castle," Cait said, slipping in between them. "What will they say when they find out he's been making free with *that*?"

"*Ai*," said Kyllan.

Roland spent most of the morning among his troops. He did not invoke the Grail again, but word of it had spread like fire. It burned away the darkness and lifted the cloud of despair.

By noon the guards on the towers could see the army advancing through the empty lands, out of the mist that veiled the world's end. It came on like a swarm of locusts. Thousands, tens of thousands, warriors innumerable, human and unhuman.

This they had let in. They had guided it here, in hope of sparing the rest of the kingdom. And yet now they saw it, not a few began to regret that they had ever done such a thing.

"We could have held the walls of air," said a lord of Caer Sidi, "until he wearied of assailing them."

They stood on the walls of stone, protected by the parapet, watching the enemy march and crawl and fly toward them. Turpin looked for Ganelon, but there were too many, and they were too far. He could not see any one face, only the swarming mass of them.

The lords near him were making no effort to speak quietly. He had seen clusters like that too often before, huddled tight, muttering to one another, shooting glances beyond their circle. "We should have kept this army out," they said. "If we had been consulted—if *he* had not high-handedly—"

He was standing somewhat apart, arms folded on the parapet, watching his enemy—his personal enemy, even beyond the wars of the Grail—advance on the castle. Turpin doubted very much that he cared what anyone was saying, in earshot or out of it.

"Arrogant," muttered the lordlings from Caer Sidi. "Blood of the Grail or no, what right or authority has he to command us?"

"The king did give him—" one of them ventured.

The others shouted him down. "The king is dying. Maybe he's dead—has anyone seen him or spoken to him since we came here? I'll wager there's a corpse in that tower he's said to be lying in, and his women are speaking for him. The chief of them—she chose that one, it's said. And not for any fitness or even purity of heart. Because he has a handsome face, and knows how to please a woman."

"He does that," Sarissa said, sweet as honey. Her smile scattered them in great disorder. She came to stand beside Turpin.

He regarded her out of the corner of his eye. "I'm sorry you heard that," he said.

She shrugged. "I've heard worse."

"The one out there—he'll feed any dissension, and turn it into treason if he can."

"That is his way," she said. She sounded little enough concerned.

"You're not afraid for him? Or for yourself?"

"I'm terrified," she said calmly. "I don't see the use in indulging it."

He pondered that; then he nodded. "Wise," he said.

"Maybe not." She wrapped her cloak a little closer about her. Though the sun was high, it was veiled in cloud, and the wind was chill.

"Father Turpin," she said in a different tone, one somewhat sharper. "Will you make a marriage for us?"

Turpin blinked. "Will I—you—*you* two?"

"Yes."

"And why isn't he asking?"

Turpin bit his tongue hard. He did not mean to sound so flat.

She seemed not to mind. "He means to. But with all that's happening—and with what he did this morning, which he has yet to see the end of—I doubt he's stopped to think of it."

"Of course he hasn't," Turpin said. "Yes, I'll do it. How could I not?"

When she smiled as she was doing now, he could almost regret the vows he had taken. Almost. She was not for him, even if he had been free to take her. "You have both our thanks," she said.

Turpin bent his head to that. "Tell me one thing," he said. "Will he be king?"

"What do you think?"

"I think he already is, but he doesn't know it. Nor do yonder idiots."

"He doesn't want it," she said.

"That should make a difference? Did you hear what he did?"

"I could hardly avoid it. The whole castle is humming with it."

"Are you as angry as the others seem to be?"

"No," she said. She let her head fall back, turning her face to the boiling sky. A shaft of sunlight broke through and pierced her. For an instant he saw her as she must be beyond the veil of flesh, as a slender pillar of light. Then she was Sarissa again, with her warm brown skin and her imperfectly disciplined brown curls.

"You knew it would happen," Turpin said in sudden understanding.

"No," she said again. "But I wasn't surprised. None of us was—not us nine. Nor the king, either."

"He can't help himself, can he? He belongs to it. It uses him as it pleases."

"He has free will," she said. "He can refuse."

"Can he? Does he know he can?"

"He has been told."

Turpin shook his head. "You trapped him. You're lucky he's forgiven you. He loves you. He'd die for you."

"And I for him." Her voice was soft, but her eyes were fierce. "I fought it—oh, too long. It nearly destroyed us. But he, with his great heart—he forgave. In his own heart he forgave me."

"Did you ever doubt he would?"

"I doubted far too much."

"And now?"

"I've taught myself to trust him. The Grail does—utterly. Else it would never have come to him."

"He didn't steal it. He called. It came."

"I know that," she said. "I felt it answer him."

"No one tried to stop it?"

"No one could." She was smiling, though the sky was growing ever darker, and the foremost ranks of the enemy swarmed on the edge of the chasm that warded Carbonek. Her eyes were on Roland.

"Arrogant," she said, but without censure. "Oh, yes. It was the most arrogant thing anyone has done in Montsalvat, and we have had our share of haughty lords."

"He is not—"

"That's the beauty of it," she said. "He puts on no airs at all. He simply does what he pleases. Sometimes he apologizes. Mostly he doesn't know that he should."

"Will he have to apologize for marrying you?"

"Probably," she said. "But not to me."

CHAPTER 56

❂ ❂ ❂

Everyone went up to the walls before that day was over, to see what they all faced. Darkness fell early, in a grey weight of cloud. The enemy's fires spread as far as the eye could see, myriad ruddy sparks in the starless night. The lord of them all had still not shown himself. The anticipation, the fear, worked on the besiegers as he had no doubt intended. The longer they waited to see, the deeper their dread became.

Roland had been the besieger often before, but not the besieged. The sense of confinement dismayed him more than he would let anyone see. Already some of the troops were fretting, yearning for the sky.

If they were fortunate, this siege would not last long. If not ...

He was forbearing to think of that, and making his somewhat preoccupied way from one of the garrisons to what he hoped would be a night's rest, when he was way-laid by a delegation of lords and princes. They trapped him in a hall in which servants had just finished taking down the tables from the daymeal, backed him ever so politely against a wall and, with remarkable bluntness for courtiers, taxed him with what they reckoned his arrogance.

"The Grail is the greatest relic of Christendom," said one elegant creature. "It is kept hidden for its great rarity and its great power. If it were shown abroad, at will, without discrimination—"

"Has it been taken out of the castle?" Roland asked civilly. But he had interrupted the spate of words, and that was not civil at all.

These princes of the Grail were suitably offended, but suitably nonplussed as well. They could hardly rebuke him for insolence; he was set above them.

The one who seemed deputed to speak for them found his tongue quickly enough. "If it were shown to those who are not pure of heart, who have never sworn themselves to it, who were brought here to fight as levies, as conscripts, then what mystery would remain in it? What power would be left to it?"

Roland looked at them. These were the knights of legend, the sacred brotherhood, men who had been brought to this place to serve and defend the Grail. They disliked greatly to bow their heads to him, creature of muddy earth that he was, with his hawk's eyes and his half-barbarian ways.

He spoke softly, and as politely as he could. He said, "Nothing can diminish the Grail. Not even darkness and silence and the prison of a shrine."

"The Grail is never diminished," said the one who spoke for them. "But its power in the world, its strength, its capacity to drive back the evil—that must be protected."

"It is protected," Roland said. In spite of himself, his voice had gained an edge. "I do as the Grail bids me. If it chooses to reveal itself through me, what right have I to refuse it?"

He had not silenced them, nor had he expected to. "You came here," said one of those who had not spoken before. He was younger, maybe; it was difficult to tell, among these ageless people. He was angrier, certainly, or more able to show it. "You came here as one roused from the dead, and took the sword, and took the Grail. And yet what do you know of us—of any of us? You are an outlander. This is not your country."

"Nor was it Parsifal's," said Roland, "when he first came here. What was it you called him then? Parsifal the Outlander—Parsifal the Stranger. Did you resist him as strongly as you resist me?"

None of them would meet his eyes. He looked from face to face, seeing men of great power and valor, ancient in wisdom and steeped in the light of the Grail—but they were, after all, men.

They were afraid, he thought, not only of the enemy who might conquer them all, but of the stranger who had come to command them. They neither knew nor trusted him.

And maybe there was more to their resistance than that. Maybe they were jealous. They had served the Grail long and faithfully, but none of them had been chosen to lead this war. Durandal had come to a foreign hand. The Lady of the Grail had passed them by, and chosen a man whom none of them knew.

He spoke to them gently, but there was no disguising the steel beneath. "Whoever I am, wherever I was born, this land seems to have made me a part of it. Be sure of this, my lords. I serve the Grail. Maybe I didn't choose to, maybe it chose me, but now that it's done, I won't undo it. You will accept this, my lords. Or," he said, softly implacable, "you may go."

They stared at him in disbelief.

"You may go," he said again. "You may leave. We cannot have dissension here."

"But where will we go?" the youngest demanded. "How will we live?"

Roland did not answer that.

For those whose armor was words, silence was a devastating weapon. These lords of the Grail fidgeted and fretted and shifted from foot to foot.

"You have no power to send us away," the youngest said. "This is our place. We were chosen for it. We are sworn to it. You cannot cast us out. And," he said fiercely, "we will not go!"

"Then stand behind me," Roland said. "Accept what the Grail does through me. We have enemies enough without. There will be no contention here."

They did not like it. But they were men of reason, it seemed, after all. They bowed sullenly, but bow they did.

Roland was sure he had not heard the end of it. For the moment he would take what he was given, and see that word was sent to all the brotherhood and court of the Grail, that if any objected to the charge that was given

him, that one had until the morning to depart from Carbonek.

The night was endless. Roland snatched a little sleep, but
the bed was too soft and the wards of the castle too sorely
taxed by the enemy's assaults. Even with the full count of
the nine raising the shields from the shrine of the Grail, ill
things walked in the shadows. Fear crawled through the
stones. Dread thrummed in the air.

And this was only the first night. He walked among the
people, those struggling to sleep and those standing uneasy
watch, giving them such comfort as he could.

There were others doing the same. Turpin led the priests
and monks and those who were Christians in the chanting
of psalms. Their voices echoed in the vaults, long and slow.
Where that sound was, the darkness was less.

Roland went up to the walls again. Tarik had found him
among the Franks and climbed up to his shoulder. The
puca would never have admitted to fear, but the cat-body
was shivering in small convulsions. He stroked it as he
stood in the blind dark. Most of the enemy's fires had
burned low. It was nearly dawn, he thought, if indeed dawn
would ever come.

He felt rather than saw someone come up behind him.
Tarik hissed. Gemma said, "Hush, you. It's only me."

Her voice was soft, but it was its wonted self: a little
rough, a little sweet, with a brisk, practical clip to it. It
would take a great deal more than the Grail's ancient
enemy to crush her spirit.

She leaned on the parapet near him. He could see her in
the faint light of the guard's cresset. It had been a while, he
reflected, since she chose to be anywhere that he was, unless duty required it.

That pain was old, but still sharp. Knowing how wise she
had been, knowing that he could not take her back, not
ever again, made it no easier to bear. There were too many
memories.

She spoke at last, as if to herself. "We can't go on like this
for long. Waiting him out won't be the answer—it will have
to be battle."

"Yes," he said, since she could not have seen his nod in
the gloom.

"Maybe you can catch him off balance," she said.

"Maybe."

She laughed, more wry than mirthful. "Listen to me, telling you what to do. It's this creeping dark—it turns us all into babbling fools. Except you. You, it makes more silent than ever."

"I don't have anything to say," he said.

"You can say more without a word than most people can with a thousand." She moved closer to him, but never close enough to touch. "I came up here to tell you to sleep. You can't carry on day and night like this, and expect to have anything left to fight the enemy with."

"The Grail sustains me," Roland said.

"But for how long? You'll burn yourself out."

"Not till the war is over." He stretched and sighed. Was that the first faint glimmer of light on the horizon? "You should sleep, too. We all should, if we can. It's two days till the new moon. Tell them—tell the troops we'll make our move then."

"The new moon?" She sounded dubious, but she did not offer to argue.

Bless her heart and soul. She was no lord, to be prey to pride. Before she turned to go, he reached and caught her hand. "Thank you," he said.

She shrugged. "You're the king. You give orders—I follow them. If," she added, "they're not too impossible."

"I am not—"

She slipped free and was gone.

"I am not the king," he said to the air where she had been.

The king summoned him at dawn: a plucking at his spirit, a sudden sense that he must be elsewhere. He was still on the walls. The darkness was only a little less. There would be no sun today, and little light, either, unless they in the castle expended strength to make it.

He went down through the shadows. They were stronger. He heard gibbering, glimpsed a gleam of eyes. Servants struggled to go about their duties. They were white and shaking, but they were holding on. Bread was baking, the sweet fragrance as potent as magic for lightening the soul.

He caught a servant on her way to the kitchens. "Ask the

cooks," he said, "if they will make sweet things, wonderful things—things rich with spices and with heart's ease."

The woman blinked, then suddenly smiled. She nodded, bowed, and ran to do his bidding.

By the time he came to the king's tower, the first hints came to him: cinnamon, cardamom, grains of paradise. He was smiling as he mounted the stair.

Parsifal clung to life by a thinner thread than Roland remembered. It was Sarissa on guard now, who must have come out from the Grail only a little while ago. Her smile was a little startled, catching the brightness of his own.

Tarik slipped down from Roland's shoulder to curl at the foot of the king's bed. Parsifal had no strength to open his eyes, but his mind was awake. He was aware.

Roland knelt beside him. The voice that spoke had no sound at all. It was a whisper in the heart. "Soon," he said. "Soon I go. The new moon—"

"No!" The word escaped Roland without his willing it.

"It's time," said Parsifal. "When you perform the great rite, when you bind the power, I will be part of it. I will be the seal and the capstone."

"But—" Roland began.

"I waited for this," Parsifal said. "I held to life for it. That was my enemy, whom I failed to destroy. This time I shall be part of his destruction."

Roland bowed his head over the skeletal hand.

The soft voice spoke again in his heart. "Don't grieve," said Parsifal. "Be glad. I'll be free. And before I go, I'll give you strength. It may—it will—be enough to cast him down."

"And without it, we'll never be strong enough."

Roland's head snapped up. Sarissa met his eyes levelly.

"You need my strength," said Parsifal.

"How am I to take it?" Roland asked. Knowing what the answer must be. But needing to hear it, though he dreaded the truth of it.

The silence, though brief, was enormous. Roland's belly clenched. He did not want to remember what Merlin had told him. Of deaths of kings. Of old, old rites. Of sacrifices.

Royal sacrifice. High blood and great courage that went of its own will to its death. Such a sacrifice had imbued the Grail with its power.

"And will again," Parsifal said. "I'm no god's son, but I was lord in the Grail's kingdom. The power I pass to you, the power of the great marriage, the royal sacrifice—it can stand against even the ancient enemy."

"That is murder," Roland said.

"Sacrifice," said Parsifal. "Willing, with great joy. I was born for this. I was meant for it."

"Surely there is another way," Roland said. "We're not pagans, either of us. We're Christian men. Is there no Christian rite that will suffice? A high Mass—the offering of the wine that is transformed into blood—blood of the Grail—"

"You know that is not enough," said Parsifal, "any more than it was enough for the Lord Christ, who died on a cross."

Roland had been thinking him a gentle man, a saintly man, a man on the border between earth and heaven. Yet this had been a great king, a warrior of renown. He had waged the first war of the Grail. He had ruled in Montsalvat.

Gentle he might be on this his deathbed, but he was implacable. He would have this thing. And Roland's hand must do it.

"Your hand, and Durandal." Parsifal sighed. There was a rattle in it. Death stood over him, but he would not let it take him. Not until the new moon.

"So that's why," Roland said, not to Parsifal but to Sarissa. "You lied to me because you knew—when I came to the crux, I'd fail."

Her lips were tight. Was she darkly glad? Was she vindicated, after all?

He would not give her the satisfaction. He looked down at his hands. Narrow hands, long fingers. They were stronger than they looked. They had killed before—more men than he could count. He was a warrior; that was what he did. He killed men.

But not in cold blood.

"I am not an executioner," he said.

"You are, by grace of the Grail, a priest," said Parsifal.

"Did you do the same?" Roland demanded. "Is this how you took the kingship?"

"You know I did not." Parsifal sounded almost regretful.

"For each it is different. This is the need now; this is what must be."

"No." Roland staggered up. He was dizzy; he was sick. "If you simply let go—if you let God's hand take you—is that not also a sacrifice? I'll be here. I'll sing the rite of your passing. I'll take the strength as your life passes."

"The strength is in the blood," Parsifal said. Roland could barely hear him. To the eye he was dead: a corpse in a monk's robe, eyes sunken in the skull, skeletal hands folded on the hollow breast. But the spirit was bright in him still, a spark so brilliant that it could blind the unwary.

That spark was pure raw strength. Power against the dark. Victory—if Roland could pay the price.

Blood on his hands. Murder in cold blood.

Was it a sin, if the victim begged for it? If the Grail demanded it? If—

Merlin would have known what to do. But Merlin was far away, beyond reach of any power, mortal or otherwise. The enemy's treachery had bound him there.

Roland had sworn to set him free.

If he destroyed Ganelon, he would fulfill his great oath. But to destroy Ganelon, he must—

He rounded on Sarissa. "Can *you* do it?"

She shook her head tightly. That must be the truth: she was not at all happy to confess it.

In any event he had known before he asked. For some things there was no mercy. If she could have done it, she would never have troubled herself with an outland champion.

"I have to think," he said. "I have to—"

He fled. Not, this time, in hawk's shape, and not beyond the boundaries of Carbonek. Coward he might be, but he would not run so far again. Whatever he chose, he would do it here, and stand to face the consequences.

CHAPTER 57

✠ ✠ ✠

With the coming of daylight, the enemy raised siege-engines before the walls of Carbonek. Hordes of faceless men—and perhaps other than men—hammered and fitted and bound and lifted, until there was a wall outside the walls, a thicket of engines, each surrounded by its swarm of attendants.

Then the bombardment began. Most of the missiles were stones, but some were softer and smaller. Some were very small. Others tumbled awkwardly as they flew, and struck with a soft, sickening sound.

Some of them still wore the device of Poictesme. Others still had faces to be recognized. Not all or even most were whole. Teeth and claws had torn them asunder, and steel had hacked them.

It was a grim task to gather the fragments of the dead, to match them into some semblance of human form, then to bless them and lay them to rest in the crypt of the castle. And all the while they did that, the engines battered the walls with stones.

Worse than stones and even dead flesh were the bolts of darkness that fell among them. Those were not visible save from the corner of an eye. When they struck, if they struck vitals, they killed; but if they struck close by, they flung a man down in a black sleep.

There had been no parley, no call for surrender. People

on the walls saw no sign of a leader, no general on a hill,
nor any tent higher than any other. The will that ruled the
army was clear to them all, but where its focus was, no one
could see. That made it all the more terrible: that it had no
face, no substance, not even a shadow to grasp.

Roland felt the force of that absence. He had fled the
king's presence and the thing he had been brought here to
do, but he would not run away from the rest of it. He would
do what he had chosen for himself: councils of war, dispositions of troops, protection of the castle.

None of the Grail-knights had left Carbonek. When he
summoned them at noon, the full count of them assembled
in their hall beneath ancient banners and relics of old wars.
They were all in armor, some of it of very antique fashion
indeed, but serviceable enough, their weapons well tended.

Maybe, he thought, he had been too hasty to reckon
them soft. They had the look of men tempered in battle,
though the last of those had been long ago. Stern faces
turned toward him as he entered the hall. Many bore scars.
They came from nations innumerable, even to the far ends
of the earth. Dark faces, pale faces, men tall and short, bull-
broad and slender as girls, but all sworn to defend the
Grail. Each wore a blue cloak over his armor, bound with
a brooch in the likeness of a silver swan.

There were a hundred of them. The Grail had nourished
them for time out of mind; they bore somewhat of the light
of it. Their spirits were stronger for it, their endurance
greater against the enemy—but they were vulnerable
nonetheless.

"I set you on guard," he said, "over the Grail and its
tower, and the ladies who protect the shrine. Choose your
watches; and be wary. The enemy has come to seize the
Grail. He'll direct his strongest attacks against those who
guard it."

"We remember," said a stocky man in Roman armor.
The strong face, the close-cropped black hair . . . Roland
was careful not to stare. Rome's legend was strong where
he came from; to see a man of the legions alive and breathing, speaking to him—that was nigh as great a thing as the
Grail itself.

"In the last war of the Grail," the Roman said, "he
pressed us hardest. Full fourscore of us died then. I lived; I

remember. The rest, who came to us after, have studied deeply. We'll be on guard, young lord; you need have no fear of that."

Young. That stung. But it was true. "Defend your charge at all costs," Roland said, "but be aware: it may not choose to hide itself in its shrine. It has come out once. It may come out again."

"So I heard," the Roman said somewhat dryly.

"And your name?" Roland asked him.

"Titus Longinus," the Roman said. "You I know, Roland of Brittany, as I knew your forefather. Merlinus Ambrosius, we called him. He still lives?"

"Yes," Roland said.

The Roman did not smile, but his dark eyes were glinting. "Good," he said. "And maybe I'll see him when this war is over—when we've brought down the old serpent. That would be a good thing; to bring back the old times."

Roland remembered to shut his mouth. So: not everyone in Montsalvat harbored an ancient hatred of Merlin.

Longinus grinned at him. In body the man was not greatly older than Roland himself. Nor was he old in spirit, either. "We do remember how to fight," he said. "Don't fear for us."

Roland bowed to him. "Take command, then, in the king's name. And may God and the Grail protect you."

They all bowed in return, every one of them: some lower than others, but it seemed they had chosen to accept his authority.

That was well, though he was not, maybe, what they thought he was. Above all things, the defenders in Carbonek needed to be of one mind, one soul. There could be no quarrels and no division. Every crack, every sign of strain, would let the enemy in.

And what of himself?

Not now.

He had done all that he could. The Grail was guarded. Watches were drawn for the walls and the towers, and for the gates both greater and lesser. And in the halls below, where the bulk of the army lay, he had given orders that he trusted would be followed.

*   *   *

He had not taken thought for his own daymeal, though
he saw to it that everyone else was fed. Lord Huon's man
found him coming up from the Franks' hall. "My lord pre-
pares to dine," the man said. "He asks if you would deign
to share the meal with him."

Roland bit back his first thought, which was to refuse.
He had crossed paths often that day with the lord of Caer
Sidi, but neither had paused for speech. Courtesy at the
least would be served if he accepted the summons. And, he
realized, he was hungry.

He had more than half expected to find Huon dining in
the great hall with a mob of courtiers, but the servant led
him to a room much smaller, a private chamber. Only
Huon was there, with one or two of his counselors, and the
eldest lady of the Grail, the gentle-faced Nieve. They were
old friends, it seemed. Old lovers? That well might be. Certainly they were at ease with one another.

They welcomed Roland warmly and sat him down between them. There was another chair set at the table; as
he settled, one came to occupy it. He raised his brows at
sight of Turpin. The archbishop met his stare blandly,
greeted the others with suitable decorum, and accepted a
cup of wine.

It was a comfortable gathering, though dark things gibbered in the shadows. Roland barely noticed what he ate;
a great weariness had fallen on him, as if he had come to
sanctuary and could, at last, let go. He ate blindly, drank,
listened to the others' soft conversation. They spoke of
small things: the flavor of the wine, the excellence of the
dinner. There was a sleepy comfort in it, a gentleness that
he had not known in too long.

He started awake. They were still drinking wine, still
conversing: Huon and Nieve and Turpin. The counselors
were gone, and the servants. The lamps burned low but
steady. The dark things were more numerous, despite the
Grail's strong singing.

The three of them were waiting for him. He was supposed to confess, he realized. To unburden himself, so
that they could persuade him to do what Parsifal asked
him to do.

It was a low thing, to bring Turpin into it. Turpin the
priest, the bishop, whose faith above all would revolt at

blood sacrifice. He was not meeting Roland's eye. Of course he would not, if he had agreed to this.

Roland rose and left them without a word, as he had left Parsifal and Sarissa. They tried to stop him. He took no notice.

The deep chamber was dim, its lamps and torches burning far apart. The whispers were louder here, the dark wings more clearly visible. Franks and people of Montsalvat huddled together round campfires. Those who could sleep did. The others snatched such rest as they might, trusting to the safety of numbers.

Gemma and her sons gathered with Marric and Cait and some of the other recruits not far from the stair to the upper regions. It was a place they had fought for, with bruises and cuts to show for it.

Roland came down as quietly as he could, wrapped in a mantle against recognition. But they knew him. They opened ranks to let him in. With Marric on one side and Gemma on the other, he felt as safe as he had felt since the enemy came to Carbonek.

He had not meant to say anything. But even a man of few words could reach his limit. The boys were snoring. Cait was awake, but heavy-eyed, her head drooping on Kyllan's shoulder. Marric prodded the fire to rouse it. The flare put to flight something very like a bogle, but made all of shadow, with long fangs and long curved claws. Marric bared his own not inconsiderable teeth at it.

"They want me to be king," Roland said. "They want me—to—"

Gemma's arm circled him, holding him lightly but firmly as she had done when he was still a mute and witless nobody.

"To be king," Roland said somewhat more steadily, "I have to kill the king. A sacrifice. To take his power. Because, he says, there is no other way to cast down the enemy. But I can't do that."

"Why?" Marric asked.

Straight to the point as always. Roland almost laughed. "It's murder," he said.

"Sacrifice isn't murder," said Marric, "if it's willing. It's sacred. It's a holy thing. Isn't that how you Christians started? With the sacrifice of a king?"

"And we condemn forever the people who willed the sacrifice, and the people who performed it."

"Then you're fools," Gemma said, "and self-righteous too. Someone has to be the priest, if the people are to benefit. Someone has to take the burden."

"And the guilt?"

"Where's the guilt in it, if the gods themselves ask it of you? I'd think you'd be guiltier for refusing it."

"You're conspiring against me," Roland muttered.

"What," she said, "you expected us to agree with you? We're not Christians. Maybe you should have talked to your friend the bishop."

"He's in the conspiracy, too," Roland said bitterly. "Everyone is. But none of them—none of you—has to strike the blow. None of *you* will have blood on your hands."

"None of us will have the power, either," she said.

"I don't want the power."

She pulled him about, face-to-face with her. "Is that the truth? The honest, unvarnished truth?"

He blinked. He was going to nod. But he found he could not move.

"Of course you want it," she said. "It must be like glory and trumpets—like what the children thought war would be. Brightness and splendor. And it's been handed to you, but you have to pay for it. Doesn't everything have a price? And the greater it is, the higher the price."

"All I want to be," he said tightly, "is a soldier. And— yes—an enchanter. But I am that already. I never wanted to be a king. I never needed to be. To be tempted like this—oh, I could dream of it, if I let myself. But not if I have to buy it with blood."

"Hypocrite," she said. "How many men have you killed? Eh? How many lives have you ended? So this one is willing. It offers itself. And you have to think about it first, and not just do it. Does that make it so very different from any other blood you've shed?"

"Profoundly different," he said. "Different past my endurance."

"That's nonsense," she said. "That's the enemy in you. He's twisting the way you think. Can't you feel it?"

He shook his head hard. "I always thought like this."

"That's what Mabon over there said just before he tried to gut himself with a smith's hammer. He had a devil in him. Father Turpin drove it out."

"I do not have—" He bit his tongue. He did not. But she would never believe him.

He tried to rise. He had come here for peace, and to escape those who would press him to do this thing that none of them could do. Only he. And there was no peace here. No one would give him peace.

Gemma held him fast. Marric, on the other side, was suddenly a leaden weight, binding him there.

"You can't run away," the bogle said. "You can't keep refusing, either. This is what you came to do."

"I came to fight. Not to murder a king."

"It's all one," said Marric.

Roland shivered convulsively. The dark things were dancing, laughing at him. They were swarming in the hall. More and more and more of them. And this was only the second night. By the third, the dark of the moon, they would even be in the light. And by the fourth—

It could not go on. Nor could he. None of them was strong enough.

Unless—

That was the one thing, the terrible thing, the thing he could not do.

And if he did not do it, horror would eat away at them. Walls of air and stone would crumble.

Battle. They could go forth to battle.

Twenty thousand against—how many? Multitudes. They would die gloriously; but the enemy would have the Grail. And when he had the Grail, the dark would come.

It might come even if he did this thing.

Yes, and if he did not do it, it would certainly come.

He doubled up, retching. He was sick—sick to the soul. And maybe there was a devil in him after all, a small and mean one, that had crept in while he was fighting against the inevitable.

It was not—

Was it not?

Gemma's hands were on him, stroking his hair out of his cold-sweating face, pressing the knots from his shoulders. She did not speak, nor croon to him, either. She was simply there. And Marric, taking his hands in long strong fingers. And the others—when had they come awake? They were all there. They were all around him, like a wall.

"If I do this," he said through the tightness in his throat, "you are in it with me. I'll make you the king's own."

"That's a threat?" Cait asked.

"A promise," he said.

She shrugged, insouciant as ever. "Well, good. Maybe then Da will stop telling me I'm the most worthless object he ever laid eyes on."

"Won't happen," Kyllan said. "But if you're here, he'll tell it to you less often."

"There, see?" she said. "Now he's got to do it. Gemma, tell him."

"You can't tell me yourself?"

She rolled her eyes. "I'm not talking to *you*. Besides, you never listen."

"I'm listening now."

"Because we've got you cornered."

"I can't scare you off at all, can I?" Roland said.

"Not even a little." Kyllan squatted in front of him, grinning like a bogle. "Don't tell me you're sorry we've made you do this. You can blame us. Then you won't feel so guilty."

Roland gasped, choked, coughed. Too many of them pounded his back. He dropped flat.

They must have thought he was in convulsions. He was laughing. It was utterly, beautifully absurd.

He rolled onto his back. The circle of them bent over him: wide eyes, blessedly familiar faces. They were not in awe of him, nor ever would be, and they knew what he was. That was the most wonderful, the most improbable thing. He would be the Grail-king—he, the half-wild man-child from Brittany, the paladin of Francia, the witling from Greenwood—and they saw nothing remarkable in it.

Someone else was standing beyond them, drawn maybe by Roland's trouble. Turpin was not awed, either, though he looked odd. That was pain, Roland thought. Turpin had always been the strong one, the one who stood fast when everyone else gave way to fear or pain or sorrow.

He had lost his brothers in arms, too, and his king, and

everything that he lived for. He had not run as Roland had. He had held his ground.

"And you, priest of God?" Roland asked him. "Do you condone this?"

"I've come to terms with my conscience," Turpin said.

"Will you absolve me of the sin?"

"I don't believe it is a sin," said Turpin.

"But the Church would call it so."

Turpin crossed himself and bowed his head. "God is the final authority. And I believe," he said, "that God will not condemn you."

"Truth?"

"Truth," said Turpin.

Roland loosed his breath in a long sigh. He was done flailing at them all. It served no purpose. It did nothing to win this war into which his fate—and Sarissa's will—had cast him.

He would do it. He would take the burden that was laid on him. But not tonight. Tonight he would stay here, among his people. He needed them as much as they needed him. In the morning he would go to the Grail, and to the keepers of the Grail.

CHAPTER 58

✠ ✠ ✠

The siege-engines had paused at the fall of dark, giving way to the assaults of night-creatures and spirits of the shadows. With the light's return, the engines woke again.

Sarissa came down from the Grail's tower to the outer wall. She was beyond exhaustion. The night's battle had worn her to the bone. They had kept the Grail safe against the enemy's servants, but the castle was infested with them. As each hour passed, more of them slipped through the wards; and those that were inside bred and multiplied.

No one in the keep had died of shadow-sickness, yet. But people were falling ill.

She called to one of the guards on the wall. "Go to Lord Huon," she said. "Tell him to raid the treasury. The hoard of silver coins, coins of the Grail—bid him gather them, and summon his smiths and jewelers. Let them pierce them for amulets, and let his mages lay a warding on them. Give them to everyone who lacks his own defenses."

The guard bowed and ran.

She leaned against the parapet. If she had only thought of it sooner. If anyone had.

It was not, please the gods, too late.

She shivered inside her skin. Roland had come up to the wall, climbing from below. He was in armor; he had Durandal at his side. His helmet rested in the crook of his arm. His face was strikingly, almost alarmingly calm.

He stood beside her. "That was well thought of," he said, "to fashion amulets. I should have thought of it myself."

"I should have thought of it days ago." She kept her voice easy, her manner casual. As if nothing at all had happened. As if yesterday had never been.

"I'll help with the spellcasting," he said, "when they're ready. Maybe this talisman of mine will add to their strength."

"It well might," she said.

They were not looking at each other. Her eyes were on the enemy below. His, when she glanced sidelong, were the same. His profile was clean-carved, clear against the grey sky. He was as unaware of his beauty as ever. If he thought of it at all, it was as a nuisance.

She swallowed a sigh. So difficult a man. So reluctant a champion. And if he would not be king . . .

The siege-engines ground to a halt. The hordes about them stirred and shifted. They were drawing back—opening a path, a road through their camp to the castle. Figures rode along it. A banner unfurled: white for truce, golden pennons for an embassy.

Roland's breath hissed. His hand had caught hers—meeting it as it came to his. They clasped hard, almost to pain.

There were guards, servants, men in silks and lordly panoply. But the one who led them, who wore a prince's crown on his thick fair hair, was unmistakable. The face of a young Charles of Francia. Long limbs, broad shoulders. And the deformity that marred the whole: the twisted back, the hump that dwarfed and bent it.

Pepin the prince sat a sturdy brown cob at the edge of the chasm, peering up at the gate and the tower. It must have cost him pain: his face was tight.

He had gained dignity since Sarissa saw him last—and more than that. She could see the power in him. He was brimming with it, as Roland had been when she first met him. But Roland had been full of light. This prince was filled with darkness.

"I knew," Roland whispered. "I knew this would come of it. I told the king. And he—would—not—"

Sarissa pressed his hand to her lips. That seemed to calm him a little. His shoulders shook, but he stood still.

Pepin had been speaking while she engrossed herself in Roland. The words were of little enough moment: insolence and defiance, as she would have expected. "I come on behalf of the great one, the mighty one, the lord of air and darkness, who rules from the ends of the world. He bids you surrender that instrument which you keep, which he has claimed since the days of the Temple in Jerusalem. Only give it up, and he will let you live; he will set you free to do as you will."

"And not as *he* wills?" Roland asked.

Pepin started like a deer. He had not, it seemed, paid close attention to the faces along the wall, and certainly not to that one among the many. They were, just then, all men of Caer Sidi: dark-haired, hawk-faced, pale-skinned men in bright armor. Very like Roland, indeed, except for the eyes. And the voice, clear and imperious, with its Breton accent.

Pepin peered upward. His expression was blank with shock. "You—my God! You're not dead."

"It would seem not," said Roland. He had mastered his own astonishment. "Tell me—is your father here?"

He was holding his breath, Sarissa noticed.

Pepin could not have seen. His lip curled. "Not likely," he said. "He's home in Francia."

Roland's knees buckled. He steadied them before Sarissa could catch him or Pepin see. Relief, thought Sarissa, deep and almost strong enough to fell him. Charles was no part of this. It was only Pepin.

If he told the truth.

She would have scented the lie. Pepin might be a fool and a darkmage, but he was not a liar.

"Now tell me," Pepin called across the chasm. "Why are you here? How are you alive?"

"I am the champion of the Grail," Roland answered him. "I live by the Grail's grace."

Pepin blinked hard. "You are not—"

"Truth," Roland said. "My blood is blood of the Grail. Its king is my kin. Ask your master. He knows."

"I am not a servant!" Pepin cried.

Roland did not counter that.

"Surrender!" shrilled Pepin. "Surrender now. If you refuse—if you delay—worse than death will fall on you."

"We would rather die than see the Grail in that man's hands," Roland said.

"Death will be gentle beside what he does to you."

"Better us than the world," Roland said.

"The world will go down after you," said Pepin.

"Then we have no choice but to destroy him." Roland leaned over the parapet. "Tell your master," he said, "that we defy him. That we will never surrender. That the Grail remains inviolate, nor shall his hand ever touch it."

"He will have it," Pepin said. "None of you can stop him."

"We can and will," said Roland. Gently then he said, "Hooved brother, take him to his master. Keep him as safe as you may. For whatever he is or may try to be, he is my king's son."

The cob turned. Pepin sawed at the reins, but Roland's magic broke them. Reinless, bridleless, the brown gelding carried him away.

Roland did not watch them go. He turned his back on them. Erect but seeming blind, he made his way from the wall to the tower.

In the dimness of the tower, he stopped as if all strength had left him. He leaned against the wall, forehead pressed to the stones. His breath shuddered as he drew it in.

Sarissa pressed her body to his, arms around his middle. He did not tense or pull away.

"I will do it," he said. "I will do—what you all ask."

She caught herself before her arms closed strangling-tight. She made herself ask calmly, "Because of Pepin?"

"I had decided before that," he said.

"But now you're certain?"

"Now I know there is nothing else I can do. That's my king's son. Am I to see him damned by his own foolishness?"

"It is his own," she said. "Even your Christ couldn't save the whole world. Only what was willing to be saved."

"He tried," Roland said fiercely. "Can I do less?"

"My love," she said. She could not decide whether to laugh or weep.

Maybe he did not hear her. "It must be tonight, yes?"

"Yes," she said. Her voice had steadied.

He turned in her arms. His face was pale and set. "He'll

know—the enemy. There is no way we can hide such a working from him."

"We won't even try," she said.

"Will he be expecting it?"

She frowned. "He well may. The dying king, the sword, the champion—he's an older mage than any of us. And he tried to have you killed. He may have thought he succeeded. But the prince will tell him the truth of that."

"Then if we act," he said, "it will have to be at once, before he can strike at us—at me. One great blow, for victory or defeat."

She nodded.

"We'll do it," he said. "Is there time to prepare?"

"Barely," she said.

"Then we'd best get about it."

Indeed, they should. But she held him for a moment, drinking in his warmth and the solid presence of him. He kissed her with surprising heat—but briefly. They drew apart with tearing reluctance.

"Still angry?" she asked.

His brows drew together in a quick rush of temper. "No!"

"Good," she said. "Because king's blood rouses the power, but I am the seal and the binding."

He drew a sharp breath. He had known that, surely he had; but, it seemed, it needed to be spoken. He bloomed into a smile, so sudden and so brilliant and so breathtakingly rare that she could only stand and stare.

His step was light as he went away. She was glad that he could be so glad. What he had to do was a bitter thing, and a terrible one. If he could laugh at the outset of it, then that was a good omen.

The bombardment of the walls went on undiminished as the day passed. But worse than that was the assault of the spirit. Great waves of darkness crashed against the wards, crashed and crashed again.

The enemy knew now whom he faced. Sarissa could well suspect that he knew what they would try to do tonight of all nights, in the moon's dark, when the old rites were strongest. Parsifal had opposed him before without the full power of the Grail. There had been no great marriage then, for none was granted him by the gods' will. And he had not performed the great sacrifice. He came to save a king's soul, and to heal his body. The war of the Grail had come upon him in the aftermath.

Roland had come for the war. If the enemy could be destroyed, then Roland was the one meant to destroy him. And if not—who knew who would remember any of them, after a thousand years of darkness?

She had waited so long, labored so relentlessly, to come to this day and night. All her life had been bent for this one thing.

And yet she felt as if it had taken her by surprise. Surely it was not time yet. Surely the next new moon, or the one after that, would be soon enough. Could they not hold off the siege? Were they not strong enough for that?

They were not. The mortal troops had drawn inward toward the citadel and to the center of the halls beneath it. The outer reaches and the curtain wall were crawling with shadows.

Some of Huon's mages would have ventured out to try to drive back the horrors, but Roland forbade it. "We'll only waste your strength," he said. He set them instead to warding the castle's heart.

That was no safe charge. One was down already, not dead but near to it. The enemy had bent all his terrible will on halting what Roland had set in train.

Servants carried the fallen mage up to the Grail's tower. The rest closed ranks as they could, cast their spells and chanted their chants and raised the powers. Their throats were raw and their power stretched perilously thin, but they held their ground.

Once again, grey day wore toward a starless night. On the edge of dark, the western horizon caught fire. It looked like a river of blood.

All of Huon's mages joined forces about the citadel. The dark battered it and them. Black wings swooped overhead. Teeth, claws, raked at them.

It was quiet within, but for the song of the Grail, sweet and undaunted. The brotherhood of the Grail gathered with the nine ladies in the hall of the shrine. All but Sarissa, who had gone down to the ladies' pool for the cleansing of

water and air, earth and fire. No mortal hands assisted her.
Spirits of the elements granted her their blessing.

She was aware in her skin that Roland, in the knights'
bath, underwent the same. He had faithful servants to wait
on him: the bogle for earth, the *puca* for air. The gestures
were the same, the blessings, the caress of wind, the brief
searing of fire. The doubled cleansing bound them, though
in body they were separated.

They would come together soon. She rose up out of the
water, clean to the very bone. She lifted her arms. A robe
of white silk fell about her, slipping down over her arms
and her face, her shoulders, her breasts and belly, the
length of her thighs. Its caress made her think of him—of
his hands on her body, his kisses, the warmth of his skin.

Soon.

Was he thinking the same? He too would be clad in
white, his hair combed but not plaited, his brow and breast
and hands anointed with blessed oils.

The chanting had begun, with the song of the Grail its
descant: deep voices of men, high sweet voices of women.
It resonated in the stones of the walls. It thrummed underfoot. It carried Sarissa out of the bath, down the long passage, up the stair.

Roland had gone ahead of her. She saw the light of his
passing, scented the oils that were on him: myrrh and
frankincense, sandalwood and bitter aloes.

Far away she heard the howling of the dark, a crashing
like waves, a growling and cracking as if the earth itself
groaned beneath the assault. But here was pure music,
pure light.

She climbed the stair. The antechamber was empty, the
inner door open. Pale light poured out of it.

They were all within: knights of the Grail round the rim,
ladies round the altar. The king lay before it, silent and still.
He wore the monk's robe that was all he had suffered himself to be covered in through the long siege of his dying;
but they had laid over it a cloth of white samite, shot with
a shimmer of silver threads. All light in the room seemed
to gather there, casting a pale glow on his face. The crown
of Montsalvat lay on his breast: a simple circlet of silver, set
with white stones.

Roland lay on his face in front of the altar and the king.

His feet were bare. His robe was as plain as Sarissa's, all stainless white. His hair was striking against it: blue-black, like the living night before evil came to taint it.

This part of the rite was his. Sarissa slipped in among the ladies of the Grail, opened her heart and her throat and mingled her voice with theirs. It completed the cleansing; it emptied her utterly, till she was but a reed in the wind of the gods.

CHAPTER 59

❈ ❈ ❈

Her voice made the music whole. Roland, lying on the stone, damp and chilled from the cleansing, felt her presence like a waft of warmth.

The chanting drew him to his knees, and then to his feet. Parsifal lay in the stillness of death, but the soul dwelt in the body even yet. It burned brighter, the closer it came to death.

The women's voices faded in the silence. The men's chanting deepened and slowed. The youngest of the brotherhood came forward with Durandal in his hands. He walked as one well accustomed to the stateliness of processional—as well he should, who had been archbishop of Rheims.

Turpin's face was grave, but his eyes smiled. He knelt in front of Roland and held up the sword on his two palms.

Roland bowed and took the sword; but once he had it, he drew Turpin to his feet, embraced him, kissed him on both cheeks. There was great comfort in that solid body, that friendship which needed no words; which simply was.

Turpin withdrew. The chanting swelled. Roland stood alone, sword in hand, before the dying body of the king. A hundred men, nine women, a bogle and a *puca* and spirits innumerable, stood about him. And yet he had never been more solitary than he was now.

Only he could do this. Only he could strike the blow.

Sarissa left the ranks of the enchantresses. She stood near but not beside him. Turpin was beyond her. Others— Huon, Nieve, Morgan, Longinus, Tarik and Marric— poured out what strength and solace they had.

It would never be enough. He alone sufficed for that.

Now, said Parsifal's spirit, a voice so clear, so strong, and yet so remote that it seemed as inhuman as the voice of the Grail itself. *Now is the time. Strike!*

Roland's fingers tightened round the hilt of the sword. It was alive in his hands, eager, thirsting for blood. Royal blood. Blood of sacrifice.

Ego te absolvo. Turpin's voice, soft, for his ears alone.

With a sound like a sob, lost in the roll of men's voices, Roland lifted Durandal. The sword shimmered in the light of the Grail. He held it high, poised over the still breast, till his arms trembled with the effort.

He let it fall of its own deadly weight. It pierced the thin skin over the brittle bone, and sank deep in the heart.

Glory—glory and lightnings. Joy as keen as the sword, as high and white and singing as the Grail's own light. Power upon power upon power, a great surge and throb like the sea. It roared through him. It rent his flesh asunder and severed his spirit; then it knit them together again, all new, all clean, all splendid.

He had thought he knew what magic was. This was the highest of high magic, power beyond his dreaming. He had never even dared to imagine it.

He was too small. His body was too frail, his spirit too feeble. He could not hold it. He was not strong enough.

Hands closed over his hands upon Durandal's hilt. Sarissa gasped as the power struck her. Her head snapped back, her body arched like a bow.

They were one. They had been two—separate, sundered. No longer. Two souls far greater together than apart. Two powers, two magics, bound into one high and singing glory.

The magic hummed and sang between them. There was a rhythm to it, a balance. Like walking a knife-edge of stone, or riding a new-broken stallion, or wielding a sword. If they faltered, they would fall. But if they held fast, little by little they would grow steadier, until they sustained the power with ease and grace.

Together. One could not hold it. It must be two—they

two, who had been meant for one another from the beginning of the world.

They had always known it. They had not known that they knew—no, not even she, who had thought herself so wise. Her eyes on him were rueful, and touched with laughter.

He laughed aloud, startling the chant from its rhythm, rippling in sudden silence. She was laughing with him. And Parsifal—great angel of light unfurling from the withered husk, spreading wings as wide as the sky. Angel of laughter, angel of joy. He gave them all the strength that mortal bodies could hold, and gladness too, before heaven took him to itself.

Roland sank to his knees. No one spoke, no one seemed to breathe. Durandal stood upright in an empty bier. Not even dust remained. Only the shroud of white samite, and the crown resting on it, glimmering in the grey light of dawn.

Roland lifted the crown in hands that, for a miracle, held steady. It was cool and not particularly heavy. The stones glowed softly, like the moonstone in Durandal's pommel.

He set it on his head. It was hardly more confining than a fillet. It held his hair out of his eyes, which was useful. It fit well.

He rose, turned. They were all kneeling, all the knights and the ladies. Even Sarissa, but her eyes were lifted as the others' were not, and they were bold. They smiled at him.

He smiled in return. He had never thought to feel such rightness, or such peace. Even knowing what waited beyond the faltering wards—the war, the enemy, the threat of death and darkness—it did not matter. Nothing mattered here but that it was done. He had taken the place that was meant for him. He was the Grail's champion, its guardian and its king.

CHAPTER 60

✠ ✠ ✠

Turpin sang high Mass in the shrine of the Grail: Mass
of resurrection for the king who was dead, and coro-
nation Mass for the king who lived. And wedding Mass,
too, royal marriage, king and queen hand in hand before
the altar.

It was deeply familiar, and yet strange, as dreams could
be. His concelebrant was the enchantress Nieve, who sang
her responses not to God the Father but to the Mother of
the world. And when it came time to open the shrine, to
consecrate the cup, not his hands brought it forth, but the
hands of the king.

Roland lifted the Grail before them all. Roland passed it
round so that they all might drink. He too was a priest. He
was consecrated above any of them, bound to the Grail
more surely and more completely.

He had the look of one who had come into his own. He
was higher, brighter, stronger than he had ever been before, but he was still Roland.

In the embrace and kiss of peace, he held Turpin close.
"My brother," he said.

Turpin would have wept if he had had time to waste in
it. He had lost enough. He did not think he could have
borne to have lost that friendship, too, or that bond of
brothers.

The rite ended with the sunrise—too soon, and yet it

seemed a long age since that bloodstained sunset. The brotherhood parted to perform their duties. Turpin's was both weighty and pressing. Yet he paused.

Roland had claimed Durandal from the bier. The nine ladies stood in a circle about him. They were advancing on him with clear intent: each held a garment or a part of his armor.

This was not the armor he had been wearing since he came back to Carbonek. This was royal panoply: shining silver mail, great crimson cloak lined with swansdown, belt and baldric of silver and crimson, high helm in the shape of a swan.

"I can't wear that!" he snapped as the ladies closed in on him. "I need armor I can fight in."

"This is the king's armor," said one of the ladies. It was not either Sarissa or the warrior Morgan. They, Turpin noticed, were standing back. Sarissa held a length of linen—undergarments, Turpin guessed. Morgan was unfolding a tunic of padded leather, much more practical than the armor, and much less elaborate, too.

"I do not need parade armor," Roland said through gritted teeth. "Fetch me battle armor—something other than that—that—" Words failed him, but his glare at the swanhelm was eloquent.

The ladies looked ready to expostulate with him over what was proper for a king, but Morgan's voice cut across them like the slash of a sword. "Do as he says. He can be pretty later. Today, he needs to be safe."

The others muttered and scowled, but they bowed to the inevitable. By the time Turpin left, they had his robe off him—to his manifest dismay, but he had no defenders there—and were clothing and arming him in much less extravagant fashion.

Turpin took the stair as fast as he dared. The morning was fleeing. The bombardment had begun yet again. The enemy must have managed to fashion a ram that would extend across the chasm: the deep boom rocked him as he ran, and nearly flung him down the last of the stair.

He hoped that the ram spanned the chasm, and that they had not built a bridge in the night. If that defense was breached, the gate would not hold for long.

Troops were mustering in the great courts before the

gate. They were all men of Caer Sidi or of Carbonek. The Franks, with Roland's recruits, were still below.

They were just finishing as he came down among them, forming ranks, praying if that was their inclination, or standing together in circles of brothers. They all had their orders. They were ready; he could feel the strength of them, the spirit that had withstood the dark, and now would go to battle with it.

They only needed his blessing. He gave it to them from the Grail's own light, from its living presence.

The drums beat, summoning them to the march. Turpin took his place in the van with Lord Huon's green-cloaked guards and Roland's bright-eyed recruits. The Franks took up the rear as they had done in another time, for another king.

They marched through the deep places, down beneath the heart of Carbonek. People of the castle guided them. Mages protected them, casting spells of light and guard.

It seemed that it was true, what Roland and the commanders had hoped: that the tunnels were free of the enemy's shadow-armies. Sleepers in the earth there were none, not beneath Carbonek. Farther out, where they must go, that might not be so; but the Lady Nieve thought that the dragons and blindworms and their kin had drawn away toward the enemy. These passages should be open.

They could only march and pray. For men of the open sky, this was a peculiar horror. They tramped through whispering galleries, down long winding passages, up and into caverns wider than the mages' light would reach. Bats chittered high above them—or things that sounded like bats.

They were inured to creepers in shadows. That much the enemy's assault had done for them. Some tried to sing, but the echoes were too strange; it dizzied them and threatened to send them staggering down side passages. They marched in silence but for the thudding of feet and the hissing of breath.

Those breaths reckoned the passing of time. Without sun or moon to guide them, they could not know otherwise how long they journeyed under the earth. For all any of them knew, their guides were treacherous and would lead them deeper and deeper into the maze, till they could never be found again.

That was a dark thought, perhaps born of darkness. Turpin thrust it away.

It seemed gradually that the passages, which had been level or descending, began to slant upward. There was almost a sense in the still air of something moving—something alive.

His spine prickled. If there was a creature of the night ahead of them, they would have to fight their way past it. And quickly, for time was pressing.

They met nothing and no one. The air was fresher, with less of the cold scent of earth, and more of the clean sky. They came up—truly up—through a cavern like the great hall of a castle, and down a broad passage, and so out into clouded but still unmistakable daylight.

Then at last they met the guardian, there at the gate of the outer world. It rose up out of the earth, a vast shape of stone, reaching with stony hands, trampling with stony feet. It was blind with the light, but its ears were deathly keen: where it heard breath, it struck.

Lord Huon's knights, dismounted but armed with their long lances, charged against the stone giant, a hundred strong. The great thing thrashed and flailed. The rest of the army ran as fast as it could run, charging out of the cavern and down the fair green valley.

The ground heaved as they ran. The stones melted and flowed, groping like hands. People fell. The earth gaped to swallow them. Stones rose up to crush them.

Turpin halted in desperation, balancing like a sailor on a strong sea. From the heart of him, where the light of the Grail was, he spoke words that came unbidden. "Peace!" he cried. "Be still."

And the earth was still. The stone giant sank and crumbled into the earth, taking the dead with it. Far too many of Huon's knights had fallen. Those who yet lived formed in ranks again, limping but strong of will. They bowed as they passed Turpin.

He crossed himself and murmured a prayer. The earth was still under his feet. He strode in the army's wake, hand to sword hilt, back prickling. But the valley was quiet behind him.

*   *   *

As long as the march and the battle had seemed, the day had not yet passed noon. Nor were they so very far from Carbonek. As they went they heard the hollow boom of the ram, and the clatter and crash of the engines hurling their missiles. Something odd, that Turpin had not realized before, struck him then. Armies were noisy things unless they were trying to march in silence. They made a great deal of noise in sieges, what with men speaking to one another, commanders calling orders, crews on the engines cheering their missiles on their way.

Ganelon's army made no sound. His soldiers were quick on their feet and deft with their engines, but they did not speak or laugh, still less urge one another on or taunt the enemy within the walls.

"They're slaves," Gemma said when Turpin spoke his thought aloud. She and her sons and the chiefs of Roland's recruits had managed to speed their march till they were level with Turpin. He was, by then, wishing rather devoutly for a horse. There had been no way to bring any through those deep passages. He was a footsoldier, then, and not a happy one.

But Ganelon's troops must be less happy still. "We remember the story from before," Kyllan said. "He makes pacts with demons and minor princes of hell, and they serve him. And he makes men his slaves."

"Then," said Turpin, "there may be hope for them—and for us. If they can be freed—if they can be persuaded to turn, and fight with us—"

"Can we even do that?" the boy asked.

"We might," said Turpin, "if we move fast enough. And if we can spare a mage or two."

"It might not take a mage," Gemma said. "You can't see yourself. You're like a lamp in a dark room. Most of the men out there, they're Franks, yes? Or people who know the Franks. I'll wager they know you."

Turpin stumbled with the shock of sudden hope. But he could do nothing now. His orders were clear. To take this force of veterans and recruits, Franks and people of Montsalvat. To fall on the enemy from behind, while a sortie rode out from the castle in front of them. To fight as best he could, as they all could, so that Roland could do what he had been brought here to do.

It was a mad, a hopeless charge, but then what could be sweeter? He had taken it because he had died once already, and he had seen the Grail. He could give up his life without either fear or hesitation.

He pressed forward, not too fast for they all must hoard their strength, but not too slowly either. The closer they came, the more they risked discovery. The mages had tightened the wards over them, but those would not hold within reach of the enemy's own wards.

They only needed to buy a little time. They had come to the place that the guides had told them of: a long ridge that overlooked the army's camp. The ranks spread along it, keeping low, but few of them could forbear to peer over the summit. The enemy swarmed below. The engines hammered walls and gate.

High on the walls, bright helmets gleamed. Shadows crawled beneath them. Those were stronger, clearer now than they had been before. They had shape and substance: teeth, claws, weapons that looked solid enough to cleave flesh and bone.

On the topmost tower, a mirror flashed once, twice, thrice.

That was the signal. Turpin nodded to the troops on either side of him. He snatched the spear that Kyllan was carrying, which had a pennon on it, blue and silver for the king of the Grail. Turpin raised it high, so that they all could see, then swept it fiercely down.

With a cry like nothing earthly, the king's own army broke the crest of the hill and charged down upon the rear of the enemy's camp. In the same instant a horn rang, echoing in the keep. The great gate rose with sorcerous swiftness. The bridge came crashing down. Huon led the sortie from the castle, mounted on his tall white stallion, leaping through the gate, charging across the chasm. His lords and princes followed him, and the swift ranks of his foot.

The enemy received them with a low and ravenous growl. The trap, that growl said, was sprung. The battle was engaged. And he had numbers far, far more than they could begin to claim.

Men who had hidden under the shields of the siege-engines burst forth and bolted for the bridge. The gate strained against chains that had grown suddenly rigid. The bridge would not lift. Some great force held it, some vast weight of darkness.

Already the enemy had a foothold within, in his armies of shadows. Mages fought against them, but they were numerous beyond counting. They gathered together like water flowing through many rivers into a black sea.

Slaves the enemy's men might be, but they fought with relentless ferocity. They cared nothing for fear or pain. They had no care for their lives. And those that were not men, that wore human faces but shifted and changed as they fought, wielded weapons of terror as well as of steel.

Turpin drove his troops against them in waves, three ranks divided, so that some could rest and some could bolster the others. They only had to hold for a while, to drive as far forward as they might, to harry the enemy's rear and, if it were possible, to seize his camp. Just so was Huon to press past the siege-engines and engage the foremost ranks.

It was desperate—insane. So was this battle without general or leader to be seen.

Until—

At last, where Huon was, came a familiar sound: a whoop, a roar, a battle cry that stopped Turpin's heart in his breast. *"Montjoie! Montjoie!"*

The battle cry of Charles of Francia, in almost his very voice: high, fierce, pitched to carry. Pepin the prince led a horde of mounted Franks against the knights of Caer Sidi.

Turpin could have howled like a dog. To be there, and not here. To be where he could do something—rise up, wield his rank and name, wake these men of his own nation to the perfidy of what they did.

But he was a warrior, seasoned in battle. He had orders. His sanity and his salvation bade him follow them. Lead his troops—Roland's troops. Fight. Drive for the camp, where surely, for he could be nowhere else, the enemy was laired.

He could fight, even against demons, though blood ran underfoot—truly? Illusion only? No matter. Hack and drive and hack again. Pray the blow, once struck, smote the enemy down; that he did not rise again a winged horror, shrieking, clawing for Turpin's throat.

And all the while he fought for his life, as commander he must be aware of everything his people did. Who fought well; who failed. Who fell, and who died.

Gemma and her sons were close behind him. Kyllan's spear spitted a taloned thing even as it fell upon him. Cait's archers behind sent a rain of arrows down on the enemy.

They were making slow headway. Maybe they were being allowed to do it. The camp, toward which they fought, seemed more and more a trap.

Huon he could no longer see. He was too far in among the enemy. But still he heard that high voice shrilling the battle-cry of the Frankish king. It was pure mockery, and pure provocation. Turpin's Franks were snarling at it. It made them reckless. They pushed too hard, fought too heedlessly. Too many of them were going down.

"*Hold!*" Turpin roared. "Fall in! Fall together! Fight, you sons of whores! Shut your ears and fight!"

And then, like a madman, or a man whose madness had driven him sane: "*Montjoie!* For God and Saint Denis, and the holy land of Francia! *Montjoie!*"

CHAPTER 61

✠ ✠ ✠

That great voice rolled across the battlefield. Pepin, leading the charge against the faery knights—every damnable one of them as like to Roland as a brother—faltered and nearly lost his head to the sweep of a sword. Only a wild scramble saved him.

Turpin, too? And Olivier?

No; Olivier was dead. He knew it in his heart, where his magic was.

At least one of the three was gone. By tomorrow's dawn, so would the other two be. That, Ganelon had sworn in the name of his dark master.

And if Turpin was out there—come on them from some hidden bolthole—then where was Roland? He was not leading this sortie. That commander was a strange one indeed, a tall man crowned with the antlers of a stag. Demons wailed and fled where he passed. Pepin's Franks were bolder, but they were hard pressed to hold the line against him.

Not that it mattered. They had opened the castle; that was what the master had wanted.

The summons when it came was long expected. *Back to me, princeling. Now.*

Pepin left the field to his Franks. They fought bravely, laughing as they slew. He drew a mantle of shadows about himself and went where he was summoned.

* * *

Ganelon sat like a spider in the heart of its web. The tent was that one which he had brought from Francia, small on the outside, vaster than worlds within.

Pepin entered the garden slowly. The supernal light was dim. The paths were closed, all but one, that which looked on the castle of Carbonek. It was a strange vision, a fortress of stone crumbling under the attacks of stones and shadows, but in the center of it, in the citadel—nothing. Where in the outer world the tower reared up to heaven, here it was more than invisible. It was deliberately and potently not there.

There were cracks in that living absence. Tendrils of darkness crawled toward it. Once Pepin thought he glimpsed a flash of sudden light.

"Is it done?" Pepin asked. "Did they perform the rite?"

Ganelon raised a brow at the insolence, but forbore to rebuke it. He sat on a throne in the garden's center. His robe was woven of shadow. His face was as immobile and as beautiful as if carved in ivory.

"Well?" said Pepin. "Did they?"

"It would seem so," Ganelon said. "The thing within has found new strength. But I am stronger. Prepare yourself now. Strengthen your spirit. The time is nearly come for you to take the Grail."

Pepin's breath shuddered as he drew it in. His hands were cold. He knotted them together to keep them from shaking. He was ready. He was. He had studied, he had honed his magic. He was strong and his power was sure. He knew the way in, and the precise count of the steps from the tower's foot to its summit, and the shape and the heft of the door that led to the shrine.

"The king is dead," Ganelon said. "They will have raised a successor—but he will be new and weak, and not yet accustomed to his power. Now is the time to strike."

"And the battle?"

Ganelon shrugged with regal indifference. "It keeps the mortals occupied. Your battle is elsewhere."

"I'm ready," Pepin said—whether he was or not, because there was nothing else that he could safely say. "This successor—is it—"

"Very probably it is the Breton," said Ganelon.

Pepin's grin was wide, feral, and altogether unfeigned.

"You may kill him," Ganelon said as if it did not matter, "once you reach the shrine. Only be sure you do it thoroughly. These Grail-kings are more dangerous dying than alive and hale."

"I will kill him thoroughly," Pepin promised. Oh, very thoroughly indeed.

This he must do alone. Ganelon could not approach the Grail as Pepin, mortal and royal, could do. Nor would he lower himself to enter the castle until it was his.

The path from the garden that had stopped at the chasm only yesterday, now led across that narrow bridge over the abyss and into the great court of the keep. Men and shadows fought there. Men were down, dead or dying, and women too. Many bore the marks of shadow-sickness: faces pale, eyes wide and fixed on emptiness.

Pepin, mantled again in shadows, smiled as he picked his way through the living and the dead. The outer courts were as nearly won as made no matter. The faery knights, the renegade Franks, would find no refuge when they turned to retreat.

Carbonek was a maze, Ganelon had taught him, but there was a pattern to it. If one came to a division of passages, one turned sunwise. It could be difficult within walls of stone to know where the sun was, but Pepin had prepared for that. About his neck he wore an iron nail that he taken from a smith's forge. He had laid a spell on it. When he stopped or paused in confusion, he lifted it in his palm. It turned, showing him the way.

Beyond the outer courts, he met no one. Had they emptied the castle, then, to muster that poor excuse for an army?

Truly it would seem so. Even the women were fighting, dressed in armor, wielding weapons. No one was defending the inner halls or the turns of the maze.

Like Ganelon's tent, this castle was far larger within than without. When it was his, he would learn all its wonders. But now he must take as straight a path as he could. He did not pause to marvel at halls of crystal, halls of glittering tiles, halls of marble or porphyry; colonnades, long sweeping staircases, glimpses of gardens even more beauti-

ful than Ganelon's. He passed them all by, some with great
regret, but time was pressing.

There seemed to be no defenses, no wards or guards.
All the ways were empty. His magic met no barrier. It
must be true, then. Royal blood gained him passage.
Mortality won him welcome.

So much for the tales. This Grail must care nothing
after all for purity of heart. Unless it should be that his
was pure in its purpose? Maybe it did not matter to the
Grail if that purpose was dark or light.

If it was a trap, it was subtly laid. He was not afraid of it.
He had learned magic from an older power by far than the
Grail.

The tower lay at the heart of the maze, the stair ascending steeply into a glimmering darkness. Night had not
fallen, his bones knew it, but the slitted windows looked
out on stars.

He had left the mortal world. Had he been in it at all
since he stood in Ganelon's tent?

He stumbled and fell on the first step, gasping, head
whirling. All that had anchored him, all that he had been
sure of, was gone. He was cast adrift, borne as if on a strong
tide. His mantle of shadows shredded and scattered. He
was naked to the cold eye of heaven.

The stones beneath him beat like a great slow heart. The
air thrummed. The Grail—it was calling. The power—the
sheer strength of it—

He was not afraid. He must not be afraid. The Grail
would not blast him. He was royal. He was chosen. He was
meant for this.

He pulled himself painfully to his feet and crawled up the
stair. There seemed to be no end to it. With each step he retreated farther from the breast of the earth his mother. The
air grew chill and thin, as if he ascended a mountaintop. His
head ached. His limbs were heavy.

He pressed on. Terrible this might be, but Ganelon was
more terrible still. And he wanted the Grail. Ah, God, how
he wanted it.

That wanting sharpened Pepin's purpose. If this was
truly so great a thing of power, he wanted part of it. Maybe
even the whole, if he could win it. Ganelon could not touch

it. Pepin could. And if Pepin held it—who knew what he might be able to do?

As he advanced, he began to hear a sound like singing. Chanting, like sweet voices in a choir. Angels, he thought from the depths of his darkness. He could not understand their words. They sang in none of the tongues Ganelon had taught him, nor in Latin either. Their song was piercingly sweet. It nigh felled him with sudden weeping.

That too was a trap. He clapped hands to his ears. That muffled the singing somewhat, and let him go on.

The stair's end took him by surprise. The door was shut. He set hand to it: it was barred from within.

That too he had prepared for. He spoke the words Ganelon had taught him. The door resisted. He spoke the words again. And yet again: three times for greatest power.

The bolt shattered. The door fell inward. He looked in upon—

Ganelon's garden. But Ganelon was not in it. *She* was. She stood like the angel at the gate of Paradise, clad all in white, and in her hand—a spear?

Not a flaming sword. A heavy, common spear, such as a footsoldier would carry. Its blade was rusted or stained with ancient blood. It had no beauty, no elegance.

But power—before God, it was throbbing with power.

Pepin tasted blood. He had bitten through his tongue. This must be—this could not but be—

That was the meaning of her name. Sarissa—spear. She held the spear that had pierced the side of Christ, that, like the Grail, had drunk the blood of a god. That spear, Ganelon had captured once, and held, and wielded against the heir of the Grail. But Parsifal had won it back. With it he had cast down Ganelon's power and nigh destroyed him.

Parsifal was dead. Ganelon did not want the spear, nor had he sent Pepin to seize it. He wanted the great prize, the prize he should have taken at the first.

The spear barred the way. She wore armor under her white robe: he saw the glint of mail. Her hands were slender but strong. Her face was stern. He could not touch her at all with his magic.

He had no spells for this. Those that came to him were silly, trivial, useless. To curse an iron blade with rust; to draw blood from a stone. To shatter a pot, or to curdle the milk in it.

The blade of that spear would never yield to anything so simple as a dark spell. And if he shattered the Grail, he would know the power of Ganelon's wrath.

He could think of nothing better than to say, plainly enough, "Let me pass."

She stepped aside. She did not resist, nor did she cry outrage. She simply ceased to bar his way.

He had to pass her if he would go on. His back prickled. He flung up wards, as many and as strong as he might.

She made no move to strike him. She followed him, but not close enough to touch.

Again he met a door. This one opened before he could lay hand or spell on it.

This was the chamber of the Grail. He had no doubt of that. Ganelon had had no knowledge to give him, nothing but that it was a high tower, an altar, and a shrine.

So indeed it was. There was no ornament in that room, except the shrine itself. There was no richness apart from that. The only light was the light of heaven. It was too simple. It was almost ugly.

Roland stood in front of the shrine. He wore mail, of good quality but plain. The sword Durandal was at his side. He had a round horseman's shield slung on his back, and a plain helmet.

The helmet was circled with a crown—silver, set with white stones. He was as arrogant as ever. He looked down his long curved nose at Pepin. His yellow eyes were as sharp as a hawk's, and as empty of human warmth. If there was any expression in them, that expression was pity. Not even scorn, not even contempt. He *pitied* Pepin.

Pepin went a little mad, maybe. When he came to himself, he was sprawled on the floor, and there was a scent of brimstone about him. He felt oddly empty, like a ballista that had hurled its missile.

Roland was neither dead nor wounded. As far as Pepin's dazzled eyes could see, he was not touched at all. He stooped over Pepin.

Pepin surged up. His hands clamped on that cursed

throat. They were strong hands, big hands, for though his back was twisted, he was not a small man. Bigger than this one, for a surety. And he hated him with a perfect hate.

They toppled before the altar, grappling without either elegance or grace. Roland made no move to smite Pepin, only to free himself. But Pepin would never let go. No, never, until this hated creature was dead.

A force like a whirlwind swept him up and flung him reeling away. He rolled and tumbled and struck a wall with force enough to strike the breath from his lungs.

He lay wheezing. Sarissa stood between him and his quarry. The point of the spear hovered above his throat.

Roland rose behind her. His own throat was blackening already. His voice was hoarse. "No, beloved. Don't kill him."

Sarissa heard that with no pleasure at all, but she lowered the spear—from Pepin's throat to his privates. His hands clapped over them.

Her smile was feral. "What, you don't yearn to emulate your master?"

Pepin gaped.

She laughed. "You didn't know? He's a eunuch, child. He gelded himself long ago, to buy himself a scrap of power. Maybe he thought it was worth the price."

"Sarissa."

Roland's voice was recovering. The sound of her name silenced her. But it did not scour the smile from her face. She was even more arrogant than Roland, and even more hateful. But oh, so beautiful.

When Pepin had the Grail, she would belong to him.

His mind was clearing. His magic was there after all, the whole deep realm of it, dark and splendid. The Grail fed it. That was the Grail's purpose: to nourish. Whether it nourished dark or light did not matter to it.

He called that power to him. All that Ganelon had taught him, all that he had studied, labored over, wrought, came together in this one moment, this one working. Before the Grail, before its raw and new-made king, he called on the great Master, the Lord of the Dark, the Prince of the Morning.

The dark came down. Ganelon rode on the wings of it.

Plots within plots, wheels within wheels, intrigue upon intrigue. Pepin was the opener of the way. Through him the master could come to this place, could approach the Grail.

He could not touch it. But he could come near it. And he could smite its fool of a king.

CHAPTER 62

❈ ❈ ❈

"Fool and heir of a fool."

Roland looked up at Ganelon. The roof of the Grail's tower had melted away. Black wings spread across the sky. A vast cold-drake hovered above him, dark beyond darkness. Its eyes were the eyes of the demon-servant Siglorel, last and strongest of the three: chill serpent-eyes that looked down on Roland with utter lack of expression.

The sorcerer rode on its great arching neck. His black robes rippled in a wind that never touched Roland. His face was the face of a dark angel.

He had taken back all that had been reft from him. But he was not above mockery, not yet.

Roland sighed faintly. Traps within traps—and how many more within those?

Roland could not tell where he ended and the Grail began. Parsifal was in him and in the sword at his side. Sarissa's warm presence wrapped them all about. Sometimes he could not tell which of them moved or spoke. They were all bound together. The power that blazed in them—in him—was a great high singing thing.

The power was ready to stand against the sorcerer. Was he?

No doubts.

Something swooped past him. Tarik blurred and stretched and grew—grew impossibly, until a dragon of light faced the dragon of darkness. The *puca* was smaller, but therefore more agile. He leaped and curvetted and danced in the air. He laughed, altogether without fear.

He plucked Roland from the floor of the hall and winged skyward.

Roland was too wise to struggle. He climbed up the clawed leg, over the great shoulder, onto the curve of the beast's neck. Wind buffeted him. He flattened against the glistening scales.

Shadow loomed over him. A bolt of raw power hissed past him. Tarik danced away from it.

Almost too late, Roland raised wards to protect them. Carbonek lay far below. Battle raged before it and within it. Ganelon's army swarmed like locusts. Roland's few fought valiantly, but they were nigh overwhelmed.

A great blow smote the wards. Tarik dropped under the force of it. His wings beat desperately, struggling to keep him aloft.

"Down," Roland said. "Back down."

Tarik ignored him. He had steadied and begun a new ascent.

Spirit of mischief indeed. Roland looked down the long, long way to the castle where he best should be.

Time was when he would have laughed at the distance, spread wings and flown. But he had lived in human shape since he came to himself again. Thought of shifting, of blurring and changing, struck cold in his belly. If he lost himself, this time he would not come back.

Tarik leaped and darted. Ganelon ceased to waste bolts of power. He sent the cold-drake after the *puca*. Tarik was agile but he was light in the air. The wind of the cold-drake's wings caught him and sent him tumbling.

Roland lost his grip on the *puca*'s neck. He clutched at nothingness. He was falling. Above him, the cold-drake roared. He turned over in the air. Tarik had fastened himself to the creature's belly, jaws sunk in its throat. The cold-drake thrashed. Roland could not see Ganelon at all.

It seemed that Roland was hanging in space, suspended on the wind's back. But the earth drew ever closer.

His skin rippled. A stab of terror stopped it. But worse than that fear was the long, long way to the ground.

His arms flexed. Wings beat where they had been. The

hawk's mind closed in upon his own. Man—he was *man*. Armor, helm, shield fell away. But the coin of the Grail swung still against his breast; and Durandal hovered in air beside him. It had a mind, a will of its own, and magic—high magic. To his keen hawk-senses, it had a scent and a taste of Parsifal.

The sword guided him, spiraling down and down. Far above, the dragons battled. *Tarik*, grieved the man's mind within the hawk's body.

No, no grief yet. No despair. The Grail was calling.

He touched the stone floor with a man's feet, and a man's mind. Durandal settled softly into his hand. Sarissa said not a word as she wrapped him in a white robe. It was nothing he could fight an earthly battle in, but it covered him.

The war of dragons raged overhead. From so far they seemed no larger than a raven locked in combat with a sparrow. They tumbled and thrashed. Wings flailed, claws raked. Teeth slashed. The cold-drake's blood was like gouts of icy water. The *puca* bled scarlet streamers of flame.

As diversion it served its purpose, in more ways than one. Roland, standing before the Grail with the wind of the gods blowing the white wool of the robe against his body, felt the power in him with far more clarity than he had before. The hawk's shape had cleansed and focused him. The long descent had given him the time he needed to gather his strength.

Maybe Tarik had meant it to be so. The *puca* had an odd wisdom, and odder ways of showing it.

It was almost peaceful here. The Grail's song went on unwearied. Sarissa stood guard over the shrine. Pepin huddled at her feet, limp, perhaps unconscious.

The blow struck the wards with a sound like lightning splitting an ancient tree. Light flashed, blinding bright.

The wards held, just. Roland's ears were ringing. When he could see more than shadows, he saw Ganelon standing on air beyond the tower, as steady as if he stood on stone.

The battle below, the battle above, went on without them. Roland met Ganelon's dark gaze, and inclined his head slightly.

They had not stood face-to-face before. That was odd, now he thought of it. No doubt it had also saved Roland's soul. If Ganelon had not underestimated him, he would have been disposed of long ago, long before he had the strength to be a threat.

Roland was strong, but his enemy was ancient and wily. Youth had served him before against the sorcerer; but he would not be so fortunate again. He had set himself full in the enemy's path, the last obstacle he must strike down before he seized the Grail.

Roland lifted Durandal and set her point down before him, hands folded over the hilt. Sarissa moved to stand beside him, spearbutt grounded likewise, braced and on guard.

The enemy smiled a faint cold smile. "So much power," he said. "So pretty to see."

"But you can't see it, can you?" Roland said as he looked into those eyes. "You can't see the Grail. For you, we stand on nothingness. You're blinded by the light."

"I need not see," Ganelon said, "in order to grasp and hold."

He flung a bolt of darkness. The wards cracked still more. Roland set his teeth. He had felt that in his own body, as if a fist had struck his shoulder. The next bolt smote him in the belly. At the third, he flung up Durandal. The bright blade turned the bolt aside. It sang like a woman, sweet and deadly.

Ganelon's next bolt flew wide.

The song, thought Roland. Durandal's song caused him pain.

Ganelon stiffened himself against it. He struck, struck, struck again, blows so swift and so potent that Roland could only parry, never strike. There was no time. Bolts that passed him, Sarissa caught and struck aside.

Under cover of that defense, he gathered everything that he had: every scrap of strength, every bit of knowledge, every flicker of power that had ever been in him or in Sarissa or in the Grail-king who had died to give him this magic. He gathered it and held it. Ganelon hammered at him, relentless.

Suddenly, completely unexpectedly, the sorcerer laughed. Behind Roland, the Grail's song changed. It was subtle, perhaps imperceptible, but he was part of it. He felt it in his blood and bone.

Pepin had the Grail. Forgotten, unregarded, he had crawled past the combatants, crept up to the shrine, opened it. The cup was in his hands.

He danced with glee. "Mine!" he sang. "Mine!"

Ganelon's smile was a cold and terrible thing. "Well done," he said, "oh, well indeed. Give it to me."

"No," said Pepin. Roland, turning in the cessation of the barrage, saw the frown on the face so like Charles'. "You can't touch it. You can't even see it."

"In your hands I can," Ganelon said. "Bring it here."

Pepin would not do that, either. "I'll keep it for you," he said. "How it sings! You didn't tell me of that. It's beautiful."

"Give it to me," the sorcerer said. His voice was lower now, darker. More dangerous.

Pepin stood with the Grail in his hands. Light poured over them, down his arms, dripping on the floor. His eyes were rapt.

The sorcerer gathered darkness as Roland had gathered light. He flung it, all of it, not at Roland but at the Frankish prince who held the Grail.

Roland flung himself between the sorcerer and his pupil. The power that was in him, the sword in his hands, rose together. That great blow struck him full on. Darkness visible. Death, dissolution, damnation of body and soul. And a hook, a talon, to grasp and seize the Grail—that lodged in his heart, where the Grail's power was strongest.

He felt the bonds of flesh dissolve. The darkness swallowed his light—as it would swallow the world, once Ganelon had the Grail.

Sarissa cried aloud. He had shielded her, as he had Pepin. They were safe. If they fled, and fled now, beyond the world there might be refuge.

He tried to tell her. He had no throat, no tongue, no voice to speak the words. He was a mist of light fading in a tide of the dark.

The spear rose, blazing in the endless night. Durandal rose with it. Together they struck. Straight for the heart. Straight through the darkness.

Ganelon laughed at them. Without Roland they were feeble, helpless. Roland had been the key. And Roland was gone.

No.

In the beginning was the word. In the word was being. In being was substance. And in substance was strength. Roland the shapeshifter, who knew dissolution with each change of his form, reached for that part of himself which made him whole again. Wolf to stag. Stag to hawk. Hawk— all anew, and always—to man.

Naked, weaponless, but brimming, singing, bursting with power, he turned—not on Ganelon, but on Pepin. Pepin clutched the Grail to his breast. Roland held out his hand. The Grail came to him as it had come before the army of its defenders, as soft, as sweet as a child to its mother. It settled in his lifted hands.

Black winds lashed him. Lightnings smote him. He took no notice of them. He walked through them, past the shards of the wards, into the tumult of the air.

Ganelon hovered in the midst of the whirlwind. Roland entered into that zone of quiet. He held out the Grail. "Take," he said, "and drink. For this is the cup of the blood, the blood of the covenant, which binds the chains of the world."

The whirlwind died. The blasts of darkness ceased. They stood face-to-face above the wide and turning world. Roland, who had died and been brought to life by the Grail's power, faced Ganelon, who had so feared death that he sold his soul to the Prince of Darkness, and thus bought his body's immortality.

"Drink," Roland said again. "Drink of the light, and of salvation. Taste the blood of redemption."

"Mockery." Ganelon's voice was thick. "What trap is this?"

"No trap," Roland said. "Drink."

"I will not," said Ganelon. "I will take. I will not drink."

"You must drink," said Roland, "for your soul's sake."

Ganelon hammered him anew with darkness. He raised the Grail against it. The darkness struck with a sound like the rending of worlds. He rocked with the force of it.

It turned. It struck back with the full might of its maker's malice. Ganelon, advancing to take the Grail from Roland's fingers, met it head-on. It smote him down.

CHAPTER 63

Ganelon fell through the sudden stillness of the air. Roland fell with him. The power in its turning had emptied him. He would spread no wings now. That was gone. He reeled down, clutching the Grail to his breast.

Somewhat before he had expected, he struck solidity. Struck, and lived. Warmth surged under him. Tarik in dragon-shape skimmed perilously close to the earth, above the heads of men locked in battle, not quite brushing the tips of spears. With a fierce beat of wings, he climbed upward.

He had something in his claws. A rag, a tatter of darkness. Ganelon's body.

Roland was scarcely more alive than that, but he was conscious. The Grail was a hard, almost painful shape between his breast and the *puca*'s neck. He pressed his face to those beaded scales with their faint scent of fire, and clung blindly.

Tarik brought him home—if home was the castle of Carbonek and the tower of the Grail. The roof was restored, if indeed it had ever been gone. The *puca* settled there, eased him to the stones, then lay for a long while, wings and limbs splayed. He was covered in wounds, bleeding, battered, torn; but he was alive. The Grail had already begun to heal him.

Roland found that he could stand, though he reeled dizzily. He was still clutching the Grail.

Ganelon lay between the *puca*'s forefeet. He looked like a broken stick, and yet he breathed.

Roland dropped beside him, catching his breath at the pain of bruised knees. The dark eyes opened. There was no yielding in them at all. No light; no spark of redemption.

Because he was what he was—because he was the champion of the Grail—Roland could do no other than what he did. He held out the cup once more. "Drink," he said yet again, "and be healed."

"Fool," said the sorcerer, hardly more than a breath of sound.

Roland held the cup to his lips.

He turned his face away. "No healing," he whispered. "Power. Only power. If I cannot have that, I will have nothing."

"You will have damnation," Roland said.

Ganelon's eyes glittered. "Yes," he breathed. "Yes."

"You want it? When you could have the light and the glory of heaven?"

"Light." The sorcerer spat. "Weakness. Folly. In dark is the glory. In damnation is the splendor. I choose that. I—choose—"

He reached up, hands clawed. They caught the plait of Roland's hair as it fell over his shoulder. They dragged him down. His breath hissed in Roland's face. It was cold, like old stone, and rank, like the breath of tombs. "I—choose—the dark."

It opened beneath them, darker than night, colder than the deepest of winter, and no end to it ever. His grip tightened on Roland's hair. He dragged them both to the edge of the abyss. They would both fall—they, and the Grail, and all the world's light.

Victory in the jaws of defeat. Black triumph at the end of things. Ganelon exulted. He would have the Grail, and the Grail-king too, and a thousand years of night.

Roland could not even shape his refusal. There was no strength in him, no magic. Only desperation. He flung himself back, wrenching, twisting, rolling up against Tarik's bloodstained side.

Ganelon teetered for an endless moment on the darkness' edge. He would hold—he would escape. And Roland would die, because he had nothing left with which to stand against the sorcerer.

The tower swayed. The darkness heaved. Ganelon fell.

He fell forever and ever. No sound escaped him, no scream, no cry of horror. He embraced the darkness. The darkness took him.

Silence. Even the Grail had gone still. The maw of the abyss had closed. Roland stood naked on a windy tower, under a sky swept clean of clouds. The sun was still high. It barely warmed him.

And yet he was warm to the bone. A great dark thing had gone out of the world.

On the field below, the battle had fallen into confusion. Demons and spirits of the night, freed of the bonds that had held them, had turned on the mortals about them. Those mortal slaves, slaves no longer, fought for their lives against their own allies.

The army of Montsalvat found itself somewhat less overmatched than it had been only moments before. Within the walls and the keep, the shadow-army had melted away. There were no living enemies there. The castle was clean. Only one hostile presence remained, and that was Pepin, held prisoner in the chamber of the Grail.

All this Roland knew in one sweep of eye and mind. The Grail had begun again to sing. The higher, the clearer its song, the stronger he was.

Tarik stirred, lifted his fanged dragon-head, folded his shining wings. His wounds were all but healed. He yawned vastly. A curl of smoke drifted heavenward.

Roland armored himself in light, for lack of more earthly expedients. It lay on him like the sheerest of silk, but strong as steel. He found Durandal between Tarik's feet, where Ganelon had lain not so long ago. She slid joyfully into the scabbard that Roland fashioned of air and sunlight.

"Dear friend," Roland said to the *puca*. "Will you carry me once more?"

"Once and always," Tarik said in a voice like a great organ.

Roland mounted his neck. There were scars, but they were fading fast. He stroked the deepest of them. "The snake?" he asked.

"Gone," Tarik said in enormous satisfaction. His jaws clashed. He spread his wings, ran for the tower's edge, dropped with throat-catching speed. The wind caught him and carried him up and up, soaring in a long sweep over the field of the battle.

The fighting slowed and stopped. Men stared open-mouthed. Demons paused in their feasting. Durandal swept the head from one, pierced the throat of the next. The third yowled and fled, and its kinsfolk and companions with it.

Tarik hovered above the field. Men cowered and scattered beneath. Roland could see himself in their eyes: great dragon of light, and warrior armored in light, holding up the shining splendor of the Grail.

"Peace," he bade them all, soft yet clear. "Be still."

They were still. His own people, the Franks, his villagers, gazed up at him in wonder and in clear delight. He smiled at them. His smile warmed most on Turpin, and on the children from Greenwood. They were together, and alive, though Kyllan was limping and Turpin's helmet was lost, his face streaked with blood.

"Gather the armies," he said to them. "See to the wounded and the dead. Offer clemency to any who will surrender. If any refuses—do as you judge best."

Turpin nodded for them all. "As you will," he said, "my lord king."

Roland's head shook at that; his hand rose to brush away the title. But Turpin was smiling as he said it, a smile that widened to a grin. They were all grinning. He had won— they had won. The war was ended. The enemy was dead.

CHAPTER 64

✠ ✠ ✠

Roland put aside his splendor, retrieved his old plain clothes and Durandal's worn scabbard, and set to work among the vanquished and the wounded. Tarik, likewise restored to his everyday seeming, came and went in cat-shape. He was useful for soothing the frightened and calming the enraged.

It was a long labor. Roland left command to the commanders, to Turpin and Huon and Morgan and the rest. His place was to heal what he could heal, and to bring comfort where he might. He did it quietly, without pretension. Few of those he tended knew who he was, nor did he trouble to tell them. It did not matter.

They were all talking of the Grail-king, the new, the splendid, the shining lord of light. The enemy's slaves, now freed, were more enraptured than not. Roland with his plain clothes and his quiet manner, they noticed only as they would have noticed any other healer. They never guessed that he was the king they spoke of.

That was exactly as he would have it. He labored untroubled by awe or by the exigencies of princes. He could see clearly how many of the wounded there were, and reckon the count of the dead. There were far too many of both. Full half the Franks of Charles' rearguard were dead or nearly so. Of the villagers, two in three would not come home again. The enemy for their part had suffered losses as great, and too many of those to their own demonic allies after Ganelon was slain.

It was very late when he came to the camp that his villagers had made, in much the same place that it had been before they retreated into the castle.

One of the youngest recruits caught him as he came into the camp. The child's face was badly bruised. There were tears on it. "Tuan," Roland said. "What is it?"

The boy caught his hand and pulled him inward.

There was a campfire in front of the tent Gemma shared with her sons. The tent's flap was rolled up, so that the firelight could illumine the space within.

Gemma knelt beside one of the cots. Kyllan was there, and Cieran and Peredur, and Long Meg and the smith.

Cait lay on the cot. She was not a large person, but she had always stood straight and faced the world boldly. She was all shrunken now.

Kyllan held her in his lap as if she had been a child, her head cradled on his breast. His eyes were dry. They burned on Roland.

They had tried to mend her. Roland scented magic on her. One of the ladies of the Grail had tended her, Nieve who was strongest but for Sarissa. That great power barely sufficed to keep her breathing.

"It was a demon," Gemma said. "She killed it, but it had its claws in her before it died. They were poisoned, the white lady said."

"Yes." Roland ran hands over the small huddled body. Darkness ran in its veins. Fever burned it. It was all but ashes.

He could free her body from pain. He could give her peace. Life there was none, not even for the Grail to restore. She had gone too far beyond the river of light.

Before he came to Montsalvat he had been a warrior, not a healer; a slayer, not a mender of men. Through this night he had grown accustomed to the glory of healing, to seeing even the dying rise up before the power that was his to wield. It was like strong wine—dizzying, exalting.

It would not come to him here. There was no malice in the refusal. It simply was. He wept as much in frustration as in grief, but his tears did nothing to restore her. She was dead. It only remained for him to set her free.

That was the taste of victory: honey-sweet, but bitter in the dregs. Kyllan and the rest regarded him with wide hopeful eyes, but he had no hope to give them.

"Make her live," Kyllan said.

"I can't," Roland said.

"You mean you won't." Kyllan was past reason, past mercy. "You don't want to. She doesn't matter. She's not a prince or a queen. She's not—"

Gemma slapped him hard. "Stop that! Can't you see he means it? He *can't*."

"He can do anything he wants to do," Kyllan shot back, though his lips and cheek must have stung abominably.

"I wish I could." Roland spoke with all the weariness in the world. He took Cait gently from Kyllan's slack grip and laid her on the cot. Softly he closed her eyes that had fixed upon the light. He kissed her brow. "Rest you well, brave warrior," he said.

Kyllan cursed abominably and burst into tears. "What good is being a king, if you can't do this? What good is anything at all?"

"I do wonder," said Roland.

"I won't forgive you," Kyllan said.

"Of course you will," said his mother, sharp as a slap. "Enough of that now. Get yourself together and see to the burying."

Roland moved to go with them. Her hand stopped him. "Not you. Let them do it themselves. It will be good for them."

"And not for me?"

"You have ample else to do. Go and do it."

"Not unless you come, too. As mayor of the palace."

He had never seen Gemma astonished before. "As *what*?"

"It's exactly like running an inn, only bigger. And more hands to do your bidding."

"I can't do that. And what of the one who is mayor already? Won't he—"

"He is dead," Roland said. "He died in the shadow-battle."

"I can't," said Gemma. "I wouldn't know where to begin."

"You already have. You order me about with no qualms at all. Let that be the first act of your new office: to dispatch me to my duties."

She opened her mouth, then shut it again. She blinked hard. He watched it dawn on her, what she had got herself into, and how she had done it. She was a little appalled—and a little, just a little, intrigued.

"I have no noble blood at all," she said. "I'm as common as the earth under your feet."

"Earth of Montsalvat," Roland said. "That's a royalty of its own."

She shook her head. "You won't let me go, will you?"

"No," he said.

"Even if I beg? Even if I tell you I'd rather die?"

"Would you do that?"

"No," she said after a moment. "No, I wouldn't. Damn you. Have you told the queen yet? That you were rather more to me than a stable-lad?"

Roland bit his lip.

"I'll wager she knows," Gemma said. She sighed. "Very well, since you insist. I'll do it. But I'll do it my way. Is that understood?"

"Perfectly," Roland said.

"I do hope so." She squared her shoulders, drew a breath. "To the castle, then. And gods help the lot of us."

Roland had not meant to return to Carbonek so soon. But Gemma's will bore him with it, taking him back through the battered gate. The dead were gone from the courts and the halls. Servants were cleansing the blood from the stones.

Gemma took it all in with a swift and raking glance. She nodded to herself. She thrust up her sleeves, tied back her hair more securely, and set to work.

Roland went up to the tower of the Grail. The chamber was quiet, the roof secure, the shrine open. It received the cup with almost a sigh of relief.

He let it go without reluctance. The physical thing, the wooden cup, might rest here, but the heart and the power of it were woven into his own flesh and bone.

He sank to his knees, then to his face. Part was reverence. Much was simple weariness. He was still living flesh, though the Grail lived in him.

He knew when Sarissa came and knelt beside him. Like the Grail, she was part of him now.

She had been laboring as relentlessly as he, after fighting battles no less terrible than the one he had fought. Yet her presence was warm, her strength seemingly unwearied.

He rose stiffly. Her smile bathed him in light. He half-fell into her embrace.

"My poor love," she said. "You're worn to a thread."

"And you are not?"

His flash of temper only made her smile widen. He was young, that smile said, and male, and not particularly sensible. And he had done a very great thing. She kissed him, deep and sweet.

"Do you know," she said, "we had a wedding, but no wedding night."

"We had a battle," he said. "Now it's morning. I should— there is still much to—"

"That has all been seen to," Sarissa said.

"But I have to—"

"You've done everything that was required of you," she said. "All the rest, your servants are doing, and gladly. *They* slept and ate while you drove yourself without mercy. Now you will eat with me, and maybe sleep."

"With you?"

Her eyes glinted. "Certainly not with any other woman while I have a say in it."

His cheeks flamed. It was sudden and mortifying, but he could not help it. "I wouldn't—I didn't—"

"Not any longer," she said.

She rose, drawing him with her. His feet were steadier than he had expected. His face was cooling slowly.

The chamber to which she led him was not the one he had slept in since he was brought into Carbonek, which he had taken for the king's. Now that he saw the king's chamber indeed, he could not have mistaken it for any other.

It was clean and swept, fresh with scents of herbs, but he caught a faint glimmer of mustiness, as if this and the suite to which it belonged had been untenanted for some lengthy while. The appointments were very fine but surprisingly plain; there was little ornament, and much that was useful. He had seen such rooms in Rome, in old villas. Few furnishings, a good rug or two, well-wrought but faded frescoes on the walls. There was even a courtyard with a

pool that reflected the sky, an atrium as such were called in
Rome.

The bedchamber was Roman, too, not large, and gracefully uncluttered. And the bed, to his enormous relief, was
a broad couch, more hard than soft, covered with good
linen and well-woven wool. No feathers, no silk.

"Now this is to my taste," he said.

"I thought it might be." Sarissa sounded pleased with
herself. She set about freeing him from his clothing, taking
her time about it, savoring the small things: the curve of his
jaw, the breadth of his shoulder.

If he closed his eyes he would fall headlong into sleep.
He kept them open, not particularly easily, though the
sight of her made it less difficult than it might have been.

She met them steadily. She had not done that before, he
realized with a small shock. Glances, yes; but never this
clear, level stare. She had always avoided it. Because he
had hawk's eyes, Merlin's eyes—eyes of, she thought, an
enemy.

"Do you trust me now?" he asked.

"With my heart and soul," she said. It could not have
been easy for her. She drew his head down and kissed his
eyelids. "I'll never be such a fool again."

He teased her hair out of its plait. It sprang free with
joyous abandon, tumbling over her shoulders, springing
about her face. He tangled his fingers in it. "And do you
love me?"

"As much as you love me."

"Ah, wicked," he said. He slipped the robe from her
shoulders. She was naked under it, breasts high and taut
with the room's chill. He warmed them with his breath. She
shivered with pleasure.

He had dreamed of this, of limning her body in kisses.
They had had so little of it since those days in Musa's
house, and so much of that tainted with mistrust or with
the threat of war. And after that he had been so angry, so
little able to forgive.

Anger was long gone. The war was over—still the aftermath to face, still grief, still pain, still long labor, but the
cause of it, the great enemy, was vanished from the earth.
The deep realms of hell held him now. Not even the gods
could bring him back.

Her fingers worked into his hair, freeing it as he had freed hers. It was not exuberant as hers was. It was thick and determinedly straight, so that plaiting barely crimped it. It slid over his shoulders. Saints, when had it grown so long?

"Don't cut it," she said. "It's wonderful."

"You are wonderful," he said. "Beautiful. Glorious. Beloved."

"Beloved," she said, opening to him, taking him into herself.

But he drew back slightly. "Is it right? Should I love a wife so much?"

"You should do no other," she said.

She was older than he by far, and famously wise. And he had always trusted her. She tightened her arms and closed her lips on his. He let her drown him in blessed delight.

CHAPTER 65

✠ ✠ ✠

Pepin the prince lay in such comfort as he would accept, in a chamber of the king's tower. The guards on the door were mages. Wards sealed both door and window, though he would have needed wings to escape through the latter.

It was three days before Roland came to look on him. The sheer enormity of the war's aftermath had absorbed him completely. There would be a crowning before the people, and a great feast of victory at the moon's full. He had much to do to prepare, duties that preoccupied him from before dawn till long after sunset; and when he could escape from those, Sarissa was waiting, to consummate again the great marriage that had bound him to the Grail and the kingdom.

Pepin had tried twice to escape. His magery was not inconsiderable, and he had studied it well. But the mages of the Grail were stronger. After the second attempt, he lay on the bed in his chamber and would not move or eat or drink.

Roland entered the room alone. Half the royal guard would have come with him if he had allowed it, and the nine ladies of the Grail, and Marric and Tarik and Turpin, too. But he had held them all at bay, except Turpin, who insisted on waiting without.

Pepin lay on his side, drawn into a knot, back to the door. Roland sat in the chair beside the bed.

It was restful. Quiet. He could hear voices below, and the ringing of laughter: some of the king's own were playing at ball in the courtyard.

That pleased him beyond measure. They mourned their dead, none more than Kyllan, but their spirits were strong. They could laugh amid grief, and dance in the sun after their battle with darkness.

"Sooner or later," Roland said after a while, "you will have to get up and eat. I don't think you're mad enough to will yourself to death."

Pepin's back was obdurate. Had his breathing quickened?

"Your master is dead," Roland said. "You knew that, I'm sure. Have you considered what it means for you? All his human slaves have repudiated him. All of them—every last one. Some few of them, who were in your father's army, profess to be your men. They're refusing to speak with us unless you're freed."

"Good."

Pepin did not unknot or turn, but his voice was clear and bitter.

"It doesn't matter," Roland said. "They'll be sent away soon, with no memory of us; for all any of them will know, they were delayed on the road home, and wandered for a long while in the Spanish marches."

"And what will you do with me?"

"What would you like us to do?" Roland asked him.

"Kill me."

"I don't think so," said Roland.

Pepin turned at last. Roland stiffened before the hatred in his eyes. It was absolute. It fed the darkness that had bred his magic. It blinded him to reason. "You would do well to kill me," Pepin said. "The master may be dead, but I live. I've sworn to destroy you."

"Why?" Roland asked him.

Pepin's mouth twisted. "What difference does it make? It's the truth."

"I never knowingly did you harm," Roland said.

"Of course you didn't," said Pepin.

Roland hunted in that face for something, anything, that he could understand. There was nothing.

The slash of power caught him almost off guard. Almost. He had been prepared for it, but sooner than this. It struck him, but only slantwise. The second bolt, he flung back without conscious thought.

Pepin reeled back against the wall. His face was white. His eyes were staring.

"Don't ever do that again," Roland said.

Pepin spat at him.

"He's dangerous," Turpin said.

Roland had got no more sense out of Pepin than those bolts of darkness and a gobbet of spittle in the face. He left at last, unwillingly, but he gained nothing by staying.

Turpin was waiting, leaning against the wall, arms folded. The guard-mages had run in at the first blast of power; they stayed inside, standing over Pepin, weaving wards that he could not break.

Roland walked down with his friend from the tower. The game had ended in the courtyard; it was deserted except for a grey cat.

Tarik sprang into his favorite place on Roland's shoulder. His purring rasped in Roland's ear.

"Pepin is dangerous," Turpin repeated as they started across the courtyard. "You can't keep him here unless you intend to keep him under guard for the rest of his life. If you send him back to his father, you can be sure he'll keep his promise to you."

"What would you do with him?" Roland asked.

Turpin hunched his heavy shoulders. "I'd have him executed," he said bluntly.

Roland stopped short. "He is our king's son!"

"*You* are a king," Turpin shot back. "Kings do what they must. It's not always the pleasant thing—but for the good of the kingdom—"

"I will not kill Charles' son," Roland said.

"Then someone has to," said Turpin. "The old sorcerer raised him to be a viper in his father's nest. You can't let him go back there. If you keep him here, you keep him prisoner. There's no other choice."

"There may be," Roland said slowly. "It's even merciful. If—"

"If?"

"If it can be done."

"You don't know—?"

"I think I know," Roland said. "Damn the sorcerer to an even deeper hell than that he lies in, for bringing that boy here!"

Turpin crossed himself. "Amen," he said.

While Roland turned Pepin's fate in his heart, speaking as yet to no one, even Sarissa, a delegation came to him from the Franks who had fought for him against Ganelon.

He had been in the chamber of the Grail, seeking counsel and gaining only the warmth of its light. There was greater solace, just then, in the king's garden, in the scent of earth and greenery. The apple trees were in bloom, intoxicating in their sweetness.

He sat on the grass beneath the oldest of the trees, a seed of which, the gardener had told him, had come from the garden of the Hesperides. A few golden apples still lingered on the boughs amid the cloud of white blossoms.

The Franks trod uneasily toward him, shying at shadows. They never had been at ease in the castle, though they did well enough in camp outside the walls.

Roland rose to greet them. They bowed as they insisted on doing, as low as if he had been the King of the Franks. He welcomed each by name, and warmly. "Here, sit," he said. "I'll send for ale. Or would you prefer wine?"

"Neither, please, sire," said Rothulf, the captain of infantry, speaking for them all. "We won't trouble you long."

"You'll not be troubling me," Roland said.

They smiled jerkily, glancing at one another, shuffling feet until he was moved to take mercy on them.

"Tell me," he said.

It took a while, and visible gathering of courage, until Rothulf said, "Sire, we're thinking it's time we went home."

That was blunt enough.

"It's spring in the world, we hear," Rothulf said. "We have wives, children, kin. They'll have been mourning us for dead. And now with the planting, they'll be needing us."

"And the spring muster," Roland said.

"We think we may be excused from that," said Rothulf, "if we've been fighting the winter long."

"That's what you'll tell the king's men?"

Rothulf shrugged, a slow roll of the shoulders. "You let the enemy's men go, took their memory away and sent them home. We'll bow to that, if you're the one to do it. Though some of us would like to remember a dream, if you'll leave us that much."

Roland searched all their faces. "You are agreed on this?"

They nodded.

"I never meant to keep you here," he said. "There's the crowning and the festival; then you'd have been mustered out. But if you'd rather go sooner—"

"No," Rothulf said. "No, sire, we want to stay for that. But we thought—"

He stopped in confusion. He was a ruddy man as so many of the Franks were; his face had flushed scarlet.

"You thought you were prisoners," Roland said. He shook his head. "My fault. I should have spoken to you long ago. You are free men. Free to keep your memories, too, though I will ask you to take oath that the secret kingdom will remain secret. You're no more bound here than you ever were to the king's wars, once those wars were over."

"No," said one of the others—an older man than some, and smaller and darker. "That's our fault for not trusting you. When the enemy's men went out, ours started growling. We all forgot what we know of you."

"We remember now," Rothulf said. "Are you angry? That we want to go home?"

"And you say you know me," said Roland.

That abashed them into speechlessness.

"Go," he said. "Be comforted. You were the bulwark of this war. When you see your wives again, you may tell them: you defended the Lord's kingdom, and helped destroy a great evil."

"Even if they don't believe us?" the Breton asked wryly. But before Roland could answer, he said, "No, no, we'll keep it in our hearts, and maybe tell it as a story to our grandchildren. How we fought a great war outside the world, and saw a king riding on a dragon's back."

After they were gone, Roland sat for a long while. *Home,* he thought.

The sun shone through the apple-boughs. Petals drifted down like snow. Somewhere nearby, a bird was singing, achingly sweet. He had but to open the eyes of his heart to see the whole of this kingdom, cupped like a jewel in his hands.

He had not been thinking at all, only doing. Now it struck him what he had done; what he was, and was not.

He was dead in Francia. They had buried a stranger's body in his name, built him a shrine at the summit of Roncesvalles. There would be a new count in the Breton Marches, a new lord over the lands that had been his.

He could not go back. That door was closed.

But was it?

Home. For all his childhood, that had been Broceliande, the old forest of Brittany. For the years of his young manhood, it had been the court and *palatium* of the Franks, and the living presence of the king. When he thought of that, of Charles whom he had served, whom he had loved, his heart ached till he could not bear it.

He rose, turning slowly. All this beauty, this power, this magic, suddenly seemed strange; alien. They were not his. They had laid themselves on him, chosen him—but he had not chosen them.

Even Sarissa . . .

His heart clenched. She would never turn away from the Grail or from its kingdom. Her life and her spirit were given to it. Even for love of him, she would not turn her back on it.

Longinus the Roman had somewhat surprised Roland, in that he was the chancellor of the king's palace. He had not seemed the sort to be a clerk at all, and yet when Roland found him, he looked deeply content. He was reckoning long columns of figures on a frame of wires and beads, reading them off to a much more clerkly-seeming person with a roll of papyrus and a pen.

Roland sat to watch, perched on a stool. The beads rattled through their computations. Longinus acknowledged him with a glance and a lift of the brow. Roland nodded, settling to wait.

It was not so long a while. It calmed him, settled the roil in his middle. He slid into a half-dream.

In the dream he was a child again, not yet a man. He ran through the wood of Broceliande. It was spring: the new leaves were springing, the clearings carpeted with flowers. Sometimes he ran as a deer, a yearling fawn; sometimes he flew as a hawk. He was as free as living creature could be.

He shrank from fawn into boy, rolled and leaped and tumbled down a long grassy hill, and came up laughing.

There was a stranger at the foot of the hill. He had almost never met anyone else in the wood. People did not go there for ease or pleasure. Hunters and woodsmen learned quickly that the wood did not welcome them.

This was a man in worn clothes, much stained with travel. Mail glinted under the leather tunic. He had a helmet on his head, but he carried no weapon: no sword, no spear. He stood with his feet somewhat apart, like a sentry on watch.

Roland circled him warily. He did not seem dangerous, and he was unarmed, but he was a stranger.

He took no notice of Roland, though Roland was not trying to be invisible. He was facing west and south. A ray of the setting sun, glancing through a cloud, struck light in his face.

Roland froze. It was his own face, the face he wore when he was awake. Maybe he had come to find Merlin, to see whether the sorcerer's destruction had freed him; but Merlin was off to the east, where he did not seem inclined to go.

"My lord."

He blinked. The face under the helmet was not his own after all; it was Longinus', dark and strong and incontestably Roman.

Broceliande shimmered and faded. He sat in the chancellor's workroom, blinking at Longinus. "It was yours," he said out of nowhere that he could name. "The spear. You— were—"

"I was," Longinus said. He was calm about it—after so long, why should he not be? He arched his back and stretched. The clerk was gone, the papyrus rolled and bound and laid away. It was only the two of them in the small lamplit room.

"Have you ever wanted to leave?" Roland asked him. "To go home again?"

"After so long, there's no home left," Longinus said, but without either grief or bitterness. "When it began . . . yes, I did dream of it, sometimes. But I'd chosen my place. I wouldn't abandon it."

"What if the place had chosen you?"

"It did that, too," said Longinus.

"You never resented the choosing? But then," said Roland, "you came of your own will. Yes?"

"I came because I could do no other." Longinus fixed him with a keen stare. "You want to go back."

"I don't know," said Roland. "There's been no time to think. Today the Franks—my Franks—came to me. They asked to be set free. As if this were a prison and they were bound. But they are not. I—I think I am. Or am I also free to go?"

"You ask me?"

"I think," said Roland, "that you know a great deal of what passes in this kingdom."

"I think that you were raised to revere Romans overmuch," Longinus said. "We were not gods, even those of us who claimed to be. We were men. No wiser, no stronger, than any other."

"Surely," said Roland, "and you have lived eight hundred years. I've lived two and twenty. I have no wisdom at all. I fought the battle I was brought here to fight. The power wielded itself through me. But now the war is over. The enemy is gone. I'm not the king you need now, the lord of peace. All I know is fighting and guarding."

"You'll learn," said Longinus.

"What if I don't want to? What if I walk away from here?"

"Then you do," Longinus said. "You're not a prisoner, either. You can go. But if you go, you leave the Grail forever, and all that the Grail has wrought. That door, once shut, will not open again. You can never return."

Roland's breath caught. "Then I'm not free, am I?"

"You're free to choose," said Longinus, "but that choice is irrevocable."

"And if I choose to stay—am I bound here forever, too?"

"You know that answer," Longinus said.

"Does it matter if I can ride in the world without crum-

bling to dust? I can't be alive in Francia again. Not and be
king of the hidden kingdom."

"That is so," said Longinus.

"You won't advise me," Roland said.

"I won't make your choice for you, no. When the Franks
go, you can lead them. No one will stop you."

"Someone might," Roland said, but softly, to himself.

The recruits were in the field below the castle, beyond
the torn and battered remnants of the battle, practicing at
archery. A dozen of them were mounted on the white
horses of Caer Sidi, instructed by two of Huon's guardsmen. The horses were patient. The riders had little grace,
but great dedication.

"We reckon," Kyllan said to Roland, "that the sleepers in
the earth are still awake, and someone will have to hunt
them out. And now we've learned to fight, we shouldn't
forget."

"Besides," said his brother Peredur from the back of a
calm-eyed white horse, "I always wanted to be a knight."

"First you have to learn to ride like a man instead of a
sack of meal," Kyllan said.

It was odd to see him without Cait beside him. Her death
had reft away a part of him. But he carried on in spite of it.
He could still laugh; he could still taunt his brother. He was
still Kyllan.

"*You* ride!" Peredur challenged him. "See how well you
look."

They would have come to blows if Roland had not
plucked Peredur from the saddle and set him firmly on his
feet. He bristled at his brother. Kyllan grinned infuriat-
ingly.

"Mount," Roland said, "and ride."

"Ah, no," Kyllan said. "I'm not—"

"Mount," said Roland.

They were all in a circle now, archers and riders. Kyllan's
face was crimson under the crowding freckles.

He made heavy work of it, but he heaved himself into
the saddle. Once he was in it, he had some faint skill—as
his brother muttered, from sitting on the plowhorse at
planting time. He was no more graceful than Peredur had
been.

As he wobbled down the field on the patient horse, Peredur's hand flicked. The stone caught the horse on the rump. He started, leaped forward.

Kyllan left the saddle completely without ceremony. He came down rolling, fetching up at Roland's feet. The horse stood with reins trailing, visibly embarrassed.

"*Ai*," said Kyllan.

"Indeed," Roland said. "Mount again. You've much to learn if you're to be a knight of Montsalvat."

"You can't do that to me," Kyllan groaned.

"Can't I?"

"I'm happy on foot," said Kyllan. "I'm good on foot. I don't *want* to—"

"It's much faster," Peredur said. He had climbed back on the horse again, not too clumsily. "I'm going to learn to ride. Then while you're trudging in the mud, I'll be galloping over the hilltops."

"I'll cheer you on," Kyllan said. Roland stretched out a hand to pull him to his feet. He creaked as he rose, but the grin was breaking through. "Then again, maybe I'll be flying over on a dragon."

"You can dream," said Peredur.

Roland laughed. They were all grinning.

Here was home, this land, these people. He had never been born to either, but born for them—that, most certainly, he was.

Maybe they might not understand why he snatched the reins of the nearest horse, deposited Long Meg crisply on her feet, and circled the field in a mad, headlong, wonderful gallop. Though more likely they would understand it, being what they were. He was claiming this earth for good and all, as it had claimed him.

CHAPTER 66

✠ ✠ ✠

They crowned the Grail-king on the field of the battle, near the green mound in which the dead were laid. He had chosen that, the breast of earth and the embrace of the sky, rather than the great hall of Carbonek—and not only for the power that he might gain from it. All his people could come to him there, the Franks who had fought so well for a cause not their own, the villagers and levies of the domains, the lords, knights, princes. They had all come, all who could, human and not.

On this day he suffered royal panoply. The people expected it—yes, his recruits, too, bright-eyed and grinning from ear to ear in the front ranks of the crowd. It was not the dreadful and useless parade armor; this was a ceremony of peace. They clothed him in cloth of silver, so stiff in its glory that he could barely move, and mantled him in deep blue silk and swansdown white as snow.

If there was any comfort to be had, it was that all the lords were at least as splendid. The ladies of the Grail were more fortunate: their robes were simple white, as always.

Sarissa's was white samite and cloth of silver. He would have helped her to dress in it, but they were kept separate in the castle, she tended by the enchantresses, he by knights of the Grail, and by Marric, who was not to be thrust aside for any rank or pretension.

They were allowed to meet at the castle's gate. A milk-white mare waited for her. The snow-white stallion who waited for Roland had been a cat not long before.

Sarissa's face was grave as befit a queen going to her crowning, but her eyes were laughing. Roland took her hands in his and raised them to his lips. It was a promise, for later; a promise he well meant to keep.

They rode side by side across the bridge, hoofbeats echoing down the walls of the chasm. The knights of the Grail rode before them, the lords of Montsalvat behind. The white ladies led them all, bearing the shrine, and in it the Grail.

Roland's hand, reaching, met Sarissa's. Hand in hand they rode to the crowning.

"No regrets?" Turpin asked. The feast was glorious, and uproarious. The sun was setting on it, and no end of it to be seen.

Roland had left the crown and the heavy mantle in the high seat. Sarissa was there still, listening to a consort of musicians—she loved music dearly. In a little while, when the music was ended, she would make her escape.

Turpin was coming from the camp-privies while Roland went to them. When Roland came back, Turpin was still there, sitting on the hill near the gate of Carbonek.

Roland freed himself of his robes. The tunic and hose beneath were of silk, but sturdy and sensible enough. He sat beside Turpin, drew up his knees and set his chin on them, and watched the sun go down over the army of feasters.

"No regrets," he said, somewhat belatedly. "Not any longer."

"Good," said Turpin.

"And you?" Roland asked. "Are you riding out tomorrow with the rest?"

"What makes you think that?"

Roland shot a glance at him. "They're leaving tomorrow. The Franks. Rothulf will take Pepin to the abbey outside of Toulouse, where he was supposed to have been from the beginning; and where, he will swear, the good Father Ganelon died of a winter rheum. He'll remember nothing but a long dull retreat and a dark dream. Maybe he'll be easier in spirit thereafter."

"The Grail can heal him after all?"

"It can free him from the burden of memory," Roland said, "and bury his magic deep, where he cannot find it or be tempted by it. He'll go out from here a mortal man—for both good and ill."

"Do you know," Turpin said after a pause, "you're rather a terrible personage when you choose to be."

Roland blinked. "I? I'm not—"

"You are," said Turpin. "And no, I'm not going."

"Of course you're going," Roland said.

"No," Turpin said with visible patience. "This is my place now, as it is yours."

Roland's eyes stung with tears—sudden and not at all expected. "Swear you're not doing it for me."

"I belong to the Grail," Turpin said. "And to you—I won't lie about that. I've always been yours: friend, servant, father confessor. I only wish—"

"Olivier knows," Roland said. "He went ahead of us. When the time comes, he'll show us the way."

"That could be a thousand years," Turpin said.

Roland shivered lightly, though the evening was warm. "Do you wish at all that you could undo it? That you could be Charles' man again, and archbishop in Rheims?"

"Rather than Roland's man, and a Christian priest in a decidedly un-Christian realm?" Turpin shrugged, smiled. "Maybe I'll convert a pagan or two. Maybe I'll spend a hundred years in the bliss of the Grail. I can do that, brother. I can do whatever God calls me to do."

"God or gods," Roland said, "or the Goddess who, my queen will tell you, was before them all."

"Heresy," said Turpin with a shudder, but he was still smiling. He struck Roland's shoulder lightly with a fist. "Look, there—is that your queen?"

It was indeed, tall and white in the twilight. Roland would have hung back, but Turpin pushed him toward her. "Go on. Don't keep her waiting."

"She understands," Roland said.

"I'm sure she does," said Turpin. "And I'm sure she'll be glad to have you to herself."

Roland glanced back once as he descended the hill. Turpin sat like a stone in the gloom, heavy and solid and altogether of earth, but with a fire in the heart of him.

Turpin had told the truth. He was home, as Roland was.

This was his earth, this sky his sky; and the Grail was singing in his bones.

Sarissa opened her arms. Roland went to them as ship to haven; as lord to his own land. The stars bloomed overhead. The lights of the castle glimmered above them. Down in the camp, a lone clear voice was singing. It was nigh as pure and nigh as sweet as the Grail itself.

Hand in hand as they had ridden out to the crowning, they walked across the bridge. The castle was empty, all its people gone to the feasting. The courts were dim, the passages silent.

Roland slid a glance sidewise. Sarissa's glance met it. Hers was as wicked as his.

All alone, but for the Grail. Solitude—pure and wonderful. A flick of power shut the gate. A second raised wards that would stand till dawn.

Morning would wake them to rank and dignity and duty, king and queen in the kingdom of the Grail. Tonight was their own. Still hand in hand, laughing like wild children, they danced through the halls of Carbonek.

ENVOI

✠ ✠ ✠

CARBONEK

On a bright morning of summer in the kingdom of Montsalvat, a stranger came to the castle of the Grail. Not many passed by that road. The mortal world had withdrawn since the old enemy was destroyed. Once the Franks had been sent back with their prince, the way had grown more difficult, the lands between more remote and forbidding. There was irony in it, but safety, too. The Grail would not again suffer such an enemy.

And yet here was a stranger, alive and well and apparently untroubled by the difficulties of the journey. He traveled alone, like a pilgrim or a vagrant, but his clothes were of fine quality, his horse well bred and well kept, and there was a sword at his side, worn with the ease of a man who had long ridden armed.

Sarissa happened to be passing by the gate when he asked for admittance. She sensed no danger in him. Curiosity brought her down from the tower to welcome him herself, in the place of the gate-warden. He seemed ordinary enough as he rode under the arch of the gate, a well-made lordly man on a strong black gelding, leading a sumpter mule. His face was too sharp for beauty, his nose a fierce curve. His hair was black and thick, lightly shot with grey. His face was clean-shaven, a rarity in these days, but it suited him.

He could have been kin to the knights of Caer Sidi, with

that face and that hair and that pale skin. Or for that matter he could have been—

He lifted his eyes to meet hers. She stood rooted.

He could have been Roland's close kin. His father—forefather.

"Merlin Ambrosius," she said. Even for love of Roland, even knowing the tales that Roland had told, she could not say that name with warmth. She had hated him too long and too well.

Merlin bowed low. Was there mockery in it? She did not presume to judge. "Lady Sarissa," he said. "Well met at last."

She bit her tongue on the first words that came to it. They were not at all courteous.

He smiled—damnably like Roland—and sprang lightly from the saddle. Servants ran to take his horse and mule. He thanked them graciously, as if to rebuke Sarissa for her own lack of manners.

"You are welcome in Carbonek," she said at last, though the words caught in her throat.

"And glad I am to have come here," he said.

It was a dance, she thought. She could tread the steps, speak the words. Was she not both enchantress and queen?

She called the servants to see to the guest, to bathe him, feed him, house him in a manner appropriate for a lord of rank. It was cowardly not to attend him in her own person, but after all she was the queen. She had duties, which she would see to. Then, if she was fortunate, she could avoid the inevitable for a goodly while. Longer, if Roland stayed away, riding the kingdom between Lyonesse and Poictesme.

That was less than proper, and she paid as she deserved. Toward midafternoon, a tumult at the gate greeted Roland's return with the crowd of his escort. Dignity be damned, and cowardice, too—Sarissa ran back down to the gate, and caught him just as he dismounted, leaping into his arms, whirling about.

People grinned as they had a habit of doing in these days. It had been too long since Montsalvat had a young king. He gladdened them all, and taught even the most somber to laugh again.

When they had swum up from a long kiss to a blessed draught of air, Roland stood with his arms about her waist, searching her face with eager golden eyes. "Is it true, what the messenger said? Is Merlin here?"

Messenger?

She caught the eye of the cat that rode on Roland's shoulder. Tarik licked his paw in elaborate nonchalance.

She seared him with a glare. He ignored it as he well could, who had Roland for ally and defender.

"Merlin is here," said a voice behind her, as like Roland's as any could be.

Roland forgot her existence. She had seen such white, wild joy in him before, but never so strong. It made the stones ring underfoot.

They were like man and mirror, like father and son. Were those tears on the elder enchanter's cheeks? Certainly Roland's eyes were brimming, though he was laughing.

Arm in arm, side by side, they left the outer court. Sarissa followed. Her mood was strange. Goddess—was she jealous?

How could she be? This was as close to a father as Roland had known, preceptor and teacher and beloved kin. But for him, Roland would not have been. The Grail might have been taken and the kingdom destroyed. He had raised Roland to be the enemy's enemy, the champion of the Grail.

They took their ease on the terrace of the garden. It was so set that from it one could look over the outer wall to the wilderness of peaks, striking above the garden's green serenity.

Merlin breathed deep of that scented air. "Freedom," he said, "is sweeter than wine."

"Tell me," said Roland.

Merlin sat back in his chair, cradling a silver cup. "After you left," he said, "I had ceased to count the days again. I knew when the war began—I felt it in my bones. But I never dared hope. One long night I fell into a sleep as deep but never as blessed as death. And when I woke, the walls of air were gone. I was free."

"I didn't dare hope," Roland said. "I sent my spirit searching for you after the war. I found nothing. I thought—I feared that I'd failed."

"I was sleeping," Merlin said. "I felt you when I woke,

but you were gone. I followed the track of the sending. It led me here."

"You knew where I'd be," Roland said.

"This way was closed to me," said Merlin, "and to my blood, before you came to it."

He did not glance at Sarissa, but she felt the brush of his awareness.

She would not apologize to him or to any son of demon or old god, for protecting her own.

He smiled, nodded: absolution of sorts, if she could possibly have wanted it.

"They know you now," Roland said. "They know the truth. You'll never be barred again, going or coming."

"So one would hope," Merlin said.

Roland leaned toward him, drinking him in. "You're different. You're young. I never knew—"

"Moss and old leaves," Merlin said, "and years beyond count. I terrified the children when I came out of the wood. They tell tales now of a beast who roared like a man."

"Then how—"

"I remembered," said Merlin, "little by little, what the world was; how men were. It had been longer than I cared to know."

"The world was a dark place after Arthur went away," Sarissa said, surprising herself. "Now, slowly, the light begins to come back."

"And, it's said, there a new Arthur in the world," said Merlin, "a new king who may succeed where Arthur failed."

"Charles of the Franks," Roland said. She could not hear regret in his voice, but he was faintly wistful. "We were going to conquer Rome for him, and crown him emperor."

"That may still come to pass," said Merlin. "I saw it written in the wind, flying like a banner over Francia."

"You want to go there," Roland said.

"In a little while," said Merlin. "But first I should like to stay here a while—if you can bear my presence."

He was not looking at Roland then. His eyes were on Sarissa.

So, too, were Roland's. She had been reckoning him oblivious, but the gaze that rested on her now, saw to the heart of her.

She had learned to endure and then to love those yellow

eyes. To see them in another face, a face she had loathed for so long, made her oddly dizzy.

"I ... can suffer you," she said. "I will learn to do better than that. Though I can't ever promise to love you."

"Tolerance will suffice," Merlin said. "It's been a long while, and a bitter war."

"But for you, we would never have won it." That was far from easy to say, but she had to say it. "He created you to destroy us. Instead you destroyed him."

"The ways of the light are incalculable," Merlin said. He smiled at her. She caught herself smiling back.

"You may stay," she said, "as long as it pleases you. I make you free of castle and kingdom. I name you friend and royal kin, and ancient ally of the Grail."

Merlin rose and bowed low before her. "Lady and queen," he said, "you walk in grace."

"No," she said wryly. "I scramble to make amends. I was a fool once, and nearly lost us all. I'll not make that mistake again."

Roland took her hand and kissed it. She wove her fingers with his.

Merlin's smile grew almost gentle. "I've done much ill in my many years, but this I'll never regret: that my blood bred this child."

"Your blood bred victory," Sarissa said, "and love and laughter, and a fine bright king for this kingdom."

"There is one thing," said Roland to the air, "that I do truly hate about being king. I hate flattery."

"Who flatters you?" Merlin asked. "We're telling the truth."

Roland hissed. Merlin laughed at him. Sarissa found herself laughing, too; yet again, in common cause with that of all men.

And that was well, she decided, after all. That Merlin was free; that Roland had kept his great oath. And that she was here with both of them, sitting in the garden of the Grail, with the sun overhead and the wind blowing soft and clean in her face.

"I think," Merlin said, "when you've tired of me, I'll go out in the world again, and see this king of kings for myself. Maybe I'll teach him as I taught Arthur. And maybe this one will live to get some good of it."

"This one will live long and die in his bed," Roland said, as serene in prophecy as Merlin had ever been.

"Then I have time," said Merlin, "to make a nuisance of myself here. Tell me, is it true—there are dragons in the hills? And old powers in wood and water?"

"We'll explore the realm together," Roland said. "There's so much—so many wonders, so many splendors. And magic . . . master, I never saw the like."

Sarissa listened to them in growing contentment. Roland was whole at last, and truly happy, with the burden of the great oath lifted from his spirit. He was free now, as free as Merlin. And therefore so was she; for all that bound Roland bound her as well, even to the world's end.

That was a joyous captivity. She smiled, half-dreaming in the sun, while their two voices, each so like the other, wove a net of words about her. The Grail always sang beneath Roland's, subtle but distinct. She realized without surprise that that same song was in Merlin's. Merlin too had been chosen, though she had never known it. She had been too stubborn to see.

Ah well, she thought. She had learned to trust Roland. She was learning to forgive Merlin. She might make a passable Christian yet, though the Goddess would have something to say of that.

It was all one. It was all in the light, all in the Grail. And who could know better than she? She was the first of its guardians, its servant and its queen.

"Amen," said Merlin in reply to something that Roland had said. "So may it be."

Read on for an exciting preview of

RITE OF CONQUEST

the new historical fantasy by

JUDITH TARR

Now available in trade paperback
from Roc

Anno Domini 1047–1048

Mathilda bent over the tapestry. The branches of an oak spread under her needle, growing swiftly in threads of green and grey and brown. Her maids' chatter flowed over her like the babble of bright water.

Her mind was empty of thought, still and clear, intent on nothing more than the thread, the needle, and the image on the taut-stretched linen. She could feel the earth's turning beneath her feet, and the dance of flames in the hearth, and the concourse of spirits all around and about and through this room in which she sat. Some of them swirled about her needle, sliding down the shaft of it into the tapestry.

The oak's leaves rustled. She caught the scent of damp earth and new-fallen snow. There were tracks in the snow, marks of shod hooves. Still empty, still pure being, she drifted above them, following where they led.

They wove through the trees of a wood, then out into snowy fields. Shadows lay long and black across the expanse of white. At the road's end was a shape of old wood and raw stone, a walled village clustered about the squat bulk of a castle. A banner hung limp from the half-finished tower; no wind caught it, to uncover the device upon it. She saw only that it was the color of blood.

The courtyard was empty of horses, though there were signs enough of their presence: trampled snow, bits of hay, a scatter of droppings. There were men in a corner, hulking figures wrapped in wool and leather, bent toward one another, conversing in a soft growl.

Because she was air and magic and little else, she heard them perfectly clearly.

"Tonight?"

"As soon as the sun goes down. He'll be up in the tower; we'll trap him there."

"He'll fight."

"The castellan's in on it," said the man who stood nearer the wall. "He's made sure there's a little something in milord's wine. He'll be out cold. Get in, slit his throat, get out—quick as carving a roast in hall."

"I hope it's that easy," the other said.

"What could stop us? We've got him away from his watchdogs. He thinks he's with friends. After all these years, he's still a wide-eyed lamb. He'll go straight to the slaughter."

Mathilda swirled upward, caught like a leaf in a sudden wind. She was no longer so empty now. This dream or vision had a purpose. She was in it because she must be. The wind was carrying her over the courtyard and up, circling the tower. Its face was blank but for narrow slits of windows.

The wind thrust her through one of the highest, into the sudden darkness of walls and the wan flicker of a lamp.

The castellan's wine had found its victim. There was a bed in the room, filling most of it, and a man sprawled across it. He was a big man, broad in the shoulders, with a strong-boned, blade-nosed face. Even unconscious, she could see the strength of will in him, and what above all must have brought her here: a fire of magic that was easily the match of her own.

It had not protected him from the drug in the wine. She cast about for signs of ill workings or hostile magic, although she had not brought enough of herself into this vision for that. One thing she could see: there were no spirits here—not in the room, not in the castle. The air was empty of them, and the earth was quiet.

Too quiet. She stooped over the man on the bed. His unconsciousness was not as deep as she had thought: she saw a gleam of eye beneath the lid, and tightness in him that spoke of struggle.

Night was coming. Darkness was already in the room, and the sliver of sky beyond was dimming slowly. Mathilda gathered every scrap of will and resource that she had, and shaped it into a voice like a trumpet call.

"Messire! Wake and ride!"

His eyelids flickered. He had heard. But he did not wake, nor did he rise.

She raised the call again, though it cost her dearly in strength. "Wake! Ride! Death is behind you."

He twitched, thrashed. The drug was heavy in him. He fought it, but it was too strong.

Desperation drove her. In her hand, far outside this vision, was a needle. She tightened her fingers about it and drove it deep into linen, willing the heavy cloth to be drug-sodden flesh.

He surged up with a strangled roar, shaking his hand furiously. If there was any rational thought in him, he wasted no time with it. He burst through the door and bolted down the stair.

Mathilda hung in the air where he had been. All her strength was gone. She melted with a sigh, dissipating into the fading light.

William had a dim memory of bowling over a pair of figures on the stair leading down from the tower. He was as mindless in his stampede as a charging bull. Only much later did he recall that there had been a gleam of steel in the men's hands, and realize that they must have been coming for him.

That chill winter evening, he knew only that he must escape the place. He found his horse in the stable, threw on saddle and bridle, and flung himself onto the board back. People were running, shouting, scrambling to shut gates and doors. He rode them down.

Night closed in, with damp and penetrating cold. The air smelled of snow and of the sea. It revived him, waking him to a preternatural alertness. His hand ached and stung where something, God knew what, had stabbed him—and thereby saved his life.

He slowed his pace somewhat from a hard gallop to a

fast canter. His horse was breathing well; it was fit and reasonably fresh, and it had caught the same urgency that drove its rider. It made its way sure-footed along the narrow twisting track, through the oak-wood and out into open fields, then down toward the river's mouth and the sigh of the sea.

His spine prickled. Men could not have gathered wits to follow at the pace he set, but other things than men were on his trail. They had separated him from his escort and herded him into the castle from which he had escaped. Now they were after him again, casting nets of confusion to bind his will once more and lure him to his death.

The pain in his hand was his protection. It raised a wall of clarity against which the hellhounds behind him bayed in vain.

His horse, for all its great heart, was tiring. It stumbled as it descended a long stony slope. Water glistened below, the broad mouth of a river running into the sea.

The tide was running out. The night was black dark, without moon or stars, but his eyes saw a glimmering path, straight as the track of moon on water. His heart hesitated—was it a trap?—but his mount made straight for it.

Damp firm sand steadied the horse's strides. The baying of hounds behind seemed fainter, as if they had slowed or turned aside. Water ran beyond the track, but where he rode was almost dry.

The wind rose to a gale, edged with sleet. The cold cut through hauberk and padded gambeson, clear to the bone. He crouched down over the stallion's neck, taking in what warmth he could. The hounds were close again, howling beneath the shriek of the wind.

His death was riding there, as close as it had ever been—and he was death's dearest companion. Almost he wheeled the horse about and sent it back into the hounds' teeth. But he was a coward. He pressed onward as best he might.

The track went on as straight as ever, but rose abruptly upward. The water sank away.

The hounds were waiting where the track met the dry land. How they had come there, where they had been, he would never know. He had no weapon—that had been taken away while he lay in drugged sleep. Even his eating knife was gone.

He could bow his head now and accept the inevitable. All the promises of his childhood—that he was the chosen one, the trueborn king, the lord of wood and water—had long since proved themselves false. Bastard, men called him though he had been born of the Great Marriage between the goddess incarnate and the year-king; they scorned his lineage and sneered at the circumstances of his birth. They had hunted him, hounded him, sought his blood and life and even his soul, until he had come to this: this cold winter's night with the taste and smell of death all about him.

National Bestselling Author
JUDITH TARR

"A MASTER OF HISTORICAL FICTION."
—*BOOKLIST*

"HER CHARACTERS ARE AS ENGAGING AS
HER NARRATIVE IS ENCHANTING."
—*PUBLISHERS WEEKLY*

House of War

0-451-52900-6

National Bestselling Author
Judith Tarr

RITE OF CONQUEST

For 500 years the Saxons ruled Endland, crushing the ancient powers. Acrosss the Channel in Normandy, William is born, the bastard son of a duke and a magical woman of Druid decent.

William has power, but he needs a teacher. It will take the beautiful French noblewoman Mathilda to help him control his abilities so that he may realize his true destiny—to rule as King of England.

0-451-46002-2

**Available wherever books are sold or at
www.penguin.com**

R080

Enter the realm of

Carol Berg

SON OF AVONAR

BOOK ONE OF THE
BRIDGE OF D'ARNATH
TRILOGY

Magic is forbidden througout the Four Realms. For
decades sorcerers and those associated with them were
hunted to near extinction.

But Seri, a Leiran noblewoman living in exile, is no
stranger to defying the unjust laws of her land. She is
sheltering a wanted fugitive who possesses unusual
abilities—a fugitive with the fate of the
realms in his hands.

"A BRILLIANT WRITER." —*BOOKBROWSER*

0-451-45962-8

Coming Soon:
Book Two of the *Bridge D'Arnath* trilogy:
Guardians of the Keep

**Available wherever books are sold or at
www.penguin.com**